SPIDER'S REVENGE

"Explosive . . . Hang on, this is one smackdown you won't want to miss!"   —*RT Book Reviews* (Top Pick!)

"A whirlwind of tension, intrigue, and mind-blowing action that leaves your heart pounding."   —*Smexy Books*

TANGLED THREADS

"Interesting story lines, alluring world, and fascinating characters. That is what I've come to expect from Estep's series."
—*Yummy Men and Kick Ass Chicks*

VENOM

"Estep has really hit her stride with this gritty and compelling series . . . Brisk pacing and knife-edged danger make this an exciting page-turner."   —*RT Book Reviews* (Top Pick!)

"Gin is a compelling and complicated character whose story is only made better by the lovable band of merry misfits she calls her family."   —*Fresh Fiction*

SPIDER'S BITE

"The series [has] plenty of bite . . . Kudos to Estep for the knife-edged suspense!"   —*RT Book Reviews*

"Fast pace, clever dialogue, and an intriguing heroine."
—*Library Journal*

D0366152

JENNIFER ESTEP

BITE

AN ELEMENTAL ASSASSIN BOOK

POCKET BOOKS

New York   London   Toronto   Sydney   New Delhi

Pocket Books
An Imprint of Simon & Schuster, Inc.
1230 Avenue of the Americas
New York, NY 10020

This book is a work of fiction. Any references to historical events, real people, or real places are used fictitiously. Other names, characters, places, and events are products of the author's imagination, and any resemblance to actual events or places or persons, living or dead, is entirely coincidental.

First Pocket Books paperback edition March 2016

POCKET and colophon are registered trademarks of Simon & Schuster, Inc.

For information about special discounts for bulk purchases, please contact Simon & Schuster Special Sales at 1-866-506-1949 or business@simonandschuster.com.

The Simon & Schuster Speakers Bureau can bring authors to your live event. For more information or to book an event, contact the Simon & Schuster Speakers Bureau at 1-866-248-3049 or visit our website at www.simonspeakers.com.

Manufactured in the United States of America

10 9 8 7 6 5 4 3 2 1

ISBN 978-1-5011-1127-3
ISBN 978-1-5011-1128-0 (ebook)

To my mom, my grandma, and Andre—
for your love, patience, and everything
else you've given me over the years.

And to my grandma, who always says,
"Why ask for one million when you can ask for two?"

Acknowledgments

Once again, my heartfelt thanks go out to all the folks who help turn my words into a book.

Thanks go to my agent, Annelise Robey, and editors Adam Wilson and Lauren McKenna for all their helpful advice, support, and encouragement. Thanks also to Melissa Bendixen.

Thanks to Tony Mauro for designing another terrific cover, and thanks to Louise Burke, Lisa Litwack, and everyone else at Pocket and Simon & Schuster for their work on the cover, the book, and the series.

And finally, a big thanks to all the readers. Knowing that folks read and enjoy my books is truly humbling, and I'm glad that you are all enjoying Gin and her adventures.

I appreciate you all more than you will ever know.

Happy reading!

※ 1 ※

Digging up a grave was hard, dirty work.

Good thing that hard, dirty work was one of my specialties. Although, as an assassin, I'm usually the one putting people into graves instead of uncovering them.

But here I was in Blue Ridge Cemetery, just after ten o'clock on this cold November night. Flurries drifted down from the sky, the small flakes dancing on the gusty breeze like delicate, crystalline fairies. Every once in a while, the wind would whip up into a howling frenzy, pelting me with swarms of snow and spattering the icy flakes against my chilled cheeks.

I ignored the latest wave of flurries stinging my face and continued digging, just like I'd been doing for the last hour. The only good thing about driving the shovel into the frozen earth was that the repetitive motions of scooping out the dirt and tossing it onto a pile kept me warm and limber, instead of cold and stiff like the tombstones surrounding me.

Despite the snow, I still had plenty of light to see by, thanks to the old-fashioned iron streetlamps spaced along the access roads throughout the cemetery. One of the lamps stood about thirty feet away from where I was digging, its golden glow highlighting the grave marker in front of me, making the carved name stand out like black blood against the gray stone.

Deirdre Shaw.

The mother of my foster brother, Finnegan Lane. A strong Ice elemental. And a potentially dangerous enemy.

A week ago, I'd found a file that Fletcher Lane—Finn's dad and my assassin mentor—had hidden in his office. A file claiming that Deirdre was powerful, deceitful, and treacherous—and not nearly as dead as everyone thought she was. So I'd come here tonight to find out whether she was truly six feet under. I was hoping she was dead and rotting in her grave, but I wasn't willing to bet on it.

Too many things from my own past had come back to haunt me. I knew better than to leave something this important to chance.

Thunk.

My shovel hit something hard and metal. I stopped and breathed in, hoping to smell the stench of decades-old decay. But the cold, crisp scent of the snow mixed with the rich, dark earth created a pleasant perfume. No decay, no death, and, most likely, no body.

I cleared off the rest of the dirt, revealing the top of the casket. A rune had been carved into the lid, jagged icicles fitted together to form a heart. My stomach knotted up with tension. Fletcher had inked that same rune onto Deirdre's file. This was definitely the right grave.

I was already standing in the pit that I'd dug, and I scraped away a few more chunks of earth so that I could crouch down beside the top half of the casket. The metal lid was locked, but that was easy enough to fix. I set down my shovel, pulled off my black gloves, and held up my hands, reaching for my Ice magic. The matching scars embedded deep in my palms—each one a small circle surrounded by eight thin rays—pulsed with the cold, silver light of my power. My spider runes, the symbols for patience.

When I had generated enough magic, I reached down, wrapped my hands around the casket lid's locks, and blasted them with my Ice power. After coating the locks with two inches of elemental Ice, I sent out another surge of power, cracking away the cold crystals. At the same time, I reached for my Stone magic, hardening my skin. Under my magical assault, the locks shattered, and my Stone-hardened skin kept the flying bits of metal from cutting my hands. I dusted away the remains of the locks and the Ice, took hold of the casket lid, dug my feet into the dirt, and lifted it.

The lid was heavy, and the metal didn't want to open, not after all the years spent peacefully resting in the ground. It creaked and groaned in protest, but I managed to hoist it up a couple of inches. I grabbed my shovel and slid it into the opening, using it as a lever to lift the lid the rest of the way.

Dirt rained down all around me, mixing with the snowflakes, and I wrinkled my nose to hold back a sneeze.

I wedged the length of the shovel in between the lid and the edge of the casket so it would stay open. Then I wiped the sweat off my forehead, put my hands on my knees to catch my breath, and looked down.

Just as I expected, snow-white silk lined the inside of the casket, with a small square matching pillow positioned at the very top, where a person's head would rest. But something decidedly unexpected was situated next to the pillow, nestled in the middle of the pristine fabric.

A box.

It was about the size of a small suitcase and made out of silverstone, a sturdy metal that had the unique property of absorbing and storing magic. The box's gray surface gleamed like a freshly minted coin, and it looked as clean and untouched as the rest of the white silk.

I frowned. I'd expected the casket to be completely empty. Or for there to be a decaying body inside. If I had been extremely lucky, Deirdre would have been in there, dead after all.

So why was there a box in it instead? And who had put it here?

I stared at the box, more knots forming in the pit of my stomach and then slowly tightening. I'd recently gone up against Raymond Pike, a metal elemental who had enjoyed planting bombs before I helped plant *him* in some botanical gardens. Pike had received a letter with Deirdre's rune stamped on it and had bragged that the two of them were business associates. He'd also said she was the most coldhearted person he'd ever met. I wondered if he'd booby-trapped the box in Deirdre's casket as some sort of favor to her, to blow up anyone who might come investigate whether she was truly dead.

I reached out, using my Stone magic to listen to all the rocks in the ground around the casket. But the rocks only grumbled about the cold, the snow, and how I'd disturbed their own final resting place. No other emotional vibrations resonated through them, which meant that no one had been near the casket in years.

I crouched down and brushed away the dirt that had fallen on top of the box when I opened the casket lid. No magic emanated from the silverstone box, although a rune had been carved into the top of it, the same small circle and eight thin rays that were branded into each of my palms.

My spider rune.

"Fletcher," I whispered, my breath frosting in the air.

The old man had left the box here for me to find. No doubt about it. He was the only one who seemed to know that Deirdre wasn't actually dead. More important, Fletcher had known *me*. He had realized that if Deirdre ever made an appearance back in Ashland, back in Finn's life, I would find his file on her and come to her grave to determine whether she was dead and buried.

Once again, the old man had left me with clues to find from beyond his own grave, which was located a hundred feet away. For whatever reason, he and Deirdre hadn't been buried side by side. Something I hadn't really thought too much about until tonight. I wondered why Fletcher hadn't buried the supposedly dead mother of his son next to his own cemetery plot. Something must have happened between him and Deirdre.

Something bad.

I opened up the bottom half of the casket and ran my fingers all around the silk, just in case something else had been left behind, but there was nothing. So I hooked my hands under the box and lifted it out of the casket. It was surprisingly heavy, as though Fletcher had packed it full of information. The weight made me even more curious about what might be inside—

"Did you hear something, Don?"

I froze, hoping that I'd only imagined the high feminine voice.

"Yes, I did, Ethel," a deeper masculine voice answered back.

No such luck.

Still holding the box, I stood on my tiptoes and peered over the lip of the grave. A man and a woman stood about forty feet away, both of them dwarves, given their five-foot heights and stocky, muscular frames. I hadn't heard a car roll into the cemetery, so the two of them must have parked somewhere nearby and walked in like I had.

They were both bundled up in black clothes and weren't carrying flashlights, which meant that they didn't want to be seen. Shovels were propped up on their shoulders, the metal scoops shimmering like liquid silver under the glow of the streetlamps. There was only one reason for the two of them to be skulking around the cemetery with shovels.

My mouth twisted with disgust. Grave robbers. One of the lowest forms of scum, even among the plethora of criminals who called Ashland home.

They must have sensed my stare, or perhaps they'd noticed the massive pile of dirt that I'd dug up, because they both turned and looked right at me.

"Hey!" the woman, Ethel, called out. "Someone else is here!"

The two dwarves started running toward me. I cursed, put the box on the ground next to the tombstone, dug my fingers into the grass, and scrambled up and out of the grave. I'd just staggered to my feet when the dwarves stopped in front of me, their shovels now held out in front of them like lances.

Ethel's blue eyes narrowed to slits. "What do you think you're doing? This here is *our* cemetery. Nobody else's."

"Aw, now, don't be like that, Ethel," her companion said. "Look on the bright side. She did the hard work of digging up this grave for us already. Looks like she found something good too."

He stabbed his shovel at the silverstone box. My fingers clenched into fists. No way were they getting their grubby hands on that. Not when it might hold clues about Deirdre Shaw—where she might be and why everyone thought she was dead, including Finn, her own son.

Don grinned; his bright red nose and bushy white beard made him look like Santa Claus. With her rosy cheeks and short, curly white hair, Ethel was the perfect counterpart. If Santa and Mrs. Claus were low-down, no-good grave robbers.

"Why, we should thank her," Don said. "Before we kill her, of course."

Ethel nodded. "You're right, hon. You always are."

The two dwarves tightened their grips on their shovels

and stepped toward me, but I held my ground, my gray eyes as cold and hard as the snow-dusted tombstones.

"Before the two of you do something you won't live to regret, you should know that that box is *mine*," I said. "Walk away now, don't come back, and I'll forget that I ever saw you here."

"And who do you think you are, giving us orders?" Ethel snapped.

"Gin Blanco. That's who."

I didn't say my name to brag. Not really. But I was the head of the Ashland underworld now, which meant that they should know exactly who I was—and especially what I was capable of doing to them.

Ethel rolled her eyes. "You must really be desperate to claim to be *her*. Then again, dead women will say anything to keep on breathing, won't they, Don?"

The other dwarf nodded. "Yep."

I ground my teeth. Low-life criminals had no trouble tracking me down at the Pork Pit, my barbecue restaurant in downtown Ashland, and no qualms whatsoever about trying to kill me there. But whenever I was away from the restaurant, got into a bad situation, and tried to warn people about who I really was, nobody believed me. Irony's way of screwing me over time and time again, laughing at me all the while.

"Besides," Don continued, "even if you really were Gin Blanco, it wouldn't matter. Everyone knows that she's the big boss in name only. It won't be long until someone kills her and takes her place."

He was certainly right about that. The other bosses were plotting against me, and many of the city's criminals were waiting to see how my underworld reign played out—or how short-lived it might be—before they officially took sides. Still, it was kind of sad when even the local grave robbers didn't respect you.

I opened my mouth to tell them to stop being idiots, but Don kept on talking.

"Enough chitchat. It's freezing out here, and we need to get to work, which means that your time is up. But since you found that box for us, I'll offer you a deal. Turn around, and I'll whack you on the back of the head." Don swung his shovel in a vicious arc. "You won't even know what hit you. I'll even plant you in that grave, so you get some kind of proper burial."

I palmed the silverstone knife hidden up my right sleeve and flashed it at them. "As charming as your offer is, I'm going to have to decline."

Ethel glared at me. "So that's how it is, then?"

"That's how it *always* is with me."

The two dwarves looked at each other, raised their shovels, and charged at me. I reached for my Stone magic, hardening my body again, then surged forward to meet them.

I sidestepped Ethel and sliced my knife across Don's chest, but he was wearing so many puffy layers that it was like cutting into a marshmallow. I slashed through his down vest, and tiny white feathers exploded in my face, momentarily blinding me and making me sneeze.

Don yelped in surprise and staggered back. I sneezed again and went after him—

Whack!

A shovel slammed into my shoulder, spinning me around. But since I was still holding on to my Stone magic, the shovel bounced off my body instead of crack-ing all the bones in my arm.

I blinked away the last of the feathers to find Ethel glaring at me again.

"Look at that gray glow to her eyes," she huffed. "She's a Stone elemental. We'll have to beat her to death to put her down for good."

Don brightened, his blue eyes twinkling in his face and adding to the Santa Claus illusion. "Why, it'll be just like our honeymoon all over again," he crooned. "Remember robbing that cemetery up in Cloudburst Falls, hon?"

The two of them smiled at each other for a moment before coming at me again. Well, at least they still did things together.

Instead of trying to saw through their winter clothes and their tough muscles underneath, I reached for my magic, raised my hand, and sent a spray of Ice daggers shooting out at them. Ethel threw herself down onto the ground, ducking out of the way of my chilly blast, but Don wasn't as quick, and several long, sharp bits of Ice *punch-punch-punch*ed into his chest. But dwarves were strong, and he only grunted, more surprised than seri-ously injured. He did lose his grip on his shovel, which tumbled to the ground.

I dropped my knife, darted forward, and snatched up his shovel, since it was the better weapon in this instance. Then I drew back my arms and slammed the shovel into his head, as though his skull were a baseball that I was trying to hit out past center field.

Thwack.

Don stared at me, wobbling on his feet, his eyes spinning in their sockets. His dwarven musculature might be exceptionally tough and thick, but a cold metal shovel upside the head was more than enough to put a dent in his bowling ball of a skull. Still, it was just a dent, and he didn't go down, so I hit him again.

Thwack.

And again and again, until the bones in his skull and face cracked, and blood started gushing down his head, face, and neck. A glassy sheen coated Don's eyes, and he toppled over, more and more of his blood soaking into the frozen ground.

"Don!" Ethel wailed, realizing that he wasn't ever going to get back up. "Don!" She tightened her grip on her shovel, scrambled back up onto her feet, and charged at me again. "You bitch!" she screamed. "I'll kill you for this!"

Ethel stopped right in front of me and raised her shovel over her head, trying to build up enough momentum to smash through my Stone magic with one deathblow. But in doing so, she left herself completely open; it was easy enough for me to palm another knife, step forward, and bury the blade in her throat.

Ethel's eyes bulged, and blood bubbled up out of her lips. She coughed, the warm drops of her blood stinging my cheeks like the snowflakes had earlier. I yanked my knife out of her throat, doing even more damage, but Ethel wasn't ready to give up just yet. She staggered forward and raised her shovel even higher, still trying to gather herself for that one deadly strike.

Too late.

The shovel slipped from her hands, and her body

sagged and pitched forward. She landed facedown in the mound of loose earth that I'd dug up, as though it were a giant pillow she was plopping down on. Well, I supposed that was one way to take a dirt nap.

While I caught my breath, I watched and waited. More and more blood poured out from the dwarves' wounds, but Don and Ethel didn't move or stir. They were as dead as the rest of the folks here.

So I retrieved my first knife from the ground, wiped Ethel's blood off the second one, and tucked both of my weapons back up my sleeves. I looked and listened, but the night was still and quiet again. No one was coming to investigate. The cemetery was located off by itself on one of the many mountain ridges that cut through Ashland, and I doubted that the sounds of our fight had been loud enough to attract any attention. Still, I needed to do *something* with the bodies. I didn't want anyone to know that I had been here, much less whose grave I had been digging up.

I looked at the dwarves' bodies, then down at the open casket.

Don was right. I'd gone to all the trouble to unearth Deirdre Shaw's grave. She wasn't in her casket, so somebody might as well get some use out of it.

I grinned.

And it might as well be me.

❋ 2 *❋*

I rolled the dwarves' bodies into the casket, shut the lids, and filled in all the dirt back on top of it. Then I arranged the blocks of sod that I'd first cut out of the ground back into place on the top of the grave, so that it had a layer of winter grass that matched the surrounding ground.

While I worked, the snow intensified, morphing into a steady shower cascading down. Good. The thickening layer of flakes on the ground would help hide the uneven spots and loose bits of dirt and rocks around the grave. Not that I expected anyone else to come looking for Deirdre Shaw, but if there was one thing Fletcher had taught me, it was that you couldn't be too careful when dealing with a new and largely unknown enemy.

By the time I'd finished making the grave look as untouched as possible, it was almost midnight. I grabbed the box that had been hidden in Deirdre's casket and left the cemetery.

I walked to my car, which I'd parked half a mile from the cemetery entrance. When I first arrived, I'd stuffed a white plastic bag into the driver's-side window as if I'd had car trouble, so no one would wonder why the vehicle was sitting by the side of the road. But my car wasn't the only one here now. An old, battered white van was parked a few hundred feet away, also with a white plastic bag hanging out of the window. Most likely Don and Ethel's ride, to haul away any loot they might unearth during their grave robbing.

I ignored the van. In a day or two, someone would get curious—or greedy—enough to approach it. That person would either call the cops to report an abandoned vehicle or smash in a window, hot-wire the van, and drive it away to sell for scrap. I'd bet on the second option, though. This was Ashland, after all. Land of criminal conspiracies and malicious opportunity.

I unlocked my car, took the bag out of the window, and slid inside. Then I placed the casket box in the passenger's seat, cranked up the heat, and drove home.

The roads around the cemetery were dark, curvy, and covered with snow, forcing me to drive slowly. Every time I reached a relatively straight patch of pavement, I glanced over at the box, wondering what secrets it held. The spider runes in my palms itched with anticipation, but I wrapped my hands around the steering wheel and forced my gaze back to the road. Fletcher had taught me to be patient, and I could wait until I got home to open it. Besides, I wanted to go through the box slowly, calmly, and carefully, despite my burning desire to pull over, crack it open right this very second, and dig through all the contents like a kid tearing through Christmas presents.

Twenty minutes later, I turned off the road and steered my car up a rough, steep driveway. The wheels churned through the snow and down into the gravel beneath, but I kept gunning the engine, and the car slowly crept up the ridge.

I crested the top of the slope, and Fletcher's house, my house now, loomed into view. Snow could hide a multitude of sins, and the falling white flakes masked much of the mismatched brick, tin, and other materials that made up different sections of the ramshackle structure. For once, the house had a cohesive look, adding to the overall snow-globe atmosphere.

Normally, this late at night, the house, the surrounding lawn, and the woods that lined the top of the ridge should have been dark and deserted.

But they weren't.

A navy sedan was parked in the driveway, and the front porch light was on, a bright beacon in the still, snowy night.

Bria was here.

Surprised, I took my foot off the accelerator. But the car stalled in the snow, so I gave it some more gas, steered over, and parked next to her sedan. I cut the engine, then looked over at the house. She must be waiting up for me. I wondered why.

My sister seemed fine when she'd come to the Pork Pit for lunch. But any number of things—good and bad—could have happened since then. Everything from Bria finally having a lead on where Emery Slater, a giant enemy of mine, was hiding out to wanting help with one of her cases. But of course, my paranoid mind immediately seized on worst-case scenarios, like one of our friends being injured, held hostage, or dead.

Worry and dread chewed up my stomach like acid, but I forced myself to stay calm, pull my phone out of my jacket pocket, and turn it on. I hadn't wanted Silvio Sanchez, my personal assistant, to track my phone and realize where I was going, so I'd shut off the device before my trip to the cemetery.

I didn't have any missed calls, texts, or messages. No one had tried to reach me, which meant that my friends should be okay. Instead of easing my worry, the knowledge only cranked it up another notch. What had been so important that Bria had come here tonight?

And that wasn't my only concern.

I looked at the silverstone box on the passenger seat. The porch light's golden glow made the spider rune carved into the top glimmer like an all-knowing eye staring back at me. Part of me wanted to leave the box out here so Bria wouldn't see it and start asking awkward questions.

But this wasn't a secret that I could keep for much longer. At some point, I was going to have to tell Finn about his mother being alive, and Bria and Finn loved each other. Maybe my sister could help me figure out the best way to break the news to him. At the very least, she would be a sounding board to help me decide how to handle this.

So I got out of the car, grabbed the box, and headed for the porch. I scanned the house, the lawn, and the woods, searching for intruders and using my Stone magic to listen to the rocks buried in the snow. But they only whispered about the cold, wind, and steady shower of flakes—no notes of alarm, fear, or malice rippled through them. Bria was the only one here.

I stepped onto the porch, then unlocked and opened the front door, scuffing the snow off my boots and making plenty of noise so she would know that I was home.

"Gin?" Bria's light, lilting voice drifted through the house to me.

"Yep."

"I'm in the den."

"Be right there."

I locked the door behind me, tossed my keys onto a table, and walked into the back of the house, still holding the box under one arm. I stepped into the den to find Detective Bria Coolidge sitting on the couch, checking her phone.

In some ways, we were mirror images of each other, with our matching dark jeans and warm layers. But of course, her hands and clothes were clean and spotless, and her primrose rune glinted a bright silver against her navy turtleneck sweater. She was also far more relaxed, with her boots off and her socked feet propped up on the coffee table. Her gun and gold detective's badge were on top of the scarred wooden surface, lying right next to . . . Fletcher's file on Deirdre.

I froze. I'd been in such a hurry to dig up Deirdre's grave before the snow hit that I hadn't thought to hide the file before I left. Then again, I hadn't expected to have a visitor tonight either. If an intruder had been hiding in the house, I would have killed him, and he wouldn't have had a chance to tell anyone about anything.

But Bria was here, and she'd seen the file. She knew something was up.

Bria tilted her head to the side, making her golden hair gleam, and her blue gaze swept over my black toboggan, fleece jacket, jeans, and boots. Despite my dark attire, her sharp eyes easily spotted the dirt and blood crusting my clothes.

"Well," she drawled, an amused note in her voice. "I see that the Spider has been busy tonight. Care to tell me where you were, what you were doing, and how many people you killed?"

"That depends on who's asking—the cop or my baby sister?"

Bria grinned, a mischievous expression on her pretty face. "Well, this cop knows you've been up to something shady at Blue Ridge Cemetery."

I blinked. "How do you know I was there?"

She started ticking off points on her fingers. "For one thing, it's after midnight, and you're wearing your usual assassin attire. You're also covered with dirt and blood, which means that there was at least one body involved somewhere along the way. A cemetery seems like a perfect place for something like that to go down." She paused. "And I might have tracked the GPS on your car when I showed up after my shift ended and you weren't here."

I frowned. "I don't have GPS on my car."

"Correction. You *didn't* have GPS on your car . . . until Silvio placed a tracking device on it a couple of days ago." Bria grinned again. "He wanted another way to keep tabs on you, now that you've started turning off your phone when you don't want him to know where you are. Silvio is rather determined to 'save you from yourself,' as he puts it. Watch out, Gin. Next thing you know, he'll be sewing GPS trackers into your underwear."

"And I'm going to cheerfully throttle my overefficient assistant when he comes into work in the morning," I growled. "*After* I take away his phone and tablet."

She laughed. "Oh, taking away his electronics will be punishment enough. Silvio is rather attached to them."

But her laugher faded, along with her grin, and she focused on the casket box. "You want to tell me what happened tonight? And what's so important about that box that you're clutching it like it holds all the secrets of the universe?"

"That depends," I countered, shifting on my feet. "You want to tell me what *you're* doing here? Not that I don't love unexpected visits from my sister . . ."

"But you didn't expect me to be here tonight. That's why you sat in your car for so long. You were thinking about what to do, and especially what to tell me."

I shrugged.

Bria put her feet down on the floor and gave me a serious stare. "I'm here because you've been quiet this past week."

I frowned again, not understanding what she was getting at. "Okay . . ."

"It's the same kind of quiet I remember from when we were kids. The quiet that always fell over you whenever you were thinking about something serious. Whenever you were trying to solve a problem that no one else even knew about." She smiled, but sadness tinged her expression. "Like when I broke Mom's favorite snow globe, even though she had told me not to play with it, and you were trying to figure out how to cover for me. Do you remember that?"

Images flashed through my mind. Bria staring in wonderment at a globe filled with a lovely garden scene, the flowers crusted with real, tiny diamonds and other sparkling jewels. Her hand grabbing the globe and shaking it just a little too hard, making it slip from her grip and crash to the floor, shattering into a hundred pieces. My sister crying, not just because of the trouble she was in but because she'd destroyed something so delicate and beautiful. Such an ordinary memory but one of the few relatively happy ones I had from my childhood . . .

"Gin?"

"Yeah," I rasped through the hard knot of emotion clogging my throat. "I remember."

"And do you remember how you handled it?"

I shrugged again, still not sure what she was getting at.

Her sad smile brightened, just a bit. "Annabella was planning on sneaking out of the house to party with her friends, so you blackmailed her into buying the same snow globe with her allowance, even though it cost a fortune. Mom never even knew that I'd broken the old one."

Bria's gaze drifted up to two drawings I'd sketched that were propped up on the fireplace mantel. One was a snowflake, symbolizing icy calm, and the other was an ivy vine, representing elegance. Matching pendants were draped over the respective frames. The runes for Eira Snow, our mother, and Annabella, our older sister, both murdered long ago.

Bria's hand crept up to her throat and her own primrose rune, the symbol for beauty. The motion made two rings glint on her hand, one embossed with snowflakes and the other with ivy vines. I wore a similar ring stamped with my spider rune, a gift from Bria, with a matching pendant hanging around my neck, buried under my layers of clothes.

My sister stared at the drawings a moment longer before dropping her hand from her necklace and focusing on me again. "That was the very first time I realized how much you loved me . . . and just how sneaky you could be."

I cleared my throat, pushing away the memories and the melancholy heartache they always brought along with them. "So you came over here tonight because I've been quiet?"

"Too quiet, as they say." She kept staring at me. "Your special kind of quiet that means something is up. If it makes you feel any better, I don't think anyone else has noticed yet. Not even Silvio, despite all his GPS trackers."

Bria was right. I did have a tendency to get quiet—too quiet—when something was on my mind, just like when we were kids. I didn't know whether to be flattered or annoyed that she knew me so well. Or just plain worried I hadn't been able to hide my inner turmoil any better.

"Now," she drawled, "I am a trained detective, so I figure that whatever has been bothering you most likely has to do with that file on the coffee table."

I tensed, my arm curling even tighter around the box I was still clutching.

"I didn't look at the file," she said. "I respect your privacy too much for that."

"But . . ."

"But I would like for you to tell me what's going on, since it's obviously much more serious than a broken snow globe." Stubborn determination filled her face. "And I especially want you to tell me how I can help. No matter how bad it is, we can figure it out—together."

I suddenly wanted to confess everything to her, but still, I hesitated, shifting on my feet again, moving the box from one arm to the other. Despite Bria's desire to help, I was still *me*, still the suspicious assassin Fletcher had molded me into, one who knew that secrets could be more dangerous than anything else.

Sure, I had a burning desire to know every little thing that was in the box, especially since the old man had carved my spider rune into it, a clear message that he had wanted me to find it. But an even bigger part of me was worried about what might be inside—what dark, ugly, painful truths Fletcher had gone to such great lengths to bury, literally.

Truths that could hurt Finn.

Bria sensed that I was wavering, and she kept her gaze steady on mine. "Let me help you. Let me carry some of the load. Please, Gin."

Her voice was even softer this time, but her tone was sincere, strong, and filled with understanding. She got to her feet, stepped in front of me, and held out her arms, waiting for me to let her help, waiting for me to let her in.

And just like that, all the resistance drained out of me.

I slid the silverstone box into her arms. Then I stepped back and massaged first one arm, then the other, trying to ease the dull ache that had built up in my muscles. Funny, but I hadn't realized how heavy the box was until now.

Bria nodded at me, then put the box down on the coffee table, right next to Deirdre's file. She eyed my spider rune carved into the top of the box but didn't say anything or make a move to open it. Instead, she waited while I shrugged out of my dirt-and-blood-crusted jacket, spread a blanket out on the couch, and plopped down on it. Bria dragged the coffee table over to the couch and sat down next to me.

We both stared at the box, quiet and still. The only sounds were the steady *tick-tick-tick*s of various clocks in the house, along with the whistle of the wind whipping around the windows.

I drew in a breath. "Remember Raymond Pike and how he bragged that he was working with what sounded like a whole group of people?"

"Yeah . . ."

"Well, I found out who one of them was."

"And?"

"Her name is Deirdre Shaw." It took me a second to force out the rest of my confession. "And she is Finn's not-so-dead mother."

Bria's eyes bulged, and her mouth dropped open into a wide O. For a moment, she was frozen in place, her entire body stiff with shock. She sucked in a breath, then exhaled and shook her head, as though she were trying to rattle my words right out of her mind. Her gaze flicked to the file on the table, then the box, then back to the file.

"Are you sure?" she asked, her voice barely above a whisper.

"I'm sure. I found that file in Fletcher's office, hidden in a secret desk drawer, as if he didn't want anyone to discover it *ever*. That file claims that Deirdre Shaw is Finn's mother and that she is very much alive." I paused, once again having to force out the words. "So tonight I went to Blue Ridge Cemetery to dig up her grave to see if she was actually buried in it . . ."

I handed Bria the file, then told her everything that had happened tonight. My sister stayed quiet through my cold, clipped recitation, absorbing and analyzing everything I said as she read through Fletcher's file.

By the time I was finished, she'd gone through all the information. She studied a recent photo of Deirdre in the file, then leaned down, staring at the rune Fletcher had inked onto the folder tab, that heart made of jagged icicles.

Bria frowned and tapped her finger against the symbol. "This might sound crazy, and it's certainly not going to make you feel any better, but I've seen that rune somewhere before."

"Yeah, it was on that letter you found in Pike's penthouse. The one you gave to Lorelei Parker, along with the rest of her half brother's stuff. Lorelei gave me a copy of it. There was no name on the letter, just that rune. I recognized the symbol and started digging through Fletcher's files. That's how I found the information on Deirdre."

Bria shook her head. "No, I've seen that rune somewhere else. I thought it looked familiar when I first saw Pike's letter. So I did a search in the police rune databases, trying to figure out where I knew it from. But there was no mention of anything like it in the databases, so I wasn't able to track it down. Still, I know it from *somewhere*."

I chewed my lip, trying to think of where Bria might

have possibly come across Deirdre's rune before, but of course, I didn't have an answer. She was right. Her having seen the rune before made me even more uneasy.

"So what's in the box?" Bria asked. "And why did Fletcher leave it in Deirdre's grave?"

"Time to find out."

I dragged the box to the edge of the table. No locks or latches adorned the silverstone, but it was still securely sealed. So I palmed a knife and worked the tip of the blade into the seam that ran between the lid and the rest of the box. I ran my knife around the entire seam, wiggling the tip back and forth. It didn't want to open any more than Deirdre's casket had, but I finally managed to split the seam. A loud *pop* sounded, like when you cracked open a pickle jar, as though the box had been vacuum-sealed. Maybe it had been.

I put my knife down, grabbed the lid, and lifted it off the box before setting it off to one side. Beside me, Bria leaned forward, as curious to see what was inside as I was.

The answer?

Photos.

Dozens of photos, all of them old, slightly yellow, and faded, with smooth, worn edges, as though someone— Fletcher—had rubbed his fingers over them time and time again in thought.

And Deirdre Shaw was in every single one of them.

In the photos, she was young, twenty or so, and quite beautiful, with pale blue eyes and long golden hair. The first photo showed her in a grassy field, wearing a blue sundress, with a crown of blue peonies perched on her head, as though she were a fairy-tale princess. She looked at the camera out of the corner of her eye, as if she were too shy to enjoy having her picture taken, although her lips were turned up into a small, satisfied smile.

The next few photos were of Deirdre and Fletcher together, holding hands, walking through the woods, even sharing a chocolate milkshake at the Pork Pit. It was obvious that this was in the beginning of their relationship, because they were staring dreamily into each other's eyes. They made a lovely couple, Deirdre slim, blond, and beautiful, Fletcher tall, strong, and handsome, with his dark brown hair and green eyes.

But as I looked through more of the photos, they slowly started to change.

Fletcher remained as happy as ever, but Deidre smiled less and less in the pictures, especially as her stomach grew larger and rounder, and it became apparent that she was pregnant. One shot showed Deirdre deep into her pregnancy. Fletcher had his arm slung around her shoulder and was smiling at the camera, but Deirdre's expression seemed more like a grimace than a grin, as though she had screwed on a smile just to have her picture taken.

And finally, I saw the first and only photo of Finn.

It must have been taken a few days after he was born, because he was just a tiny, blanket-wrapped bundle, cradled in Fletcher's arms, his sleeping face turned toward the camera. Fletcher was positively beaming, his face stretched into an enormous grin. Deirdre was standing next to him, looking at Finn, but her eyes were empty, and her face was strangely blank, as though she were staring at someone else's baby instead of her own son.

That last photo made even more cold worry pool in

my chest, as though my heart were made of the same jagged icicles as Deirdre's rune.

"It's like a chronicle of their relationship," Bria murmured, studying the photos as I handed them to her one by one. "Only without saying how or when they finally broke up."

"I'm guessing that part didn't make for such a pretty picture."

Bria set the photos aside, and I fished out the other objects in the box. An engagement ring with a hole where the diamond should be. An empty, cracked, heart-shaped perfume bottle that still smelled faintly of peonies. A blue cameo of a mother holding a child, split down the middle into two pieces.

"Mementos Fletcher saved from happier times?" Bria suggested.

"Maybe," I said. "Or maybe they're a message."

She held up the cameo pieces. "What kind of message does a broken pendant send?"

"Not a good one."

A soft blue baby blanket was also tucked into the box, with Finn's name stitched across the bottom in white letters. I lifted up the blanket, expecting it to be the final thing in the box, but two items were buried underneath it, two letters in sealed envelopes, one addressed to me and the other to Finn.

I gasped, but Bria was looking through the photos again, so she didn't notice my surprise. I dropped the blanket back down where it had been, hiding the letters. I loved my sister, but I wanted to read Fletcher's words in private, wanted to have some time to myself to think about them and digest them. Not to mention Finn's letter. I didn't even know *what* to do with that right now.

"That's it?" Bria asked. "Just a baby blanket? That's all there is?"

"Yeah," I lied. "Why?"

She shrugged. "All this stuff is interesting, for sure, but there's nothing here that's earth-shattering. Overall, it seems a bit . . . disappointing."

"You're not the one with a suddenly not-so-dead mother."

"True," Bria said. "But Fletcher has left you clues and letters before. Far more detailed ones. This seems like a keepsake box more than anything else. I just thought there would be something *more*. Records, certificates, maybe even a diary that would tell you about Deirdre, like why she apparently faked her own death and left town and why Fletcher went along with it."

I shrugged, making sure not to look at the baby blanket and the two letters buried under it. "The old man always left me the information that he thought was the most important. In this case, maybe he thought it was the pictures. Maybe he wanted me to see Deirdre as she was back then."

"Well, you knew Fletcher best. Maybe things will make more sense after you've gone through everything again."

Bria bit her lip, dropped her gaze to her hands, and started twisting her two rune rings around on her fingers, something she only did when she was thinking hard or worried about something. Her own giveaway, just like quietness was mine.

After a few seconds, her hands stilled, and she looked at me. "So what do we tell Finn?"

I scrubbed my hands over my face, but the motion did nothing to ease the dull ache in my temples. "I don't know. I was hoping that I'd be able to track her down and do some reconnaissance before I told him anything. But so far, she's been a complete ghost. No driver's license, no property or tax records, no trace of a Deirdre Shaw anywhere in Ashland." I gestured at the box, photos, and other items. "Even with all of this, all I really know about her is that she's not dead like she's supposed to be."

"You have to tell Finn that his mother is alive," Bria said in a soft voice. "He's already going to be upset and hurt that you didn't tell him the second you found out. The longer you wait now, the worse it will be. You know that."

I did know that, but that didn't mean I liked it. How do you break something like this to someone? How do you go about rocking the foundation of his world to its very core? Changing everything he thought he knew about his parents? All that would have been bad enough if this was a stranger. But this was *Finn*. The guy I'd been raised with. The guy I had been through so much with. The man who was my brother in all the ways that truly mattered.

I didn't know, and now I was in the damned awkward position of having to find out.

"Well," I said, trying to make a joke of things, the way Finn would have if our positions had been reversed. "I say we ply him with food and booze and then spring the news on him. Have all his favorite things around to help soften the shock."

Bria nodded. "That's actually not a bad idea. We're supposed to go to a cocktail party at his bank tomorrow night. Finn is schmoozing with some new client he wants me to meet. You and Owen could tag along, and we could all go to Underwood's for dinner afterward. Tell him everything and then figure out what our next move is."

I winced.

"What's wrong?" Her eyes narrowed. "Wait a second. You haven't told Owen about this either?"

I winced again. "I haven't told anyone anything, except you. I wanted to actually know what I was talking about before I spilled the beans. But all I have is this." I waved my hand over the faded photos and cracked mementos. "Not exactly a whole lot of beans to spill."

"Still," Bria said, "it all has to mean *something*. Fletcher wouldn't have buried all these things in Deirdre's casket if they weren't important. If it wasn't some kind of message."

I sighed. "You might be right, but I have no idea what he was thinking. Not this time."

Bria picked up the folder and stared at Deirdre's icicle-heart rune again. "Well, whatever Fletcher was trying to tell you, I have a bad feeling about this, Gin."

My gaze dropped to the photo of Fletcher holding Finn, and Deirdre with that cold, blank look on her face. "Yeah. Me too."

✳ 3 ✳

Bria promised to tell Finn that Owen and I would be crashing the party tomorrow night. Then she bundled up, and I walked her to the front door. The snow had stopped while we were talking, leaving three inches of white, fluffy powder coating the ground.

I waited until I heard her car pull out onto the road at the bottom of the ridge before I shut the door and headed back to the den.

I stopped in the doorway and stared at the casket box, where the two letters from Fletcher were hidden under Finn's baby blanket. But instead of tossing the blanket aside and ripping into my letter, I sat down on the couch and carefully went through all the photos and other items again.

I studied each image in turn—not just the pictures themselves but all the corners, edges, and backs, in case Fletcher had scribbled a note or left some other clue I hadn't spotted. Nothing.

I did the same thing with the diamond-less engagement ring, the empty perfume bottle, and the broken cameo. Once again, a big fat lot of nothing. No runes, no symbols, not even a maker's mark stamped on any of them.

I pulled the baby blanket out of the box and ran my fingers over the fabric, but it was just a blanket, the cotton so soft and thin you could practically see through it. Three strikes, and I was out.

Except for the letters.

I put the blanket down and finally pulled the two letters out of the box. I studied the envelopes as carefully as I had everything else, but they were plain except for the single word on each of them. *Gin* on one and *Finn* on the other, each written in the old man's distinctive, spidery scrawl.

Finn's letter wasn't mine to open, so I wrapped it back up in the baby blanket and set it aside. I turned the other envelope over and over again in my hands, as though I might suddenly see something different besides my name inked on the front. Then I picked up my knife and sliced open the top, trying to ignore the sudden churning of my stomach.

A single sheet of paper was tucked inside. The faint scent of peonies tickled my nose as I pulled out the letter and unfolded it, reading the old man's words.

Gin,

If you are reading this, then I am gone—but Deirdre Shaw is back in Ashland. I don't know exactly what brought you to her grave. If you found the file hidden in my office, if Deirdre made some move against you, or if something else entirely drove

*you to look in her casket. But you've found the box.
The things inside are all that I have left of Deirdre.
Small, hollow, fragile things, but I hope that you'll
share them with Finn when the time is right.*

*I could tell you many stories about Deirdre. How we
met. How happy she made me. How much I loved her.*

*How the bitter bite of her betrayal almost destroyed
me.*

*But none of that really matters. All that matters is
that she is back in Ashland, which means that she is a
danger to you and especially to Finn. No matter what
she says, no matter what she does, no matter what
lies she tells, remember this—the only person Deirdre
Shaw has ever cared about is herself.*

*And her rune perfectly matches her own cold, cold
heart.*

*Watch out for Finn. He'll need you after
everything is over and Deirdre has done whatever
foul, manipulative thing she's planning. Give him the
second letter once she's gone. You'll understand why
then.*

I love you both so much.

> *Now and always,
> Fletcher*

I read the letter a second time, then a third. Fletcher
hadn't given me any specifics, but he didn't really need
to. Deirdre being a ghost for so long told me the most
important part of the story: she didn't care enough about
her own son to tell him that she was alive.

Curiosity burned in my heart, and my fingers itched

to grab Finn's letter and slice it open, but I pushed down the urge. Fletcher had wanted me to save it for Finn, and I would honor the old man's words and wishes.

Even if I still had no idea where Deirdre Shaw was. Or when or even if she might appear in Ashland—and Finn's life.

Despite how late it was and how emotionally drained I felt, I couldn't leave everything on the table for just anyone to traipse in and find, especially not before I'd talked to Finn.

So I slid the two letters from Fletcher in between the pages of a copy of *Diamonds Are Forever*, the latest book I was reading for the spy literature course I was taking at Ashland Community College. Then I gathered up the photos and mementos and placed them all back inside the casket box. I crossed the den and crawled into the empty fireplace. I stood on my tiptoes, hefted up the box, and shoved it onto a secret ledge high inside the stone column.

Once everything was secreted away, I headed upstairs to take a shower and wash off all the blood and grime. By the time my head finally touched the pillows, it was after two in the morning, but my sleep was fitful, and I spent the rest of the night tossing, turning, and worrying about how Finn was going to react to all of this.

In the morning, I got up and went to the Pork Pit. I might be the head of the underworld now, but like Don the grave robber had said, all the other criminals were still plotting against me, so I did my usual checks to make sure that no one had planted any deadly surprises inside the restaurant.

Once I had determined that everything was clean, I started getting ready for the day. Normally, wiping down the tables and booths would have brought me some kind of peace.

Not today.

Instead, my stomach churned in time to my quick swipes as I mopped the blue and pink pig tracks that covered the floor and worried about how to break the news to Finn. Regardless of how I did it, Bria was right—he was going to be hurt that I hadn't told him right away.

Maybe I would feel better when I had talked to Finn, and we could get on with the business of tracking down Deirdre and finding out what she had been doing all these years. Or maybe the answers would make me feel even worse—not to mention what they might do to Finn.

Damned if I did, doubly damned if I didn't. Yeah. I had a bad feeling that's how this whole thing would ultimately play out.

The bell over the front door chimed at exactly eleven o'clock, and in walked Silvio Sanchez, my personal assistant. The middle-aged vampire looked quite dapper in a dark gray fedora, overcoat, and matching suit. A small spider rune pin winked in the center of his silver tie.

Silvio nodded in greeting, took off his hat and coat, and arranged his smartphone and tablet on the counter. Soft chimes rang out as he fired up his electronics.

"Are you ready for the morning briefing, Gin?" he asked.

I barely heard him. Instead, I stared at a photo on the wall close to the cash register, one of a young Fletcher standing with his friend Warren T. Fox during a fishing trip. Fletcher seemed plenty happy in the photo, but his smile was dim and faint compared with the big, beaming grins he'd worn in the pictures of him with Deirdre. The way he'd looked at her . . . it was like she had been his whole world. I wondered just how badly she'd broken his heart—and why.

"Gin?" Silvio asked. "Are you okay?"

I turned away from the photo. "Forget about the morning briefing. I have someone I need you to start digging into. Her name is Deirdre Shaw. She's an Ice elemental."

I reached down, grabbed a copy of Deirdre's file from a slot under the cash register, and passed it over to him.

Silvio stared at the icicle-heart rune I'd inked on the folder tab. "And what is so interesting about Ms. Shaw?"

I couldn't tell him the whole truth. Not when Finn deserved to hear it first. So I went with the next-best thing. "She's the one who was friendly with Raymond Pike. I think she's the person Lorelei Parker did business with."

Silvio's eyebrows arched. "You mean the person who revealed Lorelei's real identity to Raymond? The person who pointed him at Lorelei so he could try to kill his own sister?"

"Among other things."

"Have you talked to Lorelei about this?" he asked. "If she's had dealings with Ms. Shaw, then she might have some insight into her. Mallory might too."

It was a good point and one I'd thought of myself, although I'd wanted to confirm that Deirdre was actually alive before I started asking questions about her. But I couldn't keep this from Finn any longer, so I might as well use all the resources at my disposal.

"Please add Lorelei and Mallory to my to-do list." My

voice took on a snarky note. "Exactly how long is said list today?"

Silvio perked up, completely missing my sarcasm, and started swiping through screens on his tablet. "Well, it's actually a light day, since you haven't let me schedule anything for this week, but I can make some calls, and we can squeeze in a few pertinent last-minute meetings . . ."

My eyes glazed over as Silvio rattled off a long list of people I needed to meet with, bruised egos that required soothing, and other complaints, rivalries, and problems that demanded my time and attention, both as the head of the underworld and as the owner of the Pork Pit. While he talked, I started chopping up vegetables for the day's sandwiches, letting the steady *thwack-thwack-thwack* of my knife drown out most of his words.

Everyone thought that running the underworld was *so* glamorous. That I had *so* much power. That I inspired *so* much fear in *so* many people. Fools. All I really did was take meetings, sit in on conference calls, and listen to people complain about things, just like any other CEO. Granted, they were all criminal things, like who was selling knockoff designer goods in someone else's territory, who was jacking a rival's gun shipments, who was knee-capping the competition.

Blah, blah-blah, blah-blah.

I wondered if Mab Monroe, the former queen of the underworld, had to listen to as many people complain before I killed her. Probably not. Mab had been known far and wide for her cruelty and ruthlessness. No doubt, she'd been able to shut up most people with a mere withering glance or a bit of elemental Fire flashing on her fingertips. And of course, she could have always just used her Fire power to roast the most excessive whiners outright.

Maybe I should start doing something similar with my magic. Let little Ice spikes shoot out of my fingertips when someone annoys me. Maybe even give them a cold glare and casually threaten to freeze them on the spot. Silvio would complain that scaring people into submission wasn't the best policy, especially with the crime bosses who were already plotting against me. Then again, he wasn't the one who had to listen to them whine.

I'd despised Mab for murdering my family and had taken great satisfaction in ending her existence. But maybe—just maybe—I should strive to be more like her in this one small way. Food for thought.

The first of the day's customers stepped into the restaurant, saving me from the rest of Silvio's recitation of my ever-increasing to-do list. Catalina Vasquez, Silvio's niece, was already here, rolling up straws and silverware into napkins, along with the other waitstaff, and we all got busy, cooking, cleaning, and checking on our customers.

In addition to my regular, law-abiding customers, several underworld crooks came in during the lunch rush to subtly pay their respects to me, the big boss, by eating in my gin joint. A few folks, like Dimitri Barkov and Luiz Ramos, were less than thrilled by my reign and spent most of their time glaring at me in between big bites of barbecue. They were under the mistaken impression that their petulant pouts actually bothered me.

Barkov ran some shipyards along the Aneirin River, importing and exporting everything from guns and drugs to shoes and uniforms. Ramos focused on illegal sports betting and high-stakes gambling. The two of them were minor-league players but with ambitions to move up to the big time.

A couple of weeks ago, they'd been fighting over the right to buy some coin laundries from Lorelei Parker, but I'd given the businesses to someone else instead. Dimitri and Luiz were still plenty pissed about that and no doubt plotting some sort of foolish move against me. But for now, they seemed content to sit in my restaurant, get their barbecue on, and give me dirty looks.

Dimitri realized that I was staring at them. His dark eyes narrowed to slits, his cheeks reddened, and his entire body puffed up with anger. Even his very bad, very obvious, very shaggy black toupee seemed to bristle with indignation. But instead of returning my stare with another hate-filled one, the Russian mobster grinned, picked up his soda, and saluted me with it. Then he put the glass down, leaned forward, and started whispering to Luiz, who gave me a quick, nervous glance over his shoulder before dropping his head and focusing on his food again.

Luiz didn't have either the stupidity or the balls to come at me head-on. But Dimitri . . . Dimitri was going to be a problem.

I cleared my throat, and Silvio looked at me.

I tilted my head in Dimitri's direction. "Our Russian friend looks positively smug today. Which means that he's probably decided to strike back at me. Care to nose around and see what you can find out?"

"Of course," Silvio murmured, a bit of sarcasm creeping into his tone. "I live to serve . . . when you actually let me *do* anything. I've been meaning to diagram his organization anyway."

"Diagram it? What do you mean?"

Silvio turned his tablet around so that I could see it and swiped through several screens of pie charts, bar graphs, and more. "Diagram it. You know, break down his operations into manpower, money earned, front businesses, and so on and so forth. Just in case you ever needed to, shall we say, *dismantle* it in a hurry."

I arched my eyebrows. "Pie charts are going to help me dismantle a criminal organization?"

The vamp straightened up and smoothed down his tie, affronted that I would mock his precious pie charts. "Absolutely. As an assassin, you should know that information is often the key to cutting off certain problems before they get started."

"Of course, you're right," I drawled. "Silly me for thinking that I had been cutting off certain problems with my knives for years now."

Silvio sniffed and gave me a chiding look, not at all amused by my black humor. Sometimes my assistant was a little too prim and proper for his own good. I resisted the urge to lean across the counter, muss his hair, take away his tablet, and give him a time-out.

Luiz slid out of the booth, threw enough bills down onto the table to pay for ten meals, and skedaddled out of the restaurant. But Dimitri took his sweet time, making a big show of giving me one more soda salute and a smug smirk before peeling some bills off a fat roll, tossing them onto the table, and ambling out through the front door.

Oh, yes. The mobster was definitely going to be trouble. But trouble was another one of those things that I specialized in, along with cutting off problems. I'd handle Dimitri the same way I had the rest of the lowlifes who'd come after me: permanently.

The lunch rush wrapped up, and the day wore on. I was sliding a batch of chocolate chip cookies into one of the ovens when the bell over the front door chimed.

"I hear we're going on a double date," a low, familiar voice murmured behind me.

I almost dropped the tray of cookies, but I tightened my grip at the last second, shoved the tray into the oven, and shut the door. To give myself a few more moments to prepare, I set the timer on the counter. Then I plastered a smile on my face and turned around.

Finnegan Lane, my foster brother, was perched on a stool next to Silvio. The vamp might look dapper in his suit, but Finn was positively resplendent in his. The navy Fiona Fine jacket stretched across his shoulders, the matching shirt underneath clinging to his sculpted muscles. Add the sharp suit and hard body to his bright green eyes, walnut-brown hair, and dazzling smile, and you had a devilishly handsome package, as Finn would proudly tell you himself. He knew exactly how gorgeous he was and used it to his advantage whenever he could.

I wondered if that was a trait he'd inherited from Fletcher—or his mother.

Finn kept grinning at me, and I forced myself to act casual and step forward, so that I was standing on the opposite side of the counter from him, just as I'd done a thousand times before.

"Yep. Owen and I are crashing your swanky shindig,

and then I'm taking you and Bria out to dinner at Underwood's. My treat."

"Your treat?" Finn asked, a teasing note creeping into his voice. "Is something wrong?"

My hands curled around the edge of the counter, but I managed to crank up the wattage on my smile. "Why would you think that?"

He waggled his eyebrows. "Because you hardly ever offer to pay, especially at Underwood's."

I snorted. "That's because whenever I do, you always insist on ordering the most expensive things on the menu, regardless of whether you actually like them."

Another, wider grin stretched across his face. "What can I say? I have expensive tastes, baby."

I snorted again, but Finn cackled with glee before ordering a barbecue chicken sandwich, sweet-potato fries, and a triple chocolate milkshake. I laughed and joked and smiled as I fixed his food and slid it across the counter to him. But every time I glanced at Finn, every time I heard his suave voice, every time the rich timbre of his laughter washed over me, a single image filled my mind: that photo of Fletcher holding Finn while Deirdre stared down at her newborn son with a flat, distant expression.

Finn chattered on about tonight's party, some new client he wanted me to meet, and how everyone was going to be so jealous of how gorgeous Bria was. I chimed in when appropriate, but every forced grin and fake chuckle made my heart sink and my stomach knot up. Tonight was supposed to be fun for Finn, and I was going to ruin it by telling him about Deirdre.

Finn's lunch seemed to drag on forever, even though

he strolled out through the front door less than forty-five minutes later with a grin, a wink, and a playful warning for me to bring my credit card to Underwood's. I snarked back that I might have to take out a bank loan just to pay for his dinner. Finn laughed a final time, then left the Pork Pit.

The second he was gone, the smile dropped from my face faster than a body hitting the floor. My jaw ached from grinding my teeth and holding on to the fake expression for so long. I reached up and massaged my temples, trying to ease the pounding there.

Silvio slid over, taking the stool that Finn had just vacated. "Something's wrong. Care to tell me what it is? And what it has to do with Finn?"

I eyed him, but Silvio's face was neutral. He hadn't seemed to be paying all that much attention to Finn and me, but I should have known better. His keen observational skills were one of the things that made him such a great assistant. First Bria, now Silvio. I was really going to have to work on my fake smiles.

"I have to give Finn some bad news, and I'm not sure how he's going to take it."

Silvio kept his gray eyes steady on mine, but I didn't volunteer any more information. "Would this have something to do with Deirdre Shaw?" he asked. "Because I find it extremely odd that you want me to drop everything and focus on this one Ice elemental."

I gave him a short nod, confirming at least that much. "I'll tell you all about it tomorrow. After I talk to Finn."

Curiosity flared in Silvio's eyes, but he knew better than to push me. He nodded back at me, slid over onto his previous stool, picked up his tablet, and went back to work.

I stared at that photo of Fletcher hanging on the wall. Dark hair, green eyes, great smile. My heart twisted with loss and longing. The young Fletcher in that photo was the spitting image of Finn today. The only real difference was in their temperaments. Finn had always been much more cheerful, boisterous, and outgoing than the old man, who had been serious, quiet, and reserved, sometimes to the extreme.

I wondered how Finn was going to react to the news that his mother was still alive. No doubt, shocked and confused for starters. I wondered if he would be curious about her. Hurt that she had never reached out to him. Angry that I hadn't told him the second I found Fletcher's file on her.

My heart twisted a little more, this time with dread.

I'd find out tonight.

❖ 4 ❖

At seven o'clock that evening, a knock sounded on the front door of Fletcher's house. I opened it to find a man wearing a dark navy suit. He was a little more than six feet tall, with a solid, muscular frame that was the result of many long hours of working in his blacksmith's forge. His blue-black hair gleamed under the porch light, which also showed off the rough, rugged planes of his face and his vivid violet eyes. His nose was slightly crooked, and a jagged scar slashed across his chin, but the imperfections only added more character to his features.

"Hey there, handsome," I drawled. "Here to show a girl a good time?"

Owen Grayson, my significant other, grinned. "Always."

He stepped inside, looked me over, and let out a low whistle. "Nice dress."

A little black cocktail dress with long sleeves and a

short skirt hugged my body in all the right places. My dark chocolate-brown hair was pulled up into a sleek ponytail, and smoky black shadow made my gray eyes seem larger and lighter than they were. I wore my spider rune pendant over the dress, the silverstone shimmering against the black fabric.

"As Finn would say, I clean up good." I laughed, but the sound was weak and hollow.

He frowned, hearing the tension in my voice, but before he could ask me about it, I wound my arms around his neck, drew his head down, and planted a long, lingering kiss on his lips. Owen responded in kind, and we didn't break apart until a minute later, both of us breathing hard.

He leaned down so that his forehead rested on mine, his warm breath caressing my face. The heat of his hands on my waist soaked through the fabric of my dress, making me want to kiss him again and again, until the rest of the world—and all my problems—melted away.

But I couldn't do that. Not tonight. Not with Finn waiting for me to ruin his world, even if he didn't know it yet.

"Not that I'm complaining," Owen murmured. "But what was that for?"

"Luck."

"Luck? What would you need luck for?"

I should have made some airy, flippant excuse, but the lie got stuck in my throat, and I ended up shrugging instead.

He drew back, his gaze searching my face. "What's up, Gin? What's wrong?"

I grimaced. I was really going to have to get a better poker face. Or maybe I could get Jo-Jo Deveraux, my Air elemental friend, to give me some tips on how to fake a smile. Either way, I definitely needed to quit wearing my emotions on my face for everyone to see.

"Gin?" Owen asked again. "What's wrong? Did something happen?"

"Not yet."

"Yet?"

I sighed. "I have to give Finn some bad news at dinner. Or maybe after dinner. It depends on how long it takes me to work up my nerve. But there's no use ruining the evening before I absolutely have to. We should go. We don't want to be late. Okay?"

Owen studied my face again, questions filling his features as he mulled over my cryptic words. But he trusted me enough not to press me for answers, and he nodded. "Okay." He stared at me a second longer, then grinned, crooked his arm, and held it out to me. "Well, then, my lady, your chariot awaits."

I laughed, grabbed my black clutch, and slipped my arm through his.

Thirty minutes later, Owen pulled his car over to the curb in front of a seven-story building that took up its own downtown block. *First Trust of Ashland* was carved into the gleaming gray marble over the entrance, and a genuine red carpet stretched across the steps and all the way down to the curb. First Trust was the city's most exclusive bank, known for its stellar security, along with its utmost discretion and extreme dedication to seeing to all the needs of its insanely wealthy clientele, no matter how illegal those needs might be.

A giant dressed in a gray guard's uniform with the words *First Trust* stitched on the breast pocket hustled over and opened my door, while a second giant acting as a valet took Owen's keys. Still two more giant guards, also in gray uniforms, manned the double doors. Both wore bulletproof vests under their jackets, making them seem even larger and bulkier than they really were.

One guard was taking invitations from people and checking names off on a clipboard. The other guard rested his hand on the gun strapped to his waist, staring at a blond woman a few feet away, suspicious about why she was loitering outside on this cold November evening.

The woman turned toward the street, and I realized that it was Bria. My sister looked lovely in a royal-blue dress with three-quarter sleeves, a scoop neckline, and a short flared skirt. Her hair was pulled back into a loose, pretty braid, and her primrose rune pendant glinted in the hollow of her throat.

Bria caught sight of me, smiled, and waved. I took Owen's arm again, and we walked up the steps. I handed the guard my invitation, and he checked off our names. Once that was done, we strolled over to Bria. I hugged my sister, and Owen and I told her how beautiful she looked.

"What are you doing out here?" I asked. "Why didn't you go on inside where it's warm?"

Bria shook her head. "I wanted to wait for you guys. Because of, well, you know."

She gave Owen a tight smile, not sure if I had told him anything yet. He looked back and forth between the two of us, but he didn't comment on how strange we were acting. Instead, he offered Bria his other arm, and together, the three of us walked inside.

First Trust's decor definitely matched its highfalutin reputation. Tonight's schmooze fest was meant to show off the bank's recent remodeling and upgrades. Wispy patches of white swirled through the gray marble floor, making it seem as though we were standing on a bed of clouds. The same motif continued up through the walls and spread out onto the ceiling, which soared a hundred feet overhead. Chandeliers shaped like starbursts dropped down from the ceiling, the sparkling clusters of crystals stretching ten feet wide in places.

The lobby was a wide, open space, with antique desks and chairs set up throughout the room, each set of furniture several feet away from the others, so people could talk about their finances in private. A long marble counter took up the back wall. During normal business hours, tellers would have been working at each station along the counter, but tonight bartenders in white shirts and black tuxedo vests held court there, mixing drinks and pouring glasses of champagne. They then handed everything off to the waiters, who dispensed alcohol and hors d'oeuvres to the crowd.

Behind the counter, three cash cages were set equidistantly into the wall, each one covered with a grate of silverstone bars to protect the shrink-wrapped bricks of money stored inside. Of course, the cages were locked up tight for the night, and so was the steel door in the back left corner of the lobby. Behind that door, a staircase led down to the basement, where many of the bankers' offices—including Finn's—were located, along with another, much larger vault.

First Trust had several secure areas, but the basement vault—jokingly dubbed Big Bertha by Finn—was reserved for the bank's most important and wealthiest clients. That's where the real money, power, and secrets were hidden, carefully stowed away in silverstone boxes not unlike the one I'd found in Deirdre's casket.

"Do you see Finn?" Bria asked, peering out over the crowd.

This might have ostensibly been an informal cocktail party, but everyone was dressed to impress, with coiffed hair, perfect makeup, and sparkling gems, each rock bigger and flashier than the last. All around the room, the gemstones proudly whispered of their own beauty, their light, trilling chorus blending in perfectly with the classical music playing in the background.

Owen pointed across the lobby. "There he is."

Finn was perched on a stool at a wooden bar that had been set up along the left wall. He wore a different suit from the one he'd had on at lunch, this one a polished pewter that gleamed under the chandeliers. He clutched a glass of Scotch, his gaze fixed on the woman sitting next to him, a wide smile on his face, as though he found their conversation exceptionally entertaining. The woman must have said something truly funny, because Finn threw back his head and laughed, a loud, hearty laugh and not the small, polite chuckle he used with clients who thought they were more amusing than they really were.

The woman had her back to me, so all I could really see was her blond hair. Maybe that was why Finn was laughing so long and hard. He might be involved with Bria, but he was also a shameless flirt who wasn't above using his manly wiles to charm a female client, no matter her age, occupation, or marital status.

Finn must have sensed our stares, because he turned, caught sight of Bria, Owen, and me, and waved us over. Whispers sprang up in our wake, most of them having to do with me, since more than a few underworld bosses were here tonight. Even criminals had to store their ill-gotten gains somewhere, and First Trust didn't discriminate. Rumor had it that the bank even offered a money-laundering service—literally, to get all those pesky bloodstains off stacks of Benjamins that had been rather violently acquired.

Actually, it wasn't a rumor at all. Back when Finn was a lowly junior clerk, he had spent many hours in the bank's lab, spritzing money with a special cleaning solution and then carefully scrubbing stains off the bills. Once Finn had even enlisted Sophia Deveraux, Jo-Jo's sister and my body disposer, to use her Air magic to help clean some particularly blood-soaked bricks. With Sophia's help, he'd salvaged more than a million dollars for the bank—and got his first promotion.

More murmurs sounded, and I focused on the folks around me again. A couple of weeks ago, I would have ignored all the stares, glares, and sly whispers. But these were my people now, so to speak, so I made eye contact with every mobster I knew, nodding at the head honchos and their crew members and paying them the proper amount of respect. Many of the bosses nodded back, but a few eyed me with open hostility, including Dimitri Barkov, who alternated between glaring and smirking at me. Lucky me, getting to see him and his bad toupee twice in one day.

I made note of his sour expression and all the others to pass along to Silvio later. Perhaps my trusty assistant could diagram the best way for me to take out the more troublesome bosses all at once. If nothing else, Silvio would relish the challenge.

But there were two familiar—and friendly—faces in the crowd. Mallory Parker and her granddaughter, Lorelei. They were sitting at a table in the middle of the lobby. I pointed them out, and Owen steered us in that direction.

Mallory was a wizened dwarf who was well into her three hundreds and still going strong, as evidenced by the half-empty bottle of bourbon and the large glass on the table in front of her. Despite the liquor, her blue eyes were sharp, and her hair had been teased into a fluffy white cloud around her head, making her seem far more angelic than she really was.

More than a few folks stared at her, their envious gazes focused on the inch-wide diamond choker that ringed her neck, the matching bracelet on her wrist, and the solitaire rings that sparkled on her gnarled fingers. Mallory wholeheartedly believed that diamonds were a girl's best friend. I'd never seen her without an array of gems, and I was willing to bet that she slept with at least some of them on.

In contrast, Lorelei Parker seemed plain and subdued,

her only jewelry the rose-and-thorn rune ring that flashed on her hand, though it too featured a generous helping of diamonds. Still, Lorelei received her own share of admiring and envious glances, given her pale blue eyes, pretty features, and black hair pulled back into an elegant French braid.

Lorelei was texting on her phone, and Mallory was talking to the man sitting next to her, a stocky dwarf with wavy silver hair who was wearing a black suit that cost more than most cars. His styled hair and clothes were at odds with his hard hazel eyes, lined face, and hooked nose, which looked like it had been broken more than once. I'd only seen him a few times during my visits here, but I knew exactly who he was: Stuart Mosley, the founder of First Trust.

Several people hovered around Mosley, everyone from tellers and investment bankers trying to get a moment of face time with the head honcho to clients trying to impress upon him how important they were. But Mosley ignored them all in favor of sipping his bourbon, staring at Mallory, and nodding at whatever she was saying. Mosley wasn't a social butterfly by any stretch of the imagination—he didn't have to be—but he seemed downright friendly with Mallory. Interesting. I hadn't realized that they knew each other so well.

Mallory saw us approaching and waved us over. The hoverers grumbled, but they fell back to make room for us.

"Mallory, you're looking positively brilliant this evening," I said, then turned my attention to her granddaughter. "Lorelei."

Lorelei nodded at me. "Gin."

All around us, the other mobsters tiptoed forward, trying to overhear our conversation. Lorelei was one of the major power players in the Ashland underworld, a notorious smuggler known for her ability to get anything for anyone at any time. Us talking to each other in public was sure to set the other bosses to buzzing, since she was the only one of them I'd deigned to speak to. No doubt, the others were already worrying about what sort of alliances we might have made. Truth be told, Lorelei and I hadn't gotten that far yet, but she was the closest thing to a friend I had among the city's criminals besides Phillip Kincaid. And I was going to need all the friends I could get if I wanted to survive.

Mallory gestured at Mosley. "Gin, this is my good friend Stuart Mosley. Stuart, Gin Blanco. I'm sure you two have heard all about each other."

"Indeed." Mosley got to his feet and extended his hand to me. "A pleasure, Ms. Blanco."

We shook hands, and then he did the same with Bria and Owen. The three of them started chatting, along with Lorelei, but Mallory crooked her finger at me. I bent down, and she jerked her head in Finn's direction.

"Finn seems quite wrapped up in his client," Mallory drawled in her twangy hillbilly voice. "He barely said hello to me before skedaddling over to the bar to meet her." Her words were innocent enough, but a hard tone tinged her voice. Mallory gave me a long, pointed look, as if she was trying to tell me something.

I shrugged. "You know Finn. He would try to sell water to a fish if he thought he could make a quick buck."

"Mmm." Mallory's noncommittal response had me

raising my eyebrows, but the dwarf waved her hand again, making her multitude of diamonds sparkle and flash. "We'll talk more tomorrow. Your man Silvio called me earlier to set it up. We'll have tea out by the garden. It will make for a lovely afternoon. Won't it, Lorelei?"

"Mmm."

This time, her granddaughter was the one who made the noncommittal sound. Lorelei might be the closest thing to a friend that I had in the underworld, but we were still trying to figure out our relationship, despite the fact that we'd worked together to take down Raymond Pike, her half brother.

"Anyway," Mallory said, "you should go see to Finn now."

Once again, that hard tone colored her voice, one that I couldn't quite decipher, but I nodded. "See you then."

Lorelei and Mallory both nodded back at me and returned to their drinks, while Mosley finally deigned to wade into his crowd of admirers and start making nice with them.

"What was that about?" Owen asked as he escorted Bria and me over to where Finn was sitting at the bar.

"I have no idea."

Finn saw that we were finally on our way over to him, and he leaned forward, talking to his client and pointing at the three of us. The woman nodded, then finished her drink.

We reached his side, and Finn slid off his stool, grabbing Bria's hand and twirling her around.

"You look positively smashing," he said.

"Don't I always?" Bria arched her eyebrows, but the

blush in her cheeks told me how much the compliment pleased her.

Finn twirled Bria around again, making her laugh, before lowering her into a dip. They stayed frozen like that for a moment, staring into each other's eyes, before he kissed her, long and deep. Finn set Bria back up on her feet, leaned forward, and whispered something in her ear that made her blush even more.

I started to make a snarky comment about the two of them getting a room, but a floral aroma tickled my nose, and I had to clear my throat to hold back a sneeze. It took me a second to realize that it was the mystery woman's perfume. She still had her back to me, so I drew in another breath, trying to identify the scent, since it seemed so tantalizingly familiar. My heart stopped as I realized exactly what it was and where I had smelled it before.

Peonies—the same scent that was in the empty perfume bottle in the casket box.

Finn strode over to the mystery woman's side, gave her his hand, and helped her slide off her barstool. Together, the two of them turned to face us.

"And now, let me present my favorite new client," Finn said. "Everyone, this is Deirdre Shaw."

✳ 5 ✳

Deirdre Shaw, Finn's definitely-not-dead mother, was standing right in front of me. In the flesh. And not just in Ashland but *here*, at Finn's bank, schmoozing with him like they were old friends.

I thought back to all the times Finn had mentioned his new client over the past few weeks. Someone he was really hitting it off with. Someone he wanted to introduce us all to tonight. Someone who was far more to him than he realized.

It all made sense now—and it was all so twistedly, horribly *wrong*.

Beside me, Bria sucked in a surprised breath. I reached down, grabbed her hand, and squeezed it in warning. After a second, she squeezed back, realizing that I was asking her to hide her shock and her knowledge of who Deirdre really was.

Owen saved us both. He realized that something was

wrong, stepped up, and held out his hand, making Deirdre shift her focus to him instead of wondering why Bria
and I were both suddenly so slack-jawed.

"Owen Grayson," he rumbled. "It's nice to meet you,
Mrs. Shaw."

Deirdre looked Owen up and down, then gave him a
slow, exaggerated wink. "Well, aren't you just a cold drink
of water on a hot, hot day?" A sultry Southern drawl
added even more charm to her fun, flirty voice.

She winked again, then shook his hand. "Actually, it's
Ms. Shaw, but call me Dee-Dee. All my friends do."

Finn tucked his arm through Bria's. "Dee-Dee, I want
you to meet my lady love, Detective Bria Coolidge."

Deirdre smiled at Bria, her expression warm and invit-
ing. "Why, you're even lovelier than Finnegan described.
Charmed."

"Yeah," Bria replied in a dry tone. "Me too."

Finally, Deirdre Shaw faced me.

Her shoulder-length blond hair had been styled into
elegant pin curls, the soft, golden waves catching the light.
Her eyes were a pale blue, bordering on gray, as though
her gaze were filled with the elemental Ice she could control. Her porcelain skin was flawless, while her lips were a
perfect red heart in her face. I didn't know if she indulged
in a strict regimen of Air elemental facials, like Jonah
McAllister did, but she looked a decade younger than her
fifty-some years. I had thought her lovely in all those old
photos, but in person she was truly stunning.

Deirdre didn't seem to go in for subtle, since her knee-
length, flapper-style cocktail dress was a bloody scarlet
and covered with sequins and crystals, as was the match-

ing shawl draped around her arms. Her outfit was bold, flashy, and vibrant, the type of dress a gorgeous woman would wear to attract maximum attention and compliments. And Deirdre's jewelry was also meant to impress. Ruby chandelier earrings framed her face, while a square ruby ring glinted on her right hand.

But her most interesting bauble was her rune necklace, that heart made of jagged icicles.

Or diamonds, in this case.

The heart pendant was as big as the palm of my hand, the diamonds in each individual icicle flashing and sparkling. Even among all the jewelry here tonight, I could easily pick out the diamonds' proud, boisterous song as they continuously trilled about their own beauty. The gemstones alone must have cost a fortune. Add them to the exquisite silverstone setting and chain, and Deirdre Shaw easily had a million bucks of cold ice hanging around her neck.

Bria noticed the necklace too, and her face creased into a frown, as she tried again to remember where she had seen the rune before.

"Dee-Dee," Finn said, "this is Gin Blanco. Gin, Dee-Dee."

Deirdre looked me up and down the same way she had done with Owen and Bria, but she didn't offer me some bawdy compliment. Instead, she simply held out her hand for me to shake, as if she knew that her charming words would be wasted on me.

I took her hand in mine. Her fingers were cool to the touch, but I expected that, given the chilly air that flooded the open, drafty lobby every time someone went in or out. What I didn't expect was the Ice magic pulsing through her body, lying just beneath the surface of her skin. The cold, sudden shock of touching her was worse than plunging my hand into a bucket of ice water. It was a wonder my fingers didn't turn blue from frostbite.

The truly troubling thing was that Deirdre wasn't actively using her magic. If I could sense this much of her power just by touching her, I shuddered to think what she could do when she summoned up the full, frosty depths of it. She could easily Ice over the entire lobby with a single wave of her hand. Fletcher had said that Deirdre was strong in her magic, but I hadn't expected this level of power. She was even more dangerous than I'd thought.

"Gin," Deirdre said, smiling widely. "It's so lovely to finally meet you, honey. I've heard *so* much about you." She gave my hand a friendly little squeeze.

I squeezed back, although all I really wanted to do was yank my hand out of hers and try to rub some warmth and feeling back into my numb fingers.

"I just bet you have," I drawled. "Although Finn hasn't told me *nearly* enough about you. I'll have to get him to rectify that, since the two of you have become such good friends these past few weeks."

Deirdre's hand tightened around mine, and she frowned, the faint lines around her eyes crinkling a little deeper as she tried to figure out what I meant. After a moment, she shook off her confusion and finally released my fingers. I bit my tongue to keep from hissing in relief.

Finn looked back and forth between the two of us, also wondering at my strange words. But he charged right on past the awkwardness and gestured to a man sitting at the bar, on the stool next to Deirdre's.

"And this is Hugh Tucker, Deirdre's personal assistant," Finn said.

Tucker was a tall, wiry man in a black suit jacket with a dark gray shirt and tie underneath. His skin was a rich bronze, while his hair and eyes were midnight-black. A trimmed goatee clung to his chin. I would put his age close to Deirdre's, around fifty or so, but the years had been as kind to him as they had been to her, and he could easily pass for someone ten years younger.

Despite his distinguished air, he was as subdued and forgettable as Deirdre was boisterous and flashy, although his understated diamond cuff links had definitely cost a pretty penny. No magic emanated from him, but fangs flashed in his mouth as he tossed back the rest of his Scotch. So he was a vampire, then.

Tucker slid off his stool and nodded politely at all of us, but he didn't step forward, and he didn't offer to shake anyone's hand. Instead, he gave us all a bored, disinterested glance, as if he could care less about who we were. Not what I would expect from an assistant. If Silvio were here, he would have been examining Tucker and whoever else might be in Deirdre's entourage to make sure they weren't a threat to me and our friends. Before doing multiple background checks just to make sure.

What Tucker did seem interested in was all the other folks here. His black gaze flicked around the lobby, coolly assessing each person in turn. Maybe it was her dazzling diamonds, but he kept glancing over at Mallory Parker.

At least until Lorelei noticed his attention and stared back at him, wondering who he was and what he was up to.

Tucker arched an eyebrow, as if he was amused by Lorelei's dirty looks, then turned around, flagged down a passing waiter, and got a refill on his drink.

"Well, I should let you talk to your friends," Deirdre said. "I'll see you here tomorrow morning as scheduled, yes? And we'll go over the final details for the exhibit?"

My eyes narrowed. Exhibit? What exhibit?

"Of course. I'm always happy to meet with my favorite client."

Finn winked, then grabbed his mother's hand, bowed low, and pressed a kiss to her knuckles, as gallant as any knight. He wasn't an elemental, so he couldn't sense her Ice magic. I forced down a shudder at how long his skin touched hers.

Deirdre grabbed her red beaded clutch off the bar, then playfully tapped Finn on the shoulder with it. "Oh, you flatterer. You certainly know how to dazzle this ole gal, don't you? Why, I bet you're the most charming man in three counties."

Finn grinned. "But of course."

Deirdre looked at Tucker, and the two of them started to walk away, but I stepped up and blocked their path.

"Actually, why don't you and Tucker join us for dinner at Underwood's tonight? My treat. After all, any friend of Finn's is a friend of mine."

I kept my voice smooth and my features schooled into a polite mask, but Deirdre's forehead wrinkled, as if she was wondering whether I knew who she really was. Apparently, she wanted to find out, because a pleased smile brightened her face. "Why, nothing would give me greater pleasure, honey," she cooed in a syrupy-sweet tone. "I've just been *dying* to meet all of Finnegan's wonderful friends."

"Family," I corrected. "Finn and I are *family*."

"Mmm. Yes. Family."

We stared at each other. My face remained smooth and blank, but Deirdre tilted her head to the side, her gray-blue eyes sharpening with interest. She was wondering what I really wanted with her. I didn't quite know myself. All I knew was that Deirdre Shaw was right fucking *here*, and I wanted to know every single thing about her—including what game she was playing with Finn.

"Well, then, that's settled," Finn chirped, either oblivious to or ignoring the tension between us. "Let me just take a quick lap around the room to say good-bye to some folks, and then we can head out—"

Crack!

Crack! Crack!

Crack!

The noises were faint and muffled, no louder than glasses breaking against the floor, but I still recognized the sounds of gunfire. Owen, Finn, and Bria did too, and the four of us whirled around, turning toward the front of the lobby.

The doors slammed open, and several men ran inside, each clutching a gun.

❋ 6 ❋

The gunmen stormed into the lobby, firing their weapons into the air.

Crack!

Crack! Crack!

Crack!

Bullets zinged skyward, punching into the chandeliers and shattering the crystals. The lights flickered, sharp shards rained down, and screams, shrieks, and shouts filled the air as people dived for cover under the tables and chairs scattered around the lobby. The bartenders ducked down behind the tellers' counter, while the waiters hit the floor, dropping trays of food and drinks and causing even more loud crashes and bangs to ring out. In an instant, the elegant scene had disintegrated into complete chaos.

Finn grabbed Bria and forced her down to the floor, even though my sister was cursing and trying to yank her gun out of her purse the whole time. Owen did the same to me. Deirdre dropped to the floor beside me, with Tucker on her other side.

The gunfire seemed to go on forever, although it couldn't have lasted more than thirty seconds. Finally, the *crack-crack-crack*s faded away. People stopped screaming, and a tense, heavy silence descended over the lobby.

"This is a robbery!" the lead gunman yelled. "Nobody moves and nobody dies!"

Everyone did as he demanded and stayed completely still as the other gunmen spread out through the lobby. There were six of them, all wearing black clothes and ski masks and all regular-sized men.

The lead gunman, however, was a giant, although his seven-foot frame was lean and lanky instead of thick and bulky like most giants. He swiveled to the side, turning toward me, and I realized that he had pushed up the sleeves of his black shirt, revealing a rune tattoo on his left forearm. I was huddled on my knees, so I raised my head and inched to my left, trying to get a better view. His tattoo looked like . . . a snake wrapped around and biting into . . . something. I squinted. Maybe a snake biting into a dollar sign? Classy.

Once the giant gunman was certain that he had control of the lobby, he glanced down at his watch. I was no watch connoisseur, not like Finn was, but it was obviously expensive, given the silverstone band and blue stones ringing the face. Sapphires, maybe, or blue diamonds. My eyes narrowed. What kind of bank robber wore a watch that flashy?

"Two minutes, gentlemen. Starting now." The giant jerked his head at the others.

Three of the robbers stepped forward, reached into their pockets, and pulled out black garbage bags, which they snapped open. The other three robbers remained spread out through the lobby, their guns sweeping back and forth over the crowd, ready to cut down anyone who thought about playing hero.

"Now, be good little girls and boys, and hand over your jewelry, watches, phones, and wallets," the giant growled, "and we'll be out of here before your fancy snacks get too cold."

He laughed, but it was a harsh, mocking sound. He paused, then raised his gun and fired off another few shots into the ceiling, just because he could. Almost everyone screamed and ducked down a little more, which made him laugh even louder. The giant might claim that he didn't want any trouble, but he wouldn't be upset by any either. We'd be lucky if he and his crew left without killing anyone.

The giant was only about ten feet away from me, so I could easily use my Stone magic to harden my skin, then leap to my feet, sprint forward, and tackle him. But he might get off a shot or two before I reached him, killing someone in the crowd, and the rest of the robbers were too far away for me to take down—yet.

I looked at Bria, who shook her head. Owen and Finn shook their heads too, all of us realizing that we'd have to bide our time. Or, at worst, let the robbers escape and go after them later.

The giant checked his watch again. "Sixty seconds, gentlemen!"

The three robbers moved through the lobby quickly

and efficiently to collect the partygoers' valuables. None of them so much as glanced at the three cash cages behind the tellers' counter. The robbers must have realized that someone was sure to have seen them shoot the bank guards outside and storm in here, which meant that they didn't have time to crack open the cages before the cops arrived. Trying would only get them caught.

"Thirty seconds, gentlemen!"

This was a well-trained, professional crew, not some smash-and-grabbers who'd gotten above their raisings, as Jo-Jo might say. They knew exactly what they were doing. Which made me all the more curious about why they would rob First Trust, especially on this particular night.

Sure, the jewelry, phones, and watches would be a nice haul but hard to unload. Besides, if you were planning a robbery, why not hit the bank during the day and grab as much cash as possible from the tellers and cages? Or why not sneak in at night, disable the security system, and take a crack at Big Bertha, the basement vault?

Cold, hard cash was much easier to spend than trash bags full of rings, watches, and necklaces. If they'd wanted maximum profit for minimum risk, the robbers should have come up with another plan—a better plan.

Finn often claimed that I was the most paranoid person ever. He might have been right about that, but I couldn't help but think that the robbery had everything to do with Deirdre Shaw.

She showed up in Ashland after being gone for decades, weaseled her way into Finn's life under false pretenses, and managed to get an invite to tonight's party—a party that was ruined by robbers an hour after it started.

Those were a whole lot of coincidences, even though I couldn't see how setting up this sort of small-time score would benefit her at all.

I looked at Deirdre, but she was on her knees, her arms wrapped around her chest, staring down at the floor. She didn't seem scared, not like other folks who were trembling, crying, and shaking, but she wasn't making eye contact with the robbers either, like some of the underworld bosses were. Those fools were glaring at the robbers and practically daring the men to shoot them.

And more than a few of the underworld bosses were also staring at me, expecting me to do something, expecting me to rise up and save them and their baubles. If it had just been me in the lobby, I would have been happy to unleash the wrath of the Spider, confront the robbers, and kill every single one of them. But there were far too many innocent people here for me to take out the robbers without some collateral damage, something I tried to avoid at all costs.

Until one of the robbers yanked Bria to her feet.

"Hey, hey, pretty lady," the robber crooned, pressing his body up against hers. "Why don't you be a doll and take off your shiny necklace?"

Bria glared at the robber, not responding to his taunts, although her fingers twitched, as if she was thinking about blasting him in the face with her Ice magic.

"I said take off the bling, bitch," he growled, twisting her arm up and behind her back and dragging her even closer.

Finn surged to his feet. "Get your hands off her!" he hissed, shoving the robber away from Bria.

The robber stumbled back a few feet and stopped. Beneath his black ski mask, his dark eyes narrowed, and his lips twisted with rage. I knew that look all too well. The robber wasn't going to be happy with just taking Bria's necklace. Not after Finn had challenged him.

So I scrambled to my feet, putting myself between Finn and the robber. Owen got up too. So did Deirdre, although Tucker remained sitting on the floor, staring up at the gunmen instead of trying to help his boss. Some assistant.

The robber looked back and forth at all of us, before tossing aside his bag of loot and snapping up his gun. "What do you think you're doing? Get your asses back down on the floor! Now!"

Everyone froze, even the other robbers, and all eyes focused on us.

I stepped up so that I was right in front of him, with his gun pointed straight at my heart. "You're making a big mistake, pal. You have no idea who you're jacking."

"Listen up, bitch," he growled again. "Unless you're Gin Blanco herself, then I don't give a fuck who you are. And I especially don't care how important you think you are."

A cold smile curved my lips. "Why, sugar, you said the magic words. Because I do, in fact, happen to be Gin Blanco. And if you know anything at all about me, then you know that you've just gotten yourself into a whole heap of trouble."

The robber snorted. He didn't believe me any more than the grave robbers had. But I kept staring at him, my face as hard as marble, my gray eyes glinting with deadly intent, my fingers curling into tight fists. Whispers rippled through the crowd, confirming my claim.

Confusion filled the robber's eyes, along with the realization that I was telling the truth, and his anger quickly melted into a horror that I found quite satisfying. Everyone might not know me on sight, but they at least knew my fucking name—and the death that came along with it.

"Oh, shit," he whispered. "Shit, shit, shit!"

"Yeah," I drawled. "That about sums it up."

Desperate, the robber glanced over his shoulder at the giant gunman for help.

But I didn't give him the chance to get any advice.

The second the robber turned his head, I stepped up, punched him in the throat, and yanked his gun out of his hand. I tossed the weapon over to Finn, who easily caught it and aimed it at the next-closest robber, while I palmed one of the silverstone knives tucked up my dress sleeves.

The robber I'd punched tried to stagger away, but I grabbed his arm, spun him around, and pulled him up against my own body, using him as a human shield, even as I jabbed my knife against his throat.

"If I were you, bitch," I hissed in his ear, "I wouldn't move. Unless you want the closest and last shave of your miserable life."

The robber started to nod but stopped as the blade dug into his skin. Once I was sure that he wasn't going to do anything stupid, I looked out over the lobby. The other five robbers had their guns trained on me, except for the giant leader, whose weapon was pointed at Finn. Weird. Sure, Finn had a gun, but you'd think that the giant would be targeting me, since I was the one with the knife at his guy's throat. Maybe there truly was no honor among thieves.

My stomach clenched at Finn being in the line of fire, but I didn't let any of my worry show. Instead, I fixed my gaze on the leader. "I'll give you a choice. You and your men drop your weapons, and I'll let the cops deal with you."

The giant narrowed his eyes. "Or?"

I smiled again, my expression even colder than before. "Or you can be an idiot and try to fight your way out of here. A few of you might even make it. But you won't be breathing for long, since I will make it my mission to track you down and end you myself. Now, you seem to be a fan of precision timing, so you have ten seconds to think it over."

The giant's mouth flattened out into a harsh line. He didn't want to give in to my demands. He couldn't, not without looking weak in front of his own crew. But he didn't seem overly concerned by my threats either. No anger sparked in his dark brown eyes, no fear either, just cold calculation as he tried to think about the best way to get out of here.

All the while, I kept waiting for his gaze to skitter sideways, to lock with Deirdre's, and get some silent order from her.

But it didn't happen.

The giant kept his focus squarely on me, and he didn't so much as glance at Deirdre, Tucker, or anyone else. Unease crawled up my spine. Could I be wrong? Could Deirdre be innocent of planning the robbery? Could she be just another rich target, like everyone else?

"Five seconds," I called out. "Lay down your guns right now."

The giant's ski mask rode up on his face, as though he'd raised his eyebrows. "Or?"

I tapped my knife against the neck of the robber who was still in front of me. "Or I'm going to slit your man's throat before I do the same thing to you."

A collective gasp rippled through the crowd at the poison promise in my voice. The other five robbers shifted on their feet, staring at me, then at one another. Two of them decided to be smart about things, slowly bending down and setting their weapons on the floor. Those two robbers raised their hands and stepped away from the people around them, so that they were standing side-by-side near the middle of the lobby.

Those two robbers were close to Lorelei and Mallory Parker. More whispers sounded as Lorelei slowly stood up, tiptoed forward, and picked up their guns, staring at the other three robbers the whole time. But those three men didn't know whether to shoot her or me, and they kept swiveling their guns back and forth between us.

Lorelei tiptoed back, so that she was standing in front of Mallory, shielding her from harm. Mallory took one of the guns from Lorelei, and then the two women trained their weapons on the three remaining armed robbers.

Lorelei gave me a short, sharp nod. I nodded back, then focused my attention on the giant gunman again. I made a show of twisting my knife point into the neck of the man I was still holding on to, deep enough to draw blood this time.

"Time's up," I called out.

"Santos, man, just give up already!" My robber sputtered out the giant's name. "I don't want to die just for some lousy jewelry!"

"No names, you idiot!" Santos snarled.

He pointed his gun at the other man and shot the robber three times in the chest.

Crack! Crack! Crack!

Everyone screamed and kissed the floor again. The robber's blood sprayed everywhere, the coppery stink of it filling the air, and he slipped from my grasp and hit the ground, dead weight now.

Santos gave me an evil grin and raised his gun again. I reached for my Stone magic, hardening my skin, but instead of shooting me, he whipped around and fired at the two robbers who had surrendered.

Crack! Crack! Crack! Crack!

Santos coolly executed his own men, putting two bullets in the chest of each. More screams sounded as the men toppled to the floor, blood pooling underneath their bodies.

"Run, you idiots!" Santos screamed at the remaining robbers.

The three men sprinted for the front doors. I was too far away to stop them, but Lorelei and Mallory both stepped up, guns still in their hands.

Crack! Crack! Crack! Crack!

Lorelei got one of the fleeing robbers in the back, and he toppled to the floor. Mallory shot a second, also in the back, and he hit the ground too, but the third man managed to dart outside unscathed.

Knife still in my hand, I headed toward Santos, who was backing toward the doors.

Santos fired off a couple more shots. At first, I thought he was targeting the partygoers huddled in the middle of the lobby, but his aim was too wide for that, and the bullets harmlessly punched into the floor. But the shots made everyone panic, rise to their feet, and stampede toward the back of the lobby, running over and even knocking one another down as they tried to scramble to safety behind the tellers' counter.

I stormed after Santos but got caught in the crush of people going the other way. Every time I took a step forward, someone bumped into me and shoved me back.

"Move! Move! Move!" I yelled, but the continued screams drowned out my words.

Santos took advantage of the chaos. He made it all the way over to the doors before stopping and raising his gun again. I didn't care if the bastard shot me, but I was shoving other people out of the way, hoping that I could at least get everyone else out of his line of fire.

But Santos had other ideas. He whipped his gun to my right, aiming it at someone else. I looked over my shoulder, my blood freezing in my veins as I realized whom he was targeting.

Finn.

"Gin! Gin!" Finn shouted. "I'm coming!"

Gun in hand, he was also fighting his way through the crowd, trying to come help me. Bria and Owen were doing the same thing, but Finn was the closest, about ten feet behind me. He pushed one of the waiters out of his way and skidded to a stop, realizing that Santos was aiming at him. Finn snapped up his own gun, but he wasn't going to get the other man first.

Santos shot me a wicked grin, then focused on Finn again, his finger curling back on the trigger. He realized that shooting Finn would hurt me more than if I were wounded myself.

I raced in Finn's direction, but I was no superhero, and I wasn't even close to being faster than a speeding bullet. My foster brother was going to die, and it was all my fault.

"Finn!" I screamed. "Finn!"

Too late.

Santos pulled the trigger.

❖ 7 ❖

The shot rang out, that one sharp, single *crack* seeming louder than all the previous ones put together.

All the while, I could hear myself screaming—Bria too—but it was like I was underwater, and everything seemed to happen in slow motion. Finn's eyes widening, his mouth falling open, his entire body tensing, waiting for the bullet to tear through his chest.

But it never happened.

At the last instant, Deirdre shoved Finn out of the way, making him fall to the floor. The bullet hit her instead, and she screamed and spun around before stumbling into a cluster of chairs. She bounced off a chair and slid down, landing on her ass and clutching her left arm, her face white with shock. Given her scarlet dress, I couldn't tell how badly she might be injured.

And I didn't care. Finn was okay.

Santos's lips moved, but I couldn't hear the curses he

was spouting. He turned tail, pushed through the front doors, and disappeared.

I kicked off my black stilettos, palmed a second knife, and sprinted after him. I wanted to end this *now*, before Santos escaped, holed up somewhere, and started plotting his revenge against me. Not only that, but I wanted to know if Santos had decided to rob the bank on his own or if someone had hired him to do it. And since the bastard had tried to shoot Finn, I was going to carve the answers out of him one slow slice at a time.

Bria and Owen started to follow me, but I stabbed one of my knives toward Finn, who was still sprawled across the floor. He must have taken a harder tumble than I'd thought.

"Stay with him!" I yelled.

Not only because Finn was injured but also because I didn't want to leave him alone with Deirdre—not even for a minute.

I shoved a few more screaming people out of my way, rammed my shoulder into the door, and barreled down the stairs, which were still covered with that red carpet—

Crack! Crack! Crack!

Santos fired at me, hanging out the front passenger window of a black van idling at the curb. But I was still holding on to my Stone magic, so the bullets bounced off my body instead of punching through my chest. Still, the blows made me stagger back, and it took me a few seconds to shake off the hard, stinging impacts and dart forward again.

Santos cursed and started to reload, but whoever was driving the van had had enough, especially with the growing *whoop-whoop-whoop* of police sirens in the distance. The getaway driver gunned the engine and peeled away from the curb, tires smoking.

But I wasn't ready to give up, so I sprinted out into the street, fell to my knees, dropped my knives, and slapped my palms flat against the asphalt. In an instant, I reached for my Ice magic, blasting it out over the entire street. The cold crystals of my power exploded out from my palms and rushed down the pavement like a tidal wave streaking toward shore. The sheet of Ice raced down the asphalt, getting closer and closer to the van's back tires. If I could just get the vehicle to skid and crash, I could still catch Santos.

"C'mon," I muttered. "C'mon, c'mon, c'mon . . ."

I poured even more of my magic into creating that solid sheet of Ice, watching it creep closer and closer to the van.

At the end of the block, the driver took a hard right, making the tires screech in protest. The van careened around the corner and vanished from sight, even as my elemental Ice continued to shoot straight down the street.

"Dammit!" I snarled.

Gone—Santos was gone.

And so was my hope of getting any answers about the robbery.

I released my magic, grabbed my knives, and stood up. The elemental Ice coating the street burned my bare feet as I walked over to the curb. I slid my knives back up my dress sleeves, pushed through one of the doors, and stepped back into the bank.

All sorts of debris littered the floor—overturned tables

and chairs, trays of spilled food and drinks, shattered shards from the crystal chandeliers, trash bags of valuables, bullet casings. The waiters and bartenders were clustered along the tellers' counter, shell-shocked expressions on their faces. The partygoers and the bank's clients wore similarly stunned looks. No surprise there. Things as low-down and dirty as strong-arm robberies simply didn't happen at a place like First Trust.

As for the bank staff, all the tellers, investment types, and other hotshots were nervously gathered in the middle of the lobby around Stuart Mosley to see what his orders would be. Mosley had his phone clamped to his ear, his eyes narrowed, and his voice chillingly low as he demanded answers from the person on the other end about how this had happened.

The crime bosses were also on their phones, texting and talking to their crews, telling them what had happened and trying to get info on who the robbers were and where they might be headed. I would be doing the same and calling Silvio soon enough, if the vampire hadn't already heard what had happened.

But first, I had to deal with Deirdre Shaw.

She was sitting on the same stool as when I'd first come into the lobby. Her scarlet shawl lay crumpled on top of the bar in front of her, along with her purse and several bloody cocktail napkins. A long red gash sliced along her upper left arm, but the wound didn't look deep, and it wasn't even bleeding anymore. She'd thrown herself in front of a bullet and had only gotten grazed. I was certainly never that lucky. Then again, I'd long ago lost count of how many times I'd been shot.

But it seemed to be a new, thoroughly horrible experience for Deirdre. The robbery itself might not have scared her, but getting shot certainly had. Shock still whitened her face, her eyes twitched, and her fingers shook with small spasms before she clasped her hands together to try to hide the tremors.

I studied her carefully, but her surprise seemed one-hundred-percent genuine. I didn't want to admit it, but perhaps she really was an innocent victim tonight, like everyone else here.

What really concerned me, though, was the fact that Finn was right by her side, smiling and chatting while he dabbed at her minor wound with another cocktail napkin, even though he had a much more serious, oozing cut and a purple knot on his forehead from where he'd hit the floor.

Bria was standing right next to him, dabbing at Finn's wound the same way he was dabbing at Deirdre's. Owen was there too, a thoughtful expression on his face as he watched Bria watch Finn watch Deirdre.

Hugh Tucker had resumed his previous seat on Deirdre's other side. He eyed her wound for a moment, then started texting on his phone, probably trying to find an Air elemental to heal his boss. That's what Silvio would have been doing.

I stopped long enough to find my stilettos and slip them back on so I wouldn't cut my feet on the shattered crystal and broken glass, then headed in their direction. Bria sopped up another bit of blood from Finn's face, tossed her dirty napkin aside, and hurried over to me, making sure we were out of earshot of the others.

"Did you get him?" she asked in a low, hopeful voice.

"Sadly, no, but I'll sic Silvio on him. Santos won't be able to hide for long. If he's smart, he'll leave town."

"Well, here's hoping that he's not so smart." Bria jerked her head at Finn and Deirdre. "And what do you want to do about *that*?"

"I have no idea," I muttered.

Finn realized that I had come back into the lobby, and he waved at me. I let out a breath and walked over to him. Owen stepped up beside me, hugging me to his chest. I gave him a quick kiss before turning to Finn.

"Gin, there you are. I was just finishing up with Deirdre's wound." He shot her a grin. "Just a graze. Nothing to worry about. Why, you don't even need stitches. A few minutes with one of those Air elementals I told Tucker about, and you won't even have a scar."

Deirdre drew in a deep breath and let it out, pushing away her shock and steadying herself. Then she winked back at him. "I'll take your word for it."

"You were lucky," Finn said.

"Yeah," I muttered. "Lucky."

His eyebrows drew together in puzzlement, as he wondered why I was being so snarky to the woman who had just saved his life, but I wasn't about to explain the irony to him.

"Oh, don't mind her," he said in a cheery voice. "She's just upset that the bad guy got away, and she couldn't give him the smackdown she wanted to. Right, Gin?"

I ground my teeth, but Finn didn't notice that I didn't answer him. Instead, he fixed his green gaze on Deirdre, curiosity filling his face.

"Although I have to ask you something, Dee-Dee," he said. "Why did you shove me out of the way of that bullet? Not that I'm complaining, mind you. But it was a really brave and heroic thing to do, especially for someone you've only known a few weeks."

"Well, good investment bankers are hard to find. I didn't want my favorite asset to get hurt." She winked again, then let out a loud laugh, trying to play it off as a joke, trying to charm him the same way he'd done to countless other people over the years.

But Finn wasn't that easily swayed. "No, seriously," he said. "I really want to know. Why did you risk your life to save mine? Why did you think to protect me like that?"

Deirdre froze, her smile slowly slipping away, her expression turning serious, until she was staring at Finn like he was the only thing that mattered. She clamped her lips shut, then opened her mouth, then clamped her lips shut again, as if she was having trouble getting out the words.

My stomach twisted with dread. I knew exactly what she was going to say, but there was nothing I could do to stop her.

"I'm your mother."

❄ 8 ❄

Everyone had a different reaction to Deirdre Shaw's bombshell.

Bria bit her lip and stared down at the floor. Owen blinked and blinked, trying to process Deirdre's words. Tucker glanced at his boss, his black eyebrows arching a bit, then went back to his phone, still searching for a healer. My hands clenched into fists so tight that my nails dug into the spider rune scars in my palms.

And then there was Finn.

He stared at Deirdre for several seconds. Then his eyes crinkled, his lips twitched, and he burst out laughing.

He just . . . *laughed*.

And laughed . . . and laughed some more . . .

Maybe he'd hit his head harder than I'd thought.

"Oh, Dee-Dee, you're a hoot, all right," Finn said between deep belly laughs. "But my mother died in a car accident when I was just a baby. You know that. We've talked about it several times now."

My jaw clenched, and my hands fisted together even tighter. I wondered exactly what Finn and Deirdre had talked about. How long had she been pumping him for information? How long had she been insinuating herself into his life? How long had she been laying the groundwork and buttering him up for this moment?

Deirdre lifted her chin and squared her shoulders, still staring straight into his eyes. "That's what Fletcher wanted you to think. But it's true, Finnegan. I'm your mother, and I'm alive. I've been alive this whole time."

Finn kept chuckling for a few more seconds, until he realized she was serious. His laughter died on his lips, his entire body stiffened with shock, and he didn't even breathe for several seconds. He blinked, then blinked again, peering at Deirdre in a close, intense way that he never had before. I could practically see the gears grinding in his mind, all the memories he was calling up, all the mental calculations he was doing, trying to reconcile the woman in front of him with what little Fletcher had told him about his mother.

Deirdre's red lips creased into a sad, wistful smile. "You're even more handsome than the photos I've seen," she said in a soft voice. "I always thought you had my smile, ever since you were a baby."

She reached out and slowly placed her hand on top of Finn's. He started at the contact, but he didn't automatically jerk his hand away. Instead, something flashed in his eyes, something I had never seen before.

Longing.

A raw, naked longing that made him seem much younger than his thirty-three years. An old, aching longing he would do anything to ease. A bone-deep longing that worried me even more than all the pretty words Deirdre was spouting. In that moment, Finn seemed . . . *vulnerable*, in a way that I had never seen him be vulnerable before.

Finn shifted on his feet. From one moment to the next, he accepted what Deirdre was telling him as truth, that she was his mother. I could tell by the way he intently scanned her face, trying to find himself in her smile, her nose, her cheekbones. But the worst part was the way the longing in his eyes immediately flared up into a bright spark of hope.

"But . . . but *how* . . . *why* . . ." Finn stammered, for once at a loss for words.

Deirdre squeezed his hand. "I know you have a lot of questions and that I have a lot of explaining to do. Why don't I give you some time to process this? Then maybe we can meet tomorrow and talk about . . . everything."

No words escaped from Finn's gaping mouth—he just kept blinking and blinking at her. So I stepped up beside him, put my hand on his shoulder, and took charge of the situation. I didn't want Finn spending any more time alone with Deirdre. Who knew what lies and misinformation she had already fed him? Besides, I wanted to hear *exactly* what she had to say about Fletcher.

"Why don't you come by the Pork Pit tomorrow?"

I said. "Say three o'clock? Surely you haven't forgotten where it is."

Deirdre kept that soft, winsome smile on her face, but she couldn't quite hide the annoyance that flickered in her pale gaze. She didn't like me butting in on her re- union with her long-lost son. Too damn bad. Finn was my brother, and I was going to watch out for him.

"Why, that's a fine idea, honey," she said. "I'll see Finnegan then."

"We're looking forward to it, *honey*," I drawled right back at her. "After all, it's not every day that a dead rela- tive digs her way out of her own grave."

Deirdre's smile tightened at my sarcasm, but she ig- nored me and looked at Finn again. "I'll tell you anything you want to know," she said. "But most of all, I want you to know that I never wanted to leave Ashland. I never wanted to leave *you*."

Finn stared at her, his eyes empty, his face blank now. That wasn't the response Deirdre wanted. Her lips puckered, and she opened her mouth, as though she was thinking about making some other calculated confession. But in the end, she just nodded and squeezed his hand a final time. "Until tomorrow, then."

He still didn't say anything.

Deirdre favored Finn with another sad, soft smile, then slid off her stool. "Right now, I'm going to go have a drink, get patched up, and pretend like that bastard didn't shoot me and ruin my favorite dress." She let out a laugh, trying to make a joke of things, but it was a thin, brittle sound, and we could all hear how badly she'd been rattled. "Did you find me a healer, Tucker, honey?"

"Of course," the vampire murmured, his voice as bland and forgettable as the rest of him. "Mr. Lane's info was most helpful. I've already made the arrangements. Please, allow me."

He held out his arm. Deirdre looped hers through his, leaning on him for support. Given the shock and adrenaline still coursing through her body, she wasn't all that steady on her feet, and she wobbled in her heels as Tucker escorted her away.

Finn watched them go, his gaze locked onto his mother, while Bria, Owen, and I hovered around him.

All around the lobby, people talked and texted, chattering in louder and louder voices to one another and the cops who had arrived on the scene. But our group was still and silent. I squeezed Finn's shoulder, letting him know that I was here for him.

He shrugged off my hand without even looking at me.

"Finn?" Bria asked. "Are you okay?"

He didn't answer her. Instead, he watched Deirdre slowly cross the lobby. She reached the front doors, stopped, and looked over her shoulder at him. Their eyes locked, and she smiled at him a final time before leaving the bank. The door banged shut behind her, seeming as loud as a clap of thunder, but Finn kept staring and staring at that spot, as if he couldn't believe everything that had happened, all the bombs that Deirdre had dropped on him.

Deirdre Shaw might have lost some blood and her favorite dress, but she'd also gained something from being shot. Something far more valuable than the jewelry, watches, and phones that Santos had tried to make off with. Something far more important in the grand scheme of things. Something she wanted most of all.

Finn.

Finn continued to stare at the door that Deirdre had stepped through.

Bria looked at me. I shrugged, so she eased up and put her hand on Finn's shoulder. He blinked, as if her gentle touch had finally roused him from his fuguelike state.

"I can't believe that Dee-Dee is my mother. That she's alive. That she's in Ashland . . ." His voice trailed off, and he stared at the door again.

Bria looked at me, then at Owen, who shook his head. He didn't know what to do for Finn any more than we did.

Suddenly, Finn whipped around on his wing tips, throwing off Bria's hand. He stared at her a moment, before fixing his gaze on me, his green eyes growing colder and harder the longer he looked at me.

"You *knew*," he accused in a loud, harsh voice. "The two of you knew that Dee-Dee was my mother. Owen was as shocked as I was, but you two? Not so much. Not at all, really."

My heart dropped, and my stomach clenched. This was the moment I'd been dreading ever since I found Fletcher's file, but I had no one to blame for it but myself.

"You're right. I knew about Deirdre. Now, let me explain—"

"That's the reason for all the soft touches and sympathetic looks," Finn said, cutting me off. "How long? How long have you known, Gin?"

Before I could answer, Owen nudged me with his elbow and jerked his head to the right. I looked past him and realized that Finn's coworkers were staring at us, along with Stuart Mosley. So were the cops and everyone else still in the lobby. They all knew a juicy bit of drama when they saw it. Finn hadn't exactly screamed his accusations at me, but he hadn't whispered them either.

I turned back to Finn. "This isn't a conversation I want to have here," I said in a low voice. "And I don't think you want to have it here either. Besides, we need to get you to Jo-Jo's so she can look at that knot on your head. Let's go to the salon, and I'll tell you everything."

His gaze flicked around the lobby. His mouth tightened, and an angry flush stained his cheeks as he realized that we were the center of attention. "*Fine.*" He spat out the word. "But you'd better hope that Jo-Jo has some alcohol hidden in the cabinets somewhere. Because I need a drink. Several of them."

He whipped around again and strode away without another word.

Bria gave me a worried look.

"It's okay," I said. "Go with him, and make sure he doesn't do anything crazy. Owen and I will finish up here and meet you at Jo-Jo's."

Bria nodded, grabbed her purse off the bar, and hurried across the lobby after Finn, catching up with him just before he reached the doors. She shot me one more worried glance before following him outside.

"Well," Owen rumbled. "I guess I know what the bad news is."

I winced. "I'm sorry I didn't tell you earlier. But I wanted to let Finn know first. I just never thought that Deirdre would beat me to the punch. That she would be here tonight. That she would already have her hooks into Finn."

Anger surged through me, and I kicked the stool where Deirdre had been sitting. The metal chair skidded across the marble floor before banging into the wooden bar and teetering to a stop. The noise made everyone stare at me again, but I didn't care right now.

"I'm such an *idiot*," I growled. "Finn has been going on and on about his great new client for weeks now. I should have realized there was more to it than just him schmoozing with someone. I should have considered the possibility that it was Deirdre, trying to get close to him."

Owen took my hands in his and stroked his thumbs over my skin. "You're not an idiot," he said. "Finn always talks about his clients, ad nauseam sometimes. There was no reason to suspect that this client was different from any other. Although . . ."

"Yeah?"

"How long *have* you known about Finn's mother?"

I had started to answer when I realized that people were sidling closer and closer to Owen and me—all the criminals still left in the lobby. Gun runners, loan sharks, bookies, and more. All standing in a loose knot, all with their arms crossed over their chests, all waiting for me, the big boss, to tell them how I was going to fix this, how I was going to find and take down the people who had dared to try to rob them.

I sighed. "I'll tell you all about it on the drive over to Jo-Jo's. But first, let me deal with this."

Owen squeezed my hands, then stepped back.

I squared my shoulders, lifted my chin, and waded into the middle of the mobsters. Everyone clustered around me, talking at once, their voices growing louder and louder as they demanded that I find the robbers *right fucking now* and have them strung up from the nearest streetlight. For once, I was in total agreement with them. I wanted the robbers found, all right, especially Santos, so I could make him pay for trying to hurt Finn.

But I put my game face on, made all the appropriate *I'm-going-to-find-and-kill-these-bastards* noises, and promised all the bosses that this sort of behavior would absolutely not be tolerated on my watch.

The only ones I didn't have to placate were Lorelei and Mallory, who stood on the fringes of the crowd. Lorelei was busy texting on her phone, while Mallory watched me soothe the bruised egos of the other criminals, an amused expression on her wrinkled face.

By the time I got done playing my part as the head honcho and the other bosses had finally drifted away, more cops had streamed into the lobby, including a seven-foot-tall giant sporting a black leather jacket. Despite the cold night, he wasn't wearing a hat on his shaved head, and his ebony skin gleamed under the lights. Xavier, Bria's partner on the force.

Xavier spotted Owen and me and walked over to us. The giant looked around the lobby, his dark eyes taking in all the overturned furniture, smashed glasses, and trampled food.

"This reminds me of that robbery at the Briartop art museum during the summer," he rumbled. "Minus a few bodies."

I grimaced at the mention of the other heist. I'd thwarted that one too but not before several innocent people had been killed. At least tonight only the robbers had died.

"Roslyn won't be sorry she missed this," he added.

Roslyn Phillips was Xavier's significant other and a vampire friend of mine who ran Northern Aggression, a decadent nightclub.

"She's on vacation with Lisa and Catherine, right?" I asked, referring to Roslyn's sister and niece.

Xavier nodded. "Yep. Took them to the beach at Blue Marsh for two weeks. Roslyn called me this afternoon to tell me how great the weather was down there."

We chatted for a few more minutes before the giant pulled a notepad out of his pocket, and Owen and I told him what had happened. Xavier asked several questions, writing everything down, then looked at me.

"Bria texted me," he said. "She told me about Finn's mom."

I rubbed my aching head. "Yeah."

"Go make sure he's okay," Xavier said. "If I need anything else, I'll call. And tell Bria that I'll check in with her later."

I stepped forward and hugged him. "Thank you."

Xavier hugged me back, then winked. "That's what friends are for, right?"

One of the other cops called his name. Xavier waved at the man, smiled at Owen and me a final time, then headed off in that direction.

"You ready to leave?" Owen asked.

I looked out over the lobby, just like Xavier had

done. In a matter of minutes, the elegant space had been ruined. The marble walls scorched and cracked by bullets, the floor littered with glass, crystal, and shell casings, the antique furniture smashed to pieces. This destruction was bad enough, but worry iced over my heart as I thought of how Deirdre might hurt Finn—and how much more permanent that damage might be.

"Gin?" Owen asked again.

I shook my head, trying to squash my troubling thoughts, but I wasn't the least bit successful. "Yeah," I said. "Let's go check on Finn."

❊ 9 ❊

Owen and I left the bank and drove over to Jo-Jo's house. During the ride, I told him about discovering Fletcher's file on Deirdre, digging up her grave, and finding the box of photos and mementos that had been hidden inside. I even told him about the letter that the old man had written to me. The only thing I didn't mention was the second letter to Finn. I still wasn't sure what to do about that.

When I finished, Owen let out a low whistle. "That is all kinds of messed up," he said. "Why do you think Deirdre left Ashland? And stayed away and let everyone think that she was dead? Do you think she and Fletcher had some sort of falling-out?"

I shrugged. "Something had to have gone down between them. Something bad, judging from what little Fletcher said about her in his letter to me. I wonder why he didn't write more, why he didn't tell me exactly what happened between them."

"Maybe Fletcher wanted you to make your own judgments about Deirdre and not be biased against her based on their history together," he said. "Maybe he was hoping that she had changed, that she had become a better person than the one he knew, for Finn's sake."

"Maybe, but all I have now are more questions than answers."

"I imagine Finn has the same," Owen pointed out.

I sighed and leaned my head against the window. "I know, and I hate that I can't give him those answers. But Fletcher said that Deirdre is dangerous. That she only cares about herself. If she really loved Finn like she claims, then why didn't she come back to Ashland years ago? Why didn't she reach out and try to have some kind of relationship with him before now?"

Owen looked at me. "You think she's up to something."

"It's the only thing that makes sense. She didn't just mosey into the bank and get hooked up with Finn by accident. She planned it, just like she planned on using that initial connection to squirm her way into his life. And then there's the robbery."

"What about it?"

I snorted. "I find it more than a little suspicious that First Trust, which has never, ever been successfully robbed before, just happens to get hit the night that Deirdre and Finn are there. That Deirdre just happens to get shot in the process of saving Finn's life but that, miraculously, her wound is not serious at all. No one is that lucky." I paused. "Well, not me, anyway."

"But you saw Deirdre," he said. "The shock on her

face, the tremors, all of it. Whatever else she might be guilty of, she wasn't faking how upset she was about getting shot."

I let out a breath. "I know. And she did seem like she was a victim tonight, like everyone else. But something about her just doesn't sit right with me."

Owen frowned. He was as well acquainted with my paranoia as Finn was, although he didn't tease me about it nearly as much.

He steered his car into a subdivision, then up a hill, and parked in front of a three-story white plantation house. Bria's sedan was already here, and the front porch light was on, along with several more lights on the first floor.

We got out of the car, stepped onto the porch, and went inside. Owen followed me down a long hallway, which opened up into an old-fashioned beauty salon. Cherry-red chairs lined the back wall, and tables filled with beauty magazines were scattered throughout the room. A counter along one wall bristled with combs, curlers, and blow dryers, along with pink plastic tubs filled with lipstick, nail polish, and eye shadow. The air smelled of hairspray and other chemicals, along with a faint, soothing hint of vanilla.

Finn was leaning back in a salon chair, his suit jacket off, his shirt unbuttoned at the neck, a glass of Scotch in his hand. It wasn't his first drink, judging from the half-empty bottle sitting on the table at his elbow.

Jolene "Jo-Jo" Deveraux was perched on the edge of a chair next to him. The dwarf must have gotten out of bed, since she wore a long pink housecoat. Her middle-aged face was free of its usual soft makeup, and her white-blond hair was done up in pink sponge rollers for the night. Rosco, her basset hound, was sprawled across her bare feet, as though he was trying to keep her toes warm with his tubby body.

Bria was sitting on a couch off to one side of the room, along with Sophia Deveraux, Jo-Jo's younger sister. The Goth dwarf was wearing a black microfleece robe decorated with silver skulls that had red sequined hearts for eyes. The sight made me think of Deirdre's icicle-heart rune, and more cold worry balled up in my stomach.

Jo-Jo was healing Finn, and a milky-white glow coated her palm and glimmered in her eyes. Her Air magic gusted through the salon, the pins-and-needles sensation brushing up against my skin and making me grind my teeth. Jo-Jo's Air power was the opposite of my Stone magic, so I never liked the feel of it, which was as harsh and grating as sandpaper rubbing against my skin. Ironically, for as badly as Deirdre's Ice magic had chilled my hand, it was similar to my own Ice power, so it hadn't made me want to snarl, not like Jo-Jo's power did.

Jo-Jo moved her palm back and forth over the gash in Finn's forehead, using the oxygen and all the other molecules in the air to stitch his skin back together, fade out the bruising, and smooth out the bump he'd gotten from his hard fall.

A minute later, she dropped her hand and gave him a tentative smile. "There you go, darling. Good as new."

"Thank you, Jo-Jo," Finn said in a stiff voice.

He threw back the rest of his Scotch, then poured himself another. Everyone remained quiet, except Rosco, who whined, sensing the tension in the room. Finn downed the second Scotch, then poured himself a third one, before he finally deigned to look at me.

He stabbed his finger at me. "Start talking, Gin. *Right fucking now.*"

His voice was as sharp, clipped, and cold as I'd ever heard it. Anger rolled off him in almost palpable waves, and a storm of emotions flashed in his green eyes. For the most part, Finn was a cheerful, happy-go-lucky guy. But the angrier he got, the more that cheer crystallized into something else—something dark, dangerous, and deadly. I hadn't seen this level of cold, contained rage from Finn in a long, long time.

His rage increased my own worry, but I stepped up so that I was standing directly in front of him, drew in a breath, and told him everything. He stared at me the whole time, analyzing and cataloging every single word I said. He didn't interrupt, he didn't ask questions, and he didn't offer any comments of his own. All he did was sit there and stare at me, his face solidified into a chillingly empty mask.

I kept my own face and voice neutral, reciting the facts, just the way Fletcher had laid out the information on Deirdre in his file. I also told Finn and the others about the mementos and the letter that Fletcher had left me in the casket box, including what the old man had said about how dangerous Deirdre was and how she didn't care about anyone but herself.

Bria gave me a sharp look, obviously wondering why I hadn't told her about the letter when we'd first gone through the casket box. I gave her a guilty, sheepish shrug in return. But I still didn't mention the second letter that Fletcher had written to Finn. I'd already mangled things enough. I'd tell Finn about the letter later, in private, so he could decide whether he wanted to share it with everyone.

After I finished, no one moved or spoke, and the salon was so quiet that I could hear the steady *tick-tock-tick-tock* of the grandfather clock in the hallway. Finally, Finn downed his Scotch, leaned forward, and poured himself yet another.

"So you've known that my mother is alive for *days* now, and you kept it to yourself this whole time," he said. "That's why you were so eager to pay for dinner at Underwood's tonight. When exactly were you going to break the news to me? After we got the bread basket? Or were you going to wait until the dessert course? *Oh, hey, Finn. By the way, your mother, the one you thought was dead, is actually alive. Pass the fucking cheesecake.*"

I winced. "I didn't know what I was going to do, how I was going to tell you. But I *was* going to tell you."

He snorted and gulped down some more Scotch.

"Believe me, it was just as much of a shock to me as it is to you. I don't remember Fletcher talking about your mother all that much. Finding that file, realizing that she might still be alive, and then seeing her in the flesh tonight, sitting with you at the bar like she was just another client . . . it threw me too."

"But not as much as it did me." He took another hit of Scotch.

"No," I replied in an even voice. "Not as much as it did you."

A thought occurred to Finn, and he snapped his head around and glared at Jo-Jo. "And *you*," he snarled. "You had to know that Dee-Dee was alive too."

Jo-Jo stayed calm in the face of his anger, shaking her head. The motion made her pink sponge curlers sway back and forth. "Darling, I promise you that I didn't know anything about your mama until tonight when you came in here ranting and raving about her."

"How could you not?" he snarled again. "You and Sophia were Dad's best friends. You knew all his secrets."

"Not this one," Sophia muttered.

Jo-Jo gave her sister a pointed look, but Sophia just shrugged back.

"Of course, we knew Deirdre Shaw," Jo-Jo said, focusing on Finn again. "From the day they first met at the Pork Pit, your daddy was plumb crazy about her, always talking and telling stories about her. He brought her by the salon a few times, but they mostly kept to themselves. That's how in love they were."

Finn's eyes narrowed, but he waved his hand, telling her to continue.

"They'd been together a few months when Fletcher dropped by and told us that Dee-Dee was pregnant." The dwarf's face softened with memories. "Fletcher said it was the happiest day of his life, knowing that he was going to be a father."

Finn shifted in his seat, some of the cold rage leaking out of his face. "So what happened?"

"Family emergency," Sophia rasped.

Jo-Jo nodded. "We had an elderly cousin up in Cypress Mountain who was dying of old age and didn't have any close family to help her. So Sophia and I packed up and went to stay with her. We thought we'd only be gone a few weeks, but it was much longer before our cousin passed. Of course, we came back to Ashland every now and then, but we didn't see much of Fletcher. By the time we got through our cousin's funeral and settled up her estate, several months had passed."

"And?"

"And you had been born, but your mama was gone," Jo-Jo said. "Fletcher told us that someone had figured out that he was an assassin. This person had stormed into the Pork Pit one night with several giants while he was there with you and your mama. Fletcher said that he had to make a choice whether to save you or Deirdre—and he chose you. He said that the giants murdered your mama right in front of him. He managed to kill them all in the end, and he got rid of all the bodies except your mama's. He made it look like she'd died in a car accident. He told everyone that was how she died, and he made Sophia and me swear to tell you the same story too."

"Why? Why would he do that?" Finn demanded.

She hesitated. "Fletcher thought it would be easier on you if her death seemed like an accident. He claimed that he didn't want you to blame yourself because he chose to save you and not her."

"And you believed him?" Finn asked. "Just like that?"

"He didn't want to talk about it," Sophia chimed in.

Jo-Jo shook her head again. "Of course, we had questions, but Fletcher was so heartbroken that we didn't press him about it. Besides, why would he lie about something like that? What reason would he have? After that, Fletcher threw himself into raising you, and Sophia and I helped him as much as we could. The years passed, and eventually, Gin came along, and well, here we are tonight."

Everyone fell silent, digesting Jo-Jo's story, and once again, the only sound was the *tick-tock-tick-tock* of the grandfather clock, punctuated every once in a while by a soft whine from Rosco.

Ever since I'd found out that Deirdre was alive, I'd wondered what the Deveraux sisters might know about her, and I'd thought about asking Jo-Jo and Sophia about her a dozen times. Jo-Jo's voice had been strong, her tone sincere, her clear, almost colorless eyes steady on Finn's the whole time. She'd told him everything she knew, but it only increased my frustration, since I still had more questions than answers.

If I couldn't find out anything about Deirdre's past, then I'd have to focus on who she was now. So I turned to the one person who could shed some light on that: Finn.

His nostrils flared when he realized that I was staring at him, but the rest of his features remain fixed in that cold, blank mask.

"Why don't you tell us what *you* know about Deirdre?" I said, struggling to keep calm. "When did you meet her? You said that she's a client of yours?"

Finn jerked his head. I thought he might stay quiet, just to get back at me for keeping this from him, but he sighed and finally set his glass of Scotch aside. "It all started back over the summer," he said. "A couple of weeks after that mess with Harley Grimes up on Bone Mountain. One of the bank higher-ups came into my office and said that a big fish had just walked in the door, wanting to move her accounts and other business interests over to First Trust. He asked me to see what I could do for her. The next thing I know, Dee-Dee is strolling into my office. She was just like you saw her tonight—big, bold, confident. We hit it off right away."

A faint smile pulled up his lips, easing some of the anger that tightened his face.

"At first, I didn't think anything of her. She was just another client with old family money who spends most of her time lunching with the ladies and doing charity work. Your typical society broad. Apparently, she'd heard about me and wanted to see what I could do with her investment portfolio. Seemed like her last guy had been skimming and mismanaging funds from her charity foundation, and she wanted to get back on track."

"And . . ." I prompted.

Finn shrugged. "And things just progressed from there. I looked at her finances, straightened out a few things, recommended some investments. She would come by the bank to check on things whenever she was in town. A few weeks ago, she rented a penthouse in Ashland to stay in while she puts together a local charity exhibit. After that, we started seeing each other more often, having coffee, meeting for drinks. Dee-Dee started getting a little friendlier, opening up to me. It happens once a client feels comfortable enough. We talked about movies, TV shows, books. All your usual chitchat."

"What about tonight?" Bria asked. "What were the two of you meeting about tonight?"

"A couple of weeks ago, Dee-Dee asked me to put her in touch with some folks who could help with her charity exhibit, and she was telling me how well everything was going." He paused. "Although she wanted to take me out to dinner, said that there was something else she wanted to talk to me about. Something personal. I guess I know what *that* is now." He barked out a harsh, humorless laugh.

"What about Hugh Tucker?" I asked. "What's his story?"

Finn shrugged again. "Your typical assistant. Fetching coffee, taking messages, and the like. He's come into the bank with Dee-Dee several times now. She rented some safety-deposit boxes in the basement vault for her jewelry, and he carried in the briefcases for her. Nothing unusual there."

Nothing unusual at all. Many wealthy people in Ashland employed personal assistants. Still, the wealthier the person, usually the more obnoxious the assistant was, some of them even more aggressive than giant bodyguards about not letting you get close to their bosses. At least, not without an appointment. And most assistants were actually concerned with, well, *assisting* their bosses, not drinking, texting, and being bored like Tucker had been tonight. Silvio would have given him a stern talking-to about proper decorum.

Finn fell silent again and stared at his glass of Scotch, brooding.

"That's all?" I asked. "That's all the contact you've had with her?"

"Yeah. Why?"

I could have told him that something about Deirdre just rubbed me the wrong way. I could have told him that long-lost relatives didn't appear out of thin air for no reason. I could have told him that it was obvious that she wanted *something* from him.

But I held my tongue and kept my suspicions to myself. Finn had gotten a brutal shock, one he was trying to drink into oblivion, and he wasn't thinking straight right now. He was too close to the situation, too involved, too hurt and curious and hopeful and a hundred other things to wonder exactly why his mother had chosen this exact moment to reappear in his life after being gone for the previous thirty-three years of it.

But I was here, I was thinking clearly, and I wondered all those things. More important, I was determined to get answers to every single one of my questions. And if Deirdre was, in fact, conning Finn, then I was going to rain down a whole lot of hurt onto her for daring to think that she could sashay back into his life and use him for her own dark, devious ends.

But first, there was something else I needed to do.

"I'm sorry," I said. "I'm sorry that I didn't tell you sooner, that I didn't tell you the second I found her file. I just . . . didn't know how. Of all the bad things that have happened to us, of all the secrets the old man kept from us, your mom being alive . . . it's not something that I had ever even *considered*."

Finn snorted, but his face softened, and a little more of the cold anger leaked out of his eyes. "You and me both, sister," he muttered, sounding much more like his usual cheerful self. "So what do we do now?"

I grabbed the glass out of his hand and set it on the table. "You are going to go upstairs, take a shower, and crash here for the night. Then, in the morning, you're going to call in sick so you can sleep off your hangover. After that, you're going to put on your best suit, come to the Pork Pit, and talk to your mother."

Finn nodded. "Sounds like a plan to me."

He got out of his chair, took a step, and wobbled. He would have done a header onto the floor if Bria hadn't rushed up and grabbed hold of him. Even then, he kept wobbling back and forth.

Owen started forward to help Bria with Finn, but Sophia got there first. She swung Finn up into her arms, as though he didn't weigh any more than Rosco.

"My Princess Charming," Finn drawled. "Sweeping me off my feet."

Sophia snorted. "Lightweight," she said, a fond note in her gruff voice.

He gave her a drunken smile, his glassy eyes indicating that he was feeling no pain now, and pointed toward the hallway. "Yep, that's me. Finnegan Lane, lightweight drinker. Now, to the shower, my lady!"

Sophia carried Finn out of the salon, with Bria following them. That left me with Owen, Jo-Jo, and Rosco. The basset hound had apparently had enough drama for the night, because he hauled himself to his feet, waddled over, and curled up in his wicker basket in the corner.

"I wish I could tell you more, Gin," Jo-Jo said. "But Fletcher kept Dee-Dee to himself."

I nodded and rubbed my temples, which were throbbing like I'd just downed as much Scotch as Finn had. I started pacing back and forth, even though the *snap-snap-snap-snap* of my stilettos against the floor added to my headache. My troubled thoughts were as quick as my steps, and more and more questions crowded into my mind.

"You really think she's up to something?" Owen asked.

"For Finn's sake, I hope she's not. This is one instance where I would be happy to be wrong."

"But?" he asked.

That photo of Deirdre staring down at newborn Finn with no expression on her face popped into my head again. Funny, but that was exactly how Finn had looked at me tonight, as if I didn't matter to him at all, and it had shaken me far more than I cared to admit.

"Gin?" Jo-Jo asked.

I stopped pacing and looked at her and Owen. "But something tells me there's a lot more to Deirdre Shaw than just a mother trying to reconnect with her son."

☀ 10 ☀

We left Finn at the salon, and Owen drove me back to Fletcher's. He offered to spend the night, but I sent him home. I wasn't good company right now. Not when so many thoughts and questions kept swirling around in my mind about Finn, Fletcher, and Deirdre.

I had just locked the door behind Owen and slipped out of my stilettos when the phone rang. I sighed, knowing exactly who it was—and that he would just keep calling until I answered him.

So I went into the den and grabbed the cordless phone. "Hello, Silvio."

Silence. "How did you know it was me?" The vampire's voice flooded my ear.

"Because I turned off my cell phone before I went to the bank, and no doubt you have been trying to reach me ever since you heard about the robbery." I sat down on the couch. "Not to mention the fact that the phone

rang a mere minute after Owen left. How would someone know that I was home right this very second? Unless,
of course, he had planted a GPS tracker on Owen's car."

Silvio cleared his throat. "I will neither confirm nor
deny that."

"Of course not."

I didn't say anything more as I leaned back and put my
feet up on the coffee table. The silence stretched on . . .
and on . . . and on . . .

Finally, Silvio sighed. "You're going to make me ask
what happened, aren't you?"

"Would I do something like that?"

"Absolutely," he grumbled.

Even though he couldn't see me, I still grinned. "Sadly,
it's the most fun I've had all night."

I filled him in on the robbery and Deirdre's big reveal. When I finished, he was silent, although a series of
*clickety-clack-clack-clack*s sounded through the phone, as
if he was typing out notes on our conversation. Now, *that*
was what a good assistant was supposed to do.

"I have some preliminary information on Ms. Shaw,"
he said, still typing away. "I'll have it and more waiting at
the Pork Pit in the morning."

"Thank you. You're a good friend, Silvio."

"I do try," he said, an amused note in his voice. "Now,
get some sleep. I've got work to do."

We hung up, and I went upstairs, took a shower, and
got into bed. I thought I would have trouble falling
asleep, since my brain was still in overdrive, but as soon
as my head touched the pillows, I dropped off into the
land of sleep, dreams, and memories . . .

"I don't think this is a good idea."

Finn rolled his eyes. *"Of course, you don't think it's a good idea. You never think anything fun is good."*

He went back to stringing up white lights along the fireplace mantel in the den. I shifted from one foot to the other, my stomach twisting into tight knots, but I didn't try to stop him. I had no right to. After all, this was his dad's house. I was just a guest here. At least, that's how I still felt sometimes, even though I'd been living with Fletcher for almost a year now.

The old man had gone off on some assassin job as the Tin Man and wouldn't be back until morning. He'd wanted Finn and me to spend the night at Jo-Jo's, but Finn had griped that he was sixteen now and Fletcher had to start leaving him alone sometime. After an hour of arguing on Finn's part, the old man had reluctantly agreed. Even though I would never tell him so, I'd thought Finn was right. Neither one of us was a kid. Not after all the bad things we'd seen and done.

What I hadn't realized was that Finn had a secret agenda.

Sure, he wanted to be trusted enough to be left home alone. But he also planned to throw a massive party.

The second the old man left, Finn had started calling up all his friends.

"Hey, man. Yep, my dad's gone, just like I planned. Why don't you guys come over about eight? Sure, it's cool if you bring your own beer . . ."

He'd had the same conversation with a dozen people. After he'd finished his calls, he raced up to the attic, carried down several boxes of Christmas lights, and strung them up all over the house, as if the small white glows would hide all the clutter, mismatched furniture, and assorted junk that

Fletcher had accumulated. Finn also taped up a couple of old silver disco balls on the ceiling.

He had gone into the kitchen and arranged cold cuts, carrot sticks, and more food from the fridge on platters and then filled bowls with chips, pretzels, and popcorn. He had also set out cans of soda, along with bottles of gin, Scotch, and other liquor from Fletcher's office. For a final touch, he'd hooked up an old stereo system in the den and tuned it to a popular radio station.

"Hey, Gin," Finn called out now. "Hand me some more tape. I need to get this final string of lights up before anyone gets here."

I crossed my arms over my chest. "You're going to get into so much trouble. Fletcher's going to find out. You know he will."

The old man was downright spooky when it came to figuring out Finn's latest schemes and how he was plotting to get around Fletcher's rules, whether it was about homework or curfew or doing his chores. But Finn was just as stubborn as the old man, and he kept right on doing exactly what he wanted, no matter how many times Fletcher punished him.

Finn grinned, but his smile was more calculating than kind. "He won't find out if you don't tell him. And since you haven't called him or Jo-Jo yet, well, I'd say that makes you just as guilty as me now. Wouldn't you?"

I shifted on my feet again. I hadn't called anyone because I hadn't wanted to get into trouble. Fletcher said that he loved me, that I was part of his family, now and forever, but we weren't related.

We weren't blood.

The truth was that Fletcher could kick me out anytime he

wanted to, and I couldn't help but think that he would if I ever pissed him off enough. Like by letting a bunch of kids eat his food, guzzle his booze, and trash his house.

"Come on, Gin," Finn said, his voice taking on a wheedling note. "If you think we're going to get into trouble anyway, then we might as well go ahead and have the fun now. Make all that punishment really worth it in the end."

He winked and slowly widened his grin, trying to charm me the way I'd seen him charm countless other girls. Finn was cute, but I wasn't stupid enough to get suckered in by a pretty face. Still, it was easier to go along with him than it was to protest. Besides, he was right. He'd already done all the work and called everyone, so it wasn't like he could cancel the party. Not without looking like a complete loser in front of his friends, something Finn would do anything to avoid. Being cool and popular was more important to him than anything else.

"All right," I muttered. "But you can tell Fletcher that it was all your idea."

Finn grinned again, knowing that he'd won. "Sure. I'll tell him that very thing. Now, grab the tape and help me with the lights."

I sighed, thinking that no party was going to be worth the weeks of no TV, extra chores, and other punishments we'd get from Fletcher, but I helped Finn finish stringing up the lights.

We'd just taped the last strand to the mantel when a knock sounded on the front door.

Finn gave me a sharp look. "Just be cool tonight, okay? Or as cool as you can be. As long as you don't act like a whiny Goody Two-shoes, everything will be fine. You'll see."

He gave me one more warning glare, then hurried down the hallway and opened the front door. "Hey, Steve! Tony! Glad you guys could make it. Come on in . . ."

Over the next hour, more and more kids arrived, streaming into Fletcher's house like it was the site of the greatest party ever. Maybe it was. More than a hundred kids packed into the house, smoking, drinking, laughing, talking. The stereo was cranked up so loud that you could barely hear what anyone else was saying. Then again, everybody was too busy drinking, smoking, and making out to care about having a real conversation.

All the kids were older than my fourteen years, and many of them were older than Finn's sixteen. In fact, several guys with facial stubble and girls with big hair and even bigger breasts looked like they should have been in college, rather than hanging out at a high-school party. And beer and cigarettes weren't the only things they'd brought with them. One of the downstairs living rooms reeked of pot, with thick, hazy, suffocating smoke filling the air. And it wasn't just that folks were drinking and smoking things they shouldn't. They were bumping into furniture, breaking dishes, and making a mess of everything.

One guy staggered out into the hallway right in front of me. He grinned, his eyes bright and glassy, then bent over and puked all over the floor. I jumped back so I wouldn't get any of it on my sneakers, but I couldn't escape the hot, sour stench, and my nose wrinkled in disgust.

Once he was finished, puke boy lurched over, grabbed a random can off one of the tables lining the hallway, and chugged back all the beer inside. Several cheers sounded, and people gathered around and clapped him on the back, as if *puking your guts out and then immediately guzzling down more beer was totally awesome. Whatever.*

Enough was enough. I wasn't going to get kicked out of Fletcher's house because Finn had decided that he just had to throw a stupid party for all his stupid friends.

I shoved through the kids crowding the hallway, searching for Finn. It took me forever to move from one part of the house to the next, and more than a few guys were drunk enough to throw their arms around my shoulders and hit on me, even though I was as flat-chested as a girl could be. But I supposed all that beer had already soaked into their puny brains, making me look prettier than I actually was.

I sidestepped another guy with grabby hands and pushed my way into the den. Finn was standing in front of the fireplace, a red plastic cup in his hand, talking to a gorgeous blond girl who looked a year or two older than him. Finn had his elbow propped up on the mantel and the collar of his black polo shirt popped up, like he was supercool. I rolled my eyes. Super-idiot was more like it.

I went over and tugged on Finn's arm. The music was so loud in here that I could barely hear myself think.

Finn glanced over his shoulder. When he realized it was me, he narrowed his eyes and jerked his head, a clear leave-me-alone-right-now *signal. But I tugged on his arm again.*

"People are throwing up everywhere!" I yelled over the music. "And they're breaking things and going through Fletcher's stuff. You need to tell them to leave. Now. We'll have a hard enough time as it is cleaning up this mess before he gets home."

Finn looked out over the den as if he were just now noticing how many kids were packed inside and what a colossal mess they were making. The drinking, smoking, and puking were bad enough, but one particular drunk idiot was standing on top of the coffee table, scuffing his boots all over the wood as he tried to do some sort of lame-ass cowboy line dance.

Finn winced. For a second, I thought he was going to tell people to start clearing out. But the girl he'd been talking to peered around his shoulder at me.

The girl's nose wrinkled in disgust, the same way mine had a few minutes ago. "Who *is* this? And why is she at your party? I didn't think you had invited any losers, Lane."

I looked at Finn, expecting him to tell the girl that I was his cousin, since that was the cover story Fletcher had concocted to explain my living here.

But he gave me a sneer that was even crueler than the girl's. "I didn't invite any losers, Ella. She must have snuck in." He flapped his hand at me, like I was a bug he was trying to shoo away. "Am-scray, kid. Go away and leave us alone."

I stared at him, my mouth hanging open and hot tears stinging my eyes. For a moment, guilt flickered in Finn's eyes, but then his face hardened into a cold, uncaring mask, and he made that shooing motion again.

"Go on," he growled. "Get out of here. Can't you see I'm busy?"

Then he deliberately turned his back to me and started talking and laughing with Ella again, as if I had never been here to start with.

I bit my lip, trying to focus on that small, sharp pain, instead of the much larger ache in my heart, but it didn't work. Two tears streaked down my face before I could blink *them back. Ella noticed and laughed again. Finn turned to see what she thought was so funny, but I scrubbed my hands over my face, whirled around, and shoved my way out of the den before he realized just how much he'd hurt me.*

It was bad enough that he'd humiliated me in front of that girl. I didn't want him to know that he'd made me cry too. Especially since I had promised myself that I would never cry again. Not after my family had been murdered and I hadn't been able to save them.

Besides, Finn insulting me wasn't so bad. It wasn't anything compared with living on the streets. I could put up with a little humiliation, as long as Fletcher let me stay here, as long as I had a warm, safe place to sleep and enough food to eat. At least, that's what I told myself as I pushed through the dancing, laughing kids in the hallway, twisted the front doorknob, and staggered outside.

I stumbled all the way across the porch over to the wooden railing, clutching one of the posts for support as more tears traitorously trickled down my face. A sob rose in my throat, but I choked it down. It was bad enough that Finn had made me feel so small, so stupid, so worthless. I wasn't going to start bawling like a little kid too. Finnegan Lane wasn't worthy of my tears.

I stood there, clutching the railing with one hand, wiping away the tears with the other, wishing that I could stop them completely, when a sharp bang sounded over the loud, thumping music.

I froze, wondering if I'd only imagined the sound, but the bang came again, followed by some cursing.

Curious, I let go of the railing, walked the length of the porch, and peered around the corner.

Three guys were at the side door, hauling a safe out of the house—a safe that was filled with guns and silverstone knives, along with other valuables. I sucked in a breath. They were using the distraction of the party to steal from Fletcher.

This was bad—so very bad.

But instead of being afraid, anger roared through me. Anger that these lowlifes were stealing something that didn't belong to them. Anger that someone would do that to Fletcher, who had been nothing but good to me. And especially anger at Finn for being stupid enough to throw the party in the first place. He was the one who'd invited all these people over, he was the one who was getting the house trashed, and he was the reason Fletcher was getting robbed.

Well, fuck Finn. I wasn't going to get into any more trouble. Not for him. Finn didn't deserve my silence. Not anymore.

"Hey!" I called out. "What do you think you're doing?"

The three guys stopped and stared at me. For the first time, I saw that they were much older than the other kids, well into their twenties. I frowned. Maybe Finn hadn't invited them after all.

The three guys looked at me, then at one another. They set down the safe and hurried in my direction, their lips pulling back into snarls, revealing the fangs in their mouths. Vampires, all of them. The men came closer, and I suddenly realized that Fletcher getting robbed wasn't the worst thing that could happen tonight . . .

I woke up wrestling with my blankets, as though the soft layers of fabric were the three vamps closing in on me. Several seconds passed before I realized that I was safe in Fletcher's house and that the party was just another one of my ugly memories.

I flopped back against the pillows and closed my eyes. This wasn't the first time I'd dreamed about the awful things that had happened to me, but this particular nightmare hadn't bothered me in a long, long time. But my subconscious was tricky like that, and it didn't take a genius to figure out that this dream, this memory, had everything to do with Finn.

I wondered if he remembered the night of his first—and only—party. We'd never talked about it afterward. Sadly, it wasn't the worst thing that had happened to either of us. It wasn't even the worst thing that had happened in this house—

A floorboard creaked downstairs.

My eyes snapped open. I lay there, waiting and listening. Five seconds later, another creak sounded. Not only that, but I realized that the stones were muttering. The bricks that made up parts of the walls and floors whispered of danger and dark, deadly intent.

Someone was in the house.

☀ 11 ☀

I grabbed the knife under my pillow, slipped out of bed, and tiptoed across my bedroom. I eased the door open, making sure that it didn't creak and give away the fact that I was awake and alert. I wasn't surprised that someone was here. More than a few of the underworld bosses had sent their minions to kill me, although most of them waited in the woods outside, rather than trying to break into the house.

But someone had stepped into my parlor tonight, and it was going to be the last fucking thing he ever did.

I sidled down the hallway and stopped at the top of the stairs, listening all the while. The creaks had definitely come from the first floor, but I didn't hear any more as I tiptoed down the stairs, hugging the wall so as not to make the floorboards moan under my bare feet. I'd been creeping around this house long enough to know just where to step.

But the intruder also knew where to step, because I didn't hear any more creaks, cracks, or *pop-pop*s of wood that would tell me what room he was in. Maybe he'd found a comfortable spot to hide. Maybe his plan was to break in while I was asleep, lie in wait the rest of the night, and then take me out when I woke up and came downstairs in the morning. Not a bad idea and certainly more creative than most of the other folks who'd been foolish enough to come here over the past few months.

I reached the bottom of the stairs and looked left and right, searching for the telltale glow of a flashlight, but I didn't see one. If my intruder was smart, he would be wearing night-vision goggles so that he wouldn't need a flashlight.

I could have started searching the house, winding my way through the labyrinth of rooms and hallways until I came across my would-be killer. But eventually, I would make some sort of noise doing that, so I stood at the bottom of the steps, my back against the wall, and waited—just waited. My intruder might be quiet, but he wasn't a ghost, and he had to make a sound sooner or later. I had the patience to wait him out all night if that's what it took.

A minute ticked by, then two, then three. All around me, the stones kept muttering, whispering about the intruder and his ill intentions, but their dark murmurs didn't increase in volume, which meant the intruder wasn't nearby and getting ready to strike. So I held my position and waited. Another minute, then two, then three. Finally, my patience was rewarded with another faint creak.

He was in the den.

I headed in that direction, still hugging the wall and being as silent as possible. I reached the den entrance and carefully eased up so I could peer inside. Moonlight streamed in through the white lace curtains, painting the room a shadowy silver, which was more than enough light for me to spot the giant standing in the corner.

He was dressed all in black, a gun clutched in his right hand. A pair of night-vision goggles were clamped over his face, hiding his features, but his shirtsleeves were pushed up, revealing a tattoo on his left forearm: a snake biting into a dollar sign.

Santos.

The bank robber was here to kill me. I wondered why. Because I'd ruined his plans earlier tonight? Was this just about payback for costing him a sweet score? Or was it something else, something more?

Either way, I was going to carve the answers out of Santos.

The giant thought I was asleep, and he had settled in to wait, leaning against the corner of the fireplace and looking at the framed drawings lined up on the mantel. I grinned. If he was so curious about the drawings, then I should turn on the light so he could see them in all their glory. Those night-vision goggles only gave him an advantage while it was dark. Any sudden influx of light would temporarily blind him.

So I crept forward another step, then reached my arm around the doorjamb, feeling the light switch under my fingers—

My shoulder cracked at the motions.

Damn.

Santos snapped around in my direction. I hit the switch, but he realized what I was up to and yanked off his goggles. Light flooded the den, and we both squinted against the harsh glare.

Black hair slicked back into a ponytail, cold brown eyes, a puckered white scar that zigzagged like a lightning bolt down his left cheek, marring his bronze skin. I cataloged Santos's features even as I darted forward, slashing my knife down toward his gun hand.

But he was quicker, and he whirled out of the way, spinning around in a tight circle and snapping up his gun so he could shoot me in the face. I reached for my Stone magic, hardening my skin, especially my head, neck, and shoulders—

Crack! Crack! Crack!

Two bullets slammed into my throat, while a third clipped my right cheekbone, before they all rattled off my body and *ping-ping-ping*ed through the den. All of them would have been kill shots if I hadn't been protecting myself with my Stone power. But the close range and the force of the bullets still threw me back against the wall, hard enough to rattle the framed photos of Finn, Fletcher, and me hanging there.

Santos cursed and raised his gun again, but I flung out my left hand and sent a spray of Ice daggers shooting across the room at him. He cursed again, turned to the side, and hunkered down, protecting his head with his arms. He might be lean and lanky, but he was still a giant, with more than enough tough musculature to survive my magic strike.

Too late, I realized he was wearing a protective vest,

probably lined with silverstone, since my Ice splattered against the garment and fell to the floor in harmless chunks. Still, Santos grunted as one long needle of Ice punched through his right shoulder, outside the vest. Even better, the needle must have clipped a nerve, because his fingers spasmed, and his gun slipped from his hand and thumped to the floor.

I rushed forward, trying to drive my knife into his other shoulder to make both of his arms useless so I could question him and then finish him off. But Santos raised his forearm and blocked my blow. I lashed out with my left hand, trying to sucker-punch him in the throat, but he blocked that blow too and responded with a head-butt that made stars explode in front of my eyes.

This time, Santos surged forward, grabbed my wrist, and bent it back, forcing me to drop my knife or risk getting my wrist broken. I let go of the weapon and twisted into his hold, ramming my elbow into his stomach.

It was like hitting a brick wall. Pain jolted up my arm, but I gritted my teeth and followed up that first elbow strike with another, harder one. Santos let out a loud *oof* of air and let go of my wrist, and I whipped around, raised my fists, and went at him again.

Santos lurched to his left, grabbed the photos off the mantel, and chucked them at me. I ducked again and again, the sounds of the frames crashing to the floor and the glass splintering making me growl with rage. The bastard was destroying my rune drawings.

He was going to pay for that.

Santos ran out of pictures. I expected him to pull out another gun, but the photo bombs had just been a distraction. He sprinted forward, leaped up onto the coffee table, grabbed the ceiling fan with one hand, and swung himself right past me.

It was truly an impressive move, worthy of a world-class gymnast, especially given his seven-foot frame. But Santos was faster and far more limber and flexible than most giants. Even more impressive, he landed on his feet as nimbly as a cat and sprinted down the hallway.

I growled again, whirled around, and charged after him, but I stepped on a couple of broken bits of my own elemental Ice rolling around on the floor. My bare feet slipped, and I had to windmill my arms back and forth to keep from falling on my ass.

It only took me a few seconds to regain my balance, but it cost me dearly. I staggered out into the hallway to see the front door slamming shut. A few seconds later, a car engine roared to life in the driveway. I cursed again and picked up my speed, even though I knew I was already too late.

I yanked open the front door and raced out onto the porch. A dark, anonymous sedan was already zooming down the driveway, fishtailing wildly through snow, ice, and gravel. I hadn't even made it to the porch steps when the taillights disappeared. I cursed, knowing that I wouldn't be able to hop into my own car and catch up with him.

Gone. Santos was gone.

Again.

I stood on the porch for the better part of a minute, fuming at myself for letting Santos get away twice in one night. But there was nothing I could do to bring him back, so I moved on to what I *could* do: learn more about the bastard.

I went inside, wrapped a blanket from the couch around my shoulders, and shoved my cold, bare feet into a pair of snow boots. Then I snapped on the porch light, stepped back outside, and peered at the front door, trying to figure out how Santos had gotten into the house.

Silverstone bars covered all the windows and side doors, so he had to have come in through the front door, a solid slab of black granite shot through with thick veins of silverstone. It wasn't the sort of door that a giant could pound through or that an elemental could blast through with magic. Not without a lot of effort and a whole lot of noise—much more noise than Santos had made.

There was no damage to the door, so I bent down, examining the lock. A few scratches gleamed in the metal, so small that I wouldn't have noticed them if I hadn't been looking. Santos had picked open the door instead of trying to punch his way through it. Smart and not something I would expect from a giant, since most of them relied on their great strength to solve whatever problems came their way.

I frowned. Santos was seeming less like a common robber and more like a highly trained thief, especially given his acrobatics with the ceiling fan. You didn't develop slick, nimble moves like that by knocking over convenience stores. At the bank, I'd thought he was a professional, but he was a far higher class of thief than I'd given him credit for. I wondered what other skills he had—and how deadly they might be.

I went back inside, locked the front door behind me, and wedged a heavy chair under the knob for good measure. Then I turned on more lights, going through the rooms one by one to see if anything was missing.

But the rest of the house was undisturbed, and the only mess was the one we'd made fighting in the den. It seemed as though Santos had come in through the front door, gone straight down the hallway, and headed into the den to wait for me. No doubt, he would have stayed in there all night, then casually stepped up to the door-jamb and shot me as I went into the kitchen for breakfast. It was a good plan, and it would have worked, if my nightmare hadn't already startled me awake enough to hear his faint creeping through the house.

I frowned again as another, more troubling thought occurred to me. Fletcher's house was a labyrinth, given all the rooms and additions that had been tacked onto the original structure over the years. So how had Santos known exactly where to go? How had he realized that the den was the closest room to the kitchen and the best place for him to wait to kill me? Santos had never been in here before.

But Deirdre had.

She'd certainly spent many hours with Fletcher here, both before and after Finn was born. Even if her memories were fuzzy, which I doubted, it would have been easy enough for her to draw a crude map for Santos and suggest where he might lie in wait to murder me.

Deirdre could have done this. But had she?

Santos hadn't looked to her for help when the bank robbery went sideways, and he hadn't hesitated to shoot her. Not exactly the actions of a minion. Sure, he'd never been inside the house before, but he could have easily walked the perimeter and peered in through the windows, scouting out the best place to lie in wait for me. Maybe my bias against Deirdre was clouding my judgment and making me think that she was at the center of some grand conspiracy when she wasn't.

Because I *was* biased against her. Even if Fletcher hadn't left me that warning letter, I still would have questioned any person who just showed up out of the blue after thirty-some years. People didn't do things for no reason. Especially not in Ashland, where practically everyone had at least one ulterior motive, along with two angles they were working from at any given time. Deirdre had to want *something*. I just had to figure out what it was.

Too bad I had absolutely nothing to help me do that.

I didn't have Santos, much less a confession about whom, if anyone, he might be working for. I didn't have *anything*, not so much as a single scrap of proof linking him to Deirdre. All I had were smashed picture frames littering the floor, muddy boot prints from where Santos had stepped on the coffee table, and a ceiling fan drooping down at a sad angle from where his weight had pulled it loose.

I waded through the shards of glass and melting bits of elemental Ice and picked up one of the rune drawings—a pig holding a platter of food. The same sign hung over the front door of the Pork Pit, and the sketch was my way of memorializing Fletcher and everything that the old man and his restaurant had meant to me.

I picked the rest of the broken glass out of the frame and tossed it aside, then ran my fingers over the paper.

"I'm going to get to the bottom of this, Fletcher," I whispered. "I promise you that."

As soon as I finished speaking, a gust of winter wind howled around the house, hard enough to rattle the windows in their frames. Just as quickly as it started, the wind died down, and a still, heavy silence settled over the house again. I didn't much believe in omens, but I was going to take that as a sign of Fletcher's approval.

But there was nothing else I could do tonight, so I placed the rune drawings back on the mantel, snapped off the lights, and went to bed.

✲ 12 ✲

The next morning, I cleaned up the mess in the den and went to work at the Pork Pit as usual. All the while, I kept stewing about Santos and how he'd escaped. If only I'd been quicker, faster, stronger, I could have nabbed him and cut him open for answers about the bank robbery and why he'd tried to kill me in my own home. Instead, I was back to square one, with no clue to what was really going on.

At least, until Deirdre showed up this afternoon.

I got started on the day's cooking by whipping up a batch of Fletcher's secret barbecue sauce. Smelling its rich blend of cumin, black pepper, and other spices bubbling away was my own sort of aromatherapy, and it soothed me, the way it always did. While I stirred the sauce, I thought about all the angles I could work and how I could get to the bottom of things.

Silvio came in early, an hour before the restaurant was

set to open, knowing that I would want to have a private chat with him. A great assistant in addition to being a good friend.

I gave him a few minutes to fire up his phone and tablet, then finished wiping down the counter, put my elbows on top of the shiny surface, and stared at him. "Tell me what you found out. I want to hear everything, no matter how small the detail."

Silvio blinked, not used to me being so interested in our morning briefings. He pulled his tablet a little closer and began swiping through screens. I grabbed a knife and started slicing tomatoes while he filled me in.

"By all accounts, Deirdre Shaw is a wealthy Ice elemental who hails from a prestigious Ashland family," he began. "We're talking old, old money and a lot of it. She's the last of the Shaws, although she hasn't lived in Ashland in years. She has a number of homes around the country where she divides her time, including a summer cabin in Cloudburst Falls, a town house in Cypress Mountain, and a penthouse in Bigtime."

"Let me guess. Deirdre spends her days flitting around the country on her private jet, staying in her swanky pads, guzzling champagne, and spending all of that old, old money."

"Naturally," he replied. "But she also spends quite a bit of time raising money for charity. Supposedly, one of the causes near and dear to her heart is an after-school art program for kids from broken homes."

I snorted. "I just bet it is."

Silvio arched his eyebrows at the sarcasm in my voice. "Actually, her charity work is where it gets interesting.

Ms. Shaw is involved with numerous charities, but they all fall under one corporate umbrella, Shaw Good Works, which she heads up. Other people actually run the charities so that Ms. Shaw can spend her time fund-raising and then deciding where to put all that capital. So, really, she's an investment banker, just like Finn."

I'd always thought that Finn must take after his mom, since he wasn't all that much like Fletcher. The old man had been perfectly happy to bury his money in tin cans in the backyard, instead of buying and selling stocks, investing in bonds, and all the other financial shenanigans that Finn engaged in. Finding out that Deirdre was in the same business as her son was a bit disconcerting.

I didn't want to think that Finn was *anything* like her. But at the party last night, Deirdre had basically been an older, female version of Finn—suave, flirty, boisterous. It had been a little jarring just how much the two of them were alike. I supposed that nature had won out over nurture in this case.

"Now, before you go and start thinking too highly of Ms. Shaw, you should know that not all the money she raises and then recoups from her investments goes into her charity foundation," Silvio said. "In fact, a great deal of it—tens of millions a year—goes down the rabbit hole for expenses, operating costs, and the like."

I realized what he was getting at. "You think her charity, Good Works, is a front for something."

"Absolutely. There's no way those charities have that much overhead. But she's clever, and she moves the money around faster than a street hustler doing a card game. I'm still researching, but I'll figure out where all that money is going and exactly who's getting it." His gray eyes gleamed with excitement. There was nothing Silvio loved better than untangling puzzles. I supposed it fit in with his detail-oriented personality.

I frowned. "Wait a second. Someone else is getting the money? Who? It sounds like Deirdre has a nice little scam going. Why would she want to share the money with anyone?"

"I don't know. Ms. Shaw might have come from old money, but she burned through it all years ago. Homes and private jets and champagne fountains cost money, you know. She started her charitable foundation about the time she was scraping the last few nickels out of her original trust fund. Even then, someone else bankrolled her and got her started."

"So maybe that's where the money is going," I murmured. "To pay back her investors, whoever they might be."

Silvio swiped through some more screens on his tablet. "That's my theory. I'll keep digging."

Maybe this was all about money. Maybe Deirdre had heard what a financial whiz Finn was and had come to Ashland to get his expertise to help increase the profits from her charity scam, without letting him know what a crook she really was. Finn had said that he'd been working on her portfolio. It made sense, but I still felt like something else was going on, something far more sinister than skimming money from good causes.

I finished with my last tomato, grabbed a red onion, and started slicing it. "What about Tucker, her assistant?"

Silvio shook his head. "Hugh Tucker. I've just started drilling down on him, but nothing suspicious so far. Although he and Deirdre have something interesting in common: the Tucker family has been in Ashland for generations, just like the Shaws, and Hugh is also the last one left of his family."

Not that unusual. Despite the sky-high crime rate, Ashland was a beautiful place to live, with its rugged ridges, lush forests, and mountain streams. My family, the Snows, had also been here for generations. So had the Monroes. Come to town, enjoy the mountains, start a blood feud with another family. It was practically the Ashland tourism motto. Still, it was a bit odd that Deirdre and Tucker would both be from Ashland and also be the last living members of their families. I wondered if Deirdre had known Tucker before he started working for her.

"All right," I said. "Keep digging into Deirdre and Tucker. And there's one more person I need you to track down."

"Who?"

"Santos. After his failed bank robbery last night, he decided to pay me a house call."

I wiped off my hands and grabbed a napkin and a pen. While I filled Silvio in about the attack at Fletcher's house, I made a crude sketch of the snake-and-dollar-sign tattoo on Santos's forearm.

"Here," I said, passing the sketch over to him. "See if you have more luck with the tattoo. People can change their names a lot easier than they can change their ink."

He took the napkin from me. "I'll get right on it. And there's one more thing."

"What?"

"Ms. Shaw has been visiting Ashland on and off for several months, even before she first approached Finn." He grabbed his tablet again. "She's been putting together an exhibit of fine jewelry and rare gemstones at the Briartop Art Museum. Ticket sales will benefit her charitable foundation."

Silvio turned his tablet around to show me the museum's website. A photo of a diamond ring was front and center, the design a smaller version of Deirdre's icicle-heart necklace.

"Ms. Shaw has donated several of her own personal pieces to the exhibit," he continued. "It's the first big event the museum has hosted since—"

"Since Jonah McAllister hired Clementine Barker and her giants to rob everyone and swipe Mab Monroe's will from the Briartop vault," I said, finishing his thought. "Do you think Jonah is involved with Deirdre?"

Jonah McAllister was another thorn in my side. The smarmy lawyer had tried to have me killed multiple times, including that night at Briartop.

Silvio shook his head. "I don't think so. Jonah is holed up in his mansion, waiting for his trial to start. He hardly ever leaves it. As far as I can tell, he's never had any contact with Ms. Shaw. Not so much as a phone call, text, or email."

The fact that Deirdre and Jonah didn't seem to know each other and probably weren't working together was an unexpected bit of good news. But Silvio's intel still didn't tell me what Deirdre was really up to. If she was already skimming millions from her charity foundation, then why go to all the time and trouble to set up an exhibit here in Ashland? Why sashay into First Trust, give the bank access to her accounts, and run the risk of someone realizing where all that charity money was really going?

It didn't make sense, unless . . . unless Deirdre truly did want to get close to Finn.

Could I be wrong? Could Deirdre be legit? Well, as legit as a charity scammer could be? Could she genuinely want to reconnect with her son?

No—no way. I didn't know Deirdre, but I *did* know Fletcher. If the old man claimed she was dangerous, then that's exactly what she was. Besides, Deirdre had had thirty-plus years to reappear in Finn's life. So why the sudden interest in her son now?

Something was going on here, and I was going to figure out exactly what it was—and how best to protect Finn from whatever his mother might be planning.

❋ 13 ❋

The day passed by like any other, with the usual blur of cooking, cleaning, and customers. But as three o'clock crept closer, my friends started to appear.

Owen was the first one through the door. He kissed me on the cheek, told me that he was here if I needed anything, and then sat in a booth out of the way. I was grateful for his strong, silent support.

Jo-Jo arrived next, wearing a white cashmere cardigan over a pale pink dress patterned with tiny pink roses. Her usual strand of pearls hung around her throat, and she had white kitten heels on her feet, making her look every inch the Southern lady she was. Jo-Jo always looked elegant, but she had taken a little extra care with her appearance today, her white-blond hair curled just so, her makeup flawless, her nails gleaming with a fresh coat of pale pink polish.

Jo-Jo slid onto the stool closest to the cash register. She

murmured hello to Silvio, who returned her greeting, although he kept his eyes locked on his phone as he texted. Jo-Jo leaned forward and waved at Sophia, who was sliding a tray of sourdough buns into one of the ovens. Sophia turned, and I caught sight of her black T-shirt, which featured a white heart that had been broken in two and was dripping blood off both sharp, jagged ends. I grimaced. The image reminded me of Deirdre's icicle-heart rune.

I looked at Jo-Jo. "How's Finn?"

She shrugged. "After you left last night, Bria, Sophia, and I all tried to talk to him, but he just took a shower and went to bed. He stayed shut up in one of the spare bedrooms until late this morning, then crept out after I was busy in the salon. He didn't say good-bye, and he didn't even drink any of the chicory coffee I made for him."

Finn had left without guzzling down his usual pot of coffee? Not good. I hadn't texted or called him this morning, figuring that he might need more time to cool off after the whopper of a secret I'd kept from him. But it sounded like he was angrier than I'd thought.

Bria arrived about five minutes later, telling the same story as Jo-Jo. She'd tried to talk to Finn last night and again this morning, but he hadn't responded to any of her messages.

There was nothing I could do until he showed up, so I kept on cooking, cleaning, and cashing out customers.

Finally, right at three o'clock, the bell over the front door chimed, and Finn strolled into the restaurant . . . arm in arm with Deirdre.

Not good. Not good at all.

Jo-Jo wasn't the only one who'd taken a little extra

care with her appearance. Finn was sporting his snazziest charcoal-gray suit, his walnut-brown hair carefully styled, while Deirdre was decked out in another tight-fitted dress, this one an electric blue that was almost too bright to look at. Her blond hair was once again done up in pin curls and held back from her face with several long diamond pins, while her icicle-heart rune glimmered around her neck.

Deirdre was laughing at some joke Finn had made, her voice as light and happy as wind chimes tinkling out a merry tune. Her carefree chuckles made me grind my teeth.

Finn didn't deign to glance at me or anyone else as he led Deirdre over to the booth in the front right corner of the restaurant and helped her sit down. Then he turned and snapped his fingers at me, as if he didn't already have my full attention.

Annoyance spurted through me. I wasn't his servant, and I thought about ignoring him, just out of spite, but I was too curious and worried about Deirdre. So I plastered a smile on my face and went over to the booth.

Bria was already sliding into the side across from Deirdre, with Finn sitting down next to her. Once again, my sister stared at the Ice elemental's rune necklace, still trying to remember where she had seen it before.

"Why, hello, Gin," Deirdre chirped in a cheery voice. "So lovely to see you again."

Before I could unclench my jaw and force out some semi-polite response, Jo-Jo walked up to stand beside me.

"Hello, Deirdre," the dwarf said.

"Why, hello, Jolene. I thought that was you sitting at the counter. And I see that Sophia still works here." Deirdre's blue eyes flicked over to the Goth dwarf, who had her arms crossed over her chest and a cold expression on her face as she eyed Deirdre right back. "Both of you look exactly the same as I remember."

Jo-Jo nodded. "The years have been kind to you too."

The two of them engaged in some meaningless chit-chat, with Deirdre asking about the salon and Jo-Jo inquiring about the other woman's charity work, but they quickly exhausted those topics. Jo-Jo looked at Finn, obviously hoping that he would invite her to sit down and join them, but he tapped his fingers against the tabletop, as if he wanted her to just go away already.

Jo-Jo's head dropped, her shoulders sagged, and even her curls seemed to deflate a bit. Anger sizzled in my chest. The dwarf was the one who'd helped Fletcher raise Finn, she was the closest thing to a mother he'd ever had, and he was ignoring her in favor of some stranger. Ungrateful brat.

I opened my mouth to tell Finn exactly what a thoughtless jackass he was being, but Jo-Jo cut me off.

"Well, y'all enjoy your lunch," she said, trying to inject some false cheer into her soft, sad voice.

"You do the same," Deirdre chirped back.

Jo-Jo nodded at her again, then turned toward the door as if she were going to leave. But Owen got up, took her arm, and led her over to his booth. I flashed him a grateful smile, and he winked back at me. At least someone around here knew how to treat his friends right.

I turned back to the booth and pulled a notepad and a pen out of the back pocket of my jeans. "Well, now that you're here, you might as well eat. What can I get you?"

"I'll have a grilled cheese and a sweet iced tea with lemon."

Deirdre didn't bother glancing at the plastic menu on the table, as if she already knew every single item on it. She probably did. The menu hadn't changed much over the years. Instead, she looked out over the restaurant, her gaze taking in everything from the other booths and tables to the blue and pink pig tracks curling across the floor, walls, and ceiling. I expected her scarlet lips to curl up into a sneer and derision to fill her pretty face, but Deirdre's features remained calm and serene.

"I see that you've done some remodeling," she said after she'd completed her inspection. "I was looking in the windows, admiring everything, when Finnegan came up to me on the sidewalk."

So they'd run into each other outside the restaurant. No doubt waiting outside for Finn had been a deliberate move on her part, since it was another opportunity for Deirdre to ingratiate herself with him just a little bit more.

"Good for you," she said. "Fletcher wouldn't have let you upgrade so much as a dish towel if he were still alive. He never was much for change, no matter how beneficial it might have been."

Her voice was perfectly pleasant, but my jaw clenched a little tighter. She had no right to come in here and comment on anything—not one fucking *thing*. Not when she'd left Finn, Fletcher, and the restaurant years ago.

But Finn apparently didn't see anything wrong with her words, because he nodded his agreement. "You're absolutely right. You wouldn't *believe* how long it took me to persuade Dad to get new menus printed up a couple of years ago. The pictures were faded, and you could practically wipe the grease off the pages, but he still didn't want to change them."

The two of them looked at each other and chuckled, coconspirators in their own little joke at Fletcher's expense. I mashed my lips together, biting back a sharp retort. Deirdre had already charmed her way into Finn's good graces, so my snapping at her would only make Finn take up for her that much more. I held my tongue and my temper—for now.

"A grilled cheese and an iced tea, coming right up," I muttered.

I took Finn's and Bria's orders of barbecue chicken sandwiches and onion rings, then handed the tickets off to Catalina. Across the restaurant, Sophia gave Deirdre another hard, flat stare, but she fixed the other woman's food in silence, along with the rest of the order.

When everyone's food was ready, I grabbed the hot plates and deposited them on the tabletop. Bria and Finn were sitting on one side of the booth, with Deirdre across from them. Rather than slide in next to the Ice elemental, I drew up a chair to the end of the booth and sat down.

Since it was just after three, the dinner rush hadn't started yet, and the restaurant was largely deserted. Good. I didn't want any of the underworld bosses coming in and seeing what might turn into an ugly confrontation. I had enough problems already without giving them any more ammunition.

Finn finally noticed that I wasn't nearly as delighted to have his mother here as he was. He gave me a stern look, telling me to be nice, but I glared back at him, still pissed at how he'd brushed off Jo-Jo. After a moment, his gaze slid away from mine, and he focused on Deirdre again.

Silence fell over the booth as the three of them picked at their food. Deirdre kept sneaking little glances at Finn, a smile stretching her scarlet lips wider and wider all the while, as if she were just *thrilled* that she was finally sitting here with her son and just couldn't contain her enthusiasm any longer. In that moment, she looked exactly the same as she did in all those old photos—soft, sweet, beautiful— and I could see why Fletcher had fallen under her spell all those years ago, just like Finn was doing right now.

Deirdre turned her attention to Bria, her gaze dropping to the primrose rune that hung around my sister's neck. For a second, just a second, something flared in her eyes, some thought or memory, but she quickly cranked up the wattage on her smile, hiding the emotion. I got the sense that she did that a lot—just smiled and smiled at folks long and hard and bright enough so that they eventually forgot how dangerous she truly was.

"You met Bria last night, remember?" Finn said, noticing his mother's gaze. "And you've heard me talk about her the past few weeks."

"Yes, of course," Deirdre said. "I was just admiring what a lovely couple the two of you make. Bria is quite striking. And your rune, honey. That's a primrose, right? The symbol for beauty? It fits you perfectly."

"Mmm," Bria replied, her face thoughtful as she stared at Deirdre's icicle-heart necklace again.

Deirdre looked at me. "Why, Gin, honey, you don't have to sit all the way down there. I promise I won't bite."

She winked, let out a merry laugh, and patted me on the shoulder the way she might a child she found particularly amusing.

I wanted to palm one of my knives and shish-kebab her hand to the tabletop, but I settled for giving her a grin that was all sharp, pointed teeth. "Oh, no," I drawled. "I know that you won't bite—but I just might."

Deirdre laughed again and shook her finger at me. "Finnegan told me all about you, but he failed to mention what a hoot you are."

"Oh, I doubt that, *honey*," I drawled again. "Finn doesn't usually go around telling people that I moonlight as an assassin. But I imagine you know all about my sideline business already. After all, you were involved with Fletcher."

Deirdre's chuckles died on her lips, and she opened, then closed her mouth, as if debating whether or not to claim that she hadn't known anything about Fletcher being an assassin. But she squared her shoulders and owned up to it. "Yes, I was well aware of Fletcher's . . . proclivities. I had hoped that his . . . distasteful activities had ended with him, but I see now that my hopes were in vain."

Her gaze flicked over me, taking in my blue work apron before lingering on the long sleeves of my black T-shirt. She knew that I had a knife tucked up either sleeve, just like Fletcher always had.

After a moment, she shook her head. "How very sad. That Fletcher dragged an innocent young girl like you into his sordid world."

"Fletcher didn't *drag* me into anything," I snapped.

"He saved me, he taught me everything he knew, and I will always be grateful to him for that—*always.*" Below the table, out of sight, my hands curled into tight fists in my lap, my fingers digging into the spider rune scars in my palms. I hadn't meant to let her rile me so easily, but she'd hit the big red button of my emotions with her first jab.

Deirdre cleared her throat. "Yes, well, Fletcher always did have a soft spot for strays."

Her voice was kind, without a hint of malice, but my fingers dug even deeper into my scars. Shish-kebabing would be too good for her. Now I wanted to slice that indulgent smile right off her pretty face.

Bria shot me a warning look.

Finn, however, seemed oblivious to the rising tension and mama drama, and he pushed his plate aside. "So," he said. "You said that we should . . . talk."

Deirdre focused on him again. "Yes. I know that you have a lot of questions, so I brought along a few things that might help give you some answers."

She reached into the enormous electric-blue purse that she'd set down in the booth beside her. I tensed, ready to palm one of my knives, but she only came up with a thick manila folder. She put the folder down on top of the table, then slowly opened it.

Photos lay inside—the exact same photos that had been in the casket box.

Deirdre, Fletcher, newborn Finn. I recognized the pictures immediately, but the sight shocked me all the same. I'd never even considered that Deirdre might have copies of the photos, much less show them off in my gin joint.

Unease rippled through me, along with more than a

little disappointment. I'd thought that Fletcher had left the photos in the casket box for me—and me alone—to find. That he'd entrusted me with them. That they'd been some sort of message or warning about Deirdre, even if I hadn't been able to figure out exactly what he'd been trying to tell me.

But what if they were just, well, *photos?* Just keepsakes, like Bria had suggested when we first opened the box. What if there was no message or warning or hidden meaning in the pictures? And if I'd been wrong about that, then what else was I wrong about?

Maybe even Deirdre herself?

Maybe she was different from the person Fletcher had known. Maybe her intentions were genuine. Maybe she really did want to reconnect with Finn. The only thing I knew for sure right now was that all the *maybes* were driving me plumb crazy.

Bria drew in a ragged breath. She recognized the photos too. I shrugged at her. The cat was out of the bag now, and there was no putting it back in.

"These are all the photos that I have of us," Deirdre said in a soft, hesitant voice. "Fletcher always got two sets of photos made, one for him and one for me. I thought that you might like to see them too."

One by one, she laid out the pictures on the table in front of Finn, who leaned over and studied them with wide eyes. The casket box was still tucked away in the chimney at Fletcher's house. I'd been planning to take Finn home and show him the photos, mementos, and Fletcher's letter to him after this meeting, so he could decide for himself whether he wanted to read it. But once again, Deirdre had beaten me to the punch and wrapped another silken thread around Finn's heart, snaring him that much more tightly in her web.

He wouldn't care about me showing him the photos and broken mementos, and he wouldn't take whatever information or warning that was in Fletcher's letter seriously. Not now. Maybe that's why Fletcher had asked me to wait to show Finn the letter. Maybe the old man had known that Finn would be too swept up in Deirdre's charms to listen as long as she was in Ashland.

Finn scooped up the pictures one by one, looking at them with eagerness, curiosity, and questions filling his eyes. I'd never seen him seem so excited before, not even when we were kids, it was his birthday, and he was tearing into a pile of presents. But I kept my mouth shut while he examined the photos. Anything I said right now would just sound like sour grapes.

"I met your father when I was nineteen," Deirdre said, steepling her hands together. "Another boy brought me here on a date, but once I saw your father, I only had eyes for Fletcher, and he for me. One thing led to another, and before I knew it, we were engaged. It was one of the happiest times of my life."

Well, that explained the engagement ring in the casket box. Although I still wondered about its missing diamond.

Finn looked up from the photos, and Deirdre favored him with another smile, which he returned with an even wider one of his own. I don't know how long they would have kept smiling at each other if Bria hadn't cleared her throat.

"So what happened?" Bria asked. "If you were so happy, then why did you leave Ashland?"

Everyone could hear the sharper, unasked question in her words. *Why did you leave Finn?*

Deirdre winced, her shoulders slumping. "Fletcher and I were planning our wedding when I found out I was pregnant. My parents were very traditional, very old-fashioned, and more concerned with their magic, money, and social status than anything else. They didn't approve of Fletcher, said that he was beneath my station. But they especially didn't like the idea of my having his baby. They were both very strong Ice elementals, you see, and I inherited their magic. They wanted me to marry someone who also had Ice magic, to keep our family legacy intact. Not someone like Fletcher, who didn't have any elemental power at all. Of course, I didn't care about any of that, but when I told my parents I was pregnant, they threw me out and cut me off financially. They wouldn't even speak to me."

She paused and pinched the bridge of her nose, as if she were fighting back tears. After a few seconds, she dropped her hand, cleared her throat, and continued.

"But I loved Fletcher, and I was determined to be with him, despite my parents. And we were happy, especially after you were born. See?"

She tapped her long red nail on the photo of Fletcher holding newborn Finn, with her standing off to the side. I thought that Finn might say something about how unhappy Deirdre looked in the photo, but he didn't seem to notice her flat expression. Or maybe it was just my bias against her that made me see her that way.

"So what happened?" Bria asked again, a snide note creeping into her voice. "If y'all were one big happy family?"

I raised my eyebrows at my sister, who was rarely that snarky. Bria didn't seem to like Deirdre any more than I did. She shrugged back at me, completely unapologetic. Well, if she wanted to be the bad guy for a change, I wasn't going to stop her. More power to her.

Deirdre drew in a breath, as though the next part was particularly painful for her to recall. "Fletcher worked a lot of late nights, but running a restaurant means long hours, and I knew how devoted he was to the Pork Pit. But one night, he came home covered in blood. And that wasn't the worst part. Some men stormed into the house after him." Her voice dropped to a whisper. "And I finally learned what Fletcher was really doing all those late nights. That he was an assassin."

She shuddered, as if the memory still horrified her. "He killed the men right in front of me. Laid their throats open with his knives like it was *nothing*. But not before one of them attacked me."

Deirdre fell silent for several seconds, her gasps of breath coming quicker and quicker, until she was almost panting for air, as though she was still traumatized by what had happened. Even I might have believed that she was genuinely upset, if not for Fletcher's letter warning that every word out of her mouth was a lie.

But Finn? He swallowed it hook, line, and sinker, leaning over and squeezing her hand. Deirdre threaded her fingers through his, as if drawing comfort from his touch. Once her breathing had returned to normal, she continued her story.

"After that, it was . . . hard for me to be with Fletcher. Of course, he claimed that he would never hurt *me*, but I just couldn't believe him. Not after what I'd seen him do to those men. Even though I had been trained to use my Ice magic to defend myself, I was afraid to even leave the house, for fear that one of his enemies would be waiting to try to hurt me—or you, Finn. That was my greatest worry."

Finn nodded, his face as somber as a preacher's on Sunday, as if her words made perfect sense. I thought her story had more holes than a sack full of doughnuts.

"Fletcher and I started fighting about him being an assassin," Deirdre continued. "I begged him to stop, to give up being the Tin Man, but he said the work he was doing and the people he was helping were too important. I asked him if they were more important than his own family. That started the fighting all over again."

She shook her head. "Finally, I just couldn't take it anymore. I told Fletcher that he had to choose—his family or being an assassin. And he chose being an assassin." She tightened her grip on Finn's hand. "I'm so sorry, Finnegan. Truly, I am. I wished that things had worked out between us. I really did love your father at one time."

"But why did Dad tell everyone you were dead?" Finn finally asked the big, obvious, glaring question.

Deirdre sighed, let go of his hand, and leaned back, as if what she was about to say was breaking her heart all over again. "I told him I was leaving him and that I was taking you with me. Fletcher . . . he . . . hit me." Her hand crept up to her cheek as if she could still feel the sting of that phantom blow. "He said that I wasn't taking his son anywhere. He told me to pack up my things, leave his house, and never come back. He told me that if I ever returned to Ashland or tried to contact you, he would kill me. I believed him. He was an assassin, after all, and he had already shown me *exactly* what he was capable of."

Deirdre hung her head but not before a couple of tears streaked down her cheeks. One of them plopped onto the photo of her, Finn, and Fletcher, oozing across the paper.

"I'm sorry, Finnegan. So sorry. And so *ashamed*. I should have been stronger. I should have found some way to contact you years ago." A few more tears rolled down her cheeks, dripped off her chin, and splattered onto the photos. "But Fletcher always kept such a close watch over you, and me too. Although I did try a few times to reach out to you."

"What happened?" Finn asked in a low, strained voice. "What did Dad do?"

Deirdre let out a tense breath. "I got a packet of photos in the mail, of myself, from where Fletcher had been spying on me, along with a note warning me about what would happen if I ever came back to Ashland. That he would make good on his promise to kill me."

She shuddered, wiped the tears off her cheeks, and raised her head, staring at Finn again.

"When I heard that Fletcher had died, I knew that I finally had a chance to reconnect with you. But I was still a coward, so instead of immediately coming to town, I thought about the best way to approach you. The best way I could have some sort of relationship with you. I knew that you were a banker, and I needed some help with my charity investments, so that seemed like the most logical place to start. I was working up to telling you who

I really was. Last night, during the bank robbery, I realized that I needed to just go ahead, take a chance, and make the most of the time I'd been given with you."

She let out another breath.

"So that's it. That's my story. I'm sorry, Finnegan. So sorry. For everything. But I'm here now, and I want a second chance, if you'll have me. Even though I know that I don't deserve one."

Deirdre stretched out her hand, a pleading look on her face. The sunlight streaming in through the windows added a golden glow to her hair, making her look like a fallen angel, begging for forgiveness and a chance at redemption. Her words, voice, gesture, expression—it was all beautifully done, right down to her trembling fingers and the fresh tears glistening in her eyes. Even I might have been suckered in by her, if I hadn't known Fletcher. If I hadn't known down to the very bottom of my black, rotten heart that he would never, *ever* hit a defenseless person, much less threaten the mother of his own son, unless he had a damn good reason.

But Finn . . . he couldn't see that. He didn't *want* to see it. Not right now, anyway. Maybe not ever.

Finn reached out and wrapped her trembling hand in both of his. "There's nothing to forgive," he said in a rough, raspy voice. "What matters is that you're here now, and we have a second chance, just like you said."

"Oh, Finnegan, you don't know how happy that makes me."

Deirdre smiled, and the two of them stared at each other, lost in their own little moment.

I rolled my eyes. "Oh, please. Finn, don't tell me that

you're buying this bullshit story. I've seen better acts at the carnival."

Finn's mouth gaped. He was shocked that I was raining all over this tender, tearful moment. Oh, it was raining, all right. And it was about to fucking *pour*.

"I know that Fletcher was your mentor," Deirdre said in a soft voice, as though she were talking to an idiot and didn't want to use too many words too quickly. "I know that he took you in off the streets and that you loved him very much. But just because you love someone doesn't mean that you know everything they've done or everything they're capable of."

"And I know that you're lying through your teeth about Fletcher," I snapped back. "Maybe Finn is too starry-eyed to see the holes in your story, but I'm not."

"What holes?" Deirdre said, her voice still annoyingly calm. "Ask me anything. I'll tell you whatever you want to know, Gin. Anything to set your mind at ease."

I leaned back in my chair and crossed my arms over my chest. "All right, then. Let's play Twenty Questions. How many times did you think about Finn? Every day, once a week, once a month? How many times did you try to contact him? When? I could go on, but there's really only one question that matters in the end. Why didn't you try harder?"

She frowned. "What do you mean?"

"If I had a kid, I would do everything in my power to be a part of his or her life," I said, my voice as cold as ice. "Not let someone keep me away because of a few threats. But that's exactly what you've done, by your own admission."

"I know this is difficult for you to accept, Gin, but Fletcher is the reason I stayed away for all these years," Deirdre said. "He threatened me, just like you said."

"Bullshit," I countered. "Fletcher's been dead for more than a year now. If you were *so* concerned about Finn and *so* truly desperate to finally see your son again, then you would have come to town the second you knew that Fletcher was dead. But you *didn't*. You didn't come back to Ashland after the old man died because you had other things to do. You stayed away because you *just didn't fucking care*. Not about Fletcher and certainly not about Finn."

Deirdre gasped, and more tears streaked down her face, as though my words had cut her to the core. I certainly wanted to do that to her with my knives but not in front of my customers. The few folks dining in the restaurant might not have heard my exact words, but the icy rage in my tone had been unmistakable and threatening enough to make them all freeze in their seats, eyes wide, sandwiches and sodas halfway to their lips.

Deirdre wiped away her tears, lifted her chin, and stared back at me. "I know that this is hard for you to accept . . ."

She started her spiel again, but I was tired of listening to her lies, especially the ones she was telling about Fletcher, trying to poison his own son against him. The old man wasn't here to defend himself, but I was, and I *would* defend him. And Finn too, whether he liked it or not.

"You should know this," I said in a cold, hard voice. "When you hurt Finn, I *will* kill you."

Deirdre gasped again, her blue eyes widened, and her hand flew to her heart, as though she were truly startled by my poison promise. As if I were Fletcher threatening her all over again, like she claimed. In that moment, I supposed that I was exactly like the old man.

I was okay with that.

Her chin quivered, and her fingers trembled. I wondered if she'd practiced those moves in the mirror. Probably. She was certainly the best con artist I'd ever seen.

But her shocked, scared look had the desired effect on Finn.

"Gin!" he hissed, anger sparking like fireworks in his eyes. "What do you think you're doing?"

"Watching out for you," I snapped. "I can't believe you're falling for her lies. If she tells you that Santa Claus is real, are you going to believe that whopper too?"

Finn opened his mouth, but Bria cut him off before he could snap back at me.

"Okay," she said. "That's enough. Let's take a break."

"I think you're right," Deirdre said in a shaking voice.

She started to slide out of the booth but stopped when she realized that I was still sitting at the end of the table, blocking her escape.

"Gin," Bria said, a sharp note in her voice.

I slowly scooted my chair back and stood up.

Deirdre got out of the booth, being sure to stay out of arm's reach of me. Smart woman. She gestured at the photos still spread out on the tabletop. "Feel free to look at those as long as you like, Finnegan. I hope that you'll give me a chance to get to know you. I'd like that more than anything. And I want to get to know your friends too." She turned toward me. "Even you, Gin. Despite your feelings about me."

I stared at Deirdre, but she kept giving me that same hurt, wounded look, as though I'd gravely offended her by not swallowing her lies.

Finn slid out of the booth and walked around me. He hesitated, then stepped forward and hugged Deirdre. She seemed startled by the motion, but her arms wrapped around his back, and she hugged him even tighter.

I glared at her all the while, but she didn't look at me. Of course she didn't. I wasn't the one she was conning, so I wasn't important.

They hugged for a few more seconds before finally breaking apart.

"I'll call you later," Finn said. "Maybe we can talk some more then?"

"I'd like that," she whispered.

He nodded and started to step back, but Deirdre reached up and cupped his cheek with her hand. This time, he was the one who seemed startled, but he grasped her fingers and gently squeezed them. She smiled at him again, then grabbed her purse and walked out of the restaurant.

The bell over the front door chimed softly at her passing, but the sound seemed as loud as a gunshot in my mind.

Deirdre Shaw had definitely won this round. Now I just had to figure out how to keep her from winning any more.

*❖*14*❖*

Deirdre might have left, but the show wasn't quite over yet.

Everyone in the restaurant turned to look at me, whispering and wondering about the drama they'd just witnessed. No doubt, somebody here had some underworld connections, which meant that news of the confrontation would spread like wildfire among the bosses. I ground my teeth. Terrific.

I ignored the curious stares and glanced over at Silvio, who slid off his stool, buttoned his suit jacket, and went outside. With his enhanced vampire senses, he'd heard every word of our heated conversation. Silvio had realized that I wanted all the information I could get on Deirdre, even if it was something as mundane as what kind of car she was driving.

Finn waited until Deirdre was out of sight of the storefront windows before he whipped around to me. "Are you happy now? You just chased away my mother. Just like Dad did."

I opened my mouth, but he snapped his hand up.

"Forget it. I can't even *look* at you right now," he growled.

He stormed toward the front door, but Owen was already there, blocking his path. Finn glared at him, but Owen put his arm around Finn's shoulders.

"Come on, man," he said. "Let's go out back and get some air."

Owen looked at me, and I nodded my thanks. He nodded back, then half led, half strong-armed Finn across the storefront, through the double doors, and into the back of the restaurant.

Everyone swung around to stare at me again, wondering what I would do next. I glared back at the curious crowd, until they all decided it would be better to focus on their food and started shoving sandwiches and French fries into their mouths at warp speed.

"That went well," Bria drawled, still sitting in the booth. "You know you played right into her hands."

I huffed out an angry breath and ran my hands down my blue work apron, trying to rein in my emotions. "I know, I know. I should have been calm, cool, reasonable. Just like she was. But I just couldn't sit there and listen to all those damn, dirty lies about Fletcher. I just *couldn't*. And I don't get Finn. He's going to believe some strange woman who shows up out of the blue over his own father? The man who was here for him all these years?"

I shook my head. "Sometimes I don't know what is going on in that boy's mind."

Bria picked up the photos. "Think about it from his point of view. He gets a second chance with the mother he never knew. That would be tempting for anyone."

"Yeah, but this is *Finn* we're talking about. He usually has women eating out of the palm of his hand. Not the other way around."

She shrugged. "And growing up without a mother is probably one of the reasons he likes women so much and is such a terrible flirt. He's trying to have that connection he never had with her."

My eyes narrowed. "When did you go all Freudian on me?"

"You're not the only one who takes classes, you know. I've been doing some psychology stuff online through the police department." She grinned a moment before the smile slipped from her face. "You need to talk to Finn. Hash out this thing between the two of you before it gets any worse. If Deirdre really is a threat, then you need to stay close to him. Not alienate him even more."

I sighed. "I know. But he's not going to like what I have to say about Mama Dearest."

Bria shrugged again. She didn't know how to make Finn listen to reason any more than I did.

But she was right, and I had to try. So I stepped behind the counter, yanked off my apron, and hung it on a rack on the wall, just to give myself a few more seconds to cool off. When I felt calmer, I headed toward the double doors, where Jo-Jo and Sophia were now standing, both with worried looks on their faces.

I stopped in front of them. "What did you think about what Deirdre said?"

"Bullshit," Sophia growled, her nostrils flaring in anger. "Every single word."

Well, at least I wasn't the only one who thought so. Then again, Sophia had loved Fletcher too, especially since he'd saved her from a horrible situation, and she was just as biased about him as I was.

"Forget about what she said for now. Go make things right with Finn," Jo-Jo said. "He'll come to his senses, sooner or later."

I nodded and flashed her a smile, but my heart remained heavy as I pushed through the double doors. Because part of me couldn't help but wonder if it was already too late for Finn.

The waitstaff must have been as transfixed by the ugly scene with Deirdre as the customers were, because the back of the restaurant was empty. Good. I didn't need to have anyone else see me lose my shit today.

I moved past the metal shelves full of sugar, cornmeal, and ketchup and headed for the back door. I reached for the knob, but the door had already been left open a couple of inches.

I should have opened the door and gone outside to talk to Finn, but instead, I peered through the gap, wondering what he and Owen were saying—and how much Finn was probably cursing my existence right now.

My foster brother was pacing back and forth in the alley behind the restaurant, his shiny black wing tips *snap-snap-snapp*ing like rubber bands against the dirty, cracked asphalt. Owen was on the opposite side of the alley, leaning one shoulder against the brick wall, his arms crossed over his chest as he watched Finn pace.

Owen shook his head. "Do yourself a favor, Finn. Don't be that guy."

"What guy?" he growled, and kept right on pacing.

"The guy I was when Salina came back to town. The guy who doubted Gin. The guy who hurt Gin with those doubts. She's just looking out for you, man. Nothing else."

Salina Dubois had been Owen's ex-fiancée before I killed her. At the time, she'd been trying to murder me and all the people she blamed for her father's death, but her appearance in Ashland and subsequent death at my hands had driven a rift between Owen and me, one that had almost been the end of us.

But here was Owen, sticking up for me and trying to keep Finn from making the same mistake. Owen knew how much I valued my relationship with Finn, and he was doing everything he could to keep the situation from getting any worse. My throat closed up with emotion, and my heart swelled with love for him. He always did the thoughtful things that meant so much to me.

Finn snorted. "Well, she has a funny way of showing it, threatening to kill my mother."

Owen shook his head. "You really don't see it, do you? How suspicious this all is? Your mom suddenly coming back to town? Surely you can understand why Gin is worried."

"Of course I know it's suspicious. I'm not a complete *idiot*. But apparently, Gin thinks that I am. I can take care of myself, you know. I did it for years before she came along."

"And you know Gin," Owen replied. "She always looks out for the people she cares about. That's one of the things I admire most about her."

Finn snorted again. "You are such a fucking hypocrite sometimes."

"Excuse me?"

He stopped pacing and pointed his finger at Owen in accusation. "You—you're a hypocrite, Grayson. You're absolutely right. You were *that guy*. You were the guy who doubted Gin, who pushed her away, when all she was trying to do was help you. You were an idiot for believing Salina's lies. We all knew it, but Gin stuck by you anyway. She put her life on the line for you time and time again, and when the truth about Salina came out, what did you do? You walked away from Gin. Just like that."

He slapped his hands together for emphasis. Owen winced at the sharp sound.

"And now here you are, lecturing me about doing the same thing? Like I said, fucking hypocrite." Finn started pacing again.

Owen's hands clenched into fists, and he pushed away from the wall, like he was thinking about pounding Finn into a bloody smear on the pavement.

That was my cue. I opened the door and stepped out into the alley before things got any worse between them. They both turned at the faint creak of the door swinging open.

"Hey, Gin, you're just in time to bail out your boy toy." Finn sneered. "He's about to fall off that high horse of his."

"Shut it, Lane," Owen snapped back. "Or I will mess up that pretty-boy face of yours so badly even Jo-Jo won't be able to put it back together again."

"I'd like to see you try."

By this point, the two of them were nose-to-nose, jaws and fists clenched tight, eyes narrowed and glinting with anger. I put my hands on their shoulders and pushed them apart. The last thing any of us needed right now was a brawl.

"That's enough," I said. "Separate corners, boys. *Now*. Owen, I'll talk to you later, okay?"

Owen glowered at Finn another second, then leaned over and kissed my cheek. "Anything you need, Gin. You know that."

"I do know that. Now, go. Please."

He turned around and stormed back inside the restaurant, slamming the door shut behind him.

For several seconds, Finn and I were still and quiet, and the only sound was the rumble of traffic on the surrounding side streets, punctuated by the occasional honking of a car horn. Finally, Finn lifted his chin, his mouth a stubborn slash.

"Going to tear into me for daring to question your boy toy's loyalty?" he growled.

"Nope."

Finn had been ready to argue the point, and my simple answer took some of the wind out of his sails. He settled for glaring at me instead. "Good. Because in case you're forgetting, *I'm* the one who's always been here for you, Gin." He stabbed his finger into his chest, right where his heart was. "Not Owen, not Bria, nobody else. Just *me*."

"You and Fletcher," I said in a soft voice.

Finn's mouth twisted, and pain flashed in his eyes, mixing with his anger. "Well, Dad's not here anymore, but I still am. And for the past year, I've always had your back, no matter what happened and how bad things got. That hot mess with you and Donovan Caine? I was here. You taking on Mab? I was here. You battling Madeline and the underworld bosses and anyone else who came at you? I was always right fucking *here*."

"I never said you weren't."

But Finn was on a self-righteous roll now, and he threw his hands up into the air and went on as though I hadn't even spoken. "And now, when the tables are turned and I need something, when I need a little support and under-standing after getting the shock of my life, what do you do? Threaten to kill my mother right out of the starting gate."

I shrugged. "I was just making the consequences of being in your life crystal-clear to her."

"Oh, you made them clear, all right. As clear as the point of your favorite knife. It's a wonder she didn't run away screaming."

"Oh, I don't think Deirdre is quite the delicate flower she appears to be."

Finn crossed his arms over his chest and glared at me again.

I sighed. "Okay, okay, so maybe I shouldn't have whipped out the *I'll-kill-you* card right off the bat."

"But?"

"But she didn't run away, did she? And now she knows exactly what will happen if she screws you over. C'mon, Finn. Don't tell me you're actually buying into her act."

His chin jutted out. "And what if I am?"

"Then you're a fool." I regretted the words as soon as they left my mouth, but it was too late to take them back.

Finn stared at me, but instead of the anger I expected, a mixture of hurt and weary resignation flashed in his eyes. That made me feel worse than if he'd started shouting. "You really believe that, don't you?" he said, a sad note creeping into his voice. "That you're the invincible superhero who always knows what's best for everyone, and I'm just your cheerful, carefree, idiot sidekick who shoots people for you on occasion."

"I don't think that—not at all."

"Of course you do." Finn shook his head, his voice even sadder than before. "Because that's exactly what Dad trained you to believe."

I didn't know what to think about his accusations, much less how to respond to them. Of course I didn't think I was a superhero, and I definitely didn't view Finn as a sidekick. He was my brother, and I loved him, simple as that.

But the way he was looking at me right now, with such . . . *disappointment*, wounded me more than all his harsh, angry words had. Even worse, it was like every single thing I said only pushed him farther away. I had to fix this—now.

"C'mon," I repeated. "Do you really believe what Deirdre said about Fletcher? That he threatened to kill her if she ever came back to Ashland? If she ever tried to contact you?"

"You know Dad," Finn said in a gruff tone. "He was capable of it."

"Certainly," I agreed. "And I also know that the only reason—the *only* reason—he would have made a threat like that was to protect you. Deirdre might be your mother, but she's been playing you like a fiddle. She's dangerous, Finn. Surely you can see that."

"Of course I can see it," he snapped, a stubborn note creeping into his voice. "But maybe I want to give her a chance anyway."

I frowned. "Why would you want to do that?"

"Because I never had a mother," he said in a soft voice.

Finn stared at me, the same raw, naked longing on his face that I'd seen last night at the party and again here at the restaurant. A bone-deep yearning for something that he'd never had, that he'd never experienced, that he'd been missing out on his whole life.

"I never had a mother," he repeated in a louder voice. "I never had anyone to kiss my scraped knees or bake me cookies or sing me to sleep. Yeah, Dad did his best, but he wasn't exactly the most open and forthcoming person, especially when it came to his emotions. And we weren't exactly alike, especially as I got older. Not like you and he were. Jo-Jo did her best. So did Sophia, for that matter, and I'm grateful to both of them that they cared enough to even try."

"But?"

He blew out a breath. "But it wasn't the same. It was *never* the same. And now my mother—my *real* mother—is here, and I can see so much of myself in her. It's like I've suddenly found a part of me that I didn't even realize was missing. Surely you can understand that, given how long it took you and Bria to really reconnect after she came back to Ashland."

"I do understand that, probably better than anyone else." I sighed. "There's no denying that Deirdre is your mother. She says she wants to be a part of your life. Okay. But where has she been for the last thirty-some years? What's she been doing? Why didn't she find some way to contact you sooner, Fletcher and threats be damned? Don't you find all that suspicious? I certainly do."

This time, Finn sighed. "Of course I find it all suspicious. Dad raised me too, remember? I might not have your insane level of paranoia, but I've got plenty of my own to go around. I want to know what Deirdre is doing back in Ashland just as badly as you do."

"Then what's the problem with my approach?"

Finn stuck his hands into his pants pockets and drew the toe of his wing tip back and forth, as though he were drawing a line on the dirty asphalt. It was several seconds before he spoke again. "Because I'm hoping she's telling the truth. That she actually came back for me—just *me*, nothing else. Is that so wrong?"

And just like that, I realized how much this had already affected Finn and what an intense longing Deirdre had woken in him, one that I'd never even suspected he had. I'd never thought much about Finn's mom, and I'd thought even less about the fact that he'd never had a mother to call his own. Even I'd had a mother at one point, before Mab Monroe murdered her.

I remembered Eira Snow, my own mother, fondly enough, although I'd often tended to get lost in the pack as the middle child. When she died, I wasn't old enough to start becoming more of a friend to my mother, like my older sister, Annabella, but I also wasn't young enough to still need her constant attention, like Bria had back then. So I could understand Finn's longing, even if it was different from my own longing to have had a little more time and attention from my mother.

But that didn't mean I was going to let him get hurt by it. Not when Fletcher had asked me to look out for him.

"All right," I said. "All right. You win. I will give Deirdre a chance. Anything to make you quit giving me those sad puppy-dog eyes."

Finn immediately brightened. "You will? You'll *really* give her a chance?"

"Yes, yes, I *really* will."

His eyes narrowed. "No more talk of conspiracies and knives and killing her, then?"

"No more talk of killing her." I paused. "At least, not to her face."

Finn glowered at me, but I shrugged back. That was the only concession I was willing to make.

"You'll really give her a chance?" he repeated. "Cross your heart and hope to die?"

"What are you, twelve?"

He stared me down. "Cross your heart and hope to die, Gin?"

I rolled my eyes, but I drew a giant X over my heart. "Cross my heart and hope to die."

Finn whooped with glee, threw his arms around me, and lifted me off the ground. He spun me around in a dizzying circle, making me laugh, before setting me back down. Then he hugged me. "Thank you, Gin," he whispered in my ear. "You don't know how much this means to me."

I grimaced. "Oh, I think I know exactly how much it means from my bruised ribs."

"Oops. Sorry about that." He dropped his arms, drew back, and grinned at me again. "So does this mean that I have your permission to bring Deirdre back here for lunch tomorrow? I'd really like the two of you to start over."

I grinned back at him, although I had to clench my jaw to hold the fake expression in place. "Sure. Deirdre is welcome here anytime."

"Terrific! I'll text you the details later. This is all going to work out, Gin. You'll see."

He hugged me even tighter, driving the air out of my lungs and cracking my back at the same time. He beamed at me again, then opened the door and hurried into the restaurant, probably to whip out his phone so he could call Deirdre and tell her the good news.

I stayed behind in the alley, having zero desire to hear Finn chatter on with his mama. I hadn't been lying to him, though. I was going to give Deirdre a chance. In fact, I was going to give her every single chance she wanted and then some.

Because the longer the rope I gave her, the sooner she would hang herself with it.

And when she did, the Spider would be waiting to cut down that rope—and put Deirdre Shaw in the ground for good this time.

✳ 15 ✳

Sometimes keeping your word really sucked.

But I kept my promise to Finn. Much as it pained me to do so, I held my tongue about Deirdre, and I even made nice with the woman whenever I saw her.

Which was every single day.

Over the next week, Finn spent almost all his free time with Mama Dearest. Sure, I wanted to keep an eye on them, but I was witness to far more of their bonding time than I would have liked. They strolled into the Pork Pit every day, sometimes lingering two hours or longer over lunch or an early dinner. And every time—every single time—Finn would wave me over and excitedly re-count some silly story that Deirdre had told him about when he was a baby. How he had laughed at this or cried at that or always sneezed at her peony perfume.

Deirdre seemed to have an awful lot of those cutesy-wootsy anecdotes for someone who'd only been around for the first few months of her baby's life. Not that I mentioned it to Finn. Or that he would have listened anyway, given how wrapped up he was in her. So I nodded and smiled and made the appropriate noises when necessary, thinking that if this kept up much longer, I was going to grind my molars into dust. As it was, I had an almost perpetual ache in my face and squint to my eyes from holding on to all my fake smiles.

The only thing that kept me more or less calm was the fact that I was plotting just as hard against Deirdre as she was snowing Finn.

Not only did I see Mama Shaw during the day, but I saw her at night too, although these dates were far more one-sided on my part. Silvio had tracked down her car and had also pinpointed the penthouse suite she was renting at the Peach Blossom, a luxe apartment building. The same apartment building and suite that Raymond Pike had stayed in when he came to Ashland to terrorize Lorelei Parker, although Finn waved it away as mere coincidence when I told him about it, the same way he ignored my concerns about how strong Deirdre was in her Ice magic, claiming that she would certainly never hurt *him* with her power.

The night after that first tense meeting at the Pork Pit, I'd scoped out the Peach Blossom and found a sweet little spot on the roof of the building across the street that let me look directly into Deirdre's penthouse. Naturally, I took along all the spy gear that Silvio had procured for me. Binoculars, digital surveillance cameras, directional microphones, the whole package. I watched her like a proverbial hawk, studying her even more closely than I had my assassin targets when I worked as the Spider.

But she didn't *do* anything.

Deirdre didn't take meetings with underworld bosses, didn't engage in cryptic phone calls, didn't do or say anything that would confirm my rampant suspicions of her. All she did was wine and dine Finn from one end of Ashland to the other, call rich people and ask them to donate to her jewelry exhibit, and go over financial reports for her charity foundation. She liked to order caviar and escargot from room service, got a deep-tissue massage and an Air elemental facial every other day, and took a champagne bubble bath every single night.

Seriously. Champagne bubble baths. Who did that anymore? It was like she was some old-school movie star. Deirdre Shaw was definitely a diva with a capital D.

Hugh Tucker went almost everywhere with her, opening doors, fetching coffee, taking messages—just like Finn had said. Tucker's bland, bored expression and slow response time made me think he wasn't particularly happy being Deirdre's assistant. Couldn't imagine why. If I had to watch her simper and sashay all day long, I would have cheerfully smothered her in her sleep with a pillow long ago.

One night, after Deirdre had finally dismissed Tucker and gone to bed around midnight, I was heading back to my car with my black duffel bag hanging over my shoulder, when a guy stepped out of the alley and onto the street in front of me. He was big, more than six feet tall, with buzz-cut black hair and a fake diamond stud glinting in one ear.

"Give me the bag, toots," he snarled, baring his stained yellow fangs at me.

"A mugger?" I said, my mood brightening. "Excellent!"

The vampire frowned at my happy tone. Apparently,

he decided that I wasn't nearly scared enough, because he reached into his pocket and came out with a pitiful little switchblade.

"A mugger with a knife." I grinned. "This just keeps getting better and better."

His dark eyes narrowed in suspicion, and he glanced around, peering into the shadows that surrounded us. "Are you a cop? Is this some kind of undercover sting?"

"Me? A cop? Oh, that's *funny*, sugar." I chuckled. "Believe me, I am the very furthest thing from a cop."

This wasn't going at all the way he'd expected, but the vamp still thought I was an easy, if crazy, target, so he stepped forward and sliced his switchblade through the air, trying to intimidate me with the weapon.

Please. I had bread knives that were sharper than that thing.

"Give me the bag. Right fucking now. Or I'll gut you where you stand."

"Sure. This sucker's heavy anyway."

I slid the duffel bag off my shoulder and placed it on the sidewalk. Then I stepped over the bag and grinned at the vamp again.

"You want the bag?" I drawled, crooking my finger at him. "Come and take it from me, sugar."

"Crazy bitch," he muttered.

"You have no idea."

But I must not have seemed crazy enough to make him forget about mugging me, because the vamp snarled and raised his knife, getting ready to gut me, just like he'd promised.

I darted forward and grabbed his wrist, digging my

fingers into the tendons there and making him grunt and drop the knife. Then I stepped in even closer and slammed my fists into his stomach in a brutal one-two combo. The vamp's grunt was replaced by a far more ominous coughing spasm. Music to my ears.

He staggered back, but I followed him and punched him twice in the throat before smashing my fist into his nose. The feel of bones breaking, the sound of him choking, and the faint spatter of blood against my hands made me grin even wider.

As a final touch, I dropped down into a crouch and swept the vamp's legs out from under him. He fell flat on his back, his head cracking against the sidewalk. He let out a soft, squeaky noise, between a groan and a whimper, before he lost consciousness.

And just like that, the fight was over. Not that it had been much of one to start with.

Still smiling, I got back up onto my feet, cracked my neck, and swung my arms a few times. Nothing like an attempted mugging to get the blood flowing. After watching Deirdre these past several nights, it was nice to tackle a problem head-on for a change. I felt better and more relaxed than I had since she'd first come to town.

I glanced into the shadows, hoping he had a friend or two I could use to let off some more steam, but he was all by his lonesome. Ah, well. A girl couldn't have everything.

I hoisted my bag back onto my shoulder, stuck my hands into my pockets, and walked away whistling.

My relief was short-lived. Deirdre maintained all her patterns, including her simpering-sweet behavior. By the time she and Finn finished their lunch at the Pork Pit the next day, I was wound as tightly as ever.

Normally, I was good at reading people, but I just couldn't get a bead on this woman. She seemed so damn *sincere* in her desire to get to know Finn and so damn patient and understanding with me, despite all my snotty comments. She didn't show a hint of annoyance or anger, no matter what I said or did. Instead, she just kept giving me smile after smile, as if my suspicious nature and thinly veiled threats amused her. Maybe they did.

Either way, I was completely stumped about what she might be plotting—if she was plotting anything at all.

I still had no concrete proof that she was up to anything, other than trying to get closer to Finn. All I had was that box of keepsakes and that vague warning letter from Fletcher. Not exactly hard evidence.

I'd thought about giving Finn the casket box of mementos and Fletcher's letter to him a dozen times, but Finn was so wrapped up in his mother that I doubted he'd take the old man's words seriously. He'd just dismiss them outright like he had all the other things about Deirdre that didn't quite add up.

Besides, Fletcher had asked me to wait until after Deirdre was gone, whatever that really meant, before I gave Finn the letter. Maybe Fletcher had hoped that Deirdre's intentions were genuine and that Finn would never have to read the letter and learn what horrible truths it most likely contained. Either way, I was going to honor the old man's wishes, even if a big part of me just wanted to rip the letter open and read it for myself.

Still, as much as I loved and trusted Fletcher, Deirdre

was starting to wear me down with her bawdy persona and relentless good cheer, and I was beginning to doubt my own instincts about her, along with my general sanity.

Or maybe that was Deirdre's real plan. Drive me crazy so my friends would ship me off to some funny farm and she could have Finn all to herself. It was an admittedly absurd thought, but I was grasping at straws here. Yeah, my imagination and paranoia were definitely working overtime these days—

"What are you thinking about?" a deep voice rumbled.

I glanced over at Owen, who was snuggled in bed next to me, then focused on my phone again. I was spending the night at his house, and we were in his bedroom, watching a superhero movie on TV. Well, he was watching it. Along with concocting outlandish theories about Deirdre, I was reading an email from Silvio that told me all about Santos, the bank robber.

Rodrigo Santos was his real name, and the giant had a rap sheet a mile long for burglary, armed robbery, and assault that dated back to his teens. But there were no recent arrests, which meant that he had kept his nose clean—or had gotten better at not getting caught—now that he was in his mid-thirties. Rumor had it that the giant had worked his way up from a run-of-the-mill robber who knocked over convenience stores and gas stations to a highly regarded thief who specialized in getting into places that were supposed to be impenetrable. Museums, jewelry stores, bank vaults, Fletcher's house.

The more I read about Santos, the more worry ate away at my stomach. Because the bank robbery had been a simple stickup job, not something that would require

Santos's special brand of expertise. But he'd been there all the same, shooting up the cocktail party. Why? What was the point? Did he have some grudge against Stuart Mosley or someone else at the bank? Had he just wanted to ruin the party? Or had he been in need of a potential payday? I had no way of knowing, and it bothered me.

Despite all of Silvio's intel, nobody in Ashland had seen hide or hair of Santos since the bank robbery. Either he had skipped town or he was holed up somewhere, plotting some other job or his revenge against me. Or both. I was betting on both.

"Gin?" Owen asked again, nudging me with his shoulder. "I know you aren't watching the movie, but are you even listening to me?"

I sighed and put my phone on the nightstand. "Sorry. I was reading through some info about Rodrigo Santos."

"And?"

"And it's all good, solid intel, except for the fact that no one knows where he is. I can't question the guy if I can't find him."

"You'll find him. It'll just take a little time."

I sighed again. "I know, and I'm sorry that I'm such lousy company. I just keep waiting for the other shoe to drop."

"What shoe?"

"Deirdre. It's been more than a week now since she told Finn who she really is, and nothing's happened yet."

Owen turned on his side to face me and propped his elbow up on a pillow. "Well, maybe that's because there is a possibility you haven't considered."

"And what would that be?"

He shrugged. "Maybe Deirdre is actually telling the

truth about wanting to be back in Finn's life. The two of them have certainly spent enough time together these last several days. She seems like she's making a genuine effort to get to know him." His face was blank, and his voice was carefully neutral, but his hand clenched into a fist.

I grinned. "You still want to punch Finn in the face for calling you a hypocrite, don't you?"

A guilty flush crept up the side of his neck. "Yeah. A little."

I arched my eyebrows at him.

Owen's flush grew a little brighter. "Okay, so I still want to punch him in the face a whole lot. Is that wrong of me?"

"Nah. I've wanted to punch Finn in the face plenty of times. He can be quite aggravating when he wants to be. But his true superpower is being aggravating when he's not even trying."

Owen laughed, but then his face creased into a deep wince. "What really bothers me is that he was right. I was a hypocrite, telling him to trust you now when I didn't do that with Salina. I'm sorry, Gin."

I threaded my fingers through his. "You don't have to keep apologizing for that."

His features softened. "I know, but I wanted you to hear it again anyway."

"Well, apology accepted, again." I leaned over and pressed a kiss to his nose. "Let's finish watching the movie. The big fight scene is coming up, and you know how much I love those."

We both turned toward the TV again. I tried to watch the movie, really I did, but I kept glancing at my phone. All that info on Santos was right there. Maybe if I read through it just one more time, I could find a clue that Silvio had missed—

A pillow loomed up and plopped against my face before falling into my lap.

I looked at the pillow, then over at Owen, who was watching the TV and cheerily whistling along with the theme music.

"Did you just throw a pillow at me?"

"Oh, no," he said, still staring at the TV. "I'm just sitting here, all innocent-like, watching the movie."

My eyes narrowed. "Oh, Grayson. It is so *on*."

We stared at each other, then sprang off the bed at the same time. In an instant, we were grabbing pillows and hurling them across the bed at each other, both of us shrieking, ducking, and laughing the whole time. I quickly ran out of pillows, so I hopped up onto the bed and charged over to Owen's side, hoping to take him by surprise. He caught me around the waist, spun me around, and lowered me back down onto the bed.

Owen loomed over me, his laughter fading, even as his violet eyes sparked and flashed with an intense heat. "Pillow fights are fun," he said. "But you know what's even better?"

"What?"

He gave me a wicked grin, then leaned down and kissed the side of my neck. "This." He kissed the other side of my neck. "And this." He grinned again. "And especially this."

He lowered his lips to mine.

I opened my mouth, my tongue darting out to meet his. We kissed hard and deep, our tongues crashing together again and again the way the pillows had moments ago.

Heat roared through my body, sweeping away everything else but this moment. All I thought about was how warm and strong Owen's body was pressed against my own, how his rich, metallic scent invaded my lungs, how he still tasted of the chocolate cheesecake we'd had for dessert.

We kissed and kissed, our hands eagerly roaming over each other like a couple of teenagers getting hot 'n' heavy. Owen drew back, his violet eyes even brighter than before. He grinned at me again and lowered his mouth to mine . . .

Just in time for me to bop him in the head with a pillow I'd sneakily grabbed while he'd been distracted.

Owen blinked in surprise.

I grinned. "I'd say that makes us even now, wouldn't you?"

He growled, threw himself onto the bed, and plastered his body on top of mine, kissing and kissing me until my laughter faded into soft moans of pleasure. We rolled back and forth on the bed, stroking, caressing, and yanking off each other's clothes until we were both naked. I shivered as Owen trailed his tongue down my chest, then started teasing my nipples with his teeth. He groaned as I took him in my hand, skimming my fingers over his thick, hard length. Soon we were moving together harder and faster, each kiss, touch, and caress bringing exquisite pleasure.

All too soon, we were ready to come together, and Owen reached out for the drawer on the nightstand where he kept a box of condoms. I took my little white pills, but we always used extra protection. He reached . . . and reached . . .

And fell off the side of the bed.

I froze, my eyes wide. A second later, a low groan sounded. I leaned over the side of the bed.

Owen lay on his back, pillows haphazardly sticking out from under his shoulder, ass, and leg. "Ouch."

"Well," I drawled, "at least the pillows broke your fall. Sexy, Grayson. Dead sexy."

"Hey, now. Don't mock a man when he's down," he grumbled.

I snickered. Owen gave me a mock glower, which only made me snicker again. But I took pity on him, grabbed a condom out of the drawer, and got down on the floor with him. "Poor baby," I crooned, unrolling the condom and covering him with it. "Want me to see if I can kiss it and make it better?"

Owen drew me down on top of him and started kissing my neck even as his hand drifted lower and lower, his fingers rubbing slow circles as they dipped between my thighs. "How about I do the kissing?" he murmured.

I drew in a ragged gasp. "Okay."

Owen grinned, flipped me over onto my back, and put his mouth where his fingers had been. His tongue darted in and out as he kissed and licked and sucked all my sensitive areas. My fingers twisted in the pillows, and I moaned and rocked forward, riding the hot, electric waves of pleasure cascading through me.

Just when I was about to climax, Owen wrapped my legs around his waist and plunged into me with one long, smooth stroke. I drew him down on top of me, both of us kissing, moaning, and moving hard and fast until we came together.

Funny thing, though.

We never did finish watching that movie.

16

I managed to hang on to my good mood right up to when Deirdre and Finn strolled into the Pork Pit arm in arm at one o'clock the next afternoon.

"Right on schedule," Bria muttered.

"At least she's punctual," Silvio added.

Bria glared at the vamp, who shrugged and went back to his tablet.

Silvio had been at his usual seat at the counter since this morning, but Bria had only shown up five minutes ago to meet the pair for lunch. She watched Finn escort his mother over to their booth in the corner and help her sit down.

"He never does that for me," she said.

I threw a dish towel over my shoulder and waggled my eyebrows at her. "Jealousy does not become you, my dear."

Bria snorted. "Jealous? I'm not jealous. I'm just *sick*

of her. Even when Finn and I are alone together, she's all he wants to talk about. I swear, if I hear one more story about how adorable he was spitting up as a baby, I'm going to throw up myself, all over the two of *them*. We'll see how adorable they think *that* is."

Her blue eyes glimmered with dark anticipation. The more Deirdre came around, the snarkier Bria got. I kind of liked this sassier side of my sister. Or maybe I just wanted someone around who thought Deirdre was as insufferable as I did.

Bria sighed and grabbed the blackberry lemonade she'd been sipping. "Well, let's go see what Mama Dee is up to today."

"Mama Dee?"

"Yeah. That's what she wants me to call her."

Silvio snickered. Bria shot him a glare, and the vamp coughed, as if trying to clear the laughter out of his throat.

I snickered too. "I don't know whether to weep for you or fall down on the floor and start laughing hysterically."

Bria made a face. "I know, right? I want to stab myself in the eye with a toothpick every time I say it. But Finn keeps saying how great it is that Mama Dee and I are getting along so well."

"Oh, Bria! There you are!" Deirdre waved her hand. "Come join us, honey!"

Bria eyed the trash can beside the cash register like she was going to need it. After a moment, she sighed again, longer and deeper. "The things we do for love," she muttered.

She plastered a bright smile on her face, spun around on her stool, and marched over to their booth. Deirdre leaned across the table and made a couple of loud smacking noises as she air-kissed both of Bria's cheeks. Bria returned the gesture, although her smile slipped just a bit, and she started eyeing the metal napkin holder like she wanted to brain the other woman with it. I wouldn't be averse to that. Not at all.

"And where is Miss Gin at?" Deirdre exclaimed, her voice even louder than before. "Gin, honey! There you are! Come say hello!"

Then it was my turn to screw on a smile, which I only accomplished by grinding my teeth. That familiar ache in my face started almost immediately and shot up into my temples. Bria was right. The things we did for love.

"Oh, yes," Silvio said in a low, amused voice. "Do go say hello to Mama Dee, Gin."

I turned my smile to him and added a bit more teeth to my expression. "Keep in mind that I'm still an assassin. One who can make people disappear quite easily. Especially certain cheeky vampire assistants who enjoy mercilessly mocking their bosses."

He gave me an innocent smile in return. "And do say hello to Mama Dee for me too, while you're at it."

"You're a dead man, Silvio."

He chuckled and went back to his tablet.

I made sure my smile was locked in place before heading over to the corner booth. "Hey, y'all. What can I get you today?"

Deirdre ordered her usual grilled cheese and sweet iced tea. Finn and Bria both opted for fried chicken salads topped with honey-mustard dressing.

I started to turn away, but Deirdre grabbed my arm. Even though she wasn't actively using her power, invisible waves of her Ice magic still rippled off her fingers. The cold, frigid sensation soaked through the fabric of my long-sleeved T-shirt and chilled my skin underneath. But I wasn't going to give her the satisfaction of knowing that a simple touch of her hand was enough to make me hiss with pain, so I ground my teeth even tighter and kept my blank smile fixed on my face.

Bria winced in sympathy, though, since she could also feel Deirdre's magic. Like me, she avoided touching the other Ice elemental as much as possible. Bria had warned Finn about his mother's Ice power, about how she was much stronger than she was letting on, but he'd ignored my sister the same way he ignored me.

"Oh, Gin, I'm so glad I ran into you today," Deirdre chirped.

I shifted on my feet so that her hand fell away from my arm, which had already gone numb from her touch. "You're glad that you ran into me in my own restaurant?"

Bria snickered. Finn looked at her, and she covered her laughter by gulping down more lemonade.

Deirdre ignored my sarcasm. "I wanted to remind you that tomorrow night is the opening of that little jewelry exhibit I put together to benefit my charity foundation. Of course, you and Owen are invited. And on the VIP list." She winked at me.

"Of course." I ground out the words through my fake smile. "We wouldn't dream of missing it, especially since this is only the third time you've invited us now." Finn frowned at me, but I jerked my thumb over my shoulder. "Let me go put your order in. I'll be back with your food in a jiffy."

"Thanks, Gin, honey." Deirdre winked at me again. "You're a real peach."

I turned, stalked back over to the counter, and handed the order ticket to Sophia. The Goth dwarf gave me a mulish look, not liking Deirdre any more than I did, but she fixed their food in silence. I handed the plates off to Catalina to take over to the booth while I wiped down the counter, even though I'd just finished doing the same thing when Bria had first come in.

"Chicken," Silvio teased, realizing that I was avoiding going back over to the booth.

"I'm not chicken," I muttered. "Just trying to keep my homicidal rage in check. And the best way to do that is by staying as far away as possible from Mama Dee."

"If you really want to stay away from Mama Dee, then maybe you should take a break and actually keep your appointment today," he replied in a chiding tone.

"What appointment?"

"That meeting you have scheduled with Mallory Parker this afternoon. The one you were supposed to have the day after the bank's cocktail party. The one I've rescheduled three times so far." He turned his tablet around so I could see it. "See? I have it right here on today's agenda."

I opened my mouth to tell him to cancel again, that I was staying put so I could keep an eye on Deirdre, but Silvio beat me to the punch.

"You should really go see Mallory," he said. "She's been calling every day, wondering when you're going to show up, and she said she had something special to give you."

I frowned, wondering what that could possibly be. But then I remembered the dwarf's odd words at the party and how she'd told me that I'd better go check on Finn. Jo-Jo and Sophia hadn't known anything about Deirdre, but Mallory was older than both of them. Oh, I doubted that Mallory knew anything about Fletcher and Deirdre's relationship, but she might know something about Deirdre herself or maybe even the Shaw family. It was worth a trip to find out.

Deirdre busted out laughing at some joke Finn had made, her hearty chuckles bouncing from one side of the restaurant to the other. The happy sound sliced through my last nerve like cheese on a grater. Bria wasn't the only one who was sick and tired of Mama Dee. Maybe Silvio was right. Maybe I should leave before I broke my promise to Finn to play nice.

"All right," I said. "Appointment it is. Thanks for reminding me."

Silvio blinked. "You're actually going? Just like that? Without me having to nag you?"

"When do you ever have to nag me about anything?"

"When *don't* I have to nag you?" he muttered.

"What was that, oh assistant of mine?"

He plastered a big, fake smile on his face. "Nothing, boss. Nothing at all."

"Uh-huh."

Silvio promised to call if Deirdre did or said anything interesting. With his vampiric hearing, he could stay put on his stool at the counter and listen to every word she said over in the corner booth.

I left Sophia and Catalina in charge for the rest of the day, hung my apron on a hook, grabbed my car keys, and headed for the front door.

I'd hoped to leave before anyone realized what I was doing, but Deirdre's eyes were just as sharp as mine.

"Oh, Gin, honey!" she called out, flapping her hand at me again.

I plastered another smile on my face and veered in that direction.

"Where are you off to?" Finn asked.

"Just taking a break and meeting Owen for coffee," I lied.

"Why, honey, you should just ask him to come over here instead." Deirdre winked at me. "A good-looking man like that would spiff this place right up."

"Don't worry. You'll get to see plenty of Owen tomorrow night at the museum." I started creeping back toward the door.

Finn and Deirdre watched me walk away. So did Bria, although her expression was far more desperate than theirs. "Don't leave me!" she mouthed.

For once, I ignored my sister's suffering, cranked up the wattage on my fake smile, and gave the three of them a cheery wave. "Y'all have a nice lunch, now, ya hear?"

Then I whipped around and scurried out the front door of the Pork Pit as fast as I could.

* 17 *

It took me four blocks to unscrew the smile from my face. Once I'd made sure that no one had left any bombs, rune traps, or other surprises in, on, or around my car, I cranked the engine, left downtown, and drove to Lorelei Parker's mansion in Northtown.

The sprawling structure was set back by itself in the middle of the woods and would have been quite lovely if not for the boards that covered the broken windows, the chunks of stone missing from the walls, and a large burned patch in the yard. Raymond Pike, Lorelei's half brother, had laid waste to much of her mansion when he tried to kill her here a few weeks ago.

Three trucks with the words *Vaughn Construction* painted on the sides were parked next to the garage, with men moving all around the damaged windows and walls, taking measurements, making notes, and shouting to one another.

Lorelei was standing outside watching the men, her hands tucked into the pockets of her royal-blue leather jacket and a matching toboggan pulled down low over her forehead. Her black braid trailed out from underneath the winter hat, and her breath steamed in the chilly November air. She turned at the sound of my shuffling footsteps through the grass.

"Gin."

"Lorelei."

I stood beside her, and we watched the men work for a minute.

"Thanks for recommending Vaughn Construction," she said. "They've done an excellent job so far."

"You're welcome. Although it helps when you personally know the owner."

Lorelei nodded, then jerked her head to the right. "Grandma is waiting for you."

I fell in step beside her, and we walked the length of the house before rounding the corner and stepping onto a stone patio that overlooked a large garden. All the trees had already shed their leaves, while most of the rosebushes were just bare, brown clumps. But blue, white, and purple pansies poked their heads up, standing tall despite the cold, along with pink mums and other hardy fall flowers. Bird feeders had been set up here and there, tempting cardinals, finches, and sparrows to sail over and snag a beak full of seeds before flitting back into the woods.

Mallory Parker was sitting in a white wicker chair at the edge of the patio, a blue fleece blanket draped over her lap and a couple of space heaters going strong at her feet, driving back the chill. She was once again decked out in a dazzling array of diamonds, the gemstones glittering like rings of ice around her neck, wrists, and fingers. Her elbow was propped up on a glass-topped table, which held a large jug and three mason jars, along with a thick, black leather-bound book. Not exactly the afternoon tea I'd been expecting.

"Finally!" Mallory exclaimed. "I thought you were *never* going to get here."

The dwarf grabbed the jug and poured a couple of inches of clear liquid into each of the mason jars. Caustic fumes rose from the liquid, bringing tears to my eyes. Mallory didn't even wait for Lorelei and me to sit down before she grabbed her jar, chugged down the contents, and smacked her lips in satisfaction.

I arched my eyebrows. "I thought we were having tea, not moonshine."

"You can have whatever you like," Mallory chirped, pouring herself another drink. "But I am definitely having more moonshine. There's nothing like a little home brew to warm you up and loosen your bones on a cold day."

"Home brew?"

Lorelei pointed to the left. Through the trees, the sun winked off a small silver still. "One of Grandma's more interesting hobbies." She clinked her glass against mine. "Cheers."

"Cheers."

I downed the moonshine and immediately wished that I hadn't. I'd inhaled elemental Fire more than once during various battles. This wasn't much different from that. In some ways, it was *worse*, since the moonshine scorched my mouth and burned all the way down my throat, before smoldering in the pit of my stomach like I'd swallowed a burning ember.

"Smooth," I rasped, my voice sounding worse than Sophia's broken one.

Mallory beamed at me. "Isn't it?"

She grabbed the jug like she was going to pour me another, but I shook my head and held my hand out over the top of my jar.

"Can't handle your liquor, Gin?" Lorelei quipped.

"I can handle liquor just fine," I wheezed. "But that is not *liquor*. That is liquid *torture*."

Lorelei laughed. "Amateur."

I glared at her through the tears in my eyes, but she just laughed again and took another sip.

While I tried to catch my breath, Mallory and Lorelei chatted about the mansion renovations, the cocktail party at the bank, and the subsequent robbery. I chimed in when appropriate, all the while trying to think how I could steer the conversation around to what I really wanted to talk about: Deirdre.

But Mallory did it for me. After she had poured herself a third serving of moonshine, she sat back in her chair and gave me a sly look over the top of her mason jar. "So tell me, Gin, how are you liking Deirdre Shaw invading the Pork Pit every day?"

I blinked, and this time it wasn't because my eyes were still watering. "How do you know about that?"

Mallory grinned, then took another hit of shine. "I have my sources, just like you do. So how is Deirdre? Still the same spoiled, selfish brat I remember?"

A jolt zinged through me. "You actually knew her?" I'd hoped as much, but after so many frustrating dead ends, it was a pleasant shock to hear it confirmed.

"Oh, yes," Mallory said. "I knew several generations of Shaws. Stuck-up snobs for the most part, who thought that their family fortune made them better than everyone else, especially folks like me who had to do more . . . unsavory things to make a living."

"So that's why you were telling me that I should go talk to Finn during the cocktail party. You saw him with Deirdre." Another thought occurred to me. "And you've heard Finn talk about her these past few weeks, haven't you? You've known who she really is all along. Why didn't you tell me about her? Why didn't you tell *Finn*?"

Mallory shrugged. "For one thing, I was a bit preoccupied when Raymond came back to Ashland. For another, it wasn't my place to spill that sort of secret. Besides, I figured that Deirdre would tell him herself sooner or later, probably in some grand, overly dramatic fashion. Am I right?"

I winced, thinking back to that first lunch at the Pork Pit. "Oh, it was certainly dramatic."

"So we heard," Lorelei chimed in. "You probably shouldn't threaten to kill long-lost relatives in your own restaurant. Could make the customers think twice about what you might be putting in their food."

I winced again. So news of our initial confrontation had made the rounds through the underworld just like I'd feared. Terrific. But I couldn't do anything about that now, and this was too good an opportunity to pass up.

I looked at Lorelei. "Deirdre's icicle-heart rune is the

one that was stamped on that letter you found in Raymond's things. She's his business associate, the one he mentioned in the botanical gardens the night he died. She's the one who told him about your real identity and that you were here in Ashland. Do you remember smuggling anything for her?"

Lorelei tapped her fingers against her jar. "I noticed her rune necklace at the bank, and I've been thinking about that myself. But I never met or even saw Deirdre before the party. If I ever did any business with her, it wasn't face-to-face, and she used an alias."

I stared at Mallory. "And you? What do you know about Deirdre?"

The dwarf shrugged again. "Not much, I'm afraid. She and Lily Rose were a year apart in school, but they were involved in the same activities, went to the same parties, that sort of thing. So I saw her the way a parent would see someone else's child. Deirdre always struck me as being totally self-absorbed, but then again, most teenage girls are."

Lily Rose had been Lorelei's mother and Mallory's beloved granddaughter. I hadn't realized that she'd gone to school here in Ashland, though, much less that she had known Deirdre back then. Sometimes it truly was a small world.

Mallory opened the black leather-bound book sitting on the table, revealing a stack of old loose photos. I groaned.

"Something wrong?" Lorelei asked, still sipping her moonshine.

I shook my head. "I've had just about enough of old photos lately."

"I think you'll be interested in these," Mallory said. "I came across them in an old dresser a few days ago, while we were cleaning it out before putting it in storage during the renovations. I set them aside just for you, Gin."

Mallory pulled a photo off the top of the stack, her blue eyes misting over with tears. She cleared her throat, then slid the photo across the table to me. The picture featured a row of teenage girls in white dresses, with white lace gloves crawling up their arms and blue ribbons braided through their hair. It looked as though it had been taken at an old-fashioned cotillion. Debutante parties like those were still quite popular in Ashland, especially among the moneyed folks in Northtown. There was a whole season of them, each event designed to introduce rich young women and rich young men who would make suitable couples to further their families' wealth, power, and prestige.

Mallory tapped her finger next to one of the girls. "That's Lily Rose."

A pretty girl with Lorelei's black hair and blue eyes smiled shyly at the camera.

She tapped her finger next to another girl. "And that's Deirdre."

Blond hair, blue eyes, big smile, icicle-heart necklace. I recognized Deirdre immediately. Unlike Lily Rose, who was standing behind two other girls as if she wanted to blend into the background, Deirdre was front and center in the photo, her hands planted on her hips, obviously enjoying having her picture taken.

Mallory tapped her finger next to a third girl, who was standing next to Deirdre. "And I'm sure you know who that is."

Blond hair, blue eyes, snowflake pendant.

My breath caught in my throat, and I leaned forward, wondering if my eyes were playing tricks on me. "That looks like . . . *my* mama." More shock zipped through me. My mother had known Deirdre? Or had at least been at the same party with her?

"That *is* your mama," Mallory said. "From what I remember, Eira Snow was a lovely girl. Quiet thing, though. I don't think I ever heard her say more than a few words at a time."

I frowned, my mind spinning as I studied the photo. The Snows had been another old-money Ashland family, so it made sense that Eira had gone to the cotillion balls. Now that I'd seen the photo, I dimly remembered my mother telling Bria bedtime stories about how lavish and fancy some of the high-society parties had been. Bria had loved those stories and spent hours playing dress-up in our mother's old gowns and jewelry, pretending that she was a Southern princess.

"Could I borrow this photo? Bria would love to see it."

Mallory nodded, closed the book, and pushed it over to me. "Take the whole thing. There are more party photos in there, and you might find some more shots of your mama. Feel free to have some copies made, if you like."

I nodded my thanks, my chest tight with emotion. I didn't have any photos of my mother—not a single one—and neither did Bria. They'd all been destroyed the night Mab Monroe murdered her and Annabella and burned our mansion to the ground.

This . . . this must have been what Finn had felt like the first day he met with Deirdre at the Pork Pit. The shock, the surprise, the unexpected delight. Although more than a little melancholy was mixed in with my emotions. Because, unlike Deirdre, my mama was dead. I had watched a ball of elemental Fire reduce her beautiful face to ash in an instant. I breathed in, and the fumes from the moonshine took on a smoky, charred scent, the same way my mama's body had smelled after Mab killed her—

I shook my head to chase away memories that were better left buried. Focus. I needed to focus right now. "Is there anything else you can tell me about Deirdre? Anything at all?"

Mallory fingered one of her diamond bracelets. "Well, there is one other thing you might be interested in. Some lackey of hers came 'round here last week, asking if I would donate some of my jewelry to that charity exhibit she's putting together."

"Was it a vampire?" I asked. "A guy named Hugh Tucker?"

Lorelei shook her head. "It was some woman who said she worked for Deirdre's charity foundation. Apparently, Deirdre and her minions have been making the society rounds, asking everyone to show off their Sunday jewels." She paused. "For the children, of course."

"Moonshine makes you catty." I grinned. "I like it."

Lorelei toasted me with her glass and took another sip.

"Well, I didn't like her attitude," Mallory said. "She swaggered in here, acting like she was doing me some big favor by asking for my jewels. And she had the nerve to talk down to me. I'm three hundred and thirty-three years old. I'm not senile. Hmph."

I grinned again. I could imagine Mallory dressing down the charity worker. "So what did you tell her?"

"I told her no, that I liked my diamonds right where I could see 'em—namely, on me—and not behind some flimsy sheets of glass."

Hmm. Now, that was a possibility I hadn't considered. Clementine Barker and her cadre of giants had almost pulled off the crime of the century at the Briartop museum back during the summer. Perhaps Deirdre was planning to do the same. All that jewelry would make for a nice score.

It made sense . . . but then again, it didn't. Why bother cozying up to Finn if she was going to rob the museum? Deirdre had already put her exhibit in motion before she'd first contacted him. What was I missing? What angle was I not seeing?

Maybe Deirdre's scheme and her interest in Finn were two different things. Maybe she really did want to be part of his life but without giving up her criminal enterprises, whatever they might be. Or maybe Deirdre wasn't planning to rob the museum at all. Maybe I just thought that was her plan because of the previous robbery attempt. Surely she wouldn't be so obvious and so dumb as to repeat Clementine Barker's mistakes.

"What did the charity worker say when you told her no?" I asked.

Mallory shrugged. "She thanked me and went on her way."

"That's it?"

"That's it." She shook her head, making her diamond choker sparkle. "I'm sorry, sweetheart. I know it's not much, and I wish that I could tell you more. I wish that I could give you some of the answers you want, and Finn too. He's a sweet, lovely boy, and I consider you both dear friends. But I'm afraid that all I have are old photos and memories."

She gave me a sympathetic look. So did Lorelei. But it wasn't their fault that I hadn't found anything on Deirdre yet. I was going to keep right on searching and spying on Mama Dee, no matter how long it took. No matter how many lunches I had to cook for her and no matter how many times I had to sit and smile when all I really wanted to do was punch her in the face.

"Are you okay, Gin?" Lorelei asked. "You look like you want to hit someone."

I gave them a bright smile and pushed my mason jar back over to Mallory. "You know what? Pour me some more of your liquid torture. After the week I've had, I could use it."

✳ 18 ✳

The next night was the grand opening of the jewelry exhibit. Even if I hadn't been invited by Mama Dee herself, a whole passel of assassins couldn't have kept me from seeing what was supposed to be her crowning achievement.

The event was being held at Briartop, Ashland's largest, fanciest, and most self-important art museum. And, lately, the most maligned, given all the deaths and injuries that had resulted from Clementine Barker's almost-successful heist back during the summer.

Briartop perched on top of a rocky ridge of an island in the middle of the Aneirin River and was accessible only by crossing an old-fashioned whitewashed covered wooden bridge. Given the previous robbery attempt, the police had come out in full force for tonight's event, and groups of officers were stationed at both ends of the bridge, shining their flashlights into every car and examining invitations before they let anyone cross over to the island itself.

Owen showed our invitation to the cops, who waved us on through, then steered his car across the bridge and into the receiving line of vehicles crawling up the hill. He handed his keys off to a valet, and we walked arm in arm toward the museum.

Even by Ashland standards, Briartop was impressive: five stories of gleaming gray marble, with a coal-black slate roof and fat, pointed turrets that made it look like the Southern version of a fairy-tale castle. Crenellated balconies clung to the front of the building like square, narrow spiderwebs, adding to the castle illusion, while four massive columns flanked the main entrance.

More cops were stationed outside the entrance, along with the museum's own guards, all of them check-ing invitations a second time just to make sure that no one slipped past them who wasn't supposed to be here. If Deirdre was planning to steal the exhibit jewelry, she would have a hard time getting through all the security. But if that wasn't her plan, then what was? Worry wiggled like a worm on a hook in the bottom of my stomach. Try as I might, I still couldn't see what her endgame was, much less how or even if it involved Finn.

Owen and I got in line to have our invitations checked again. Tonight's event was black-tie to the max, and the folks milling around the museum entrance had risen to the occasion, with the men in classic tuxedoes and the women in glittering gowns. Even among the highfalutin crowd, Owen attracted more than his share of attention. His blue-black hair gleamed under the lights, and his black tuxedo jacket stretched perfectly over his broad, muscled shoulders, making him even more ruggedly handsome than usual.

I attracted some glances too, mostly because of my dress. The blood-red velvet that was always my color hugged my body like a second skin, but what made the dress really stand out was the spiderweb pattern done in black crystals stretching across the bodice. Smaller webs, also done in black crystals, flowed down the skirt before trimming the entire bottom of the garment, making me look like a black widow spider come to life.

More than one person did a double take at the dress's obvious association with my assassin alter ego, and whispers sprang up all around me. I ignored them. Let people think what they wanted to about me. I had much more important things to worry about tonight.

"Why, Blanco, fancy seeing you here," a snide voice murmured.

I looked to my right to find Dimitri Barkov standing a few feet away, a blonde with sky-high hair and over-inflated breasts clinging to his arm like wet tissue paper. The Russian gangster was wearing a tux, and he'd even gone to the trouble of styling his shaggy black toupee into an elaborate pompadour. All the grease in the fake hair made it look like an oil slick spreading across his scalp.

Dimitri's cold brown eyes flicked over my dress. He opened his mouth to deliver some insult, but his date thrust her breasts up against his side and stuck her lower lip out in an exaggerated pout.

"Come on, Dimi," she crooned in a baby-doll voice. "I want to go inside and see the jewels like you promised."

He looked at her, his face flat. "And I told you never to interrupt me when I'm talking business."

The blonde heard the threat in his words loud and

clear. Despite her heavy makeup, her face paled, and she dropped her head in apology. Her body started trembling so hard that her breasts threatened to jiggle right out of the top of her dress.

Dimitri turned back to me. "See you around, Blanco," he said, sneering.

He gave me another cold glare, then headed for the entrance and disappeared inside the museum, since he and his date had already been cleared. I didn't like his smug smirk, not one little bit. Dimitri was definitely up to something, but this wasn't the time or place to confront him.

"What was that about?" Owen asked.

"Just a minor mobster trying to be threatening. Forget about it. I could kill him with my eyes closed."

Finally, Owen and I reached the front of the line, where a familiar face was checking invitations.

Xavier looked us both up and down, then let out a low whistle. "Nice duds, Grayson. You too, Gin."

"Well, you know me. I saw the pattern and couldn't resist the irony." I nodded at the giant. "You look pretty spiffy yourself."

Like all the other cops, Xavier was wearing black wing tips, dark blue dress pants, and a dark blue jacket with a double row of silver buttons marching down the front. A matching blue hat was perched on top of his shaved head, while a black leather utility belt was cinched around his waist. His gold badge gleamed on the belt, right next to his holstered gun. A metal baton dangled from another slot on the belt, along with a flashlight.

"Chief's orders," he rumbled. "Everyone in dress blues for the fancy shindig."

Owen grinned. "Taking names and kicking ass like usual?"

"Well, someone's got to do some work around here, since my partner decided to take the night off." Xavier jerked his head. "Bria and Finn are already inside, along with Mama Dee."

I groaned. "Don't tell me you're calling her by that ridiculous nickname too."

"She's got everyone here calling her that." Xavier stamped our invitations, then handed them back to Owen. "Enjoy the show."

"Fat chance of that," I muttered.

Xavier chuckled and waved for the next couple in line to step forward.

Owen and I entered the museum, walked down a hallway, and stepped into the exhibit area, an enormous rotunda topped by a high, domed ceiling. I'd expected the setup to be the same as the last time I was here—glass cases filled with baubles, subdued white lights wrapping around the columns, soft classical music trilling in the background.

But Mama Dee didn't do anything halfway, and the rotunda had been converted into an old-fashioned Prohibition speakeasy. A large bar had been set up along one of the walls, complete with a champagne tower at either end, and all the waitstaff were dressed in either old-timey white suits or white flapper dresses. Clusters of white feathers, black beads, and red crystals decorated everything and wound all the way around the second-floor balcony. Upbeat big-band music pulsed through the air, and I wouldn't have been surprised if the waiters stopped serving drinks and broke out into an elaborate song-and-dance routine at any second.

Still, the bright, elegant atmosphere didn't even come close to outshining all the jewels on display.

Diamonds, sapphires, emeralds, rubies, and more winked from behind three-inch-thick glass cases throughout the rotunda. The jewels themselves were impressive enough, but the settings were even more extravagant: gold, silver, and platinum that had been hammered into all sorts of shapes, from classic princess-cut diamond solitaire rings to an owl pin with quarter-sized emeralds for eyes to a clutch purse covered with rubies that had been fitted together in the shapes of roses. It was like standing in the middle of the world's most impressive and expensive rainbow. There was easily more than a hundred million dollars' worth of stones in this room, each one vainly chirping about its own sparkling beauty. The gemstones' boasting voices perfectly punctuated the fast-paced music.

"Deirdre owns all these jewels?" Owen asked.

"Just a few pieces," I said. "Most of the items belong to folks here in Ashland. Apparently, Deirdre knows everyone who's anyone, especially among the society crowd, and she got them all to loan their jewelry to her."

"Impressive," Owen said.

And it truly was. The display of Mab Monroe's personal effects here back during the summer had been a sight to see, but this was something else. I'd never been much for jewelry, but even I couldn't help gawking at all the unique and interesting pieces on view. I could almost admire Deirdre for putting together such a lavish, over-the-top show.

Almost.

"Let's find Finn and Bria." I paused. "After we have a drink. Or three."

"Sounds like someone needs a little liquid courage for her next encounter with Mama Dee," Owen teased.

"Absolutely." I elbowed him in the side. "Now, shut it, wiseguy, and take me to the bar."

Owen and I grabbed a couple of drinks—a Scotch on the rocks for him and a gin and tonic for me—then walked around the rotunda, looking at the jewelry and searching for our friends. In addition to Ashland's upper crust, several underworld bosses were here tonight, and I once again had to stop and make nice with the more important ones, just as I had done at the bank's cocktail party. Once again, my cheeks started to ache from all the fake smiles and inane pleasantries. But as Silvio had told me many times before, it was all part of my job as the big boss now. Lucky me.

Mama Dee had also invited Silvio, who was already here, making the rounds and seeing what info he could dig up to pass on to me later. The middle-aged vampire looked quite distinguished in his tuxedo, his silver hair glistening under the lights. A younger man whom I didn't recognize was giving Silvio come-hither looks over the top of his champagne flute, but Silvio ignored him.

The vamp caught sight of Owen and me and waved. I waved back and made a motion with my hand, telling him that we would catch up later. Silvio nodded back, walked away from his admirer, and continued circulating through the room, chatting up a few people here and there as he passed.

Owen and I walked on. I said hello to a few more folks, rounded another case, and there they were, standing in the center of the rotunda—Bria, Finn, and Deirdre. Of course that was where Mama Dee would be.

Bria was a vision of ethereal beauty in a lavender dress that floated around her like a cloud, while Finn looked as handsome as ever in his tuxedo, a diamond pin winking in the center of his bow tie. But they both paled in comparison with Deirdre.

She wore a tight, fitted, floor-length gown made of dazzling silver sequins that sparkled even brighter than many of the jewels. A couple of long, thin diamond pins held her blond curls in place, while her scarlet lips were a perfect pop of color in her beautiful face. Her only other jewelry was her rune necklace—that heart made out of jagged diamond icicles.

I wondered when she would finally reveal her own cold heart. Silvio was still digging up info on her, insisting that there was something seriously off about her charity foundation finances, but that didn't help me combat her growing hold on Finn.

A hold that was on full display tonight.

Even though Bria was with them, Finn was completely focused on Deirdre, his gaze locked onto her face even as he belly-laughed at some joke she'd made. So did everyone else who was gathered around them. Before his mother had come to town, Finn wouldn't have been able to take his eyes off Bria, especially given how gorgeous she looked tonight, but that wasn't the case anymore. No wonder she was sick of Deirdre.

Bria saw me and waved. She murmured something to

Finn, probably telling him that Owen and I were here, but all he did was nod distractedly and go right back to his conversation with Deirdre.

Bria stared at him, the hurt flashing in her eyes quickly flaring up into annoyance and then outright anger. Not that he noticed. She sniffed, turned her back to him, and stormed over to Owen and me. The sharp *crack-crack-crack-crack* of her stilettos against the marble floor rang out above the music.

Bria stopped a passing waiter, downed a glass of champagne, and grabbed another one before coming over to us. Owen got waylaid by one of his business associates, so then it was just my sister and me, drinks in hand, watching Deirdre smile, bat her lashes, and entertain the growing crowd around her and Finn.

"The more I see of that woman, the less I like her," Bria muttered. "It's like she and Finn are joined at the hip. It's getting on my last nerve."

I scoffed. "You think it's getting on *your* last nerve? You're not the one who has to be a dear and fetch her iced teas and grilled cheese sandwiches until the cows come home. She and Finn had a three-hour lunch at the Pork Pit earlier today, which meant *three whole hours* of listening to her laugh and talk and simper and make an ass of herself and Finn. My face still hurts from smiling at all her stupid jokes."

Bria snorted her agreement, her gaze never leaving the necklace around Deirdre's throat.

"Did you ever figure out where you had seen her rune before?"

"Not yet," she said. "I haven't had much time to work

on it the last few days, and last night I was busy with all of Mallory's old photos. Thank you for giving them to me. I've only gone through about half of them, but it's been really great, seeing Mom's face again."

As soon as I'd left Mallory and Lorelei's mansion yesterday, I dropped the photos off at the police station for Bria, knowing how much she would enjoy them. I'd look through them later. Right now, I needed to focus on Mama Dee, not get all misty-eyed and maudlin about my own mother and my dim memories of her.

"I'd almost forgotten what Mom looked like." Bria's voice rasped with emotion. "I just wish I had a picture of Annabella too."

I linked my arm through hers. "You'll never forget Mom or Annabella, because you see them every time you look in the mirror. You're the spitting image of both of them." I winked. "Only prettier."

A wry smile curved her lips. "Thanks, Gin." She drew in a breath. "But I need to talk to you about the photos—"

"Bria! Honey! There you are!" Deirdre's voice boomed through the rotunda, and she sashayed over to us. "I was wondering where you'd run off to."

"I doubt that," Bria muttered.

Deirdre turned her dazzling smile to me. "And Gin, so nice to see you tonight. You look lovely. Red really is your color."

I smiled back, my eyes as cold and hard as hers were warm and soft. "You have no idea."

Some other people came up to us, insisted that they

just had to introduce Deirdre to their friends, and whisked her away. Since Mama Dee was otherwise occupied, Finn finally deigned to wander over and grace Bria and me with his presence. Still, all the while, he looked across the rotunda and beamed at Deirdre, proud of her splashy success.

"She really is something, isn't she?" he crowed.

"Mmm." Bria and I made the same noncommittal noise in unison.

Finn crooked his eyebrow at our less-than-enthusiastic response.

"The exhibit is impressive," Bria admitted. "Especially when it comes to the security."

She tipped her champagne flute at a giant standing guard at the back of the room. And he wasn't the only one. More guards were stationed throughout the rotunda, along with an equal number of cops, not to mention the security cameras mounted on the walls that swiveled around and around, recording everyone here tonight.

"Mama Dee didn't spare any expense," Finn said, his voice warm with pride. "She knows that the exhibit is a potential target, and after what happened at the bank's party, she's determined to make sure nothing jeopardizes it. She's promised everyone that their jewels will be safe."

Of course the exhibit would be a target. This much jewelry in one place . . . it was like offering candy to Ashland's criminals. I thought of Rodrigo Santos and the thief's expertise in breaking into places like Briartop. But I just didn't see how he or anyone else could get past all the cops and security guards, much less snatch the jewels and actually make off with them. It would be suicide to even try. Still, something about the whole situation nagged at me, like an itch between my shoulder blades that I couldn't quite reach.

Finn kept prattling on about Deirdre, all the hard work she'd put into the exhibit, and how much money tonight's event and subsequent ticket sales would raise for her charity foundation. I tuned him out.

Deirdre was now talking to some society ladies, and she gestured for Finn to come join them. He headed over to her without so much as a backward glance at Bria or me, leaving my sister to glare at his back.

"Have you talked to him?" I asked. "About how much ignoring you like this hurts?"

"I've thought about it."

"But?"

She sighed. "But then he starts going on and on about what a connection he feels with Deirdre. How he's so glad that she reached out to him. How he wants to make up for lost time with her. And I just don't have the heart to burst his bubble. Besides, it's not *all* his fault."

"No," I replied. "It's not all his fault. Deirdre came along and offered him something that no one else could. Anyone would be taken in by her. Even I might believe she was legit if not for Fletcher's letter to me. Even then, all I really have are the old man's warnings and this vague, uneasy feeling that slithers up my spine every time Deirdre smiles at me—and especially at Finn. But she can't keep up this act forever. She's bound to show her true self sooner or later. All we can do is be there for Finn when it happens."

"Even if we want to murder him ourselves in the meantime?" Bria snarked.

I grinned and threaded my arm through hers. "Even if."

Xavier entered the rotunda to take the place of one of the other cops, and Bria headed over to speak to him. Owen was still chatting with his business associate, so I got a fresh gin and tonic and wandered through the room, looking at all the jewels again.

I finally reached the center of the rotunda and the pièce de résistance: a diamond choker that featured dozens of exquisite, sparkling carats. Each diamond was shaped like a heart, with a large heart in the center and subsequent hearts gradually becoming smaller and smaller until two tiny hearts hooked the whole thing together in the back. According to the identification card inside the glass case, this necklace actually had a name—Hearts of Ice—and was from Deirdre's private collection, with an estimated value of more than ten million dollars. Now, that was some nice ice.

"Impressive, isn't it?" a voice murmured.

Mallory Parker stepped up beside me. The elderly dwarf wore a long-sleeved blue ballgown and was decked out in almost as many diamonds as were in the entire exhibit. Large solitaire rings flashed on every one of her fingers, diamond studs the size of small pebbles glinted in her ears, and an impressive tiara sparkled on top of her head, nestled in the fluffy mound of her teased white hair.

"Mallory."

"Gin."

I looked around and spotted Lorelei Parker talking

with Bria and Xavier. I waved at Lorelei, who returned the gesture and then went back to her conversation with my friends.

I turned back to Mallory. "I didn't think you'd be here tonight, especially since you didn't donate anything to the exhibit."

The elderly dwarf grinned. "I might not have donated anything, but I'm always happy to lust after someone else's stones." She nodded her head at the display case. "That necklace has been in the Shaw family for generations. Deirdre's mama wore it to plenty of parties. I even tried to buy it from her when I heard that she was looking to unload some of her jewelry, but she was too snooty to sell it to me."

I had started to respond when the scent of peonies filled the air. I bit back a groan.

"Gin! Honey! There you are!" Deirdre said, walking up to us. "I see that you're admiring the heart of the exhibit. Hee-hee-hee. Isn't it lovely?"

"Lovely," I said in a wry voice.

Deirdre favored Mallory with a dazzling smile. "And Mallory Parker, how wonderful to see you again."

"I wish I could say the same," the dwarf replied in a tart voice. "But we both know that ain't the case."

Deirdre let out a trilling laugh and waggled her finger at the other woman. "I see that the years haven't dulled that sharp tongue of yours. Why, you're just as charming as ever, honey."

Mallory slapped her hands on her hips and glared up at her. "You can spout your pretty words all you want, but I know it was you who sicced Raymond Pike on my

Lorelei. I will get you for that, *honey*. You have my word. And unlike you, Deirdre, I *always* keep my word."

The dwarf nodded at me again, then picked up her skirt and moved over to where Lorelei was standing with Bria and Xavier. Lorelei looked at me and raised her eyebrows. I shook my head, telling her that now was not the time to talk.

"She never did like me," Deirdre murmured, still staring at Mallory. "Not even when Lily Rose and I were young. I have no idea why."

"You know exactly why," I snapped. "She just told you. Or did you forget about that letter you wrote Raymond Pike? The one wishing him happy hunting when he came to Ashland to murder Lorelei? The one with your icicle-heart rune stamped on it?"

She shook her head. "I have no idea what you're talking about, but I see that Mallory has been bad-mouthing me. Not that you need any added incentive to dislike me. Do you, Gin?"

"None at all, sugar."

Deirdre's scarlet lips turned down, and frown lines wrinkled her forehead, as though my obvious distrust greatly pained her. Even now, when it was just the two of us, she wasn't breaking character, not even for a second. "I wish that you would give me a chance, a real chance. For Finnegan's sake."

I sneered at her. "Finn's sake is the only reason—the *only* reason—you're not dead yet. You should remember that and stop whatever scheme you've hatched against him. Before it's too late—for you."

Deirdre was completely unruffled by my threat, although her gaze slid past me for just a moment. I turned my head and saw Hugh Tucker, who was standing off by himself and checking his phone. He didn't pay the slightest bit of attention to her, though. If Deirdre was expecting her assistant to come over and save her from me, she was going to be sorely disappointed.

She turned her full attention back to me. "I see that Fletcher made you as paranoid as he was." She shook her head. "For that, I am truly sorry, Gin. I didn't come back to Ashland to hurt you. I just want to get to know my son. That's all. But I suppose that it's only natural for you to feel jealous and threatened by little ole me. After all, you were supposedly the only family Finnegan had left, after you got his daddy killed."

I gasped, more surprised than if she'd slapped me across the face. Shock, grief, and guilt surged through my body like electricity, burning every single part of me before charring my heart.

"Finnegan told me all about it," Deirdre continued in an innocent voice, as if she were just making conversation and not talking about one of the worst moments of my life. "How some assassin job of yours went wrong and how Fletcher ended up tortured to death inside the Pork Pit because of it. That must be a heavy, heavy burden for you to bear. No wonder you're so protective of Finnegan. You don't want history to repeat itself, now, do you?"

I didn't say anything. I *couldn't* say anything. All I could think of, all I could feel, was my own failure coursing through my veins like venom, reducing everything inside me to brittle ash. Just as it had the night I'd found Fletcher's broken body in his own restaurant.

"But you don't have to worry about me, Gin," Deirdre went on, as if she couldn't see the soul-crushing despair in my eyes. "Despite what you think, my intentions are good. All I want is to have a real relationship with Finnegan. I hope that you'll finally give me that chance. Just think about it. Okay, honey?"

Despite all her hurtful words, I forced myself to nod at her and not let her realize how deeply she'd wounded me. "You're right," I said, my voice as empty and hollow as my heart was right now. "I haven't treated you well. I apologize. I won't stand in the way of you and Finn. Not anymore."

"Oh, Gin, honey!" she squealed. "I'm so glad to finally hear you say that!"

Before I could stop her, Deirdre swooped me up into a tight hug, her hands pressing into my back, her body plastered against mine, her peony perfume snaking down my throat, making me want to vomit. Even through the thick velvet of my gown, I could feel how cold her hands were and the elemental Ice magic pulsing through her entire body. My chest and back went numb in an instant, the cold so swift, sudden, and intense that it brought tears to my eyes.

At least, that's what I told myself was causing the waterworks. Not Deirdre's words and especially not the ugly, ugly truth in them. That I was jealous of her and threatened by her. That I was the reason Finn didn't have any family left.

That I was the reason Fletcher was dead.

"And what are two of my favorite ladies up to?" Finn called out, striding over to us.

Deirdre dropped her arms, stepped back, and gave me a conspiratorial wink. "Oh, nothing special. Just some long-awaited girl talk. What about you, handsome?"

The two of them started chatting, but I just stood there, my face frozen in a hollow smile, tears trapped in my eyes, and my gaze locked on Deirdre's icicle-heart rune.

Cold, broken, and jagged—just like my own heart right now.

✸ 19 ✸

It took the better part of two minutes for the chill of Deirdre's Ice magic to leave my body, but her words continued to sting my heart. I mumbled an excuse to her and Finn, but they'd already turned away to talk to some other folks, and neither one of them heard me.

Owen had finally extricated himself from his business associate, and he met me in the middle of the rotunda. He took one look at my face and frowned. "What's wrong?"

"Do you care if we leave now?"

"Are you sure? I thought you wanted to keep an eye on Finn."

I looked over at Finn, who was still standing by Deirdre's side, chatting with her latest round of admirers. "Don't worry," I said in a sad voice. "He won't even realize that I'm gone."

And he didn't.

Owen and I stopped long enough to say good-bye to

Bria and Xavier and wave to Mallory and Lorelei as we made our way toward the exit. Finn never once looked in our direction.

On the ride back to Fletcher's, Owen tried to get me to tell him what was bothering me, but I just didn't have the energy to recount how Deirdre had rubbed my face in all my past mistakes and failures—and that she'd been right about every single one, especially Fletcher being dead because I hadn't been good enough, strong enough, fast enough to save him.

Owen offered to stay the night, but I told him I was tired and was going to bed. He kissed me, told me to call him if I wanted to talk, and left.

I stripped off my spider gown and took a long, hot shower. We'd left the exhibit early, and it was just after nine, but I was exhausted, so I crawled into bed. I drifted to sleep almost immediately.

The three vampires who'd been robbing Fletcher's house crept closer and closer to me.

The smart thing would have been to sprint back around the porch, throw open the front door, and run inside. But it wasn't like I would have gotten all that far. Not given the logjam of kids still partying in the house. Besides, I was too angry to think straight, so I stood my ground.

The three vamps spread out in a line across the porch in front of me.

"Lookie here, boys," the guy in the middle crooned. "A little girl's come out to play with us."

My hands clenched into tight fists. If there was one thing I wasn't, it was a little girl. Not anymore. Not for a long time now.

Another vamp laughed. "Well, I say we play with her. Right, Paul?"

Paul, the vamp in the middle, nodded. "Yep."

But I was still too angry—at them, at Finn, at everything—to back down. Besides, they'd be on me like a pack of hyenas the second I turned my back.

"Leave now, and we can pretend like this never happened," I said. "Like you weren't trying to rob this place."

Paul laughed and looked at his friends, who joined in with his chuckles.

"What's so funny?" I muttered.

Paul stared at me. "You know why we like parties? Because the kids are too busy drinking, smoking, and screwing to notice who comes in the front door, much less what they take out the back with them. You're not ruining that for us."

So they'd done this before. Slipped into a house during a party and walked out with whatever they could stuff into their pockets and carry away. And if the homeowners noticed that their valuables were missing, then it was just too bad, and they'd most likely chalk it up to their kids' friends having swiped it and ground their own kids as a result.

It was a sweet little scam. I wondered who had told them about Finn's party. Someone had to have clued them in, especially since Fletcher's house was out in the boonies. It wasn't like they'd seen or heard the noise from down the street and had come to investigate. No, someone had to have tipped them off. Otherwise, they wouldn't be here.

But my main problem was that there were three of them and only one of me. I glanced at the windows. The other kids were still inside, just a few feet away, but the music was so loud that I doubted anyone would hear me if I screamed.

Even if they did, they'd probably think somebody was just messing around and not in any real danger. Either way, none of them would come and help me.

I'd have to take care of myself, just like always.

So I studied the vampires. Paul, the guy in the middle, was obviously the leader, with a tall, strong body that made him the most dangerous. The other two guys were short and lean, closer to my size than his, but they were still vamps, and the blood they drank would make them stronger and quicker than me. I couldn't let any of them get close enough to put their hands on me, much less sink their fangs into my neck. Too bad I didn't have any of the knives Fletcher had been training me to use. In fact, there were no weapons on the porch at all, just a few small gardening tools that Fletcher had been using to clean up the yard for the coming winter.

"You need to leave," I repeated. "I called the cops. They'll be here any minute."

For a second, worry flashed in Paul's dark eyes, but he must have realized that I was bluffing because he grinned again. "Cops, huh? Well, then, I guess we'll just have to be quick about our fun." His gaze flicked up and down my body. "Or maybe we'll just take you with us. You're a little skinny for my tastes, but some guys like 'em just like you."

My anger vanished in an instant, and bile bubbled up in the back of my throat. Not only did they want to steal from Fletcher, but now they wanted to steal me too.

I bolted.

I turned to run, but Paul was quicker. He grabbed my ponytail and jerked me back. I used the change in momentum to ram my elbow into his stomach. He gasped and doubled over, losing his grip on me. I opened my mouth to scream, even as I surged forward again.

But I'd forgotten about the other two guys.

One of them caught my left arm from behind, and I smashed my foot down onto his instep. He hissed, but he didn't let go of me. The other guy stepped up and clamped his hand on my other arm. No matter how hard I struggled, I couldn't break free of their tight, bruising grips, so I screamed and screamed, but the blaring music swallowed up my terrified cries. No one so much as looked out a window to see what might be happening outside.

Paul straightened up and marched over to me. He stared at me for a second, then slapped me across the face. "Bitch."

Pain exploded in my face, and I would have fallen back against the porch railing if not for the two vamps holding me upright.

Paul hit me again and again, making my head snap back and forth. My lips split open, and blood filled my mouth. When he had finished with my face, he rammed his fist into my stomach, almost making me vomit on the spot. I groaned, but the thumping music once again swallowed up the sounds of my misery.

"Get her down on the ground," he growled. "I want to sample the goods first to see if this bitch is worth hauling back to town."

"And if she's not?" one of the other vamps asked.

Paul shrugged. "Then we'll have our fun, take her blood, snap her neck, and throw her body into the woods. Now, hurry up, in case she really did call the cops."

Even though my head was spinning, I fought harder than ever before, biting, clawing, kicking, scratching. But it was no use, and the two vamps threw me down onto the porch. One of them pinned my arms down, while the other gripped my legs.

Paul loomed over me, a smile splitting his face as he reached for his belt buckle . . .

I woke up screaming and pounding my fists into my pillows, just as I'd tried to hit the three vamps so long ago. It took me a minute to remember that I was safe in Fletcher's house, longer still to calm my ragged breathing and racing heart.

But the feeling remained—that awful, awful feeling that I was all alone. That danger was closing in fast all around me.

That no one was coming to help me.

It was the same feeling I got whenever I looked at Deirdre. That Fletcher was gone. That she'd taken Finn away from me, and that there was nothing I could do to get him back.

That I was all alone again.

I knew that it wasn't true, that it wasn't *rational*, that Finn, Bria, Owen, and the rest of my friends loved me. But my worried, traitorous heart still made me feel alone and small and empty.

And scared—so very scared.

I lay in bed for several minutes, catching my breath and trying to get my emotions under control. But the truth was that I had been decidedly out of control ever since Deirdre waltzed into Finn's life. I could be hard when I needed to, as cold as ice even, but Deirdre . . . she was in a league by herself. With just a few soft sentences, she'd brought all my guilt, grief, and heartache about Fletcher's death roaring back to the surface.

I kept waiting for her to slip up, to crack, to finally reveal her true nature to Finn and everyone else. I was the Spider, I was patience itself, but nothing I said or did so much as rattled Mama Dee. She was much better at this game we were playing. She was *winning*, and Finn was going to be her prize.

And I'd be damned if I could see a way to stop her.

Even though it was just after eleven, I didn't even try to go back to sleep. Not when there were more nightmares swimming around in my subconscious like sharks waiting to take another bite out of my heart. Instead of tossing and turning, I decided to get up and do something useful.

Spy on Deirdre.

I put on my usual black clothes, topped off with a black silverstone vest, and made sure that I had all five of my knives. Then I grabbed a duffel bag full of extra knives and other gear, threw it into my car, and drove over to the Peach Blossom. It was just after midnight when I parked my car in a lot close to Deirdre's building. I looked up and down the street, but it was deserted at this late hour, so I got out of my car, grabbed my gear, and hurried over to the building across the street.

This building didn't have any external security cameras, but I still kept to the shadows as I sidled up to the side door. I looked left and right again, but no one was out and about, so I reached for my Ice magic, holding my palm close to my chest and turning my back to the street to hide the cold, silvery glow of my power. A second later, I was clutching two long, slender Ice picks, which I used to unlock the door, just as I'd done all the previous times

I'd come here. I threw the Ice picks onto the ground to melt away, then slipped inside.

The building was used for office space, so no one was creeping around this late on a Friday night, not even janitors taking out the week's trash. I climbed to the top of the fire stairs, used another set of Ice picks to open the door there, and stepped out onto the roof.

The Peach Blossom was roughly the same height as the building I was on, and the roof here gave me a clear, direct view of Deirdre's penthouse on the top floor. But the windows were dark, and no one moved through the shadows there. Deirdre wasn't home yet. Not surprising. She'd be the last person to leave her swanky gala.

So I pulled out my binoculars, a digital surveillance camera, and a directional microphone from my duffel bag. I'd thought about leaving everything here so I could record Deirdre 24-7, but I didn't want to risk someone coming up to the roof and finding my equipment, alerting her to the fact that someone was spying on her.

I'd just finished checking my gadgets and making sure that everything was in working order when lights winked on in the penthouse. I checked my phone. Not even one in the morning yet. Deirdre hadn't enjoyed her night of triumph nearly as long as I'd expected.

I turned on the microphone, set it and the camera on the ledge, and aimed them just so. Then I picked up my binoculars and peered through them at the penthouse, which took up the entire top floor. The spacious suite was largely furnished in cool whites, from the marble counters in the kitchen to the sofas in the living room to the thick carpet underfoot. Pale blue paint covered the walls, with matching pillows and chairs adding a bit more color to the rooms. The kitchen and living room were one open space, with a hall leading to two bedrooms, each with its own attached bathroom.

Deirdre strode through the kitchen and into the living room, still wearing her sparkling silver gown, along with a scarlet silk wrap, which she pulled off and tossed onto one of the sofas, along with her silver clutch. Hugh Tucker trailed in behind her, texting on his phone.

She eyed him a moment, then went over to the wet bar in one corner of the living room and poured herself a healthy amount of whiskey. She threw back the drink, poured herself another, and tossed it back too. She could give Mallory and her moonshine a run for their money.

Tucker finally looked up from his phone and raised his eyebrows at her. Deirdre snorted, but then she poured drinks for both of them, even going so far as to walk across the penthouse and hand it to him.

She kicked off her stilettos, sprawled across a sofa, and propped one foot up on the glass table in front of her. The entire sequence of moves was eerily similar to what I'd seen Finn do a hundred times before. Like it or not, he had more than a little of his mother in him.

Tucker sat down on the other end of the sofa, his drink in one hand and his phone in the other.

"I thought that tonight went exceptionally well, didn't you?" Deirdre asked.

"Mmm." That was Tucker's only response.

"The exhibit was lovely, and everything went off without a hitch," she continued, obviously fishing for a compliment, but Tucker kept ignoring her.

Deirdre frowned, but either he didn't see her annoyed expression or didn't care about it. No assistant worth his salt would treat his boss like that. Not if he wanted to keep his job. So why didn't Deirdre just fire him and hire someone who would fawn over her night and day?

"Are you sure everything's set for tomorrow?" Tucker asked, finally setting his phone down. "You can't afford to have any problems."

I frowned. The way he said that—"*you* can't afford to have any problems"—was rather ominous. Tucker made it sound like Deirdre was in more dire straits than I'd imagined. She was a rich, powerful, and well-connected Ice elemental, so what did she have to worry about? The more I learned about Deirdre Shaw, the less sense I could make of her.

"Everything is set," she said. "Don't worry, Tucker, honey. Everything will go exactly according to my plan. I guarantee it."

"Yes, you have guaranteed it, haven't you?" Tucker raised his glass in a toast. "Well, then. Here's to your guarantees."

Her eyes narrowed, but she raised her glass too, and the two of them downed their drinks.

Deirdre's phone beeped. She took it out of her clutch and read the message, a smile curving her lips. She sent back a quick text, then put her phone down on the glass table, got to her feet, and wandered over to the windows. She stared out into the night, almost as if she could see me watching her from across the street, but I was too well hidden in the shadows for that.

Not for the first time, I wished that I could just take

her out with a sniper rifle. *Bing, bang, boom.* But Finn would never forgive me, especially not now, when he was so certain that her intentions were good.

"Is Blanco going to be a problem?" Tucker asked in a bored voice, texting on his phone again. "I heard your conversation at the museum. Nice way to twist a knife in her back, bringing up your ex the way you did. Then again, that's something you excel at."

My ears perked up. That was the first time Tucker had said anything remotely interesting since I'd been watching him and Deirdre, and it was the first time he'd done anything to acknowledge my existence besides nod at me whenever he came into the Pork Pit with her. Plus, a snide tone sharpened his voice, as if he was almost mocking her.

"Of course not," Deirdre said. "I told you that I would deliver, and I will. You should have more faith in me."

Tucker snorted, but he kept right on texting, as if he'd already dismissed me and any potential problems I might cause from his thoughts.

"Gin Blanco is a suspicious little bitch," Deirdre said, coldness creeping into her voice. "But she is predictable. Just like Fletcher was."

And that was the first time Mama Dee had ever let her true feelings for me show through her big, bawdy persona. Maybe tonight would *finally* be the night I got something that I could take to Finn, some sort of proof that she wasn't what she seemed. I made sure that the microphone and camera were picking up her every word and movement. Then I leaned forward, willing her to say more about Fletcher, willing her to spill her guts to

Tucker about everything that had really happened between her and the old man.

"Do you know what the bad thing is about being predictable?" Deirdre continued. "It makes you weak. It makes you vulnerable."

She paused a moment and leaned even closer to the windows, smiling all the while. "Isn't that right, Gin?"

I gasped, shock zipping through me like a lightning bolt, and I almost dropped my binoculars. Everything just *stopped*, as though Deirdre had frozen me in place with her Ice magic. Even my brain ground to a complete halt. When it finally started sputtering again, I frowned, wondering if I'd heard her right. If she'd actually said my name. If she knew that I was watching her.

Deirdre stared out the windows again, and this time, she did look straight at me, her face smug with triumph. More shock zipped through me, and the revelations hit me one after another, each one as brutal as a fist to the face.

She'd been playing me this whole time. She had realized that I would be suspicious enough to spy on her. It was what Fletcher would have done, and it was exactly what the old man had taught me to do. Even more than that, it was the predictable move, just like she said. I was betting it was part of the reason she'd taken up residence in this particular penthouse—to make it easier for me to keep tabs on her.

And for her to keep tabs on *me*.

I cursed, scrambled to my feet, and whipped around. Lights blazed on, illuminating me as clearly as if it were noon, and men stormed out of the access door and onto the roof. I threw my binoculars aside, palmed a knife, and stepped forward, ready to drive the blade into the chest of the first man. But he was closer than I'd expected, and he was already swinging the butt of his gun straight at my face.

I reached for my Stone magic to harden my skin and tried to twist out of the way of the coming blow, but I wasn't quick enough.

His gun slammed into my temple, and the world went black.

❊20❊

I woke up in a cage.

My eyes fluttered open, then snapped shut again as the bright glare from the bare bulbs overhead stabbed into my brain. My head was already pounding from the hard hit I'd taken, but I swallowed down the groan that threatened to escape my lips. Because I had no idea where I was, only that I was in serious trouble.

And so was Finn.

My eyes snapped open again at the thought of Finn. I had to warn him that Deirdre had finally shown her true self. That she was up to something—something big. So I forced myself to blink and blink until my eyes adjusted to the light and I could examine my surroundings without adding to the constant throbbing already in my head and face.

I was in a warehouse, sprawled across a cold, dirty concrete floor. The walls were made of gray cinder blocks, but the sloped roof was metal and soared about fifty feet overhead. Forklifts of all shapes and sizes squatted here and there in the warehouse, along with heavy-duty wooden pallets that supported large crates and shrink-wrapped boxes. I had no idea what the containers held, but some of the writing on the sides was in another language. Russian, maybe.

I was lying in the center of a cage made out of bars that stretched from the floor all the way up to the ceiling. It probably served as a secure storage space for more valuable items like guns, drugs, and money. I looked from one side of the warehouse to the other. No guards, no gangsters, no goons of any sort. The lights were on, but nobody was home except me. Good. That gave me time to escape.

I pushed myself up onto my hands and knees, then staggered to my feet and took stock of my injuries. Aside from the continued ache in my head and face, I was in one piece. After I was knocked out, they hadn't done anything other than drag me in here. Fools. They should have already put a bullet in my head.

And that wasn't their only mistake. The cage was sturdy, and the bars didn't move at all when I tried to rattle them, but they were made out of regular iron and not silverstone. That meant that I could blast my way out of here with my Ice and Stone magic if I needed to.

But I decided to try something a little quieter first. I went over to the cage door, which was secured with a heavy padlock on the outside. Whoever had put me in here had taken my phone and all five of my knives, so I couldn't jimmy it open that way. I could easily freeze the lock and then shatter it open with my Ice magic, but I didn't know where Deirdre might be lurking, and she might sense me using a large, sudden burst of power like that.

So I reached for the smallest trickle of my magic, letting it pool in the palm of my hand, until I had a single shard of Ice about as long and thick as a needle. I held my breath, looking and listening, but no one came running into the warehouse, so I felt safe enough to add another layer of Ice to my needle, then another, then another . . . until I had formed my usual Ice pick. I stopped, looking and listening again, but the warehouse was as silent and empty as before, so I reached for another trickle of magic and made a second Ice pick.

Once I had two picks, I released my magic, stuck my arms through the gaps in the bars, and went to work on the padlock. It was an awkward position, and the pounding in my head didn't make it any easier. Time and time again, my picks slipped out of the lock.

"Come on," I muttered. "Come *on.*"

If Finn were here, he would have already opened the lock, stuck his hands into his pockets, and been whistling while he strolled away. The thought made me smile and redouble my efforts.

Finally, the picks hit the necessary sweet spots, and the lock clicked open. I started to pull it off the door so I could open it and get out of the cage, but voices sounded outside the warehouse, along with several *beep-beep-beep*s, as though someone was punching in a security code.

So I put the lock back together as close as it would go without actually snapping it shut. It wasn't my most brilliant plan, but as long as I was still in the cage, I could hope no one would do more than glance at the lock. I also reached up and probed my left temple. A goose egg had formed there, and I could feel the slash of a long cut that was still oozing blood. I dipped my fingers in the blood and smeared it down the side of my face. Then I leaned wearily against the cage bars, as if I were more seriously injured than I really was.

A giant guard opened the door, and Deirdre strode into the warehouse. She had changed out of her silver party dress and was now wearing a neon-purple pantsuit and matching stilettos. Her blond hair was sleeked back into a low bun, and her icicle-heart rune glinted under the lights. No doubt, the peacock was here to strut her stuff and crow about capturing me.

Tucker entered the warehouse next, dressed in a navy suit, although it was the two people trailing him who caught my attention: Dimitri Barkov and Rodrigo Santos.

Dimitri stopped in front of the cage and smirked at me. He was still wearing his tuxedo from the museum gala, although he'd ditched his bow tie and jacket and rolled up the sleeves of his white shirt. Despite the styling grease on his toupee, pieces of his fake black hair had curled up in all directions, as though he'd sprouted a dozen devil horns on his head.

Given his sneers at the museum earlier tonight, it had been obvious that Dimitri was plotting something against me. Of course he would have aligned himself with Deirdre. She wouldn't have even had to offer him anything other than my death to make it happen. I could have smacked myself for not realizing it sooner.

But Santos was the far bigger surprise. I'd thought that

Deirdre might have had a hand in the bank robbery, but her genuine shock when Santos shot her had made me back-burner that theory. Just one of the many things I'd been wrong about lately.

Either way, it seemed as though Santos had been hiding out with Dimitri this whole time, which was why Silvio hadn't been able to track him down. But Santos and Dimitri weren't going to be problems for much longer.

And neither was Deirdre.

Santos also smirked at me. Instead of his usual dark, anonymous clothes, he was wearing a long, expensive black overcoat and shiny black boots. The front of his coat was open, giving me a peek at the dark gray clothes he wore underneath, although it seemed more like a uniform than a suit. Weird.

Tucker kept his distance from the cage, texting on his phone. Deirdre eyed me a moment, making sure that I was exactly where she wanted me, then turned to Santos.

"Is everything set?" she asked, her voice clipped and much colder than her usual syrupy-sweet drawl.

Santos nodded. "My crew and I are ready. Everything will go according to plan. Don't worry."

She gave him a flat look. "Well, perhaps this time you can manage not to shoot me."

"I had to make it look good, didn't I? Shooting Lane and slapping you around wasn't going to cut it after Blanco started playing hero. Besides, you got the added bonus of saving your dear son. I got him to trust you, just like that." The giant snapped his fingers.

So the whole point of the bank robbery had been about Deirdre ingratiating herself with Finn. No wonder she'd seemed genuinely upset. Santos shooting her hadn't been part of the plan, but he'd done it anyway. Too bad he'd only grazed her instead of putting a bullet through her chest.

Deirdre's red lips puckered, and anger filled her eyes at his mocking tone. It was obvious that there was no love lost between the two of them. Perhaps the giant would double-cross and kill her for me. Yeah, right. No way could I ever be that lucky. Besides, I wanted to end Mama Dee myself.

"Oh, yeah, the bank job went so well that you had to shoot your own men and leave with nothing," I sniped, slurring my voice to add to my weakened appearance. "What are you going to do for an encore? Swipe some poor kid's lunch money on the playground? That seems to me like that's about all you can handle, Rod."

Anger stained Santos's cheeks. He opened his mouth to snipe back at me, but Deirdre held up her hand. "Don't be an idiot. She's just baiting you."

I snorted and leaned a little more heavily on the cage bars. "Sugar, from where I'm standing, it looks like you've surrounded yourself with idiots."

"Mmm." Deirdre's noncommittal murmur had Dimitri and Santos eyeing her with suspicion. "Regardless, they were clever enough to capture the great Spider. Interesting nickname Fletcher gave you."

I shrugged. "He thought it was appropriate."

"Just like his name, the Tin Man." Deirdre paused, her eyes gleaming with sly satisfaction. "Do you know why he decided on that particular moniker?"

I shrugged again. I had no idea what she was getting at.

She smiled. "He told me it was because he didn't have a heart anymore. That I had ripped it right out of him. I always liked the idea of him never forgetting what I did to him."

I gripped the bars. "What *did* you do to Fletcher? What's the real story with you two?"

She glanced at her watch. "I suppose I have time to indulge you in this one last thing. Before I let Mr. Barkov dispose of you. He's been so very helpful these past few weeks. He should be rewarded, don't you think?"

Dimitri sneered at me again, his whole body puffing up with self-importance. He actually started cracking his knuckles, as if the thought of him beating me would frighten me. Idiot.

I focused on Deirdre again. "So what happened with Fletcher?" I didn't even try to keep the eagerness out of my voice. This might be my last chance to get the truth out of her before one of us killed the other, and if I had to grovel to do it, then so be it.

"Just a typical story of a girl rebelling against her parents. We never got along. They thought that I should be a prim, proper prude like they were, with no more ambition than catching a rich husband to prop up the Shaw family fortune." Deirdre shook her head. "But I had other plans. I was supposed to get my trust fund when I was eighteen, but my parents realized that I was going to leave Ashland the second I got the money. They changed the terms so I couldn't access it until I was twenty-five. Even then, I realized that they'd just keep putting it off. My parents had already blown through their fortune, and they were going to spend mine too."

"So?" I asked, not seeing her point.

"So I decided to stop them."

"This is about your trust fund? Seriously?"

She shrugged. "Are you really that surprised? You're an assassin, Gin. You know better than anyone else what people will do for money."

She had me there.

"Once I realized that my parents weren't going to give me my money, I decided to do whatever I wanted. Smoking, drinking, boys." She grinned, but it was a sharp, predatory expression. "*Lots* of boys."

"What about Fletcher?"

"Another boy took me to the Pork Pit, where I met Fletcher. He was quite handsome, charming too. Even better, I knew that my parents would *never* approve. He ran a barbecue restaurant, which was about as low-class as you could get, according to them. So I decided to have a little fun. I seduced Fletcher, made him think that I was this sweet young girl who totally adored him, and he fell for it. He was totally in love with me. It was amusing enough while it lasted."

Deirdre paused, her gaze distant, as if she were seeing Fletcher as he had been back then. Her hand crept up to her icicle-heart necklace, her fingers stroking over the rune.

"So what happened? What changed?"

"I got pregnant." Her nostrils flared with disgust, and she dropped her hand from her necklace. "I didn't want the baby, but Fletcher was over the moon about it. He thought that we were going to get married and be this perfect little family. He was wrong."

I thought back to the casket box full of mementos. "Fletcher gave you an engagement ring. I found it in a box of old photos. What did you do with the diamond from it?"

"I hocked it, of course, the day after he gave it to me, and had the diamond replaced with a glass chip. Fletcher didn't know the difference until it was too late." She chuckled.

The mocking sound made me grind my teeth, but I wanted to hear the rest of her story, so I forced my voice to stay steady. "What about Finn? Why did you keep him?"

"The idea of a baby put Fletcher even more under my spell, so I went along with it. I could see how useful it was going to be in the end."

Her voice and face were cold, flat, and emotionless, as if she were reciting some history lesson she'd memorized long ago. It was such a complete change, such a total role reversal from the warm, over-the-top persona she'd shown until now. I'd thought all along that Deirdre was coldhearted, but seeing her complete lack of compassion or feeling up close jarred me much more than I'd expected. I had to keep reminding myself that this was the *real* Deirdre Shaw—and exactly what Fletcher had warned me about.

"Useful for what?" I asked.

"Once I realized that Fletcher was an assassin, it was easy enough to wait, plan, and set things up. I went ahead with the pregnancy, even though it was the longest, most miserable nine months of my life, pretending that I was excited about the baby." She rolled her eyes. "But Fletcher never even suspected what I was really up to. Not until it was too late."

Deirdre started walking up and down in front of the cage, trailing her long red fingernails over the metal bars like a cat sharpening her claws. I made sure not to look at the padlock, even though I was holding my breath the whole time, hoping that she wouldn't jar it loose and make it drop to the floor. If that happened, I was dead. Deirdre and her Ice magic were dangerous enough, but Dimitri, Santos, and Tucker were still here, standing behind her. One of them could easily pull a gun and put a bullet in my head while I was battling her.

She ran her nails along the bars a final time, then stepped away from the cage and faced me again. "After I had the baby, I told Fletcher that I wanted to reconcile with my parents. So I said that I was taking Finnegan to see them."

"What did you do?"

"I took the money I got from the diamond in that pathetic ring and paid a homeless bum to slap me around. I also ripped up Finnegan's clothes, as if he'd been attacked right along with me. Then I rushed over to the Pork Pit, crying my eyes out, and told Fletcher that my father had hit me and that my mother had tried to take the baby away from me. He never even questioned me." She let out a dark, satisfied chuckle. "As for what happened next, well, you knew Fletcher. You knew all about his savior complex and *exactly* how far he would go to protect his family."

My heart plummeted into my stomach. "Fletcher killed your parents."

"Just like that." Deirdre snapped her fingers, the sound

as loud as a gunshot. "With my parents dead, I got my trust fund *and* what was left of the Shaw fortune. I wanted to leave right away, but of course, I had to wait for the estate to be settled. Three months was better than a lifetime of waiting, though, so I stuck around and pretended to be the grieving daughter and doting new mother. I'll admit that the thought of all that money made me a wee bit impatient and that I didn't play the parts as well as I should have. I think that's when Fletcher first suspected that I had set him up. But I didn't care. He was nothing but a tool, and I was done with him."

"What happened?" I asked, wanting to hear the rest of it, even though I could guess how bad it was going to be.

"As soon as the estate was settled and all the money was mine, I went to that monstrosity that Fletcher called a house and packed up my things. I'd been planning to disappear without a trace, but he came home and caught me right before I left. He was devastated at the idea of my leaving him. He begged me to stay, if you can imagine that." She laughed again. "Told me that he knew how much I was hurting over my parents' deaths but that Finnegan needed me, that he needed me, and we could work things out. What a blind fool he was."

"What did you do?" I whispered.

She looked at me, her blue eyes colder than I had ever seen them. "I told him the truth. About how I'd used him to get my money. You should have seen the look on his face. It truly was priceless. One of my fondest memories."

My heart dropped again, like an elevator that just kept plummeting down, down, down. I'd once killed an innocent man, been tricked and manipulated into it much the same way Fletcher had been, so I could imagine how he'd felt. The anger, the guilt, the shame at how completely Deirdre had fooled him. The icy sting of her betrayal would have eaten away at him the rest of his life.

"Once he'd realized what I'd done, Fletcher actually tried to stop me. Pulled one of his little knives and came at me as if he thought he had a chance against my Ice magic." Deirdre shook her head. "He put up more of a fight than I expected, and we beat each other up pretty good. Fletcher even had a chance to kill me."

"So why didn't he?" I muttered.

She shrugged. "Because I grabbed hold of Finnegan's cradle. I threatened to freeze him to death if Fletcher didn't let me go."

Despite all the bad things I'd done, all the people I'd killed, all the gruesome torture I'd endured and dished out in return, even I sucked in a ragged breath at that. Dimitri and Santos both winced and shifted on their feet. Tucker kept messing with his phone, as bored as ever. Fletcher had warned me that Deirdre didn't care about anyone other than herself, but the casual, matter-of-fact way she talked about killing her own son . . .

She wasn't coldhearted—she didn't have *any* heart at all.

"Of course, Fletcher let me go. I told him that if he ever threatened me in any way, I would kill Finnegan, along with those two Deveraux busybodies. Then I walked out the door and never looked back." She shook her head again. "Although the same can't be said for Fletcher. I knew that he kept track of me, crept around in the bushes and took pictures from time to time. As if there were ever any reason for me to come back to Ashland."

"Not even for your son?" I asked, already knowing the answer.

"Finnegan?" She shrugged again. "He's just another tool that I happen to need."

"And once you're done with him?"

"Then I'll dispose of him, just the way I did Fletcher all those years ago."

Her words chilled me to the bone, because I knew she meant every single one of them.

But she still hadn't told me the most important thing: exactly what she needed Finn for. I opened my mouth to ask, but Tucker cleared his throat, cutting me off. Deirdre looked over at him, and he waggled his phone at her, reminding her that it was time to wrap up our little tête-à-tête. Whatever was going on, whatever their plan was, it was starting now.

"Santos," she called out. "I believe you have an appointment to keep."

The giant nodded and pivoted on his heel. The sudden motion caused his coat to fly out from his body, revealing his dark gray clothes again. I frowned. I'd been right about him wearing some sort of uniform, complete with a company name stitched on the breast pocket, but the coat dropped back into place, and he walked away before I could make out what it was.

"And I also have my part to play." Deirdre fixed her icy blue gaze on me again. "Good-bye, Gin. Say hello to Fletcher for me when you see him. And do tell him that I'll be sending Finnegan along shortly to join the two of you."

"You bitch!" I hissed, my hands clenching around the

cage bars. "If you so much as touch Finn, I will rip out your heart with my bare fucking hands."

"Oh, I doubt that, since you'll be dead long before Finnegan will be. He is still useful, while you are not." She tilted her head to the side, studying me as though I were some odd specimen. "You really are just like Fletcher. So protective and so predictable. He couldn't see the big picture until it was too late. And you? You'll never even get the chance."

"Well, enlighten me, then," I snapped.

"I'm not that foolish." She smiled. "I only indulged your whim about Fletcher because it amused me, and I knew how much it would hurt you to knock him off that pedestal you've put him on. Besides, I rather like the idea of you going to your grave knowing that you failed to protect your so-called brother."

"I'm more Finn's family than you are, you coldhearted bitch."

"As if I would care about something as silly as that." She looked at me again, that cold, cold smile still on her face. "The only thing your precious family has gotten you is dead, Gin. Think about that when Dimitri starts torturing you. I'll be sure to remind Finnegan of it when I do the same to him."

Her smile widened at my horrified expression, and she threw her head back and laughed, the light, pealing sound ringing like a death knell as she turned and left the warehouse.

✤ 21 ✤

Tucker didn't even glance at me as he slid his phone into his jacket pocket and trailed outside after his boss. Santos was already gone, so that left me alone with Dimitri Barkov. He snapped his fingers a couple of times, and the guard standing at the door stuck his head outside and let out a loud whistle.

A minute later, two more guys entered the warehouse, and the three of them swaggered over to the cage. All were giants, seven feet tall, with big, beefy bodies, and I recognized them as some of the enforcers in Dimitri's crew. The kind of guys tasked with breaking arms, knees, and even necks when the occasion called for it. They were all carrying long, heavy tire irons, one of which they handed over to Dimitri.

The Russian mobster grinned and slapped the tire iron against the palm of his hand several times, trying to intimidate me. Idiot. He was already dead. So were his men. They just didn't know it yet. I could have busted out of my cage anytime I wanted to, but I intended to give this canary a chance to sing first.

"So you wanted your revenge on me, and you threw in your lot with Deirdre to try to get it." I shook my head. "That's the last mistake you'll ever make, Dimitri."

He chuckled. "Not just Deirdre. Her entire group. They offered me a very nice compensation package to help them."

My eyes narrowed. "What group? Who else are you working for?"

He clucked his tongue at me. "Dead women shouldn't ask so many questions. I told you that I'd kill you when you humiliated me on the *Delta Queen*. You should have believed me."

"You haven't managed to do it yet." I mocked him. "Don't get too cocky, sugar. I'm still breathing, which means that you're still going to wind up dead before this is all said and done."

He growled and whipped his hand forward, trying to smash his tire iron against my fingers. I lurched back out of the way of his strike, but the tire iron still slammed into the cage, hard enough to shake the door—and make the open padlock slip out of its slot and drop to the floor.

Dimitri stared at the lock, his bushy black eyebrows drawing together in confusion. Then his eyes widened with realization. "Get her, you fools—"

Too late.

Even as the three giants converged on the cage, I rammed the door open with my shoulder, reached for my Ice magic, and sent a spray of daggers shooting out of the palms of my hands. The sharp, deadly needles caught the giant closest to me square in the throat, and he went down, choking on his own blood. I darted forward and snatched up his tire iron.

The second giant came at me with his own tire iron, but I held my weapon out in front of me and parried his blows.

Clack-clack-clack-clack.

Our makeshift swords banged together again and again, each of us determined to break through the other's defense and brain them with the metal.

"Don't just stand there!" Dimitri barked at the third giant, who was watching our fight with wide eyes. "Shoot her, you idiot!"

The giant fumbled for the gun under his jacket, yanked it free, and aimed it at my head. Just as he pulled the trigger, I ducked down and plastered my body up against my attacker's.

Crack! Crack! Crack!

The guard shot his friend in the back, making the other giant bellow with pain. While he was distracted, I yanked his tire iron out of his hand and cracked both pieces of metal against his head, one after the other, like I was playing a drum set.

Crunch-crunch.

He whimpered and dropped like a stone to the floor, blood spurting out from the cracks I'd opened in his skull.

But I was already whipping around toward the guard with the gun and using my Stone magic to harden my skin.

Crack! Crack! Crack!

Bullets *ping*ed off my body and *thunk-thunk-thunk*ed into the surrounding crates. The guard kept pulling the trigger, even as I charged at him. He ran out of ammo and threw his gun at me, but the weapon clattered off my Stone-hardened skin just like the bullets had. The guard yelped in surprise and turned to run, but I raised my tire irons and slammed them into his skull before he had a chance to take a step.

Crunch-crunch.

He collapsed onto the floor, his body twitching from the massive trauma.

That left Dimitri.

Instead of doing the smart thing and running away while his guards died, Dimitri stood his ground, yanked a gun out from against the small of his back, and started firing at me.

Crack!

Crack! Crack!

Crack!

But his bullets were as useless as all the others had been, and I was on top of him before he'd even finished firing. This time, I went low, ducking his awkward punch, and slammed one of the tire irons into his left knee.

Crack!

His kneecap shattered on impact, and Dimitri staggered back and flopped onto his ass. His gun slipped from his hand and tumbled away, and he clutched his knee and screamed curses.

"You bitch!" he yelled. "You broke my fucking knee!"

I tossed away one of the tire irons and dropped to my own knees, straddling Dimitri. He tried to fight back, so

I grabbed his ear and slammed his skull against the concrete floor, stunning him. His toupee slipped off his head.

But I had to give him credit. He blinked away his daze and raised his fists to punch at me again. So I laid the tire iron across his throat, putting my weight behind it, cutting off his air. Dimitri's dark eyes bulged, and his face turned beet-red, but he didn't dare try to hit me again. He knew how easily I could crush his windpipe.

"Start talking," I hissed. "What is Deirdre up to with Santos? Where are they going? How is Finnegan Lane involved?"

Dimitri glared up at me, a mulish expression on his face.

I eased the pressure on the tire iron, even as I dropped one hand down to my side. I reached for my Ice magic, creating a dagger, then stabbed him in the thigh with it.

Dimitri screamed, and I yanked the dagger right back out again, making him scream even louder.

"Do you want to start talking now? Or should I make you my own personal pincushion?"

"I—I don't know!" he screamed. "I don't know what she's up to! I swear!"

I scraped the cold, bloody dagger down his cheek, making him shudder. "So what *do* you know? What is she doing with Santos? What kind of uniform was he wearing?"

"It's—it's a security guard uniform!" Dimitri sputtered. "I import them for lots of businesses! That's one of the reasons they came to me for supplies!"

"Which businesses? What was the name on his uniform?"

"I don't know! It's just a generic uniform! I never saw what name Santos had put on it or any of the others!"

I stopped, the Ice dagger right next to Dimitri's left eye. "Others? How many uniforms did you give him?"

His eyes flicked to the dagger, so I bore down with it, digging the cold tip into his face, deep enough to draw blood.

"How many uniforms did you give him?" I asked again.

"A—about a dozen!"

"And what businesses employ guards with those kinds of uniforms?"

"Some jewelry stores, museums, the Posh boutique, all the downtown banks . . ."

Dimitri kept rattling off businesses, but he'd already said the magic word: *museums.*

As in Briartop.

I cursed. Deirdre was planning to rob her own jewelry exhibit, just like I'd thought. Of course she'd had an ulterior motive for getting all those gems in one place. But I still didn't understand how she thought she was going to pull it off. Even if she had a dozen men, including Santos, there were twice as many museum guards, along with at least a couple of cops. The only thing the thieves were going to get was dead. Not that I had a problem with that, but it was such a big, stupid risk to take.

According to Silvio, Deirdre was skimming millions from her charity foundation. So why would she need to steal the jewelry? Sure, it was a big enough payday to tempt anyone, but everyone knew that Deirdre was the driving force behind the exhibit. Why make enemies out of all the people who'd donated their jewelry? Folks in

Ashland had long memories and enough cash and connections to hunt her down and make her pay for stealing from them. And I still didn't see how Finn fit in with all of this. Something else was going on here. Something I just didn't see yet.

Dimitri's hand crept across the concrete, his fingers inching toward the tire iron that I'd dropped earlier. I snapped up my Ice dagger and drove it all the way through his hand. He screamed, but I pressed the tire iron against his throat again. He swallowed down his screams, although tears streamed out of the corners of his eyes.

"Tell me about Briartop. When exactly are Santos and his crew planning to hit the museum?"

His eyes twitched, and his tongue swiped across his lips in a nervous gesture. "I—I didn't say anything about Briartop. They don't use those uniforms there."

I shook my head. "I hate it when people lie to me, Dimitri. Makes me want to stab them. But since I've already done that to you, I guess I'll just have to settle for this instead."

I sent out a small burst of magic and shattered the Ice dagger still in his hand, making him scream again. But Dimitri was tougher than I'd given him credit for, because he surged up, grabbed the tire iron against his throat, and tried to wrest it away from me. Fool.

I thought about questioning him some more, but that would take precious time. It was enough that I knew where Deirdre was headed, so I decided to put Dimitri out of my misery. He didn't even manage to get a good grip on the tire iron before I had formed another Ice dagger and rammed it into his throat.

The mobster fell back, his blood sluicing across the floor and mixing in with the greasy strands of his black toupee. He let out a few wheezing breaths before his head lolled to the side and he was still.

Silvio would have been proud of me. I'd finally scratched one enemy off my to-do list.

Deirdre Shaw was next.

Once I was sure Dimitri was dead, I rifled through his pockets, taking his car keys and all the cash in his wallet. I would have used his phone to call my friends and tell them what was happening, but it required a PIN code, so I tossed it aside.

All the while, I kept glancing at the warehouse door, expecting men to come running inside, guns drawn. But no one appeared, and I didn't hear anything but a faint, steady rush that indicated I was somewhere near the water. Either no one else was around or they hadn't heard the gunshots. I checked the time on Dimitri's fancy gold watch. Just after nine on this Saturday morning.

After I searched Dimitri, I patted down the dead guards, looking for a phone I could use. But all their phones were locked the same way their boss's had been, rendering them useless. I growled, got up, and stalked through the warehouse, peering past the crates and boxes, hoping to see a landline phone sticking out from the wall.

I didn't find one, but I found something even more interesting: an office.

It was a twenty-five-foot-square space in the back corner of the warehouse. I used my Stone magic to harden my hand, then punched my fist through the glass in the door, threw the lock open, and stepped inside.

According to the brass nameplate on the door, this was Dimitri's office, but it looked more like a thief's lair. Photos, blueprints, and security specs had been tacked up to the walls, along with lists of names and times. My eyes narrowed. Those looked like guard rosters and rotations.

This . . . this was where Santos had planned the Briartop heist, and quite thoroughly from the looks of it. But I didn't have time to be impressed by the giant's planning. Not if I wanted to stop the robbery.

So I went over to the desk in the center of the room and started opening drawers . . . where I found yet more photos, blueprints, and lists. Unlike the other pages that were haphazardly taped to the walls, all this information was neatly filed away, as though someone had wanted it kept separate from everything else.

I frowned. Why weren't these pages up on the walls with the rest of the museum schematics? It seemed like there was more information stuffed in the desk than anywhere else in the office. Of course, Santos would have been thorough with such an ambitious heist, but the more drawers I opened, and the more information I spotted, the more my worry increased.

Something was wrong here.

But I didn't have time to puzzle out what it was, so I kept rifling through the desk, searching for a phone. There was no landline, but I was hoping that I might find a spare burner phone somewhere, one without a stupid PIN code already programmed into it.

I found a phone, all right—mine. Along with all five

of my knives, just tossed into a drawer like they were a pile of paper clips. Jackpot.

I slid the weapons into their usual slots, then powered on my phone, turned around, and took several photos of the blueprints to prove to Finn that Deirdre had been lying all along—

"Boss! Are you all right?" A loud voice boomed through the warehouse.

I stuck my phone into my back pocket, palmed a knife, and slipped out of the office. Several crates separated this area from the rest of the warehouse, so I sprinted over to the end of the row and peered around the last one.

A guy was standing over Dimitri's body, his mouth gaping open, a gun in his hand. "Oh, no, no, no, no . . ." he babbled, even as he dug his own phone out of his pocket to call in the rest of the crew. Soon the warehouse would be crawling with goons.

Time to leave.

I glanced around and spotted a door fifty feet past the office. It was directly in the guy's line of sight, but it was the quickest way out of here. So I pushed away from the crates and sprinted in that direction.

"Hey! Hey, you! Stop right there!" I heard him shout.

Crack! Crack! Crack!

The guy fired off a few shots, but his aim was lousy, and the bullets all went wide.

"Hey! Stop!"

I put on another burst of speed, slammed my shoulder into the door, and raced out into the bright morning sunlight.

22

A few more bullets *ping-ping-ping*ed off the closing door behind me, but I ignored them and glanced around, scanning my surroundings.

The warehouse was in the center of a large shipping yard. Rusty red, orange, and yellow metal containers were stacked everywhere, like oversized Legos. Cranes and other heavy machinery towered over the containers, and the air smelled of oil, exhaust, and fish. In the distance, the sun glinted off the Aneirin River, making the surface sparkle like the diamonds Deirdre was planning to steal.

More shouts rose in the warehouse, but instead of plunging into the container maze, I turned right and jogged around the corner of the building. I yanked Dimitri's keys out of my pocket and started hitting the unlock button. His car had to be around here somewhere—

Beep-beep.

Headlights flashed on a black Range Rover sticking out between two containers at the opposite end of the warehouse. I sprinted in that direction, yanked open the door, and threw myself inside.

"Hey! There she is! Get her!"

More shouts sounded, and men started pouring out of the warehouse, all of them carrying guns and running toward the SUV. Dimitri's crew had given chase faster than I'd expected.

I jammed the key into the ignition, cranked the engine, and stomped down on the gas. The Range Rover lunged out of its makeshift parking space, but instead of wrenching the wheel and turning the vehicle away from the men, I steered straight at them.

Crack! Crack! Crack!

Bullets *ping-ping-ping*ed against the front grille, and one punched into the windshield. I gave the engine even more gas, and the vehicle lurched forward. Dimitri's crew finally realized that I wasn't going to stop, and they all trampled one another, trying to get out of my way. One guy wasn't as fast as his friends, and he screamed as I mowed him down. He disappeared below the grille, and the tires *whomp-whomp*ed over him.

I grinned and kept going.

Shouts rose behind me again, and a few more gunshots rang out, but I had my eye on the prize: the open gate several hundred feet away at the end of the shipping yard.

I hit the gas again, zooming through the gate before the giant sitting in the guard shack could do anything more than gape in surprise, much less reach for his gun. Tires squealing, I made a hard right onto the road, leaving the warehouse and the shipping yard in my rearview mirror.

I drove fast for three miles, getting away from the shipping yard as quickly as possible. When I was sure that none of Dimitri's men was going to give chase, I slowed down, yanked my phone out of my pocket, and checked the time. Nine twenty-seven. My escape had taken longer than I'd hoped. I didn't know exactly what time Deirdre and Santos had left the warehouse, but they had at least a thirty-minute head start, if not more. But I knew where they were going—Briartop—so I headed in that direction. All I could do was hope I'd catch up to them in time.

While I drove, I checked my voice mail—two messages, one from Silvio and one from Owen. Silvio sounded especially worried, and he told me to call him back immediately. He also finally had some news on Deirdre: *She's broke. Combine her insane spending habits with some bad investments, and she's lost almost all her charity foundation's capital in the last year. We're talking tens of millions just gone up in smoke. Whoever fronted her that money has to be pissed. She's playing a shell game with what money she has left, just trying to stay afloat.*

Well, that explained why she was planning to rob her own exhibit. She desperately needed to pay back her investors, whoever they were.

And why has your phone been off all night? Silvio snapped at the end of the message, his voice a bit surly. *You know I can't locate you when it's turned off.*

I snorted. Sometimes Silvio made me feel like a way-ward puppy that kept escaping from the yard. He should just put a GPS chip in my shoulder and be done with it. I wouldn't have minded him tracking me to the ware-house and getting some help from him and our friends this morning.

Instead of dialing Silvio, I called Finn first, hoping I wasn't too late to warn him.

Hello, ladies and gentlemen. You have reached the al-luring, amazing, and all-around awe-inspiring Finnegan Lane. Leave a message . . .

His phone went straight to voice mail. Deirdre and Santos had made good use of their head start. Whatever their plan was, it was going down right now.

"Finn," I growled after his phone beeped. "Your ice-queen bitch of a mother kidnapped me last night. She's planning to rob her own exhibit at the Briartop museum. Whatever she tells you, *do not trust her.* Call me back the second you get this."

I hung up and tried him again, but it went straight to voice mail, same as before. Frustrated, I called Owen, but his phone was off too. I cursed, but then I remembered that he'd promised his sister, Eva, that the two of them would spend some time together today. I left him a mes-sage, told him what was going on, and promised that I would call him back when I had more info or Deirdre was dead, whichever came first. I was hoping for the second option.

Third, I tried Bria, and finally—*finally*—someone an-swered me.

"Detective Coolidge," she said in a cold, clipped voice.

"It's Gin. Where are you? Deirdre is going to try to rob the Briartop exhibit. Rodrigo Santos, the bank robber, is working with her. You have to get some cops over there to stop them."

Silence.

"Bria? Bria, are you there?" I asked, wondering if my phone had cut out.

"I'm here." She sighed. "But I'm afraid it's too late. Someone's already tried to rob the museum. I'm here at Briartop right now, dealing with the aftermath."

I cursed. "I'm on my way."

We hung up, but I wasn't really on my way since Dimitri's SUV ran out of gas about five miles from the museum.

"You have got to be kidding me," I muttered.

I'd been in a hurry at the shipping yard, so I hadn't paid any attention to the gas gauge. Besides, what kind of idiot let his gas get that low? Dimitri Barkov, that's who. If the mobster had been here, I would have killed him all over again.

The red light on the dash kept blinking and blinking. The Range Rover sputtered up another hill, then died completely.

"Dammit!" I snarled, and slapped my hands against the steering wheel.

There was nothing else to do but get out of the vehicle and start hoofing it toward the museum. I pulled out my phone and dialed Silvio, hoping that he might be able to pick me up, but the call went straight to voice mail. Weird. I didn't think I'd *ever* gotten his voice mail before. Maybe he was busy talking to someone else. I left him a message.

I thought about calling Bria again, but she was probably too busy to leave the museum, so I trudged on. I'd only gone about a quarter-mile when I crested another hill and spotted a familiar sign: *Blue Ridge Cemetery*.

I stopped on the side of the road, remembering my last trip to the cemetery. It had been more than a week now, but I wondered if the van was still there. Not likely, but it was the best option I had right now.

So I picked up my pace, jogging around a sharp curve, and there it was, an old, battered white van sitting on the side of the road, right where the grave-robbing Don and Ethel had left it. The vehicle looked untouched, and even that white plastic trash bag was still stuck in the driver's-side window, fluttering like a trapped butterfly. I supposed the van had looked too much like a junker for anyone to bother messing with it.

I grinned. "No good deed."

The van had a full tank of gas, but it was still after ten by the time I reached Briartop.

It looked like every cop in Ashland was at the museum. Blue and white lights flashed on more than a dozen patrol cars on this side of the covered bridge, with even more cars over on the island and clustered around the museum itself. Uniformed officers and suited detectives swarmed over everything, talking and texting on their phones or calling out to one another through their walkie-talkies.

I parked the van behind one of the patrol cars. My black clothes hid most of the blood that had soaked into them from the warehouse fight, but my face was a bruised, blood-caked mess. I couldn't exactly waltz over to the museum looking like this, so I started rustling around in the van, looking for supplies.

The grave robbers had stuffed a variety of junk into the door pockets, including a bottle of water, which I poured over an old white undershirt. It wasn't much of a wash-cloth, but it scrubbed the blood off my face. I couldn't do anything about the goose egg, but this was as respectable as I was going to look, so I got out of the van and headed for the covered bridge.

A cop who barely looked old enough to shave stepped in front of me. "Sorry, ma'am, but you can't be here. This is an active crime scene."

I had opened my mouth to make up some excuse to try to get past him when heavy footsteps sounded, and Xavier stepped out of the bridge opening.

"She's with me," he called out. "Let her through, Larry."

Larry gave me a suspicious look, but I just smiled sweetly at him, and he reluctantly stepped aside. It was good to have friends.

"Here," Xavier said, passing me a pair of black crime-scene gloves. "Put these on, and try to look official. Bria's up at the museum. She asked me to come down here and keep an eye out for you."

I did as he asked, and the giant led me through the covered bridge, up the hill, and into the museum. Cops looked at us, wondering why I was here, but Xavier nod-ded at them, and no one stopped us from entering the main exhibit space.

The rotunda was a disaster. It looked like a bomb had exploded, blowing blood, glass, bullets, and bodies everywhere. Men dressed in khakis and cheap gray suit jackets were sprawled across the marble floor, guns lying next to them and blood pooled underneath their bodies from where they had been shot so many times. Bullets had smashed through and shattered the glass cases housing the jewelry, and the resulting shards glinted like diamonds underfoot, mixed in with the brass bullet casings. More holes blackened the walls, and I could hear the marble whimpering about all the violence that had occurred here today.

Bria broke away from a cluster of cops and came over to Xavier and me. She hugged me tight before pulling back and giving me a quick once-over, eyeing the knot on my head.

"Are you okay?" she asked.

"I'm fine. Just a little banged up. What happened?"

Bria pointed at the dead men on the floor. "These guys walked in here as soon as the museum opened at nine o'clock this morning, pulled out guns, and started shooting. But given the amount of jewels, the museum's guards and the cops on duty were already on high alert. They took cover and returned fire. All the robbers were killed, and only one of our guys was hit in return. Shoulder wound. He's with an Air elemental healer, and he's going to be fine."

I frowned. From the way Deirdre had talked and the obvious planning that Santos had put into this, I would have thought the robbery would have been successful. Or at least not such a total, epic failure.

"I don't know what these guys were thinking." Xavier shook his head. "They never had a chance."

He was right. All the robbers' bodies were clustered at the front of the rotunda. They hadn't gotten twenty feet into the room before they were all killed. Maybe Deirdre and Santos hadn't been as smart as I'd thought.

One of the cops called out to Bria and Xavier, and they went over to see what she wanted. I looked over the dead men on the floor, expecting to see Santos's mug somewhere in the mess of bodies, his face frozen in pain and death.

But he wasn't here.

I frowned and walked closer to the bodies, going around the pile of them and staring at each robber's face in turn, but none of them was Santos. I hadn't expected Deirdre to be here, to do the dirty work of actually robbing the museum herself, but this was Santos's gig, his crew, his plan. He should have been here, leading the charge. So where was he? Had he managed to escape from the museum?

No. The cops would have checked the security footage to make sure that none of the robbers had escaped. Even if Santos had gotten away, they would have been combing the surrounding area for him, not camped out here at the museum collecting evidence.

And then I noticed something else missing: the jewelry.

Many of the exhibit cases had been shattered by the flying bullets, but no jewelry littered the rotunda, and I didn't see so much as a single diamond knocked loose from its setting, glittering on the floor. And all the cases that were still intact were also empty. No rings, no bracelets, no necklaces. All the jewelry was gone. The cops must have removed it and taken it to the museum's shiny new vault for safekeeping.

I stared out over the blood, bodies, and destruction, turning things over and over in my mind. The longer I studied the scene, the more cold worry pooled in the pit of my stomach. Deirdre wasn't done yet. She hadn't gone to all this trouble for an unsuccessful heist. And why worm her way back into Finn's life if she'd been planning to hit the museum all along? He didn't have any real connection to the museum. From what I could tell, Finn hadn't been anywhere near Briartop when the robbery attempt had gone down. Bria would have told me if he'd been here.

While I was waiting for Bria and Xavier to finish their conversation with the other cop, I took off my black gloves, pulled out my phone, and called Finn again, but he still didn't answer. Another brick of worry piled onto the growing stack in my stomach.

Something was wrong.

Bria left Xavier and the other cop and walked back over to me.

"Sorry that took so long," she said. "Debbie was telling us that the security company has transported the jewelry to the secondary location."

"Secondary location? Why didn't you guys just leave it here and stick it in the museum's vault?"

Bria shrugged. "Since Clementine Barker managed to crack the museum vault back during the summer, the company insuring the exhibit insisted on it. That in case of a robbery attempt, all the jewelry would immediately be taken to a more secure location for safekeeping. At least until everything could be reassessed and the museum and exhibit reopened. They briefed Xavier, me, and all the detectives on it several times and even did a couple of dry runs."

And just like that, everything made sense.

Deirdre coming back to Ashland, cozying up to Finn, putting the jewelry exhibit together. Part of me marveled at her plan. It was far more clever, devious, and intricate than I'd expected. Fletcher had been right all along. Deirdre Shaw was definitely one of the most dangerous people I'd ever met. Even worse, she'd been absolutely right when she'd mocked me about not seeing the big picture until it was too late.

An icy fist of dread clenched tightly around my heart. "Where's the secondary location? Where did they take the jewelry?" I already knew the answer, but I needed her to confirm it.

"First Trust bank. It's one of the most secure facilities in Ashland." She frowned. "Why do you care so much about where the jewelry went—"

Bria's eyes widened, and her face paled.

"That's Finn's bank."

❋ 23 ❋

"That's Finn's bank," Bria whispered again, her mind stuck on that one terrible, horrifying fact.

I nodded, my mouth set into a grim slash. This had been Deirdre's master plan all along. Santos must have told her that there was no way to heist the jewelry from Briartop, that there were too many guards and too many cops at the museum. So the two of them had sent those men in to die, all with the ulterior motive of getting the jewelry moved somewhere else—somewhere *better*.

Fletcher had a saying: *Why steal one million when you could steal two?* In this case, why just rob the museum when First Trust was a veritable treasure trove of jewelry, cash, and other valuables? But Deirdre had needed an inside man at the bank to make her plan work. Someone high up on the food chain. Someone above suspicion. Someone to squire her around and give her tours and let her into the basement vault so that she could memorize the security setups and pass all that info on to Santos.

Finn was that inside man. He just didn't realize it.

Bria stared at me, putting Deirdre's plan together the same way I had. With one thought, we both bolted out of the rotunda.

Xavier had left to check on something elsewhere in the museum, and I didn't see him among the throngs of cops and guards Bria and I darted past. There was no time to track down the giant and tell him what was going on. Every minute, every second, counted now.

Even though Finn might already be dead.

That icy fist squeezed my heart again, but I forced myself to push the thought away. Finn wasn't dead. He couldn't be.

He just *couldn't* be.

Right before Bria and I reached the front doors of the museum, I grabbed her arm and forced her to slow down to a fast walk.

"Easy," I murmured. "We don't want to attract any unwanted attention. We need to get out of here as quietly as possible."

Bria didn't like it, but she nodded and matched her pace to mine. We skirted around more clusters of cops, and she stabbed her finger to the right toward the parking lots.

"This way," she said. "My car's this way."

"Right behind you."

Still keeping to our fast walk, both of us weaved around the other cops and then ducked under the yellow crime-scene tape that had been strung up around the museum perimeter.

Bria broke free of the crowd, her strides getting shorter and quicker until she was almost running again. She couldn't help herself, and neither could I. The two of us darted around patrol cars with flashing lights and raced over to her sedan. We jumped in, and she cranked the engine and zoomed out of the parking lot. I grabbed my phone and tried Finn again.

No answer.

"How long ago did the security company arrive at the bank with the jewelry?" I asked.

"The armored truck had just pulled up to the bank when I told you," Bria said, glancing at the dashboard clock. "Ten twenty-three now. So maybe five minutes ago?"

I cursed. Santos and his crew had probably already taken down the armored-truck guards, along with those at the bank. The heist was in full swing now.

Bria drove down the hill to the covered bridge. She reached for the switch to flip on her sirens and blue lights, but I grabbed her hand.

"Don't," I said. "Santos might have someone watching the museum to make sure that the cops stay here. I don't think that anyone noticed us hurrying outside, but a car leaving with sirens and flashing lights might tip him off. If Santos and Deirdre realize that we're on to them, they'll grab what they can from the bank, execute Finn and anyone else inside, and leave before we get there. We need to be smart about this. Not go rushing in blindly."

Bria's mouth tightened, but she dropped her hand from the switch. "What do you suggest?"

"Just drive away from the museum at a normal speed. Once we're a couple of miles away, hit the gas. And let me make some calls in the meantime."

Bria nodded, her hands tightening on the steering wheel. "If that bitch has hurt him, if she has mussed so much as one hair on his head, I will strangle her with my bare fucking hands."

"Not if I get to her first," I promised, my voice as dark as hers. "Not if I get to her first."

While Bria drove, I made another round of calls. I finally got through to Silvio, who'd been talking to someone, digging up more dirt on Deirdre. I told him what was going on, where I wanted him to meet us, and, most important, what I needed him to bring me.

I'd just hung up with the vampire when Owen called. I told him the same things I'd told Silvio, and he promised to meet us ASAP.

I debated calling Jo-Jo and Sophia, but I decided not to. If Deirdre and Santos were holed up in the bank, then stealth was the best option—the *only* option. The more people I brought in to help Bria and me, the more chance there was for one of us to be spotted before we rescued Finn.

Bria drove to the downtown loop in record time. Most of the office buildings and skyscrapers were closed on the weekend, with their corporate drones safely ensconced in the suburbs, so the area was largely a ghost town. First Trust of Ashland was also closed, making it the perfect time for Deirdre, Santos, and their crew to rob the bank. Since it was Saturday morning, they could take as long as they needed to crack the cash cages behind the tellers' counter in the lobby, along with Big Bertha, the basement vault where the real payday was. The thieves could easily make off with hundreds of millions in cash, jewels, and more. At one fell swoop, Deirdre could pay back her investors, shore up her charity foundation, and have plenty left over for her champagne bubble baths. Once again, I had to admire the cleverness of her plan.

"How do you want to play this?" Bria asked when we were three blocks away from the bank.

"Drive by the bank at a normal speed. Not too slow. We want it to seem like we're just another car, cruising through downtown on our way to somewhere else."

Bria nodded and made the turn.

The block that housed First Trust was as deserted as all the rest, and I didn't spot so much as a bum digging through trash cans on a side street. What I did see was an armored truck sitting outside the bank entrance. A couple of guys were grabbing boxes from the back of the truck and passing them over to several giants, who were all wearing the gray uniforms of the bank's security guards.

Including Rodrigo Santos.

The giant had his gray cap pulled down low on his forehead and his arms crossed over his chest as he supervised the jewelry exchange, but I still recognized him. My heart sank. If Santos was out here on the sidewalk, acting as the head guard, then that meant he already had control of the bank. I wondered how many guards—legitimate guards—might be inside. Probably a skeleton crew, since it was a Saturday.

Bria cruised past the armored truck. Santos stared at

our car, and I leaned my elbow up in the window, hiding my face from him. The light at the end of the block winked to red, and Bria made the appropriate stop. She looked in the rearview mirror, while I did the same in the passenger's-side one.

The armored-truck guards finished handing over the boxes of jewelry, then closed the back doors on their truck, got inside, and pulled away from the curb. Santos watched the truck drive off, then went into the bank with the rest of his crew, leaving one man outside to stand guard. Santos might have control of the bank, but he wasn't taking any chances, and storming in through the front was out. That would only end up getting Finn and every other innocent person inside killed.

"Now where to?" Bria muttered as the light turned green.

"Go around the block. There's a garage on the back side of the bank. Drive in there, and park on the top level."

Bria did as I asked. Three minutes later, we were in the garage, which was as deserted as the rest of downtown.

She killed the engine, then looked at me. "Now what?"

"What was the protocol for transferring the jewelry? How was it supposed to work? How many guards were supposed to be at the bank? Lay it all out for me."

Bria drew in a breath. "An armored truck with three guards was supposed to drive the jewelry from the museum to the bank and unload it out front, just like we saw. The bank was supposed to have at least half a dozen guards waiting inside to take the jewelry from the lobby down to the basement vault."

She bit her lip. "Finn was supposed to be at the bank

too, running point on everything. He wanted to be sure that nothing went wrong with Deirdre's exhibit. Or if it did, that at least the jewelry would be secure in the vault."

Another reason Deirdre had needed him, so he could let her into the bank this morning.

"So he's in there," I said. "Along with at least six other innocent people."

If Deirdre hasn't killed them all yet.

I didn't have to say the words. The worry pinching Bria's face told me that she was thinking the same thing. Deirdre wouldn't leave any witnesses behind. She would execute every single person in the bank, including Finn.

"Yeah. So how are we going to get everyone out?" She pulled her phone out of her jacket pocket. "I could call in a SWAT team. They could be here in twenty minutes."

"And Finn and everyone else inside would be dead a minute after that." I shook my head. "You can't call it in; you can't call for any backup at all. Deirdre's probably paid someone in the police department to tip her off at the first hint of trouble. When that happens, either she'll kill everyone outright or use them as hostages to make her escape. Either way, they'll still end up dead. We have to do this ourselves. Are you up for that?"

"You'd better damn well believe it. I want to kick that woman's ass for what she's put Finn through." A faint smile curved her lips. "And for making me call her Mama Dee."

"You got it, sister."

I held out my fist, and Bria bumped me back before her expression turned serious again. "I've got a few supplies in the trunk but not enough for us to take out all the thieves. Even if I did have enough supplies, I don't know how we'd even get into the bank."

"Leave that to me. There was a reason I wanted you to come here."

Her eyes narrowed. "You know how to break into the bank."

I grinned. "Among other things. Let's go. We don't have any time to waste."

❋ 24 ❋

Bria popped the trunk and opened the cases inside, revealing enough guns and ammo to outfit several commandos, along with knives, flares, binoculars, and a couple of black vests lined with silverstone like the one I still wore.

I let out a low whistle. "Nice arsenal."

She shrugged. "It pays to be prepared in this town."

Bria shrugged out of her jacket and zipped a silverstone vest over her chest before stuffing extra guns and ammo into all the vest pockets. I added some extra knives to my usual arsenal. I also grabbed a tin of Jo-Jo's healing ointment and smeared it all over the goose egg and the cut on my head. The dwarf's Air magic pricked my skin, scabbing over the cut, smoothing out the swelling, and easing the ache in my face. The knot and the cut weren't completely healed, but it was better than nothing.

We'd just finished gearing up when Silvio pulled his car into the garage, Owen right behind him in his own vehicle. The two of them hurried over, each carrying a black duffel bag.

Owen dropped his bag, then cupped my cheek, his violet gaze steady on my gray one. "How can I help?"

I reached up and squeezed his hand. "Thank you for coming." I paused. "Especially since I know how much you still want to punch Finn."

He made a face, then gave me a crooked grin. "Yeah, but he's family. I'll punch him after we rescue him."

"Deal." I turned to Silvio. "Did you bring it?"

The vampire huffed and gestured at the bag at his feet. "Of course I brought it. What kind of assistant would I be if I didn't? Although I don't see how it's going to help you get inside the bank. I drove by the entrance. I saw the guard stationed out front."

"We're not going in through the front."

I crouched down, opened the bag, and pulled out a large crossbow, a long length of rope, a couple of metal handles, and a silverstone grappling hook strong enough to shoot through a stone wall. Silvio, Owen, and Bria watched in silence while I assembled everything.

Owen frowned. "Is that a zipline? What are you going to do with a zipline?"

Silvio crossed his arms over his chest. "My question exactly."

I checked to make sure the equipment was in order. "Remember back during the summer, when Finn, Owen, and I were playing that war game, and the two of them bet me that I couldn't mock-kill both of them?"

"Finn bet you." Owen held up his hands. "I was just an innocent bystander."

"Uh-huh. Keep telling yourself that. Anyway, one of the places that I scouted out to kill Finn was at the bank."

"But you didn't kill us at the bank. You killed us at my office," Owen said. "Quite easily, from what I remember."

"That's because your office wasn't nearly as secure as the bank. But no matter how locked down a building is, there's always a way in."

"You cracked the bank's security setup," Silvio said.

"Yep. It took a while, but I managed it." I got to my feet, hoisted the crossbow onto my shoulder, and looked at my sister. "You ready to have a little fun?"

Bria sighed. "I'm not going to like this, am I?"

I grinned. "Only if you're afraid of heights."

It turned out that Bria was, in fact, not the biggest fan of heights. But when I explained my plan, she sighed again and nodded. Owen and Silvio didn't much like my plan either, since it left them waiting outside while Bria and I went into the bank, but I needed my sister's Ice magic to help me get down to the lobby and then to the basement vault. That's where Deirdre and Santos would be—along with Finn. Besides, Owen and Silvio had their own parts to play.

Five minutes later, I was standing on the roof of the parking garage with Bria, Owen, and Silvio. The garage was one story taller than First Trust, giving us a clear view of the bank's roof, including an access door with stairs leading down into the bank itself.

First Trust took up its own block, and a fifty-foot-wide alley separated the parking garage from the back of the bank. The main entrance might be guarded, but no one was on the roof yet, something that I was going to take advantage of.

I peered through the scope attached to the top of the crossbow, lining up my shot, then gently squeezed the trigger. The hook shot out from the bow and sailed over and across the alley, taking the rope along with it.

Thunk!

The hook punched into the stone wall right next to the access door. I unhooked the rest of the line from the crossbow, wrapped it around one of the parking garage's columns, and yanked on it several times, making sure that it was securely anchored on both ends. Then I clipped two metal handles to the line—one for me and one for Bria.

"You're up, baby sister."

Bria nodded, took hold of the handle, and stepped up onto the roof ledge. The wind whistled over her, making her blond ponytail flap around her head. She shivered, and not because of the chill in the air.

"You don't have to do anything," I said, trying to reassure her. "Just let your weight carry you down the zipline. When you get over the bank roof, let go, drop, and roll. Easy as peach pie."

"Easy. Right," she said in a faint voice, peering down at the eight-story drop.

"It'll be over with before you know it."

Even though her face was pale, Bria nodded and gripped the handle a little tighter. "The things we do for love," she muttered.

"Better watch out," I teased. "That's rapidly becoming your new motto."

"Well, let's just hope that Finn is still alive to appreciate all my sacrifices."

As soon as the words left her mouth, she winced, and we both fell silent, hoping that Finn was indeed still alive. I wouldn't let myself think about the alternative—I *couldn't*.

"Here goes nothing," Bria whispered.

Before she could think about it anymore, she pushed off the ledge. Gravity immediately pulled her down, and she sailed down the zipline with barely a whisper of sound. As soon as she was over the bank roof, she let go of the handle, dropped down, and rolled to a stop. She lay sprawled facedown on the roof for several seconds, then slowly got back up onto her feet. Even though she was wobbling from all the adrenaline rushing through her body, Bria gave me a shaky thumbs-up and pulled out one of her guns, screwing a silencer onto the end of the barrel.

I gave the zipline several more hard yanks, making sure that it was still secure. Silvio was peering over the side of the ledge, his face as pale as Bria's had been, but Owen stepped up, pulled me into his arms, and kissed me.

We broke apart, both breathless, staring into each other's eyes.

"Don't you dare die before Silvio and I get into the bank," he whispered.

I grinned. "Never."

I kissed him again, then got onto the ledge and took hold of the second handle. On the opposite roof, Bria waved her hand, urging me to hurry.

"And away we go," I whispered, and pushed off from the ledge.

For a moment, I had the freeing, utterly weightless sensation of being suspended in midair. Then gravity took over, dragging me down the way it always did. The wind whipped around my face, making my ponytail slap against my shoulders, and I had the sudden urge to laugh. Despite the situation, despite the danger Finn was in, despite the fact that I could fall to my death, this was still *fun*.

Three seconds later, I was over the bank roof. I softened my knees, let go of the handle, and rolled to a stop, coming up into a low crouch.

Bria helped me to my feet. "Are you okay?"

"Yep. You?"

"I'm fine." Her stomach rumbled ominously. "Except for a sudden urge to throw up."

"Don't worry. It'll pass."

I went over, pressed my hand against the wall where the grappling hook was, and used my Stone magic to crack the hook out of the wall. Then I took the hook and the attached zipline, walked over to the edge of the roof, and dropped the whole thing over the side. I gave Silvio a thumbs-up, and he started hauling in the zipline and hook.

It didn't take long, and he signaled me when he was done. Then he and Owen disappeared from view to get into position in front of the bank. They were going to park down the street in Silvio's car and monitor things from there until I needed them for phase two of my plan. I didn't want to make it down to the bank lobby only to find that Deirdre had brought in more reinforcements through the front door.

But first, Bria and I had to get through the door in front of us.

Most people didn't bother to secure the doors and windows above the first two floors of their homes and offices, but Stuart Mosley and the other folks at First Trust were far more cautious than most. They had to be, given all the millions in cash, jewelry, bonds, and more stored inside. Normally, the two security cameras mounted over the access door would have been swiveling around in constant circles, covering every single part of the roof, and a faint hum would have been emanating from the door itself, since it was electrified.

But the cameras were frozen in place, with no red lights flashing on them, and the only sound was the wind continually gusting across the roof. So I made a ball of slushy Ice and threw it at the door. When no sparks flew, I went over to the door and peered at the high-end lock embedded in the metal. I also rattled the knob, just in case someone had left it unlocked, but of course, my luck could never be that good.

"Um, Gin?" Bria asked. "Do you see those security cameras pointed right at you?"

"Yep."

She frowned. "And you're not worried that Deirdre's spotted us already on the feed?"

"If you were taking over a bank and planning to pick it clean, what's the first thing you would do after you got inside?"

She thought about it. "Disable the security system and erase all the footage."

I shot my thumb and forefinger at her. "Bingo. Deirdre doesn't want any record that she was ever here, and she doesn't want to accidentally trip any alarms getting into the cash cages or the basement vault. That's why the cameras are down, along with the rest of the security system. She doesn't realize it, but she's made it a whole lot easier for us to get inside."

I looked at the lock again. I didn't want to waste precious time picking it, so I reached for my Ice magic, ready to freeze and shatter the lock—

And that's when the dead bolt clicked free, and the door started opening.

Bria dashed around the corner and out of sight, but I didn't have time to do that, so I ended up darting behind the door and hoping that whoever was opening it wouldn't think to look behind it.

A giant dressed in a gray bank guard's uniform strode through the door and took several steps out onto the roof. I held my hands up, catching the door before it slammed into my face, then peered around the edge of it. The guard looked around, his hand dropping to his black leather utility belt, as if he were going for the gun holstered there. I palmed a knife and tensed, ready to move. But instead of reaching for his weapon, the giant grabbed the walkie-talkie off his belt, hit a button on the side, and brought the device up to his lips.

"The roof is secure. You want me to hang out up here or come back down and help the other guys with the cash cages while you work on the vault?" the guy asked, then let go of the button and waited for a response.

Static crackled out of the walkie-talkie. "I've got the vault covered, and Ralph and the others are cutting through the cages right now. Stay up there. I don't want anyone trying to get in here from any angle, not even the roof."

That was Santos's voice. So he had men working in the lobby, but he was down in the basement vault. That's where Deirdre would be too, and most likely Finn.

The guy sighed and pressed the button on the walkie-talkie again. "Roger that. Call me when you need me."

"Roger that," Santos replied.

The guy sighed again, louder and deeper, disappointed that he wasn't in on the action down in the lobby. He holstered his walkie-talkie and turned to close the access door behind him.

Right where I was waiting.

His eyes bulged, but he didn't even have time to scream before I stepped up and sliced my knife across his throat. The giant clutched both hands to the vicious wound, trying to put pressure on the gaping hole, even as his legs slid out from under him and he toppled to the ground.

"I'll take that," I said, bending down and plucking the walkie-talkie off his belt.

The guy coughed, but that was the only noise he made as he bled out. I turned the walkie-talkie back on, hoping to hear some chatter from Santos and his crew, but the device remained silent. They were probably too busy breaking into the vault and the cash cages to talk right now. Good. That meant that no one would miss this guard for several minutes, if not longer. I turned off the walkie and slid it into one of the pockets on my vest.

Bria stepped out from behind the corner, gun in hand. "What now?"

"Now we go down into the belly of the beast." I held my hand out, gesturing at the dark corridor that led into the bank. "Ladies first."

She nodded, raised her weapon, and stepped through the door into the shadows.

Bloody knife in hand, I followed her.

We were in.

✢ 25 ✢

First Trust bank was housed in an old prewar building, so it wasn't nearly as tall as the modern skyscrapers that made up the downtown skyline. But it took up the entire block, which meant that there was a lot of ground to cover.

The fire stairs were wide enough for Bria and me to creep down side by side. I stopped at every floor, but the doors were all locked, and I didn't hear any movements on the other sides, much less see anyone through the narrow strips of glass in the doors. No one was working up here in the offices, and Santos hadn't bothered to station any guards on the higher floors. Excellent.

Bria and I quietly went down the stairs to the second floor. Once we were on the landing there, I leaned over the side of the railing and peered down. Sure enough, a guard was stationed in the stairwell on the first floor, leaning against the open door, thumbing through screens on his phone, totally bored by his assignment.

I motioned to Bria to draw back, then made two Ice picks and unlocked the door on the second-floor landing. I winced at the *snick* of the door opening, and Bria and I scooted through to the other side and eased the door shut behind us. We flattened ourselves against the wall, out of sight of the strip of glass in the door, and waited, but the guard didn't come to investigate.

"We're stuck," Bria said. "We can't get past that guard without letting everyone in the lobby know that we're here."

"Yes, we can. We just have to be a little more creative. This way."

The second floor was mostly offices and cubicles, re-served for some of the investment bankers and their as-sistants or rented out to real-estate and other companies that had extensive dealings with the bank. I stopped a moment, orienting myself, then went over to the opposite side of the building, pushed through a wooden door, and stopped. Bria slipped in behind me and looked around at the urinals, stalls, and sinks.

"Um, Gin?"

"Yeah?"

"What are we doing in the men's bathroom?"

"Making our own elevator shaft."

Bria gave me a strange look, but she followed me to the back corner of the bathroom.

"I spent a lot of time studying the bank's blueprints when I was trying to figure out how to mock-kill Finn here. All the bathrooms are located on this side of the building, stacked right on top of each other, which means that we're directly above the men's bathroom on the first floor," I said. "Someplace that Santos isn't likely to be, since he's down in the basement vault. So we get through the floor here, and we can get down to the lobby. After that, we'll see what's what and go from there."

Bria nodded. "Let's do it."

We both knelt down. The floor was the same beautiful gray marble as in the lobby, but it wasn't nearly as thick and had been cordoned off into three-foot squares fitted together. I reached for my Stone magic, and a cold silver light flared to life on the tip of my right index finger, burning as brightly and steadily as a blow torch. I leaned forward and traced my finger along the marble seams, using my power to crack the stone.

Bria came along right behind me, her finger glowing an intense blue with her own magic, driving her elemental Ice down into the cracks that I'd created and widening them.

We repeated the process over and over, cracking the marble with our combined magic until we were able to hook our fingers down into the broken stone and start lifting out chunks of the floor. We worked quickly and quietly, careful not to crack too much of the marble at once. The last thing we needed was for a piece of stone to fall down, hit the floor below, and make enough noise for someone to come check on things.

It took us the better part of fifteen minutes to make a jagged hole that was big enough for us to drop through. I went first, with Bria behind me. We landed on the bathroom floor below, raised our weapons, and waited, wondering if anyone had heard or sensed our magical jackhammers, but a minute passed, then two, then three, and no one came to investigate.

I had taken a step toward the bathroom door when a smear of red on the floor caught my eye. I stopped and pointed to the stain, which was in front of the largest stall door. Bria nodded and raised her gun. I tiptoed forward and opened the stall door.

A giant was inside, his knees tucked up under his body and his arm flung over the toilet as though he were about to puke. The pose was so natural that for a second, I thought he was actually alive. Then I noticed his empty, sightless gaze and the black hole in his forehead still oozing blood. Given his gray uniform, he must have been one of the real guards, killed when Santos and his crew had taken over the bank.

Bria tiptoed forward and eased open the next stall door, then the one after that and the one after that. Bodies filled all of them, stacked on top of one another like rolls of toilet paper. There were six in total, all dressed in guard uniforms.

Santos must have eliminated the real guards first thing, so none of them would make any trouble or trip a silent alarm while the heist went down. Then he'd replaced them with his own crew, dressed in the uniforms that Dimitri had gotten them, so the folks from the armored-truck company wouldn't know the difference as they handed over all the exhibit jewelry. Smart. And brutal.

There was nothing I could do for the dead guards. I just hoped that Finn hadn't met the same fate, but I shoved the cold worry down into the bottom of my heart. I wouldn't think like that. I couldn't let myself think like that. Otherwise, I wouldn't be able to do what needed to be done now.

Killing Santos, Deirdre, and every other person who stood between us and Finn.

Bria pressed her lips together in a tight line, as disgusted by the slaughter as I was. She nodded at me, and together we crept over to the bathroom door, which I cracked open. The bathroom was on the far right side of the bank, down a hallway that opened into the lobby. Faint sounds drifted over to me, but I didn't see anyone, and I slipped out of the bathroom and crept down the hallway, with Bria right behind me.

The sounds grew louder the closer we got to the end of the hallway. Men shouting back and forth. The steady whine of a power saw. The hissing of a welding torch.

I reached the end of the hallway, dropped into a crouch, and peered around the corner, Bria hunkered down right beside me. Six men, all dressed in guard uniforms, stood in the bank lobby. One of the men was stationed at the fire stairs, same as before, while the other five were behind the tellers' counter.

A second man was using a power saw to cut through the silverstone bars that covered one of the cash cages, while a third guy was doing the same with a welding torch on another cage. The third and final cage was already open, and three men were moving in and out of it, hauling out shrink-wrapped bricks of cash and stuffing them into black duffel bags sitting on the tellers' counter.

The cash was a great score all on its own, easily millions of dollars. But none of the men was Santos, which meant that he was downstairs in the basement vault, just as I'd suspected.

I memorized the guards' positions and the distances

between them, adjusting my plan. Then I nodded at Bria, and we slipped down the hallway and back into the bathroom.

I raised my cell phone. "Time to call in our distraction."

I hit a number on the speed dial, and Owen picked up on the first ring. "Update?" he asked in a tense voice.

"Bria and I are in the first-floor bathroom, watching some guys cut their way into the cash cages. No Santos, no Deirdre, and no Finn in the lobby, which means they must be down in the basement vault. Here's what I need you guys to do."

Owen put me on speaker so he and Silvio could both listen to me. They agreed to my plan, although Silvio insisted that we all synchronize our watches so that we would be in perfect time. I rolled my eyes, but he had a point, and I set my watch to match his. So did Bria.

Once that was done, I put my phone away, grabbed the walkie-talkie I'd taken from the roof guard, and turned it on. But the thieves were all busy, and nothing but static sounded, so I clicked off the walkie and left it on the sink.

Bria and I slipped out of the bathroom and back into the hallway. The thieves were still in the same positions as before, with one man by the stairs and the other five working on the cash cages.

I checked my watch. "In five, four, three, two, one . . ."

An emphatic knock sounded, hard enough to rattle the glass in the front doors. "Hey! You in there! I need to make a deposit! Immediately!"

Silvio's voice boomed through the lobby, and the vampire himself was cupping a hand around his eyes and peering in through the glass. A briefcase dangled from his other hand.

The giant guard who was stationed outside the bank stepped up beside him. "Sir, I already told you that you need to leave—*now*. The bank isn't open."

"Not open? Not open? I can see exactly how open you are! Look at all those guys inside!" Silvio pointed in through the glass, then whipped around to the outside guard. "Surely one of them can take my deposit. I *demand* to be let in right this very *second*. Do you know who I am? *I* am a very important person who works for an even *more* important person."

His voice got louder and higher with every word, drawing the attention of all the robbers inside the bank. Even the guys with the power saw and the welding torch cranked down their tools to lower settings, raised their masks, and stared at him.

"My boss knows your boss. So I suggest that you let me inside, buddy. Right now." Silvio stabbed his finger into the other man's chest. "Or the only thing you'll be guarding is a school crosswalk. And that's if you're lucky."

I glanced at Bria, who was grinning as widely as I was. Who knew that Silvio could do self-important pain-in-the-ass so well? I'd have to tease him about it later.

"Well?" Silvio sniped again, his voice booming even louder than before. "Do I need to call *my* boss and have her call *your* boss?"

That was the last thing the thieves wanted, especially when it would be far easier to lure Silvio into the bank and kill him. So the outside guard unlocked the front doors, while the one stationed by the fire stairs hurried that way, with all the men at the cash cages staring in that direction. A perfect distraction, just like I'd wanted.

"Go," I whispered to Bria.

Keeping low, she left the hallway and darted out into the lobby, ducking behind a desk that was sitting between the front doors and the tellers' counter. The second she was in position, I hurried over to and crouched down behind another desk, this one right at the end of the tellers' counter.

I peered around the corner of the desk, but the five guys in front of the cash cages were still focused on Silvio and the commotion he was making, and none of them had noticed Bria and me move. I flashed my sister a thumbs-up, which she returned.

Silvio stormed into the lobby, walking fast and putting some distance between himself and the two giants coming up behind him. The vampire looked around, his gaze locking onto the guys holding the power saw and the welder's torch. Both tools were still churning and burning at a low, steady level.

"What is this?" Silvio asked, throwing one hand up into the air. "No one told me that you were doing construction today. Ugh. I'll come back later."

He turned to leave, but the two giants blocked his path.

"Sorry, pal," one of the giants said with a sneer, his hand dropping to the gun holstered to his belt. "You wanted inside, so you're going to stay inside—permanently."

Silvio shook his head. "You really don't want to threaten me. You see, my boss takes threats to her employees very seriously. Some might even say deadly seriously."

I rolled my eyes. Now he was just hamming it up.

"Oh, I think we'll risk your boss's wrath," the other guard chimed in, also reaching for his gun.

Silvio looked back and forth between the two men, then shrugged. "Okay, if that's the way you want it."

He raised his briefcase and slammed it into the face of the closest giant. That man staggered back, howling at all the blood gushing out of his broken nose. Silvio dropped the briefcase, surged forward, and tackled the second man, driving him to the ground, then snapped his head down and buried his fangs in the giant's throat.

The guard with the busted nose cursed and pulled out his gun, but Owen stepped in through the now-unlocked front doors and shot him three times in the back.

Pfft! Pfft! Pfft!

Owen's silenced gun barely made a sound as he fired, and the giant dropped to the floor like a stone. That left Bria and me to deal with the five men in front of the cash cages.

Bria rose from behind the desk and started shooting, focusing on the three men who'd been transferring the cash from the first cage into the duffel bags.

Pfft! Pfft! Pfft!

Her gun had a silencer too, and Bria put two of the men down with head shots. The third man grabbed a couple of duffel bags full of money, ducked down behind the tellers' counter with them, and yanked a gun from the holster on his belt. He was so focused on Bria that he never even saw me creep up behind him. I punched my knife into his back, driving the blade through his ribs and into his lungs. I yanked the blade right back out, and he died with a wheezing whimper.

That left two giants—the one with the power saw and the other with the welder's torch.

Pfft! Pfft! Pfft!

Bria shot the guy with the saw in the chest. Even though the tool was on a low setting, it clattered to the floor and started whirring against the marble, making a horrible grinding noise and sending silver sparks shooting up into the air. But I didn't have time to turn it off, so I sidestepped the saw, hoping that Deirdre and Santos would think the commotion was just part of the thieves working on the cash cages.

The guy with the welder's torch realized that I was coming for him, and he slammed his protective mask back down into place and fired up the torch, brandishing the hot, blue-white flame at me. I cursed and ducked back out of the way, but my foot snagged on something, and I tripped and fell back on my ass. Something hard and flat dug into my hands, and I realized that I'd landed on one of the duffel bags and was now literally sitting on a pile of money.

The welder pressed his advantage, stepping forward and aiming his torch at my head, even as he cranked up the flame's intensity. My knife had slipped out of my hand when I tripped, so I grabbed the only other thing within arm's reach—a shrink-wrapped brick of cash—and threw it at him.

The brick wasn't even close to being a real weapon, and my aim wasn't all that great, but I managed to bean the guy in the chest, making him jerk back in surprise.

Whoosh!

The open flame hit the wad of cash, instantly igniting it and making it explode like a bomb in the welder's face. He yelped in surprise and dropped his torch, which clattered to the floor and kept right on burning, slowly chewing into the marble.

Pfft! Pfft! Pfft!

Bria and Owen both stepped up and fired at the welder, and he joined his dead friends on the floor.

As soon as the last man was down, I grabbed my knife, got back onto my feet, and sprinted to the door that led downstairs to the basement. I plastered myself against the wall next to the door, waiting for it to burst open and for giants to come pouring into the lobby from the basement.

Nothing happened.

No footsteps, no bursting door, no giants.

Behind the counter, the saw kept whining, and the welder's torch kept hissing. The whirring machinery must have largely masked the sounds of the fight, and no one was rushing up the stairs to check on things. Good. The longer we had the element of surprise, the better our chances were of rescuing Finn.

Bria, Owen, and Silvio rushed over to me.

"Now what?" Silvio said, pulling a gun from against the small of his back.

I flashed my bloody knife at my friends. "Now we go downstairs and find Finn."

Silvio turned off the power tools and stayed in the lobby to keep watch and make sure nobody else came into the bank and took us by surprise.

Bria, Owen, and I hurried back to the men's bathroom. My sister and I did the same procedure as before, with me cracking the marble with my Stone magic, then her widening the cracks with her Ice power. Even though I wanted to blast the floor away as quickly as possible, I made myself work slowly and steadily, not making any more noise and not using any more magic than absolutely necessary, so that Deirdre wouldn't sense us using our combined elemental power. But the process went much quicker this time, since Owen was here to help grab the jagged chunks of stone and move them out of the way.

As soon as we'd made a big enough hole in the floor, I dropped down to the basement level below, with Bria next and Owen bringing up the rear. Bria checked the bathroom stalls, but there were no blood and no bodies to be found. She nodded at me, and I crept up to the door, eased it open, and peered outside.

Just like on the lobby level, this bathroom also opened up into a hallway, which was deserted. Bria and Owen nodded and raised their guns. I opened the door, and we all left the bathroom.

As soon as I stepped out into the hallway, a cold gust of air swept over my face, which could only mean one thing. Someone was using Ice magic down here.

Deirdre.

We tiptoed down the hallway in a line. Once we reached an intersection, the three of us crouched down and peered around the corner. Offices branched off this corridor, but it was still a straight shot all the way down to the main vault fifty feet away.

Big Bertha more than lived up to her name. The five-foot-thick marble walls, floor, and ceiling encasing the vault were the thickest in the entire building and re-inforced with silverstone rebar. The vault itself took up a large chunk of the basement, the front of it fifty feet wide and the interior more than three times as long. Big Bertha's rectangular shape matched the hundreds of safety-deposit boxes lining her walls.

A heavy metal door about ten feet wide was set into the center of the vault. That door had already been drilled and blasted open, judging by the tools and shrapnel littering the floor, the scorch marks on the surrounding walls, and the stench of hot melted metal that filled the air.

But another door lay behind that first one.

Well, it wasn't really so much a door as it was a thick, tight mesh of silverstone bars that covered the entrance from top to bottom and side to side. Way too much silverstone to cut your way through with a power saw or a welding torch, unlike the cash cages upstairs. A keypad was attached to the right side of the mesh, the light on the front red, indicating that the mesh was locked down tight.

Several boxes were stacked to one side of the vault, each stamped with the words *Property of Briartop*. Deirdre and Santos had brought all the jewelry from the museum exhibit down here. Of course they had. They wouldn't have wanted to let any of those precious stones out of their sight, not for one second.

I didn't see Deirdre or Santos, but they had to be here somewhere, perhaps farther down from the vault in the hallway that branched off to the right and led to the lobby stairs. But I didn't care about them right now, just the chair off to the left side of this hallway. The chair had been partially turned toward the front of the vault, but I could still clearly see the person sitting in it.

Finn.

My brother looked like he had been wearing his usual suit before his jacket and tie had been taken from him and his white shirt had been ripped open and torn apart.

All the better to torture him.

Thick ropes bound Finn's wrists and ankles to the chair, immobilizing him. Pale blue-white splotches dotted his skin from his forearms all the way up to his shoulders before spreading across his muscled chest, as though he had a terrible rash. But the marks were far more painful than any rash could be.

They were Ice burns.

Deirdre had used her Ice magic to torture her own son, horribly, given the number of wounds on Finn's skin. Some of the burns were small, no bigger than a dime, as though she'd pressed the tip of her index finger against his body and let loose with her magic. Some of the wounds were much larger, like careless blasts of power. One mark right over his heart was particularly gruesome, as though she'd balled up her fist, pressed it up against his skin, and frozen that one spot over and over again.

Finn had been tortured by elemental magic much the same way Fletcher had been. Despite my best efforts, I'd failed to save the son from the fate of the father. My heart shattered, my throat closed up, and my stomach roiled. At that moment, all I wanted was to look away from his broken body, from the horrible reminder that I'd once again been too late to save someone I loved from being brutalized.

Beside me, Owen let out a whispered curse, while Bria's fingers dug into my shoulder. But I tuned them out and forced myself to focus on my brother.

Finn's head was hanging down, so I couldn't see how bad the damage was to his face. But what made my heart shatter all over again was how utterly still he was. Too still. As if he were a statue sitting in that chair. As if Deirdre had frozen him in place with her Ice magic.

As if he were dead.

My gaze locked onto that blue-white, fist-shaped burn right over his heart, willing his chest to rise and fall—for him to still be alive. A second passed, then another, then another . . .

Breathe, Finn. Just breathe. Breathe, already!

And finally—*finally*—Finn's chest moved up, then down, and he let out a weak, racking cough.

"Is that all you've got?" he snarked in a low, raspy voice. "I've had razor burn that hurt worse than that."

Footsteps scuffed on the floor, and Finn slowly raised his head and glared at the person who stepped in front of him.

Deirdre fucking Shaw.

She'd put on a pair of gray coveralls over her purple pantsuit and had replaced her stilettos with heavy black boots. Despite the work clothes, she still managed to look cool and elegant, her icicle-heart rune glittering in the hollow of her throat just like always.

Deirdre moved so that she was standing between Finn and the silverstone vault door. More footsteps scuffed, and Santos appeared, still wearing his bank guard's uniform, although he'd ditched the long black coat and gray jacket and had rolled up his shirt sleeves, revealing his snake tattoo. The giant leaned back against the wall across from Finn and crossed his arms over his chest.

Deirdre stared at Finn, her pale blue eyes chillingly empty, then shook her head. "You're a stubborn, stupid fool, just like Fletcher was. All you had to do was give me the codes to the vault doors, and we could have avoided all this unpleasantness. But now you're going to die just like your father did. Tortured to death in your beloved place of business."

She circled around him. Finn turned his head, following her movements, and I finally got a good look at his face.

Deirdre hadn't burned him there, but someone— Santos, most likely—had laid a good, old-fashioned beat-down on Finn. One of his eyes was black, blood dribbled out of his broken nose, and a deep cut slashed across his left cheekbone where someone had backhanded him. Deirdre had probably delivered that last blow, given the blood marring the heart-shaped diamond solitaire on her left hand.

Bria's fingers dug even deeper into my shoulder, hard enough to make me wince and look at her. The rage and disgust burning in her eyes made them glow a bright, piercing blue, and I could see the matching shimmer of my own gray eyes and my own raging emotions reflected back in hers. I squeezed her hand, and she let out a breath and loosened her grip. We both turned our attention back to Finn.

"Just give me the code, and this will all be over," Deirdre said. "There's no need for you to suffer needlessly. I'm not a complete monster."

"Oh, no," Finn said. "Just a stone-cold bitch who's A-OK with torturing her own son. Gin was right about you."

She shrugged. "Then you should have listened to her. But that's your mistake, not hers. She did everything but tar and feather me. Did you know that she was even spying on me in her spare time? Santos's men took her down on the building across from my penthouse last night."

"You captured Gin?" Finn's entire body stilled. "What did you do to her?"

Deirdre's lips curved into a wide, genuine smile. "I gave her to Dimitri Barkov as payment for services rendered. He was quite eager to get his hands on her. I imagine he's still torturing her. Unless he got careless and accidentally killed her already."

She waited, her smile growing wider, expecting the news of my kidnapping, torture, and supposed murder to demoralize Finn, perhaps even break his spirit enough to make him give up the keypad code to the vault door.

She really should have known better.

In many ways, Finn was Deirdre's son. A flatterer, a charmer, a smooth operator, who desired and enjoyed all the finer things in life. But Finn was also Fletcher's son, and the old man had been the toughest son of a bitch I'd ever met.

Oh, it wasn't that Fletcher had been stronger or more resilient or more immune to pain than anyone else. He had simply been more *stubborn*. The more you tried to get the old man to do something he didn't want to do, the more you tried to bend his will to yours, the more you tried to break his spirit, the harder he dug his heels in and defied you—a trait that Finn had gotten from him in spades.

So instead of being concerned or cowed by my capture, Finn actually brightened, his shoulders lifting and his face creasing into a smile, despite the blood and bruises that blackened his features.

"You gave her to Dimitri Barkov? Seriously?" He started laughing.

Deirdre frowned. "What's so funny? Barkov had Gin well in hand when I left them."

Finn kept laughing and laughing, his gleeful cackles so hard and loud that he doubled over from the force of them. Tears streamed down his face, and I had the feeling that he would have even slapped his thigh in amusement if his hands had been free.

"And these were *your* mistakes," he said in between chortles. "First, that you didn't kill Gin right off the bat. Second, that you left her with Barkov. The only one who's dead is him. Trust me on that. But none of those is as bad as your third mistake. That's the one that's really going to come back and bite you in the ass."

"And what would that be?"

"Thinking that you could hurt me and get away with it." Finn smirked at her. "Gin is going to come here and slit your throat for that. I just hope I'm still alive to see her do it."

Deirdre stared at him, her forehead wrinkling, as if she was concerned by his unshakable confidence in me. She looked at Santos. "You told me that Barkov could handle Blanco."

"Correction. I told you that Barkov *wanted* to handle

Blanco. Not that he actually *could*," Santos snapped. "You're the one who left her alive instead of killing her like I advised. Lane could be right. She could be on her way here right now. So either get the code out of him or get started on the door yourself. My guys are taking care of the cash cages upstairs, and I drilled through the outer door already. The only one holding us up right now is you."

Deirdre's hands clenched into fists. "Don't you *dare* speak to me that way."

Santos laughed, pushed away from the wall, and stepped up so that he was looming over her. "I'm the one who's done all the hard, dirty work of planning and executing this thing. All you had to do was set up the jewelry exhibit and charm your boy so that he'd give you unrestricted access to the bank and let you in this morning. But now you can't even get one lousy access code out of him. So I'll speak to you however I damn well please."

I frowned. Back at the warehouse, I'd thought that Santos was Deirdre's minion, but he made it seem like they were actually partners in this.

Deirdre glared at Santos, but he just smirked back at her. She stared at him another second, then turned back to Finn.

Deirdre reached for her Ice magic, and her hand began glowing an eerie blue that was so pale it was almost white. The light grew brighter and brighter, until small blue-white flames flashed to life, flickering on her fingertips like cold candles. Even from here, I could feel the intense chill of her power, icy enough to make me shiver, despite my heavy clothes. Having her actually touch her fingers to your skin even for an instant would be painful—so fucking *painful*. I didn't know how Finn was so calm, resolute, and resilient after being tortured by her. I would have still been screaming.

Deirdre leaned down and waggled her fingers in front of Finn's face, a clear threat that he should give up the code or else. But he stared right back at her, never flinching, never wavering, never showing the slightest hint of fear. He wasn't giving up the code no matter what. Stubborn to the end, just like Fletcher would have been.

I was so damn proud of him in that moment.

"Tell me one thing," Finn said. "Was any of it real? Did you ever feel *anything* for me?"

Deirdre leaned in even closer, trying to crack his calm façade. But Finn didn't flinch, so she pulled back and stared down her nose at him. "I suppose I could lie and tell you that I felt something. That you're my son, and some small, motherly part of me actually cares about you. But I'm just not wired that way. I never was. Fletcher was so disappointed that I didn't feel the same way about him that he did about me. That he couldn't wish me into the person he wanted me to be. I think that's the reason he didn't ever try to kill me. I think he was still hoping that I would change someday, even though he knew deep down that it was never going to happen. He was a sentimental fool that way. And so are you."

"Yeah, I was a fool when it came to you. Like father, like son, I suppose." Finn barked out another laugh, but this one held no humor. "Do me a favor, will you?"

"What?"

"When Gin tracks you down and kills you, tell her that I'm sorry I ever doubted her." He paused. "On second thought, forget it. You'll be bleeding out before she gives you the chance to sputter out so much as a single word."

"You have far too much faith in your little friend."

"Not my friend," Finn said, his voice ringing with conviction. "My *sister*."

Deirdre stared at him, the blue-white flames of her Ice magic still flickering on her fingertips. Finn lifted his chin, glaring defiantly into her eyes. In that moment, they were almost mirror images of each other—both cold, calm, and completely unwilling to crack, compromise, or give an inch.

"Forget him," Santos growled. "You've been working on him for almost an hour now and haven't gotten anywhere. Let's get this show on the road. Unless you can't hold up your end of the bargain?"

"I told you that I could get into the vault without the access code if necessary," Deirdre snapped.

"Then quit wasting time and do it already," Santos growled again.

She shot him a sneering look, but she turned away from Finn and marched over to the vault door. She stood in front of the tight, thick mesh of silverstone bars, staring at them and the vault beyond for a moment. Then she stepped forward, wrapped her hands around the bars, and blasted them with her Ice magic.

In his file on her, Fletcher had said that Deirdre was a powerful elemental, but the old man hadn't fully communicated the depths of her magic. As soon as she let loose with that first round of magic, the temperature in the basement plummeted ten degrees, and the floor, walls, and ceiling began to frost over. Not because she was targeting them but because her magic was that intense. I shivered again, my breath steaming in the air. Beside me, Bria and Owen did the same. Deirdre Shaw was definitely the strongest Ice elemental I'd ever encountered, and I didn't know how to kill her without getting frozen alive by her magic.

Deirdre was completely focused on the vault door, and she blasted it over and over again with her Ice power. At first, the bars soaked up all her magic, like a sponge absorbing water, since silverstone had the unique property of being able to hold and store elemental magic.

"What does she think she's going to accomplish?" Owen whispered in my ear. "She doesn't actually think she can get through that much silverstone, does she?"

I shook my head. Deirdre didn't think it—she *knew* it.

Slowly, the silverstone began to soak up less and less of her power, and her elemental Ice actually started to coat the bars themselves, like layers of icing covering a cake. The blue-white crystals leaped from one piece of metal to the next, getting colder and harder all the while, the bars taking on the same pale, ugly blue color as the burns on Finn's skin. That's what Deirdre was doing with her power, using the bitter bite of her Ice magic to burn right through the metal.

Soon the entire mesh door was glowing with the blue-white light of her magic, and the metal began to creak and groan from its exposure to the intense, prolonged cold. Even the access keypad Iced over, the red light on the front snuffed out by Deirdre's deep freeze.

It seemed to go on forever, although Deirdre's assault on the metal bars couldn't have lasted longer than a couple of minutes. Finally, she released her hold on her magic and stepped back, admiring her handiwork. If I'd used that much magic in such a short amount of time, I would have been huddled in a ball on the floor, too tired to even whimper. But Deirdre wasn't even breathing hard. Santos gave her a sharp, approving nod. Bria's and Owen's mouths were both gaping open, and even Finn looked impressed, despite himself. Yeah. Me too.

Deirdre stepped forward again and flicked her long red fingernail against the very center of the mesh.

Tink.

A single crack appeared in the metal and slowly spread out, forming more and more cracks, until the pattern resembled a spider's web that had been carved into the middle of all that glittering elemental Ice. Deirdre studied the bars a second, then flicked her fingernail in the same spot again.

Tink.

More spiderweb cracks spread through the metal, zipping through the entire vault door. Deirdre leaned forward and flicked her fingernail against that same spot a third time.

Tink.

With a roar, all the elemental Ice shattered, crushing the silverstone bars and the keypad. It fell to the floor in one cold wave, and left a clear, open path into the vault.

Deirdre looked at Santos. "What were you saying about getting the show on the road?"

The giant ignored her gloating and reached into a duffel bag sitting on the floor. He grabbed a crowbar out of it, then stepped into the vault. He had moved out of my line of sight, but the *screech-screech-screech* of metal filled the air as Santos dug his crowbar into the first safety-deposit box, then the next. His giant strength let him pop the heavy metal boxes out of the wall as easily as I could crack a can of soda.

"So the bank vault was your endgame all along," Finn said, his voice brimming with bitterness. "But why go to all this trouble? You could have just stolen the jewelry from the armored truck. You could have had Santos do that, collected the insurance money, and kept your cover intact. So why rob the bank too? Why blow your contacts and everything else you set up in Ashland? Why take such a big risk?"

"Big risk, big reward. You should know that. Every money man does."

Finn glared at her, but she laughed, reached out, and patted his cheek. She put a bit of Ice magic into the gesture, making him hiss with pain and jerk away from her cold, cold touch.

"Don't worry, Finnegan, honey, and don't look so glum," Deirdre crooned. "Soon you won't have to worry about me or anything else. In fact, you won't feel a thing. I promise."

She patted Finn's cheek a final time, then headed into the vault to collect her bounty.

✷ 26 ✷

Deirdre stepped to one side of the vault and moved out of my line of sight, just like Santos had. A second later, blue-white flashes of light started appearing in the vault, as she used her Ice magic to crack open the safety-deposit boxes just like she had the silverstone bars. Meanwhile, Santos kept up his own steady assault with his crowbar. Looked like they were going to force open all the boxes first before they started rifling through the loot inside them.

"Now what?" Bria whispered. "The second they see us coming, they'll kill Finn. One blast of Ice magic from Deirdre would be more than enough. All she has to do is step out into the center of the vault, and she can hit him."

"Now we do some shock and awe of our own," I whispered back. "This way."

Bria and Owen followed me back to the men's bathroom. Owen gave Bria and me a boost through the hole we'd created, then we reached down and helped him climb up. Together, the three of us left the first-floor bathroom and stepped back out into the lobby.

Silvio was standing by the front doors, his phone in one hand and a gun in the other. He hurried over when he saw us. I marched to the center of the lobby, which was directly on top of the basement vault, and the others gathered around me.

"What are you going to do?" Bria asked.

I studied the floor, listening to the low, dark mutters of violence that had sunk into the marble from the thieves taking over the bank and killing the guards, along with me cracking through the bathroom floors.

"I'm going to bust through the floor and drop down right on top of Deirdre and Santos in the vault. If I'm lucky, I'll bury them in the rubble and kill them outright. But even if they survive, they'll be too surprised and too busy dealing with me to worry about anything else, including Finn. It should give you, Owen, and Silvio enough time to get him to safety."

Bria gave me a worried look. "You saw what Deirdre did. She blasted through those vault bars like they were made out of paper. And she still has plenty of magic left."

We could all hear exactly what she wasn't saying—that Deirdre might very well kill me with her Ice magic.

"I know, but this is our best chance to rescue Finn— our only chance. We have to take it, or Deirdre will kill him as soon as she and Santos are done looting the vault."

Bria didn't like it, but she nodded her agreement. So did Silvio and Owen.

Silvio made sure that our watches were all still synchronized, and then he, Owen, and Bria hurried over to the bathroom to slip through the hole in the floor and back down to the basement.

I gave them three minutes to get into position, just like we'd planned, then closed my eyes a moment, gathering my thoughts and my magic. Big Bertha was the most secure part of the bank, encased in marble and silverstone, and I would need almost all my power to blast through it. So I reached and reached for that mix of cold and hard magic flowing through my veins, letting it pool in the palms of my hands, until my spider rune scars were glowing a bright, brilliant silver with the cold, continuous ripple of my magic. Then I tapped into the Ice and Stone magic stored in my spider rune ring and necklace.

When I had gathered up all that power, I slowly turned my hands over so that my palms—and my spider runes—were facing the floor.

I raised my hands, steeling myself, then snapped my hands down, blasting all my magic at the floor directly below my feet.

Crack!

Crack! Crack!

Crack! Crack! Crack!

The surface of the marble immediately shattered, and I slammed a wave of my Ice magic down into all the jagged zigzags. The stone shrieked at the sudden, brutal assault, but I ignored its cries and hammered at it with the brutal one-two punch of my Ice and Stone magic, pouring all my power into the growing cracks and widening them even more, shattering every single bit of stone, then all the metal underneath.

The seconds ticked by, and I reached for even more of

my power, gathering up every single scrap of it and forcing it down, down, down—

CRACK!

With one giant, crashing roar, the floor beneath my feet split wide open.

For a moment, there was just noise.

A rushing roar filled my head with a dizzying symphony of sound. I had the sense of free-falling, and I reached for what little was left of my Stone magic to harden my skin, so that I wouldn't impale myself on a piece of shrapnel and bleed out before I got the chance to kill Deirdre.

I hit the ground hard, bouncing off the rocky rubble that covered the vault floor from my blasting through the one above it. Dust clouded the air, making it hard to breathe, and I coughed and coughed, trying to clear the pulverized marble from my lungs.

I dug my hands into the loose rocks under my body and managed to push myself up and then onto my feet. I squinted, trying to see through the billowing clouds of dust, but I couldn't so much as see the walls around me, much less peer out the vault door and tell if Bria, Owen, and Silvio had managed to rescue Finn yet.

As I stumbled around the vault, trying to figure out where the door was, I palmed one of my knives, searching for someone to kill.

"You bitch!" a voice roared behind me. "You just don't know when to quit, do you?"

I whipped around just in time for a fist to zoom out of the dust and slam into my face. Thanks to my jarring landing, I'd lost my grip on my Stone magic, so the punch socked me square in the jaw, making pain explode all the way up my cheekbone.

The force of the punch threw me back through the dust and up against a bank of safety-deposit boxes, some of which had been opened. I slammed the metal drawers shut with my body, each one punching into my back like a hammer and making me groan with pain. So that was where one of the walls was. Good to know.

Santos loomed up in front of me, his black hair now gray with marble dust. Even more of it coated his face, including that jagged scar on his cheek, making him look like he'd upended a sack of flour over his head. He growled and came at me. I raised my knife to stab him, but he knocked the weapon out of my hand. He tried to punch me again, but I blocked the blow and slammed my fist into his throat, hitting the giant where he was vulnerable.

Santos coughed, wheezed, and sputtered, but he surged forward again and wrapped his hands around my throat. He lifted me off the ground and wrenched me left and right, slamming my body into more open safety-deposit boxes, like I was the silver piece in a pinball machine and he was trying to get a high score.

I punched him, slamming my fists into his face over and over again, but he just snarled and took the blows, even though I managed to break his nose with one of them. The blood mixed with the marble dust on his face and made him look even more angry and vengeful.

I palmed a second knife, but Santos realized what I was up to, and he grabbed my arm, pulled it forward, and then rammed my hand back against the wall. The bones in my left wrist shattered on impact, and I screamed, my knife slipping from my numb, nerveless fingers. The weapon clattered to the floor and dropped into a hole in the piles of rubble.

White spots began winking on and off in my field of vision, and it was only a matter of time before I ran out of air. I'd already used up most of my magic breaking into the vault, and an Ice dagger wouldn't do me any good against the giant. My eyes flicked left and right, looking for something that I could use to at least get him to let go of me. Once I had air back in my lungs, I could figure out the rest.

Santos drew me away from the wall and then slammed me right back up against it, hard enough to make some of the loose safety-deposit boxes rattle beside my shoulder. My eyes latched onto the one closest to me, and I quit hitting Santos. Instead, I reached down with my right hand and grabbed the handle on the end of the box. At least, I tried to, but the dust and sweat coating my hand made my fingers slip off the handle. I growled with frustration, although it sounded more like a whimper.

Santos must have thought that I was flailing around for no reason because he laughed. "Not so tough now, are you, Blanco? I'm going to enjoy squeezing the life out of you for all the trouble you've caused me."

I ignored his taunts and his hands tightening around my neck. My whole world had shrunk to hooking my fingers through that handle and sliding the box free from the wall. My fingers slipped, and slipped again, but I kept trying.

Santos shook me again, moving my arm just enough

for me to wrap my fingers around the handle and tug the box free from the wall. Whatever was inside was heavy—heavy enough to yank my arm down—and I almost lost my grip on the whole thing. Even though my strained muscles were screaming at me to let go, I gritted my teeth and used the downward momentum to swing the box right back up and smash it into Santos's face.

The box cracked against his left cheekbone hard enough to leave a dent in the metal. The sharp blow stunned him, making him loose his grip on my throat and stagger back. I fell to the floor, coughing and wheezing, but I hung on to the box, surged back onto my feet, and slammed it into his face again, this time catching him in his already broken nose. At this impact, the box popped open, spilling black velvet bags everywhere. Loose diamonds came tumbling out of the bags, sparkling like ice chips embedded in the rubble.

Santos growled and clapped his hands to his nose. I wrapped my hand around the handle and swung my entire body around, driving the box into his head as hard as I could. I managed to get the angle just right, and one of the metal corners stuck in the sweet spot at his temple, cracking his skull open like an egg. Blood sprayed everywhere, and this time, Santos was the one who whimpered. His shoulders slumped, his knees buckled, and he crumpled to the floor, his body sprawling at an awkward angle on top of the shattered stones.

I stood there, sucking down dusty air, and watched him bleed out on top of all those diamonds. Then I tossed the safety-deposit box aside, staggered over to the wall, and followed it over to the vault entrance.

The dust had finally started to dissipate, letting me see that Finn was gone, cut ropes hanging over the chair that he'd been tied down to. I squinted, but I didn't see him or the others. Santos must have hit me harder than I'd thought. I blinked and peered down the hallway again—

A blast of cold hit me from behind.

I screamed as the wave of magic slammed into my back, catapulting me right out of the vault. I hit Finn's chair and bounced off, face-planting onto the marble floor of the hallway. In an instant, my body burned with cold, my back turning stiff and brittle, just like the crystals that were spreading across my skin, trying to freeze the rest of me. I immediately pushed back with my own magic, stopping the crystals in their tracks, but the damage had already been done, and most of my back was frozen solid. I felt like an ice cube that had somehow grown arms and legs, but I groaned, grabbed hold of the chair, and pulled myself back up onto my feet.

Deirdre stood in front of me.

I'd been so concerned with keeping Santos from choking me to death that I'd lost track of her. She too was covered with marble dust, and blood dripped down her face, neck, and arms from where the stone shrapnel had shredded her coveralls and cut into her skin. Deirdre was wounded, but she was by no means dead. Her pale eyes glittered in her face, and the cold blue-white flames of her Ice magic shot out of her clenched fists like frosty fireworks exploding over and over again.

"You meddlesome bitch!" she hissed.

Deirdre shoved her hands forward, shooting out a spray of long, jagged Ice daggers at me, any one of which would be enough to end me if it hit in just the right spot. I covered my head and face with my good arm and ducked back behind the chair, using it as a shield.

Thunk-thunk-thunk-thunk.

The chair took the brunt of Deirdre's assault, the wood splintering apart as the Ice daggers speared it, but one of the cold, sharp projectiles punched into my thigh. I screamed and staggered back, but my knee buckled, and I sprawled in a heap on the floor. Still, I kept going, clawing at the floor with my one good hand, trying to pull myself over the slick marble and away from her.

Too late.

Deirdre marched down the hallway and kicked me in the ribs, forcing me to roll over onto my back and look up at her.

"Well, now I realize why the others were all so worried about you." A sneer twisted her lips. "At least killing you will earn me some favor with them."

Them? Who was *them*? And why were they so interested in me?

Deirdre raised her hands, Ice daggers sprouting like blue-white spikes on her fingertips. There was no way I could avoid her magic. Not this time. So I reached for the scraps of my Stone power and hardened my skin as much as I could, even though I knew that it wasn't going to be enough to stop her from skewering me—

A blue ball of magic streaked through the air, slamming into the center of Deirdre's chest and knocking her back.

Footsteps pounded on the floor, and Bria, Owen, and Silvio emerged out of the lingering clouds of dust. Bria stepped in front of me, reared back her arm, and hurled another ball of her Ice magic at Deirdre. But the other elemental sent out a spray of daggers, and the two masses of magic crashed together in midair. Shards of elemental Ice shot out everywhere, embedding themselves in the floor, walls, and ceiling. The temperature dropped another ten degrees, and everything took on a pale blue, glassy sheen.

But Bria kept right on attacking Deirdre, sending out blast after blast of magic, driving the other elemental back into the vault.

"Get Gin!" Bria yelled, summoning up more magic in the palms of her hands.

Owen and Silvio darted forward, grabbed me under the arms, and hoisted me to my feet. They started dragging me away from Bria and Deirdre, who was still in the vault. But she wouldn't stay there for long. I could feel how Bria's blasts were slowly weakening, while Deirdre's counterattacks remained at their cold, steady level. In a minute, two tops, Bria would run out of magic, and then Deirdre would step out of the vault and kill her with one Icy wave of power.

"No!" I yelled. "Let me go! I have to help Bria!"

"Forget it!" Owen yelled back. "You're in no position to help anyone!"

He was right, but I still struggled against him and Silvio, even as they dragged me backward.

Deirdre sent out another, larger blast of magic that had Bria ducking out of the way. She surged out of the vault, pressing her advantage and sending out spray after spray of Ice daggers. Bria knew when she was beaten, and she whipped around to follow us, but one of the daggers caught her in the back and sent her crashing to the floor. Her silverstone vest took the brunt of the blow, but she still grunted with pain.

"Bria!" I screamed, knowing that I wouldn't be able to save her. "Bria!"

Deirdre looked at me, a smile curving her lips. She raised her hands and focused on Bria again, even as my sister tried to crawl away from her—

Crack!

Crack! Crack!

Crack!

Finn staggered up beside Owen, Silvio, and me, guns clutched in both of his Ice-burned hands. I didn't know where he'd gotten the weapons, and I was amazed that he had the strength to even hold them, much less stand upright, given how he'd been tortured.

The hail of bullets made Deirdre lurch to one side of the hallway. She snarled, whipped around, and reached for her Ice magic again, this time to blast Finn with it. But Finn was faster, and he snapped up his guns and sent more bullets flying in her direction. Owen and Silvio also reached for their guns, and Deirdre realized that she'd lost control of the fight.

So the bitch turned and ran.

She sprinted down the hallway toward the stairs as fast as she could. Finn snapped up one of his guns and squinted down the length of the barrel, aiming square at her back so he could take her down with one shot. He took a step forward to better his aim, and his foot slipped on a patch of Ice on the floor.

Crack!

The bullet bounced off the marble wall instead of punching into Deirdre's back. But Finn wasn't about to give up. He staggered forward, pulling the triggers on both of his guns now, but she was already gone. His legs went out from under him, and he collapsed in a heap on the floor.

"Finn!" I yelled. "Finn!"

His head lolled in my direction, and he grinned up at me, his green eyes filled with pain—so much pain—that wasn't all from his gruesome physical wounds.

Owen lowered me, and then he and Silvio ran over to check on Bria, who was still groaning and trying to sit up. I crawled across the Ice-slickened floor to Finn.

He grinned at me again, even as tears dripped down his bruised, bloody cheeks. "I'm sorry, Gin," he mumbled through his split lips. "I'm so sorry. You were right, and I was wrong. She was using me the whole time . . . the whole damn time . . ."

His voice choked off, and he closed his eyes, though the gesture couldn't stop the tears flowing down his cheeks. The air was so cold that the drops froze on his face, glinting like diamonds against his bloody skin. He curled into a ball on the floor, sobs shaking his body.

I lay down next to him, slid my good arm around his shoulders, and gave him a weak, understanding hug before my own strength deserted me.

"Shh, shh, it's okay," I whispered, trying to soothe him. "Everything's going to be okay."

But things were anything but okay right now, and the tears kept streaming down and freezing on Finn's face.

✴ 27 ✴

Once they made sure that Bria was okay, Owen and Silvio ran upstairs to the lobby, but Deirdre was long gone, along with a couple of duffel bags full of cash.

Of course the bitch had escaped.

But she wasn't going to be able to hide for long.

Not in Ashland. Not from the Spider.

Silvio called Jo-Jo, who rushed over to the bank. Silvio and Owen had carried Finn and me upstairs, laying us both out on desks. Jo-Jo took one look at the Ice burns on Finn's body, slapped her hands down onto his chest, and blasted him with her Air magic. I rolled my head to the side and watched her work, too cold and exhausted to do anything else.

Once Jo-Jo was finished with Finn, she repeated the process on me. It hurt more than usual, since the dwarf had to slough off all the dead layers of skin that Deirdre had frozen solid with her Ice magic, but I clamped my lips shut and swallowed down my snarls. My pain was nothing compared with what Finn was going through right now.

When I was healed, Jo-Jo helped me sit up. Owen, Silvio, and Bria were still in the lobby, going through the thieves' pockets, looking for clues, but I didn't see Finn.

"Where is he?"

Jo-Jo jerked her thumb at the door that led downstairs. "Back down in the vault, darling."

She stayed with the others, but I trudged downstairs. I found Finn sitting in the middle of the ruined vault, picking through the rubble, scooping up the loose, bloody diamonds, and arranging them in a neat little pile.

Jo-Jo had healed all those ugly blue-white burns on his skin, but he was still a mess. Blood, dust, and other filth covered his torn clothes, which were wet in spots from the elemental Ice that had melted and soaked into the fabric. His dark brown hair was rumpled, his shoulders slumped with exhaustion, and dried blood speckled his face like freckles. Finn looked nothing at all like his usual slick, charming self, but the thing that worried me most was the dull hurt shimmering in his eyes—the sort of soul-deep, heart-rending, bone-weary hurt that you never quite got over.

The same sort of hurt that Deirdre had inflicted on Fletcher all those years ago.

Finn sighed. "What a fucking mess. Mosley and the rest of the higher-ups are going to have conniptions when they find out about this."

"They don't have to know anything," I said. "Everyone who saw us here is dead, except Deirdre. We could just walk out of here and pretend we didn't know anything about what happened."

"I can't do that. Not when this is all my fault. I'm the one who helped Deirdre get inside the bank. She told me that someone had tried to rob the exhibit and that the insurance company was moving the jewelry here." He picked another diamond out of the rubble and placed it on his stack. "So I hurried over here like her little lapdog and let her waltz right into the lobby with Santos and his men. I knew all the guards they killed. Every single one of them. Nice guys. They didn't deserve this. Neither do their families."

"Deirdre and Santos storming in here and killing the guards, that's not on you. None of this is on you. It was their plan, not yours."

"Of course it is." His mouth twisted. "It's *all* on me. And do you know what the really sad part is?"

I shook my head.

Finn picked another loose diamond out of the rubble. "Deep down, I knew that you were right. That Mama—" He stopped and cleared his throat. "That Deirdre was up to something. She was just too good to be true, but I ignored it. I ignored your warnings, my own gut instincts, everything."

"It's not your fault," I repeated.

"Yeah, it is. Because I knew that she was up to something. I just didn't care what it was."

"We'll find her," I said. "Deirdre won't get away with this. Not what she did here at the bank and especially not what she did to you. Not the torture, not the lies, none of it. I promise you that."

Finn gave me a distracted nod. "Yeah. Sure. Thanks, Gin."

I laid my hand on his shoulder, letting him know that I was here for him. He smiled at me, but his heart wasn't in it, and he went back to picking through the rubble. I looked at the diamonds that he'd already gathered. I didn't know if he'd done it subconsciously or not, but he'd arranged the loose, bloody stones into a familiar shape.

The diamonds formed a jagged, shattered heart, just like Finn's.

Finn picked up a few more diamonds while I fished my knives out of the rubble. Then I coaxed him back upstairs. I asked again if he wanted to leave, but he said no and called Stuart Mosley. Bria pulled out her phone, called Xavier, and told him what had happened, then contacted her own bosses.

"They'll be here soon," she said, after she ended the call. "Probably fifteen minutes, tops."

"You guys should go," Finn said, his voice that same dull monotone as before. "No need for you to get dragged any deeper into this."

I opened my mouth to protest, but he shook his head, not quite looking at me or anyone else.

"You've done enough for me today. Just go, Gin. Please?"

I didn't like it, but he was right. Us sticking around would just lead to all sorts of awkward questions. I squeezed his shoulder again. Finn gave me the same weak smile he had down in the vault, then turned away, staring out over the blood and bodies in the lobby.

Bria stayed behind with Finn, and Owen, Silvio, Jo-Jo, and I left the bank.

"He'll be all right," Jo-Jo said, once we were outside. "He just needs some time."

I nodded, knowing that she was right. The dwarf hugged me, then headed off to her car to drive back to her salon. Owen, Silvio, and I went back to the parking garage.

"I'm going to the Pork Pit," Silvio said. "Spread the word and get people to start looking for Deirdre."

If Deirdre was smart, she was already on her way out of town, but I didn't mention that. "Good idea. Thank you, Silvio."

The vampire nodded, got into his car, and drove off.

I climbed into Owen's car with him, and we sat there. I didn't say anything, and he didn't try to prod me into a conversation. Instead, he reached over and took my hand in his. Owen knew that Finn wasn't the only one who was hurting and heartsick.

"I didn't want to be right about her," I whispered. "I know that I didn't help matters, acting the way I did toward Deirdre, but I didn't want to be right. I didn't want Fletcher to be right. I didn't want her to hurt Finn."

"I know, Gin," Owen said. "I know."

I curled my fingers into his, soaking up all the warmth, comfort, and support he had to offer. Then I let go and buckled my seat belt.

"Will you drive me somewhere?"

Owen frowned. "You don't want to stay here? See what the cops do? Make sure that Finn's okay?"

I shook my head. "Bria will take care of him. There's nothing else I can do here."

"All right, then." Owen cranked the engine. "Where to?"

I rattled off an address. His eyebrows shot up in surprise, but he threw the car into gear and left the garage.

Ten minutes later, he pulled into another parking garage, this one underground, and we took the elevator up to the lobby. I made a call to the doorman's boss—Jade Jamison, an underworld figure that I was friendly with— who was happy to tell her guy to give me access to whatever I wanted. The doorman put his key in the elevator, and Owen and I rode it all the way up to the top floor of the Peach Blossom.

The doors slid back, revealing Deirdre's penthouse.

Knife in hand, I stepped out of the elevator and into the suite. Owen was right beside me, gripping a gun and ready to shoot anyone who came at us. After a quick once-over, we saw that no one was in the kitchen or the living room, and no one was hiding in the bedrooms and bathrooms. Even more telling, I didn't feel so much as the faintest trace of Deirdre's Ice magic. When we'd cleared the suite, Owen and I went back to the living room.

That was where the mess was.

Deirdre must have come straight back here after the disaster at the bank, because a suitcase was sitting on one of the white sofas, clothes haphazardly sticking out of it. More luggage littered the rest of the living-room floor, all of it open, with clothes, shoes, jewelry, and makeup bristling out of the tops of the bags. It looked as though Deirdre had grabbed her things and tossed them into the suitcases, not caring where or how they landed.

Someone, most likely Deirdre, had dropped a heart-shaped perfume bottle onto the floor, breaking it into half a dozen jagged pieces. The overpowering scent of peonies filling the air reminded me of the broken bottle that had been in Fletcher's casket box.

Owen poked his gun down into one of the suitcases, making bottles of makeup, hair gel, and nail polish rattle together. "Looks like she was in a hurry to leave."

"Yeah," I replied. "But she didn't take any of her stuff with her. Why not?"

He shrugged. He didn't know any more than I did.

We moved through the rest of the penthouse, but it was clean, except for the mess in the living room. No blood, no bodies, nothing that would indicate a struggle or that Deirdre had left against her will. If the luggage and her things had been gone, I would have assumed that she'd already skipped town. But Mama Dee wasn't the kind of woman to leave so much as a toothbrush behind. Since her bags were still here, that meant she was most likely still in Ashland. So where had she gone? And why had she left in such a hurry?

I didn't know, but I was going to find the answers— and her.

For Finn.

✳ 28 ✳

Unfortunately, the answers that I wanted, and the ones that Finn needed, were much harder to come by than I expected.

Despite all the feelers that Silvio put out, along with a hefty reward from yours truly for information about Deirdre's whereabouts, we got exactly nowhere trying to track her down. It was like she had vanished into thin air. She was simply *gone*, with no trail to follow. I didn't hear so much as a whisper about where she—or her body—might be.

The only bright spot was that things didn't go nearly as badly for Finn as they could have. Stuart Mosley was plenty pissed that someone had tried to rob his bank, but Bria managed to spin the story that Finn had been taken hostage and had bravely fought off the thieves until help arrived. Mallory Parker also put in a good word for Finn, since she was all buddy-buddy with Mosley and an esteemed bank client herself. But most important, Mosley didn't want anyone to know just how close Deirdre and Santos had come to grabbing everything in the vault. So he blamed it all on a gas leak and subsequent explosion, hired a crew from Vaughn Construction, made everyone from the construction workers to the cops sign confidentiality agreements, and got them to clean up the mess.

Still, the more time passed and the more things got back to normal, the more worried I became. I didn't particularly care if someone had gotten to the Ice elemental before me. I just wanted to know with absolute certainty that Deirdre was dead and rotting, not lurking in some dark corner of Ashland waiting to strike back at me—or, worse, Finn.

"You're . . . cranky," Silvio said as I slammed some dirty dishes into one of the sinks. "I don't think that I've ever seen you cranky before."

I gave the vampire a dark glare, but he merely quirked his eyebrows in a chiding response and went back to his tablet.

It was Tuesday, three days after the bank robbery, and just after seven at the Pork Pit. It was a slow night, given the cold and increasing flakes of snow outside, and I was getting ready to close up. I'd told Silvio that he could go home an hour ago, but he'd insisted on staying, just in case someone called in with a tip about Deirdre. But no one had, and no one was going to. Deirdre was a ghost, until she either decided to lash out at us again or someone uncovered her body in a shallow grave. I was hoping for the latter, although I didn't know anyone who wanted her dead as much as I did.

Still, my worry over Deirdre was nothing compared with my worry over Finn.

Despite everything he was dealing with at the bank, Finn had still come to the Pork Pit every day for lunch, just like he had with Deirdre. He seemed to have aged a decade over the last few days. Everything about him was dull, flat, and lifeless, and he had lost the vibrancy and cheer that made him, well, *Finn*. It was as though Deirdre had reached inside him and scooped out his essence, his heart, leaving nothing behind but a brittle, hollow shell.

Making him a Tin Man, just like Fletcher had been.

Finn didn't laugh or smile or joke, and he barely picked at his food, even though I made all his favorites, including triple chocolate milkshakes. More than once, I looked at Finn to find him with his fork in his hand, staring over at the corner booth where he and Deirdre had sat so many times, a blank look on his face. Mama Dee had really done a number on him, and I had no idea how to help him.

My troubled thoughts made me slam some more dishes into the sink, and I glared at the bowls and plates for making so much noise.

"You know," Silvio said, "I think that maybe I'll go on home for the evening."

I sighed. "Sorry I'm being such a bear right now."

He shrugged. "It happens, even to the best of us. You shouldn't worry so much. Ms. Shaw will turn up sooner or later, and you'll deal with her when she does."

"Thank you, Silvio."

He nodded at me. I smiled and nodded back.

Silvio packed up his gear and left. I shut and locked the

front door behind him, then turned the sign over to *Closed*. The rest of the waitstaff had already left, and I thought about heading home for the night. But I had some leftover food from a take-out order that hadn't gotten picked up—hot dogs with all the fixings, another one of Finn's favorites—so I pulled out my phone and texted him.

Want to come over to the Pit, have some food, and talk?

I waited, but there was no response. No surprise. He was probably stuck in another crisis-containment meeting with Mosley and the rest of the bank staff. I decided to give him some time to get back to me, so I mopped the floor and did several other chores, getting the restaurant ready to open up again in the morning. Then I sat down on my stool behind the cash register, pulled out all five of my knives, and set them out on some dish towels on the counter. The knives could use a good cleaning, and I might as well be productive while I waited to see if Finn would text me back or show up here.

I was about to get started when I realized that Catalina had forgotten to take out the last of the trash before she'd left. I didn't want it to stink up the restaurant overnight, so I grabbed the bag and pushed through the double doors. I cracked open the back door, looking and listening, just in case someone was lying in wait to try to kill me, but the alley was empty. Still, I was cautious as I stepped outside and heaved the trash into the closest Dumpster. I looked around the alley again, but it was as deserted as before, except for the snow, which was picking up speed.

I locked the back door behind me. My phone chimed, so I pulled it out, thinking that Finn had texted me back, but it was Bria.

Found something BIG on Deirdre's rune. Call me when you get home. Need to come over and show you in person.

I frowned, wondering why Bria couldn't just call and tell me right now. I hit reply, then pushed through the double doors and stepped into the storefront. I was so preoccupied with my phone that I didn't hear the warning rumbles of the bricks around me until it was too late.

Three giants were waiting for me inside.

They must have picked the front-door lock, because I hadn't heard them slip in, and they were clustered around the double doors, not giving me any room to maneuver. Since I'd foolishly left my knives lying on the counter, I raised my hands to blast them with my Ice magic, but they were quicker than I was.

A fist cracked into the side of my face, and the world went black.

Paul and his two vampire friends were going to rape me.

Out of all the bad things that had happened to me living on the streets, that was one horror that I'd managed to avoid. But now it was going to happen, ironically enough, at Fletcher's house, the one place where I had always felt safe.

I opened my mouth to scream, but Paul fell on top of me, covering my mouth with his hot, sweaty hand. His breath washed over my face, bringing the stench of pepperoni along with it. Smelled like he'd grabbed a slice from the pizzas that some of the kids had brought over before he'd decided to rob the house.

Paul started fumbling with his pants. A scream rose in my throat, but I couldn't let it out, not with his hand clamped over my mouth. Fear surged through me, paralyzing me, freezing me in place. But then he started fumbling with my pants, and cold rage flooded me instead, overpowering my fear. I'd already been through so many bad things. I wasn't going to suffer through this too.

Not without a fight.

I jerked my head to the side, wrenching free of Paul's disgusting hand. Then I opened my mouth, snapped my teeth forward, and bit his fingers as hard as I could. He howled with pain and managed to yank his hand free of my tearing teeth. I reached for my Stone magic, making my skin as hard as a rock, then head-butted the bastard. It was an awkward blow, and I saw just as many white stars as he did, but it got him to scream, fall off me, and cradle his aching head in his hands.

The other two vamps were still holding down my arms and legs, and one of them clamped his hand over my mouth before I could scream. I tried to jerk my mouth out from under his hand, but he dug his fingers into my face, leaned down, and gave me an evil grin.

"Feisty, huh? We're going to have some fun with you—"

Crack!

A baseball bat slammed into the side of the guy's head. The hard blow knocked him out cold, and he slumped over on top of me.

Mouth gaping, the second vamp turned to see who had attacked his friend.

Crack!

And he too got a bat upside the head.

I blinked away the white stars, and suddenly, Finn was there. He threw his baseball bat down onto the porch, then knelt by my side, shoved the two vamps off me, and helped me sit up against the porch railing.

"Gin! Are you okay?" he asked.

I nodded, although I couldn't stop the tears from streaking down my face. My entire body started shaking harder than a leaf in the wind. I curled my hands into fists to try to stop the tremors, but it didn't work.

"Don't cry," Finn said, a stricken look on his face. "Please don't cry. I'm sorry I was such a jackass before, but I'm here now. Everything's going to be okay—"

"Losers," a voice jeered. "You're all a bunch of fucking losers."

The boards creaked, and Ella, the pretty blond girl Finn had been talking to in the den, stepped out of the shadows and into the center of the porch, right behind Paul, who was still moaning softly and cradling his aching head in his hands.

Only Ella didn't look so pretty now. Instead, her face was twisted in disgust, the anger staining her cheeks a perfect match to her cherry-red lip gloss.

"You idiots," she snarled. "You couldn't handle breaking into one dumb kid's house, could you?"

Ella drew back her foot and kicked Paul in the ribs. The motion snapped his head back, and his skull hit the railing with a sickening crack. He too slumped to the porch, unconscious.

"Ella?" Finn said. "You asked these guys here?"

"Of course I did." She sneered. "Did you really think that I came to your lame-ass party just to flirt with you? Please." She laughed, but it was an ugly, ugly sound.

Finn's face hardened, and he got to his feet, his hands clenching into fists. Ella glared right back at him. Neither one of them noticed me as I grabbed Finn's baseball bat, took hold of the porch railing, and pulled myself onto my feet.

"*You were just pretending to like me so your friends could come to my house and steal from my dad.*" Finn's voice was cold and harsh, but I could hear the hurt in it. He'd really liked this girl.

Ella raised her eyebrows. "*So you're not a complete idiot after all. Good for you. Too bad you're not going to get the chance to rat me out to anyone.*"

She reached into her back pocket and came out with a switchblade, then flipped the weapon open with practiced ease. The sharp edges of the blade glinted a dull silver in the light streaming from the windows.

Ella grinned and stepped over her vampire friends, slicing the weapon through the air as she drew closer and closer to Finn—

But I stepped in front of him, raised the bat, and hit her across the face with it.

Crack!

Her eyes rolled up into the back of her head, and she dropped to the porch without another sound. I stood over her, making sure that she wasn't faking, but she was out cold, just like the three vamps.

"Home run, bitch," I muttered.

Finn touched my shoulder. "You didn't have to do that. I could have disarmed her."

"I know you could have, but I wanted to take care of her." My hand tightened around the bat. Even though Ella and her friends were out of the fight, I wanted to keep right on hitting them. I wanted to make them hurt just as much as they'd planned on hurting me. But I swallowed down my screams of rage and focused on Finn.

"I'm sorry, Gin. So sorry. I had no idea what she was up

to." His shoulders slumped. "I thought . . . I thought she really liked me."

This time, I reached out and touched his shoulder. "It's okay."

He shook his head. "No, it's not. I would promise you that it won't happen again . . ."

"But?"

"But we all know that I'm a sucker for a pretty face." Finn grinned, then winked at me.

He was trying to charm me again, trying to get me to smile and laugh and forget about the horrible thing that had almost happened. It shouldn't have worked, but his grin and the light in his eyes were both too infectious to ignore, and I found myself snickering, just a little bit.

"There we go," he said. "That's better, isn't it?"

And it was. Not a lot, not enough, but it was better than before.

Finn's gaze moved slowly, from me to Ella and the three vamps sprawled across the porch to the party inside, which was still going strong. He winced. "How are we going to explain this to Dad?"

"We?" I snorted. "There is no we in this equation. There is only you, being a jackass over a pretty girl."

Finn glared at me a moment, and then his face melted into a sheepish smile again. "Yeah, you're right. Just do me a favor, okay?"

"What?"

"Don't forget about me, since Dad will probably banish me to my room for the next ten years."

I rolled my eyes. "I couldn't forget about you even if I tried."

"Cross your heart and hope to die?" he asked, making an X over his chest.

I rolled my eyes again, but I mimicked his motion. "Cross my heart and hope to die."

"Now, that's what a guy likes to hear."

Finn slung his arm around my shoulders, grinning at me again—

Cold water hit me square in the face, snapping me out of my dream, my memory. I gasped and opened my eyes . . .

Just in time to get hit in the face by another round of cold water.

Some of the water went up my nose, while still more trickled down my throat, and I doubled over, sneezing and coughing at the uncomfortable sensations. When I'd finally gotten the worst of the water out of my lungs, I reached up to wipe the rest of it off my face.

That's when I realized that I was shackled to a chair, with silverstone handcuffs glinting on both my wrists. I rattled the cuffs, but they were securely anchored to the metal chair.

"Well, that finally woke her up," a familiar voice called out.

I raised my head.

Deirdre Shaw was sitting across from me.

For a second, I thought she was the one taunting me. Then I noticed the gleam of silver on her wrists and ankles. It took me a moment to process that they weren't heavy bracelets. They were handcuffs.

Deirdre was shackled to a chair just like I was.

❖ 29 ❖

My muddled mind struggled to catch up to my eyes and process what was going on.

Deirdre a prisoner, just like me? Then that meant . . . that meant that she was in serious trouble too. That she wasn't the one in charge.

That she was *working* for someone else—and had been this whole time.

Surprise flashed through me, burning the cobwebs out of my mind. And I realized that not only was Deirdre handcuffed, but she looked far worse for wear than I did.

Her gray coveralls were gone, although she still wore the same purple pantsuit and black boots she'd sported during the bank robbery. But her appearance was anything but elegant. Her jacket and pants were covered in blood and grime and torn in more than a dozen places. I didn't know how long she'd been chained to that chair, but it must have been a while, given the stench of urine that surrounded her and the puddles of liquid on the floor.

Her blond hair was a sweaty, frizzy mess, and her blue eyes were dull and glassy with pain. Cuts, burns, and bruises covered her face and exposed skin, along with several puncture wounds, as though a vampire had taken a bite or two out of her. She'd been thoroughly tortured, the same way she'd tortured Finn.

Good.

Deirdre realized that I was staring at her. She snarled and jerked forward, although the silverstone cuffs on her wrists kept her as securely shackled to her chair as I was with the ones on my wrists. Her ankles had also been chained down, and all she could do was rock her chair back and forth, since it was on rollers. My chair also had rollers, but my feet were free and not tied down.

I ignored her hissy fit and studied my surroundings. Bare bulbs hanging down from the ceiling. Stacks of crates and shrink-wrapped boxes everywhere. Concrete floor and walls. The metal cage in one corner where I'd woken up the last time I was here. I was back in Dimitri Barkov's warehouse.

And I was surrounded.

Several giants stood in a loose circle around Deirdre and me. They were all carrying guns under their suits, and one of them was holding a metal bucket with a leaky water hose curled up at his feet like a snake dripping venom. Nothing unusual there, but the longer I looked at them, the more worried I got. I didn't recognize any of their faces, not a single one. This wasn't Barkov's crew—it was someone else's.

"So this is where you've been hiding," I said, turning my attention back to Deirdre. "What charming accommodations. Bet you wish you were back in your penthouse right now, honey."

"You bitch!" Deirdre hissed, spittle flying out of her bloody, swollen lips. "This is all your fault! I should have killed you when I had the chance."

"Oh, yeah. You absolutely should have. I'm just sorry that I wasn't the one who got to work you over. They did a half-assed job, if you ask me. Considering that you're still breathing."

Deirdre snarled at me again, and I bared my teeth right back at her.

"Now, ladies," that same voice I'd first heard called out again, a voice that I now realized wasn't Deirdre's. "There's no need to be so nasty."

Footsteps scuffed on the concrete, and Deirdre stopped snarling at me. A mulish look settled over her face, but she couldn't quite hide the fear flickering in her eyes. She'd failed to rob the bank for her employers, whoever they were, and now there was to be a reckoning. One that included me, since I was the reason her scheme had gone sideways. Lucky me.

The footsteps grew louder and closer, until they stopped right behind me. Whoever was standing there wanted me to turn around, to strain and struggle to try to see him, but I stayed still and faced front. He'd step into the light. Every cockroach did, eventually.

I started counting off the seconds in my head. *One . . . two . . . three . . . five . . . ten . . . fifteen . . .*

I hadn't even made it to thirty before a man walked

past me, stepping into the space between Deirdre and me.

Black hair, black eyes, trimmed goatee, snazzy suit. He looked the same as always, except for the fact that he wasn't obsessively checking his phone. Instead, for once, he looked straight at me.

"Hello, Ms. Blanco," Hugh Tucker said. "So nice of you to join us."

I looked at Tucker, then at Deirdre, then back at Tucker.

"So you're the man behind the curtain," I said. "Hiding in plain sight all along."

He shrugged. "Something like that."

I'd wondered why he didn't act like a typical assistant, and now I knew. Deirdre had been working for Tucker this whole time, not the other way around like they'd led everyone to believe. But even more interesting was Deirdre's reaction to her boss. Her body trembled, her fingers curled tightly around the arms of her chair, and her tongue darted out to wet her lips. Whoever Tucker really was, Deirdre was practically shaking in her boots at the sight of him. Then again, he'd been torturing her for the last few days. Prolonged pain was enough to break just about anyone.

"You're probably wondering why I brought you here, Ms. Blanco."

Instead of the bland, polite murmur I remembered, Tucker's voice was rich and deep, with a sophisticated slant and the faintest hint of a Southern drawl. Not only that, but he seemed taller, more interesting and vibrant than before. Even his suit was brighter, a royal blue that brought out the bronze color of his skin. He'd been playing the part of the harmless assistant this whole time, and now the snake was shedding its skin to reveal its true, venomous nature.

"Not particularly. I imagine that you want to kill me for fucking up your ice heist."

He arched an eyebrow at my snarky tone. "Yes, well, I did warn Deirdre about the dangers of involving Mr. Lane and, by extension, you in her scheme. Repeatedly, I might add. Of course, Deirdre and I have already had a long discussion about that."

Deirdre couldn't hide the shudder that wracked her body.

"Despite my many warnings, Deirdre insisted that she could handle you. Obviously, she was wrong about that."

I grinned. "Why, Tuck, you flatterer. Are you saying that I'm a badass? Because I *totally* am. I told Deirdre as much the first day she sashayed into the Pork Pit, but she didn't believe me. And now look where she is. Why, you couldn't have ended up in a better spot, Mama Dee."

I smirked at Deirdre, who struggled against her handcuffs again. "You bitch! This is all your fault!" She looked at Tucker. "My plan was solid. It would have worked, if not for her."

The vamp arched his eyebrow again. "*Would haves* are for other people, Deirdre. Not you, and especially not us. All you got from the bank was a lousy two million in cash, not the hundreds of millions that you promised us, that you *owed* us. You risked everything on this plan, and it has blown up quite spectacularly in your face. You know what that means."

Deirdre had already been horribly tortured, had already sat in that chair and suffered for days on end, but her face still paled, and a sheen of sweat popped out onto her forehead at Tucker's casual promise of her impending death.

"So," I drawled, "you've already tortured Mama Dee, and now you're going to kill her. Why, exactly, am I here, then? Not that I'm complaining, mind you, as I'll be quite happy to sit here and witness her death. Bring me some popcorn, and I'll even do the play-by-play commentary."

"But?" Tucker asked.

"But this is a weeknight, and I've got a barbecue restaurant to open in the morning. Couldn't y'all have just called and told me where to find her body?"

For the first time, a spark of anger shimmered in Tucker's black eyes, belying his polite words and calm expression. "You're here because we wanted you here. To see this. To see what happens when people displease us."

"And who, exactly, is *us*?"

His lips twitched, as though I were a child who'd done something to amuse him and he was holding back a laugh at my expense. "You really don't know anything, do you? About how things actually work in Ashland?"

I shrugged. "Ostensibly, I'm the head of the underworld. So that means that everything goes through me."

This time, Tucker let loose with a hearty, amused chuckle that almost made him seem likable. Almost. "Mab never told you anything, did she?" he asked. "And neither did your mother."

I couldn't have been more shocked than if his goon had doused me with another bucket of water. Of all the things he could have said, of all the names he could have dropped, I wasn't expecting him to bring up my *mother*. This time, my hands were the ones that curled around the arms of my chair as I struggled to hide my surprise. "What does my mother have to do with anything? She's been dead for almost twenty years now."

"You always thought that Mab killed your mother because of some long-standing family feud between the Monroes and the Snows." Tucker gave me a look that was almost pitying. "You believed exactly what we wanted you to."

I frowned, not understanding what he was getting at.

"It's true that Mab despised Eira and was worried about your magic. Those are some of the reasons your mother died." He bent down so that he was at eye level with me. "But those aren't the only reasons. Why, they're not even the main ones."

Cold fingers of unease crawled up my spine. "What are you saying?"

Tucker leaned even closer to me. "Mab killed your mother because *we* ordered her to."

I sucked in a breath, my mind spinning in a hundred directions. Every word out of his mouth was like a grenade exploding at my feet, but I pushed aside my shock and surprise and forced myself to think things through. Tucker was a master manipulator. He'd been pulling Deirdre's strings this whole time without my realizing it. He was just playing me now, trying to confuse me and get me to focus on his lies instead of escaping.

He hadn't been there that night. He hadn't seen my mother and Annabella die. He hadn't heard their screams as Mab's elemental Fire had consumed them. He hadn't seen or smelled or touched their charred bodies. He hadn't been tied down to a chair and tortured by Mab. *I* had been, and I knew exactly what had happened and why. Tucker didn't know anything about my mother.

Not one damn *thing*.

"You're lying," I snarled. "Mab killed my family because she wanted to. Because she was an evil, vicious, vindictive bitch. Mab certainly never asked anyone's permission for any of the bad things she did."

"Oh, that's where you're dead wrong, Ms. Blanco," Tucker said, his eyes still on mine, a snake trying to transfix me with the depths of his black gaze. "Mab was certainly all of those things, especially when it came to Eira Snow. But Eira was the one making problems within the group. She wanted us to abandon some of our more . . . profitable endeavors, just in the name of human decency. She actually threatened to go public and expose us. So we let Mab take care of her."

"Right," I drawled, my voice dripping with disdain and disbelief. "Just like you let Mab be head of the underworld."

"Exactly," he replied. "Mab was always a bit . . . showier than the rest of us. She was the perfect figurehead for all the petty crime bosses to focus on, while we carried on with our own interests behind the scenes. But Mab knew exactly what we were capable of doing, even to her, and she went along with us because it was in her best interests to do so."

Part of me wanted to laugh in his face and thank him for the great bedtime story. But his voice, his words, his expression . . . they all held an air of cold, cruel certainty that I couldn't ignore, that made twin knots of worry and doubt twist together in my stomach. Could Tucker actually be telling the truth? Could Mab have murdered my mother for some reason other than a petty family feud?

Could I have been wrong all these years?

But . . . but that would mean that I had been wrong about *everything*—my mother, what kind of person she had been, why she'd died, even my revenge against Mab. Every single thing that made me, well, *me*. It would all be wrong. No, it would be worse than that.

It would all be a fucking *lie*.

When I first found out that Deirdre was alive, I'd been worried about shattering Finn's world and upending everything he knew about his parents. I couldn't quite believe that the same thing was happening to *me*. That this wasn't all just another manipulation on Tucker's part.

But I couldn't ignore the possibility that he was telling the truth.

I gave him a skeptical look. "I'll ask again. Who, exactly, is this illustrious *we*?"

"You can call us the Circle. We're the ones who run this town and everything in it. Mab, the underworld, the crime bosses, they're all just useful tools to hide our activities. Unlike Mab, we see no need to let everyone know our business."

"So you're telling me that some secret group, some secret society of folks, are the true forces of power, greed, and corruption in Ashland?" I laughed. "That's the most ridiculous thing I've ever heard—"

Tucker palmed a knife and pressed it against my throat, cutting off my words and cutting open my neck. I winced at the cold sting, even as warm blood oozed down my throat. The bastard was *fast*. I hadn't even seen him move. I wondered if his speed was a natural vampiric ability or the result of drinking other people's blood. Maybe both.

"You stupid girl!" he hissed. "We can reach out and crush you anytime we want. The only reason you're still alive is because it amuses us to watch your pitiful struggles."

I stared right back at him, hate blazing in my eyes. "Then do it, already. Make good on your threat. Cut my throat, right here, right now. Otherwise, drop your fucking knife, quit posturing, and tell me what it is that you really want."

Tucker dug the blade into my skin, making even more blood trickle down my neck. I glared right back at him, not showing a lick of fear. Finn might be Fletcher's son, but I was the old man's daughter in all the ways that truly mattered, and he'd passed down the same stubbornness to me, drilled it into me during all the years he'd trained me to be the Spider.

I wasn't afraid, not of Tucker and especially not of the knife at my neck. I'd accepted the inevitability of my violent, bloody, messy death a long time ago. My solace here was that I wouldn't be the only one departing this world tonight. Because as soon as he was done with me, Tucker would kill Deirdre, which meant that she would never have a chance to hurt Finn again.

Tucker dug the blade even deeper into my neck, but I didn't crack and start begging for mercy like he wanted. Instead, my eyes narrowed in challenge, silently daring him to do his worst. If I could have spit in his face without him slicing through my carotid artery, I would have done it in an instant and then lunged forward and sunk my teeth into his throat for good measure.

The vamp saw that I wasn't going to break. He nodded in approval, dropped the knife from my neck, and stepped back.

"Well, it's good to see that you're as tough as advertised, Ms. Blanco," he said. "It's time that we replaced Mab, and I think you'll make a fine addition to the Circle."

"Join you? The group who supposedly ordered my mother's murder? Not bloody likely."

He ignored me and snapped his fingers. One of the giants stepped forward, and Tucker exchanged his bloody knife for the giant's gun. Deirdre and I both tensed. Tucker could easily shoot us where we sat, have his men roll our chairs out into the shipping yard, and shove us off the docks and into the river. No one would have any clue to what had happened to us until some poor fisherman hooked our bodies and got the fright of his life a few weeks later.

Instead of shooting us, Tucker ejected the clip from the gun, then loaded a single bullet back into the chamber. He put the gun on a nearby table and pulled a set of handcuff keys out of his pocket. He held the keys up in front of my face.

"Don't do anything stupid, or my men will kill you."

The giants stepped a little closer, a couple of them pointing their guns at me. I made note of where they were all standing and of all the other obstacles around me. The crates, the boxes, the door at the far end of the warehouse, where a lone giant was posted, angling his phone in my direction.

Tucker uncuffed my right hand, then slapped the gun into it. He stepped out of the way and gestured at Deirdre. "Shoot her. Prove your loyalty to the Circle, and you can go free."

Deirdre's eyes bulged. "No! Tucker, no! You can't do this! Think about all the money I've made you and the others over the years. Think about how much more money I can still make you."

He gave her a cold glare. "We wouldn't be in this mess in the first place if not for all your bad investments and ridiculous spending habits."

I remembered what Silvio had told me about Deirdre's charity foundation, about how someone had bankrolled her when she first started out years ago. And about how she was now broke and playing a shell game with other people's money.

"All these years later, and this is still all about your trust fund, isn't it?" I said. "You blew through all your money, just like your parents did, and then you lost all your friends' money too. That's why you went for the double shot of the exhibit jewelry and the bank vault. Your friends wanted their money back, or else." I smirked. "I guess champagne bubble baths don't come cheap. Do they, Mama Dee?"

Anger stained Deirdre's cheeks a mottled red, but she didn't deny my accusations.

Tucker chuckled softly, enjoying her humiliation. "And now, because of your own incompetence, everyone in Ashland—underworld or not—knows that you tried to rob your own exhibit, along with the bank. You've exposed yourself, and potentially all of us, and you know what the penalty for that is."

He shook his head. "You should thank me. If it were only me deciding, I would stake you out here and make your death last for *days*. Ms. Blanco will probably be far more merciful and shoot you in the gut so it only takes you a few hours to bleed out."

My fingers curled around the gun, calculating distances and angles. I shifted my feet so that my toes were resting against the concrete floor.

Seeing that she was getting nowhere with Tucker, Deirdre turned her teary eyes and pathetic pleas to me.

"Gin, please, honey, you can't do this. I'm Finnegan's mother—"

I snorted. "There is nothing *motherly* about you. Don't expect me to save your lying, deceitful, sorry ass. Not after what you did to Finn. I told you point-blank that when you hurt him, I would kill you. You really should have listened. Now you're going to die here, a victim of your own lies, and absolutely no one will mourn your passing. Especially not Finn."

Deirdre realized that she wasn't going to soften my heart, which was just as cold and hard as hers was. "You stupid bitch," she snarled. "By the time they're done with you, you'll wish you were dead too."

I shrugged. "We'll see."

Tucker gestured at the gun in my hand. "Go ahead. Kill her. You know you want to."

I kept my gaze steady on him, even as I wrapped my fingers around the cuff on my left wrist, sending a small trickle of Ice magic into the locking mechanism. The silverstone soaked up that first wave of magic, so I sent out another, slightly stronger one, wanting to drop the temperature of the cuff and weaken the metal.

"Forget it," I said. "Do your own damn dirty work."

"Shoot her," Tucker snapped. "*Now*."

"Why? So you can record the whole thing and blackmail me with it? I see your man with his phone out over there."

Tucker couldn't help but look in that direction. The giant at the door winced and lowered his phone.

"Seems like the invitation to join your precious Circle is more of an order, and I don't take orders from anyone, sugar."

"Then you're a fool," Tucker snapped.

"And you're a dead man."

"If you won't kill her, then I will. And then I'll kill you too. Only I won't be so nice as to use a gun." He gestured at the knife he'd cut me with, the one the giant was still holding on to for him. "I'll carve you up, just like you've done to so many other people. But there won't be anything quick and painless about it. Your screams will be like a sweet serenade, and I won't stop cutting until you beg me for mercy."

I snorted again. "You can make me scream, certainly, but I won't beg. You want Deirdre dead, then kill her your damn self. Mab might have been involved with you, but I'm not her. I'm not one of your lackeys, and I never, *ever* will be."

The vampire glared at me, his eyes narrowed to two black slits in his face, but I stared right back at him, even as I fed a little bit more Ice magic into the cuff on my left wrist. The metal was so cold now that it was starting to steam in the ambient heat of the warehouse, but no one noticed the wisps of frost except me. Almost there.

"Fine," he snapped. "It will be easier to kill you both now anyway."

Tucker bent down, as though he was going to wrest the gun out of my hand, but I dug the toes of my boots into the floor and pushed back as hard as I could. The rollers on my chair sailed smoothly along the concrete floor, shooting me back, well out of Tucker's reach.

He swiped for me and ended up staggering to keep his balance. For a moment, everyone was frozen, but I kept digging and digging my toes into the floor the whole time, trying to roll myself toward the door at the end of the warehouse. Even as I sailed away, I whipped up the gun, pressed it against the lock on the handcuff on my left wrist, and pulled the trigger.

Crack!

The shot reverberated through the warehouse. The bullet, combined with my Ice magic, was enough to shatter the lock on the silverstone handcuff. The second the cuff fell away, I tossed the empty gun aside, lurched out of the chair, and sprinted for the door.

Crack!
Crack! Crack!
Crack!

My shot must have also jolted Tucker's men out of their shock. Bullets zinged through the warehouse in my direction, but I reached for my Stone magic and hardened my skin into an impenetrable shell. One of the bullets caught me square in the back, throwing me forward as though someone had punched me in my spine, but my magic saved me from being killed. The blow still hurt—the force of the bullet was hard enough to bruise my back and ribs and make breathing uncomfortable—but I ignored the pain and staggered forward.

Shouts rose behind me, and more bullets whizzed through the air, plowing into the crates and boxes as I ran past them, but I kept my legs churning and my gaze locked on the door at the end of the warehouse. I needed to get out of here, and not just so I wouldn't get killed. I needed to warn Finn and the others about Deirdre, Tucker, and everything he'd said. But first, I had to survive this.

A lone giant was standing by the door, the guy who'd been recording me. He was still holding his phone, and he fumbled for the gun in his shoulder holster. Something silver glinted in my field of vision, and I veered over to a worktable, snatching up a wrench. The man yanked his gun free and raised it to fire at me, but I was faster, and I cracked the wrench across his face before he could pull the trigger. He screamed and dropped to the ground, losing his grip on his gun and his phone.

I stopped long enough to drop the wrench and scoop up his gun and phone from the floor, then slammed my shoulder into the door, stumbled out of the warehouse, and sprinted into the dark night.

❖ 30 ❖

Hide-and-seek had always been one of my favorite games as a kid, mainly because I'd always had the patience to wait out whoever was looking for me and slip away to a new spot when their back was turned.

As an assassin, it wasn't so much a game as it was a necessary survival skill.

The good thing about being trapped in a shipping yard at night was that there were a lot of places to hide.

The bad thing was that Tucker had brought a whole lot of men with him.

Several giants had been guarding the perimeter, and the gunshots sent all of them racing toward the warehouse, their own guns drawn, ready to shoot any shadow that moved. The snow had stopped while I was in the warehouse, and the moon was now shining big and bright in the sky. I slipped into the closest patch of shadows and hurried down a row of metal containers as fast as I could, kicking up sprays of snow.

I came to a corridor in the containers, cut to my right, then right again, heading back in the direction I'd just come from, hugging the sides of the containers to hide my tracks as best I could. Going back to the warehouse was dangerous, but there were two more things I needed to do: find out as much as I could about Tucker's operation, and make sure that Deirdre was dead.

Less than a minute later, I was back at the front of the containers, peering over at the warehouse. I stopped long enough to fiddle with the guy's cell phone, setting it to video mode. Then I found a small crack to hide in, worming my way in between two shipping containers. My hidey hole was cloaked in shadows but still gave me a clear view of the warehouse.

Sure enough, a couple of minutes later, Tucker stormed out, a gun in one hand and a phone in the other. I held up my own stolen phone and zoomed in on him.

"Find her!" he yelled.

Giants moved all around him, yanking out their guns, spreading out around the warehouse, and heading into the maze of shipping containers beyond. One of the keys to hiding was to remain perfectly still, as though you were just another part of the landscape, dull, harmless, and completely unworthy of notice. Darting around like a wounded animal would get you caught quicker than anything else, so I stayed still and quiet in my hiding spot.

And it worked.

The guards expected me to run as far and as fast as I could, not to double back and spy on their boss. They didn't even consider the fact that I could be hiding so close to the warehouse, and more than one man ran right by me as they moved deeper into the shipping yard.

Tucker paced back and forth for a minute, texting furiously. His phone beeped back, and a smile curved his face. I frowned. What was he up to? He should be pissed that I'd escaped, not looking as pleased as punch.

Part of me wanted to slither out of the shadows, sneak up behind him, and put a bullet through his head. But two giants were standing by his side with guns out, so there was no way I could get close enough to kill the vampire. I stayed in my hiding spot, watching and waiting.

Tucker punched a button on his phone, then held it up to his ear. "Blanco escaped," he said. "No, she didn't shoot Deirdre. We have no leverage. She's not going to fall in line."

Well, he was certainly right about that.

"She has no idea who we are," he continued. "The meeting can still take place as scheduled next month."

My ears perked up. What meeting? Where? I needed more info.

"I've already put our contingency plan in place." He checked his watch. "In fact, it should be coming to fruition any second now—"

Ice magic blasted me in the back.

I screamed, and another blast hit me in the same spot, freezing and burning my skin at the same time. The pain was bad enough, but even worse, the force threw me out of my hiding spot and sent me tumbling to the ground in the middle of the row of containers, right where Tucker could see me. He casually waved his hand, and his two guards raced in my direction.

My lungs felt as though they were frozen solid inside my body, and I gasped for air, even as I tried to scramble across the snow to where my stolen gun and phone had landed. But Tucker's guards reached me first. They grabbed my arms and dragged me along the cold, snowy ground, then threw me down right in front of the vamp.

Tucker gestured for someone to step forward. A few seconds later, Deirdre limped up to his side, smirking down at me, the blue-white flames of her Ice magic dancing along her fingertips. She was favoring her right leg, and blood still oozed out of the cuts that dotted her body, but her silverstone cuffs were gone, and her face was smug now instead of fearful.

"I told you that she would double back and try to spy on you," Deirdre said. "Just like Fletcher would have done. You really need to quit being so predictable, Gin."

I huddled on my knees and focused on forcing air in and out of my frozen lungs, even as my hands curled into the snow, searching for a rock or a piece of metal or something else—anything else—that I could use to wipe that smirk off her face.

"Deirdre convinced me to give her a chance to redeem herself," Tucker said. "Said that she could get you before you got out of the shipping yard. Looks like she was right."

So that's why he'd been standing out in the open—as bait. He'd wanted me to creep close enough for Deirdre to sucker-punch me in the back with her Ice magic, and I'd fallen right into their trap. I wondered if Tucker's call had been fake too. No way to know.

He waved his hand at the Ice elemental. "Freeze her, and then my men can drop her into the river."

Deirdre loomed over me, the flames of her Ice magic burning cold and bright on her fingertips. "I'm going to enjoy this," she hissed.

I reached for my Stone magic, using it to harden my skin again, but she'd already frozen part of me, and I didn't have the strength to fend off more of her magic.

Deirdre smirked at me a final time, then drew her hands back to unload on me—

Crack!

A black bullet hole appeared in the middle of Deirdre's hand, snuffing out her Ice magic and making her scream.

Crack!

Another hole appeared in her shoulder, driving her away from me.

Crack!

And a final kill shot, straight through her cold, cold heart.

Finn was here.

My brother was the only one who could make those kinds of shots, especially on a snowy, moonlit night.

And he'd just killed his own mother so that I could live.

Deirdre toppled to the ground, her blood turning the snow a startling scarlet. I scrambled forward on my hands and knees and yanked her icicle-heart rune necklace from her throat. It was a foolish risk, but I wanted Finn to have it.

"Kill her!" Tucker ordered, ducking behind his own man for cover. "Kill her now!"

The other giant stepped forward and snapped up his gun. I tensed, ready to throw myself at his legs and try to spoil his shot—

Crack!

Finn put a bullet in the shooter's head, and the man dropped to the ground beside Deirdre. I snatched up his gun, scrambled to my feet, and fired off shot after shot at Tucker and his other guard. I was backpedaling toward the shipping containers the whole time, so my aim was lousy, but my wild shots had them ducking down and running in the opposite direction.

Drawn by the gunfire, other giants sprinted from the warehouse in my direction. I fired at them until my gun ran out of bullets, and I tossed the weapon aside in disgust. I darted forward, grabbed the stolen phone and the gun that I'd dropped earlier, and quickly emptied that weapon too.

The guards realized that I was out of ammo, and they quickened their pace, trying to catch me before I could disappear into the shadows.

Crack!

Crack! Crack!

Finn put the guards down before any of them could get close to me. I sprinted through the rows of shipping containers, looking right and left. Another giant stepped out from behind a container ten feet in front of me, already raising his weapon. I skidded to a stop and reached for my Stone magic again, wondering if I could harden my skin before he pulled the trigger—

Crack!

The giant crumpled to the snow.

That shot had been much closer than any of the others, and my head snapped up.

Finnegan Lane stood on top of one of the shipping containers.

My brother was wearing a long gray trench coat over a gray suit. The fabric glimmered like pure silver in the moonlight, which also frosted the tips of his dark hair and brought out the hard planes of his handsome face. He looked like a ghost come back for vengeance.

He waved me over, and I sprinted in his direction. He swung his legs over the side of the container and dropped to the ground, then popped right back up, slinging his rifle on top of his shoulder and grinning widely, his green eyes glinting in his handsome face. In that moment, he looked so much like Fletcher that it made my heart squeeze tight. He'd come to my rescue, just like the old man had done so many times in the past.

"What are you doing here?" I asked.

"I got your text about coming over to the Pork Pit," Finn said, still grinning. "I pulled up right as those giants were carrying you out of the front of the restaurant. Looked like you could use a little help."

He frowned, snatched his rifle off his shoulder, and fired off another round, dropping two more giants who'd been heading this way.

"You're awfully popular tonight," he drawled. "I think we should go and leave them wanting more."

Crack! Crack! Crack!

More giants caught sight of us and starting firing, the bullets *ping*ing off the metal containers all around us.

"Good idea," I said.

Finn fired off another round of shots, then held his hand out. "Ladies first."

I laughed and disappeared into the shadows, with him right beside me.

✲ 31 ✲

Finn and I made it out of the container maze and back to his car. He threw it into drive, and we zoomed away from the shipping yard. We didn't speak for several blocks.

"Jo-Jo's?" he asked.

"Yeah." I winced. "My back is burned and frozen solid from Deirdre's Ice magic. Double the fun, double the pain."

He nodded and turned onto the highway that would eventually take us to Jo-Jo's salon, and we both fell silent again.

Finally, I cleared my throat and gently placed Deirdre's icicle-heart necklace on the console between us. I'd managed to hold on to it through the fight in the shipping yard. For a moment, Finn stared at the blood—Deirdre's blood—that coated the diamond icicles. Then his lips pressed into a harsh line, and he looked away from the rune.

I'd spent the last few days tiptoeing around, trying to give him the time and space he needed to come to terms with everything, but I couldn't do that anymore. Not after what happened tonight. Not after he'd shot his own mother to save me.

"I'm sorry you had to kill her," I said in a soft voice. "I know how much you cared about Deirdre."

Finn shrugged. "But she didn't care about me, did she? Not one little bit. No matter how much I wanted her to." His voice dropped to a low rasp, hurt and longing rippling through his words. After a second, he cleared his throat. "I'm glad it was me. I think that Dad would have wanted it to be me."

"Why would you say that?"

He looked at me out of the corner of his eye. "After Santos got control of the bank and tied me to that chair, I asked Deirdre why she was robbing the bank. She told me everything. How she'd manipulated Dad into killing her parents so she could get her trust fund and then how she'd used me to get access to the bank." He paused. "She said that I was an even bigger fool than Fletcher had ever been, because you'd warned me about her, and I'd refused to listen to you. She was right about that."

I shook my head. "She was your mother. Of course you wanted to believe that she'd come back to Ashland to be with you. She was counting on it."

He sighed. "Yeah, and I fell right into her trap. I hurt you because of her. And Bria and Jo-Jo too. I'm sorry about that. Sorrier than you will ever know. And I'm going to make it up to you, all of you." His mouth hardened, and his hands tightened around the steering wheel. "But for right now, I'm just glad that bitch is dead."

His voice was cold, but hurt still flickered in his eyes.

Finn might have killed Deirdre to save me, but he'd be feeling the bitter bite of her betrayal for a long time to come, just like Fletcher had.

We rode in silence for a couple of miles before Finn spoke again.

"Tell me about the shipping yard," he said. "What did Tucker want with you?"

I filled him in on everything that had happened. Everything Deirdre had said and everything Tucker had threatened, including that there was some sort of secret group that really pulled the strings of the underworld and everything else in Ashland.

"Who do you think they are?" Finn asked.

"I have no idea, but Tucker wanted me to work for them. To be their front woman, their puppet. Just like Mab, who he said had been working for the group all along." My hands curled into tight fists in my lap, my fingers digging into the spider rune scars embedded in my palms. I drew in a breath and forced out the rest of the words. "Tucker claimed that my mother was involved with them too, although I don't know how. He said that this group, this Circle, gave Mab the okay to murder her."

Finn's eyes widened, and he looked at me. "Do you believe him?"

A wild sob rose in my throat, and I wanted to scream that of course I didn't believe Tucker, that of course it couldn't be true, that of course my mother couldn't have been working with him, with this group.

That my mother couldn't have been a monster like Tucker and Mab and Deirdre.

But I couldn't force out the denial, no matter how hard I tried, so I ended up shrugging instead. "Why would he lie about something like that? He was either going to blackmail me into working for him or kill me outright. He had nothing to gain by lying."

I cleared some of the raspy emotion out of my voice. "Whether everything he said was true or not, there's something going on here, and I'm going to get to the bottom of it."

Finn reached over and placed his hand on top of both of mine. "*We're* going to get to the bottom of it."

I tightened my fingers around his. "You're damn right we are."

Just before noon the next day, I was standing in Jo-Jo's kitchen with Finn and Owen. The dwarf had healed me, and I'd spent the last several hours resting and recuperating. Jo-Jo had packed up her supplies to go help a client who was in a beauty pageant, and Sophia was covering the Pork Pit for me. Finn and Owen were sitting across the butcher-block table from each other.

"I said I was sorry for everything I said to you at the Pork Pit that day." There was a wheedling note in Finn's voice. "What more do you want from me?"

Owen crossed his arms over his chest and glared at my brother.

I rolled my eyes. Finn had been apologizing to Owen for the last five minutes, and Owen had been pointedly holding a grudge. I ignored them and went back to layering pasta sheets, spicy marinara sauce, and mounds of mozzarella and Parmesan cheese in a large casserole dish for my homemade lasagna.

Finn snapped his fingers. "Ah. I know what you want." He got to his feet, went around to Owen's side of the table, and held his arms out wide. "C'mon, Grayson. I'll give you a free shot at me. Surely that will make you feel better."

Owen frowned, but he made no move to take Finn up on his offer. Finn waggled his eyebrows in invitation, and Owen huffed in response.

"Fine," Finn muttered. "If that's how you want to be—"

Owen surged off his stool and plowed his fist into Finn's jaw.

Crack!

Finn staggered back against the counter, a dazed look on his face.

"You're right," Owen rumbled, shaking out his hand, even as a smile quirked his lips. "I do feel better."

I rolled my eyes again. "Boys."

I reached into the freezer and grabbed two bags of frozen peas. I tossed one to Owen for his bruised knuckles and the other to Finn for his jaw. The two of them settled back down at the table, the silence between them far more companionable now.

Forty-five minutes later, I'd just taken the lasagna out of the oven and started dishing it up, along with a Caesar salad and garlic breadsticks, when the front door slammed open and Bria strolled into the kitchen.

"That smells amazing," she said, shrugging out of her jacket and placing a manila folder on the counter.

"Sit down, and tell us what you found," I said.

We all gathered around the table and dug into our food. I breathed in, enjoying the scents of cooked tomatoes, melted cheese, basil, oregano, and other spices that rose from the lasagna, which tasted even better than it smelled. It was the perfect warm, hearty dish to chase away the phantom chill of Deirdre's Ice magic that still lingered in my mind. Lasagna was also great comfort food, and we could all use a little comforting after everything that had happened.

Bria took several bites of her lasagna and sighed with appreciation before starting her story. "Xavier and I found Deirdre's body in the shipping yard, right where Finn shot her."

"But?" I asked.

"But the rest of the place was clean. All the papers and files had been cleared out, all the computers had been smashed, and Xavier found a dozen cell phones torched in a trash can. Whoever Tucker really is, he was certainly thorough. We'll follow up and chase down all the leads, of course . . ."

"But you don't expect to find anything," Owen finished.

She shrugged. "Probably not."

We finished our food in silence. Bria was the first to push her plate away, and she grabbed the folder she'd brought off the counter and placed it on the table. Owen cleared the dishes, and we all gathered around the table again.

Bria looked at me. "Remember when I told you that I had seen Deirdre's rune somewhere before?"

"Yeah . . ."

"Well, I finally remembered where, thanks to those photos Mallory gave you."

She opened the folder and drew out a photo. It was another shot of that long-ago cotillion ball, just like the one Mallory had shown me several days ago. But instead of a group of girls, this photo showed only two: Deirdre and our mother, Eira. Both of them were smiling and holding out their rune necklaces toward the camera.

Finn let out a low whistle, and Owen tilted his head to the side. All I could do was stare at the photo.

Bria tapped her finger on the picture. "Mom had a photo just like this one. I remember her pulling out a whole album of photos and looking through them with me whenever she would tell me those bedtime stories about those old cotillion balls. But it's not even the most interesting picture."

She pulled out another photo, this one of Eira and Deirdre standing with another girl, Mab Monroe.

The three girls were clustered together, with Deirdre standing in the middle and smiling at the camera. Eira and Mab were on opposite sides of her, and neither one looked particularly happy to be so close to the other. In fact, Mab had her head turned, staring at a guy standing at the very edge of the photo.

Bria tapped her finger on the photo again. "And look who Mab has on her arm."

Black hair, black eyes, confident smile. Even though I could only see the side of his face, I recognized him immediately.

"Son of a bitch," I muttered. "That's Tucker."

Bria nodded. "There are some more shots of him, talking with different people." She hesitated. "There are a couple of photos of him with Mom. He wasn't lying about knowing her."

Bria looked at me, sympathy in her eyes, then started pulling out more photos and arranging them on the counter. Eira, Deirdre, Mab, and Tucker were in many of the shots, just like she said.

"What do you think it means?" Finn asked.

I stared at the long-ago images, more questions swirling through my mind. Had Tucker been telling the truth? Had my mother really been part of some secret society in Ashland? Were the members of the Circle really responsible for her death? What had she done that upset them enough to want her dead?

I didn't know, but I felt all the stubborn denial that I'd been hanging on to burning to ash, replaced by the cold, sinking certainty that my mother hadn't been the person I'd thought she was.

Then who *had* she been?

And what did that make *me* now?

"Gin?" Finn asked again. "What do you think it means?"

I shook my head. "I have no idea. But it's a place to start looking for answers. And I'm going to find them."

☀ 32 ☀

Three days later, I found myself right back where I had
started.

Blue Ridge Cemetery.

And just like last time, I was standing inside someone
else's grave—my mother's.

Oh, I didn't expect my mother's casket to be empty,
since I'd witnessed her murder and knew that she was as
dead as dead could be. But Eira Snow had known Deirdre, Mab, and Tucker, so it seemed like a logical place
to start searching for answers. I'd already gone through
Fletcher's house and gathered up all the old man's files,
and I had been systematically going through them one by
one, but I hadn't uncovered any dirt there yet.

I was hoping that I might here tonight.

I'd arrived at the cemetery forty-five minutes ago, and
I was almost down to my mother's casket. This night was
even colder than when I was first here, but the steady

motions kept me warm, and the quiet gave me time to think about everything that had happened.

But the more I thought about things, the fewer answers I came up with, just like every other time I turned my attention to this new puzzle. For the first time, I envied Finn. At least, he had answers about Deirdre, even if they were dark, hurtful ones. People always said that ignorance was bliss, and I finally understood what that meant.

Because not knowing was driving me crazy.

I was determined to find out exactly what my mother had been involved in, even if it meant disturbing her final resting place—

Thunk.

My shovel hit something, and I frowned, knowing that I wasn't quite down to the casket yet. But I bent and cleared the dirt off the item I'd hit.

It was another silverstone box.

It was a much smaller box than the one that had been in Deirdre's casket, but my spider rune was carved into the top, just as it had been on the box in Deirdre's casket, and there was no doubt in my mind that the old man had left it here for me to find.

"Fletcher," I whispered.

It was one thing to dig up Deirdre's grave—a stranger's grave—and realize that things weren't what they seemed. But it was another to have the same realization about my own mother's grave.

My entire body went cold and numb, and I slowly sank into the dirt, the box clutched in my hands like an anchor weighing me down. My stomach churned, and dread squeezed my heart tight, but I'd come too far to stop now.

I *couldn't* stop now.

So I took a moment to gather my thoughts, and then I fished out one of my knives and cracked open the box.

Tucked inside was an envelope with my name scrawled across the front. With trembling hands, I opened it, drew out the single piece of paper inside, and read the note the old man had left me.

> *Gin,*
>
> *Don't open your mother's casket. There's nothing in there but regret and sorrow for disturbing her.*
>
> > *Love,*
> > *Fletcher*

Despite the tears streaking down my face, I still smiled. Even now, the old man was looking out for me, knowing how much it would hurt me to open my mother's casket and see the charred remains of her body. I started to set the envelope aside, but something slid around in the very bottom. So I reached inside for the object and drew it out into the light.

A second later, I burst out laughing.

It was a key to a safety-deposit box at First Trust of Ashland. The bank's name was stamped into the key, and someone—Fletcher—had scratched the number of the box into the metal: 1300. The irony made me laugh.

"If only I'd had you last week," I murmured to the key. "I could have gotten you while I was down in the vault."

But there was nothing more I could do here tonight, so I tucked the key and the letter into my pocket, got to my feet, and picked up my shovel again.

"Need a hand?" a voice called out.

I looked up to find Finn standing next to my mother's grave, wearing black clothes and with a shovel propped up on his shoulder.

"What are you doing here?"

He grinned. "You mean, how did I find you? Silvio was quite happy to download his tracking apps onto my phone."

I let out a curse. "I'm going to take away all his phones and tablets and everything else he has that's got even a hint of information on it."

Finn laughed and stabbed his shovel into the mound of earth I'd dug up. Then he sat down and dangled his legs over the edge of the grave.

"There's another reason I came here." He drew in a breath, not quite looking at me. "I finally looked through that box of stuff you gave me. The one that Dad left in Deirdre's casket. I read his letter too."

I'd given Finn the box and the letter the day after the warehouse fight. I should have given it to him sooner, the very first night I'd dug it up. Maybe if I had, none of this would have happened. Maybe Deirdre wouldn't have hurt, tortured, and betrayed him. And maybe Tucker wouldn't have hurt me by hinting at ugly truths about my own mother.

But Fletcher had wanted me to wait until after Deirdre was gone—dead—to give Finn the letter. I might have honored the old man's wishes, but we'd all suffered because of it. Still, I think I finally understood Fletcher's reasoning. He hadn't wanted to hurt Finn by telling his son all the horrible things his mother had done. He really had wanted to give Deirdre one last chance, hoping that she was a different person, a better person, for Finn's sake.

But Fletcher had also realized that she probably hadn't changed, so that's why he'd warned me about her. *Hope for the best, but always prepare for the worst* was another motto that the old man had lived by. In this case, he'd let Finn do the hoping and me the preparing. Now what was done was done, and Finn and I would have to live with my mistakes and all the painful consequences of them.

Finn pulled an envelope out of his jacket pocket and passed it down to me. "Here. I know you want to read it."

"I do want to read it, but that doesn't mean I should. Or that I have any right to. Fletcher left it for you, not me."

He grinned, but it was a sad expression. "Just read it, okay, Gin?"

I nodded and held out my hand. Finn leaned down and helped me up out of the grave. I sat down beside him, our legs hanging over the edge. Then I unfolded the letter and began to read.

> *Dear Finn,*
>
>   *If you are reading this, then I am gone, but your mother is back . . .*

It was a long letter, much longer than the one Fletcher had written me, and in it he recapped his relationship with Deirdre. For once, she hadn't been lying, and everything had happened just as she'd said. She'd accidentally gotten pregnant, tricked Fletcher into killing her parents, threatened to freeze Finn with her Ice magic. Fletcher wrote that he'd kept the few things he'd had of Deirdre's because he thought Finn might want them someday. And he also confirmed my suspicion about hoping that Deirdre was different from the woman he'd known and that she would never hurt Finn the way that she had him.

But it was the last few lines of the letter I lingered over.

> *I don't regret what your mother did to me because I have you as a result. I would suffer through it all again—and again—if it meant having you as my son.*
> *I'm so proud of you and the man you've become.*
> *I love you so much.*
>
> > *Now and always.*
> > *Fletcher*

Tears gathered in my eyes, but I blinked them back and looked at Finn to find that he was doing the same thing. I had to clear the emotion out of my throat before I could speak.

"He meant it, you know. Every single word. He was so proud of you, and he loved you so much."

"I know," Finn said. "And I loved him too. I just wish I had been more like him sometimes. That we had gotten along better. That I had told him how important he was to me more than I did."

He plucked a blade of frosted grass out of the ground and twirled it around. "I also wish that I had listened to you about Deirdre."

"You don't have to apologize again."

He looked at me, his green eyes full of regret. "Yes, I

do. I just . . . I wanted her to actually be here for me. I wanted it more than anything. You know?"

"I know. It's the same way that I feel about Fletcher. Sometimes I wish he was still here so much that it hurts. It's literally an ache in my chest that I can never get rid of."

"But at least you know he loved you."

I waved the letter at him. "And he loved you too. He kept you safe from Deirdre for all these years. The two of you might not have been that much alike, but he loved you more than anything, Finn."

He nodded, but he didn't say anything else. A few flakes of snow started falling down from the sky. Finally, he gestured at the box that was still down in the grave.

"What was in it?"

I showed him the key and the letter.

"Yep, that's from First Trust, all right." He winked. "I know a guy who can get you in there on the sly."

I laughed. "I'll just bet you do. But first, I need to clean up the mess I made here." I slid off the edge of the grave and back down into the hole.

"You want some help putting all this dirt back where it belongs?" he called out. "Or can I just sit up here and supervise and keep my clothes pristine?"

I gestured at him with my shovel. "You can stay up there, or you can take a dirt nap down here. Your choice."

Finn laughed at my teasing threat and slid into the grave with me. Then he grabbed his shovel and stuck it in the dirt right next to mine. "I'm going to have to get a manicure after this," he said. "All this dirt and physical labor will wreak havoc on my nails."

I snorted. "I think it's sad that you get more manicures than Bria and me combined."

"Hey, now. Don't diss the manscaping. Women like a well-groomed man."

I rolled my eyes. "Well, when I see a well-groomed man, I'll let you know."

Finn bumped his shoulder into mine, and I bumped him right back. "You know there's no place I'd rather be tonight than here with you, right?" he said, his voice lighter than it had been in days.

I arched an eyebrow. "Really? You want to be cold, dirty, and sweaty? Why is that?"

"Oh, come on," he said. "Skulking around a cemetery on a cold winter's night? Digging up graves and secrets? Hot on the trail of some secret society that your mother may or may not have been involved in? Honestly, what could be better than this?"

He grinned at me again and started filling in the grave. I watched him for a few seconds, and then my gaze drifted down the hill to where Fletcher was buried. Finn and the old man had had their issues, but Fletcher had loved Finn, and that love had been returned. Maybe now more so than ever before.

Finn was right. There was no place I'd rather be either.

I smiled and started working side by side with my brother.

Turn the page for a sneak peek at the
next book in the Elemental Assassin series

Unraveled

by Jennifer Estep

Coming soon from Pocket Books

❋ 1 ❋

It was the perfect night to kill someone.

Thick, heavy clouds obscured the moon and stars, deepening the shadows of the cold December evening. It wasn't snowing, but an icy drizzle spattered down from the sky, slowly covering everything in a slick, glossy, treacherous sheen. Icicles had already formed on many of the trees that lined the street, looking like gnarled, glittering fingers that were crawling all over the bare, skeletal branches. No animals moved or stirred, not so much as an owl sailing into one of the treetops searching for shelter.

Down the block, red, green, and white holiday lights flashed on the doors and windows of one of the sprawling mansions set back from the street, and the faint trill of Christmas carols filled the air. A steady stream of people hurried from the holly-festooned front door, down the snowmen-lined driveway, and out to their cars, scrambling into the vehicles and cranking the engines as fast as they could. Someone's dinner party was rapidly winding down, despite the fact that it was only nine o'clock. Everyone wanted to get home and be safe, warm, and snug in their own beds before the weather got any worse. In ten minutes, they'd all be gone, and the street would be quiet and deserted again.

Yes, it was the perfect night to kill someone.

Too bad my mission was recon only.

I slouched down in my seat, staying as much out of view of the passing headlights as possible. But none of the drivers gave my battered old white van a second look, and I doubted any of them even bothered to glance at the blue lettering on the side that read *Cloudburst Falls Catering*. Caterers, florists, musicians. Such service vehicles were all too common in Northtown, the part of Ashland where the rich, social, and magical elite lived. If not for the lousy weather, I imagined that this entire street would have been lit up with holiday cheer as people hosted various parties, each one trying to outdo their neighbors with garish light displays.

Once the last of the cars cruised by and the final pair of headlights faded away, I straightened in my seat, picked up my binoculars from my lap, and peered through them at another nearby mansion.

A stone wall cordoned this mansion off from the street, featuring a wide iron gate that was closed and locked for the night. Unlike its neighboring house, there were no holiday lights, and only a single room on the front was illuminated—an office with glass doors that led out to a stone patio. Thin white curtains covered the doors, and every few seconds, the murky shape of a man would appear, moving back and forth, as though he was continually pacing from one side of his office to the other.

I just bet he was pacing. From all the reports I'd heard, he'd been holed up in his mansion for months now, preparing for his murder trial, which was set to begin after the first of the year. That would be enough to drive anyone stir-crazy.

Beside me, a soft *creak* rang out, followed by a long, loud sigh. Two sounds that I'd heard over and over again in the last hour I'd been parked here.

The man in the mansion wasn't the only one going nuts.

"Tell me again. How did *I* get stuck hanging out with *you* tonight?" a low voice muttered.

I lowered my binoculars and looked over at Phillip Kincaid, who had his arms crossed over his muscled chest and a mulish expression on his handsome face. A long black trench coat covered his body and a black toboggan was pulled down low on his forehead, hiding his golden hair from sight, except for the low ponytail that stuck out the back. I was dressed in black as well, from my boots to my jeans to my silverstone vest, turtleneck, and fleece jacket. A black toboggan also topped my head, although I'd stuffed all my dark brown hair up underneath it.

"What's wrong, Philly?" I drawled. "Don't like being my babysitter tonight?"

He shrugged, not even bothering to deny it. "You're Gin Blanco, the famed assassin turned underworld queen. You don't need babysitting." He shifted in his seat, making it *creak* again, then shook his head. "But Owen insisted on it . . . The things I do for that man."

Phillip was right. As the Spider, I could handle myself in just about any situation. I certainly didn't need him here, but Owen Grayson, Phillip's best friend and my significant other, had insisted on it. But I hadn't protested too much when Phillip showed up at the Pork Pit, my barbecue restaurant, at closing time and told me that he wanted to tag along tonight.

With the mysterious members of the Circle out there, a little backup might come in handy. Even if said backup was whinier than one would hope.

"Why couldn't Lane sit out here with you?" Phillip asked. "Or Jo-Jo, or even Sophia for that matter? Why did I get elected to freeze my balls off tonight?"

Finnegan Lane, my foster brother, was often my partner in crime in all things Spider-related, while Jo-Jo and Sophia Deveraux healed me and cleaned up the blood and bodies I left in my wake.

"Because Finn is still dealing with the mess that Deirdre Shaw left behind at First Trust bank, and Jo-Jo and Sophia had tickets to *The Nutcracker*," I said, ticking our friends off on my hand. "And, of course, you know that Owen promised Eva that he'd help out with that holiday toy drive she's leading over at the community college."

"I would have been *happy* to help Eva with her toy drive," Phillip grumbled again. "Thrilled. Ecstatic even."

Despite their roughly ten-year age difference, Phillip was crazy about Eva Grayson, Owen's younger sister, although he was waiting for her to finish college and grow up a bit before pursuing a real relationship with her.

"Anything would have been better—*warmer*—than this." He popped up the collar of his trench coat so that it would cover more of his neck, then slouched down even farther in his seat.

"Aw, poor baby. Stuck out here in the cold and dark with me tonight." I clucked my tongue in mock sympathy. "And to think that I was just about to offer you some hot chocolate."

His blue eyes narrowed with interest. "You have hot chocolate? Homemade hot chocolate?"

I reached down and pulled a large metal thermos out of the black duffel bag sitting between our seats on the van floor. "Of course I have homemade hot chocolate. You can't have a stakeout on a cold winter's night without it."

I grabbed a couple of plastic cups out of the duffel bag and handed them to Phillip, who held them steady while I poured. The rich, heady aroma of the hot chocolate filled the van, cutting through the icy chill that had crept inside the vehicle. I breathed in the fumes as I capped the thermos and put it away. Phillip passed me my cup, and I drew in a couple more steamy breaths before taking a sip. The dark chocolate coated my tongue with its bittersweet flavor, softened by the vanilla extract and raspberry puree I had added to the mixture.

Phillip cradled his hot chocolate like a bum huddled over a trash can fire. He took a long slurp and sighed again, this time with happiness. "Now, *that's* more like it."

We both settled back in our seats, watching the mansion and sipping our hot chocolate.

The folks who'd been hosting the dinner party must have decided to go to bed, since the recorded carols abruptly cut off, and the holiday lights winked out one door, window, and plastic snowman at a time, further blackening the landscape. The drizzle picked up as well, turning into more of a steady rain, each drop *tink*ing against the windshield. It truly was a night fit for neither man nor beast, but this had been my favorite kind of environment as an assassin. The cold, the rain, the darkness always made it that much easier to get close to your target and then get away after you'd put him down. If I wanted someone dead, I would have waited for a night just like this one to strike.

And I was willing to bet that someone might have the same idea about the man in the mansion.

Phillip tipped his cup at the shadow still pacing back and forth behind the patio doors. "You really think that he knows something about the Circle?"

I shrugged. "He's the best lead I have right now—and the only person still alive who might know anything about them."

Two weeks ago, I'd been kidnapped and held hostage by Hugh Tucker, a vampire who claimed he was part of "the Circle," a secret group that supposedly pulled the strings on the underworld and everything else in Ashland. That had certainly come as news to me, since *I* was supposedly the head of the underworld these days. But Tucker had claimed that the Circle was a group of criminals so high and mighty that no one could touch them, especially not a lowly assassin like me. The vamp had also said that the Circle monitored everything from behind the scenes—and that they could kill me and my friends anytime they wanted to.

But the most shocking thing he'd told me was that my mother, Eira Snow, had supposedly been one of *them*.

My mother was murdered when I was thirteen, and it was a deep loss that I still felt to this day. But I'd viewed my mother like any other kid. She was my mom—nothing more, nothing less. I'd never really thought about who *she* was, much less about what kind of person. The good things she did, the bad things, how she felt about all of them. I didn't know any of that. But Tucker had turned my world upside down with his accusations, and I wanted to know how true they were: I *had* to know if my mother had been the good person I'd always assumed she was, or just as rotten, dirty, and depraved as the rest of this shadowy Circle.

"You know, we could just go knock on his door and ask him about all of this," Phillip said.

I snorted. "He wouldn't tell me anything. Nothing I could trust anyway. He hates me too much for that."

Phillip shifted in his seat again. "Well, at least we could get this over with and go home for the night. That would certainly keep my balls from turning into ice cubes—"

A pair of headlights popped up in the rearview mirror. I gestured at Phillip, and we both slouched back down in our seats.

A black SUV cruised down the street, passing us. The vehicle went down to the end of the block and made a right, disappearing from sight. Phillip started to sit back up, but I held out my hand, stopping him.

"Wait," I said. "Let's see if they come back."

He rolled his eyes but stayed still. "Why would they come back? It's probably just somebody who lives in the neighborhood—"

Headlights popped up in the rearview mirror again

and that same SUV cruised by our position. This time the vehicle turned left at the end of the block.

"Maybe they're lost," he said. "All these cookie-cutter Northtown streets and mansions look alike, especially in the dark."

I shook my head. "They're not lost. They're seeing how quiet and deserted the area is for whatever they have in mind. They'll be back. You'll see."

We sat still in the van, watching our mirrors. Sure enough, a minute later, that same SUV cruised by us again. Only this time, the vehicle didn't have its headlights on, or even its parking lights. It whipped a U-turn in the middle of the street, pulled over to the curb, and stopped—right in front of the mansion we were watching.

"Hello," I murmured. "What do we have here?"

The doors opened, and two people got out of the front of the SUV, both wearing long black trench coats akin to Phillip's. They were giants, each one roughly seven feet tall with thick shoulders and broad chests. Most likely they were the muscle and bodyguards for whoever was in the back of the vehicle.

Sure enough, one of the giants opened a rear door, and a shorter, thinner figure emerged, also sporting a black trench coat. This person also wore a black fedora and had a matching scarf wrapped around their neck. I peered through my binoculars, but the person's back was to me, so I couldn't see their face, although from the size and gait, I did get the impression that it was a woman.

"Some late-night visitors here for a hush-hush meeting with our old friend?" Phillip drawled.

"Maybe."

One of the giants squatted down. At first, I wondered what he was doing, but then the woman in the fedora and scarf ran over to the giant, who hoisted her up into the air. Ms. Fedora grabbed hold of the top of the iron gate and swung her legs up and over it with all the grace of an Olympic gymnast. Landing deftly on her feet in the yard on the other side, she straightened up and started striding toward the mansion with graceful purpose.

I cursed, realizing that I was about to lose my one and only lead on the Circle. I'd considered the possibility that someone might come here looking for him, but part of me hadn't thought that it would actually *happen*, since everything else I'd tried to track down the members of the Circle had been a dead end.

"Not a meeting," I growled. "They're here to kill him."

Since Fedora was already past the gate, I didn't have time to ease out of the van, sneak through the shadows, and stab the giants in the back the way I normally would have.

Thus I kicked my door open, barreled out of the vehicle, and started running down the street toward the SUV.

"Gin! Wait!" Phillip shouted, scrambling to get out and follow me.

But I needed to get to the man in the mansion before Fedora did, so I tuned him out. The giants whirled around at the sound of Phillip's voice and spotted me racing toward them. They cursed, pulled guns out from underneath their trench coats, and snapped up the weapons.

Pfft! Pfft! Pfft!

I zigzagged, and the first round of bullets went wide. But when the giants paused to take more careful aim, I reached for my Stone magic and hardened my skin into an impenetrable shell.

Pfft! Pfft! Pfft!

The second round of bullets also went wide. The giants had come prepared, and the silencers on the ends of their weapons muffled the sounds of the shots. No lights snapped on inside the neighboring mansions. They wanted to keep this quiet—well, so did I.

Pfft! Pfft! Pfft!

Two of the bullets went wide, but the third punched into my right shoulder, spinning me around. Still, thanks to my magic, it didn't blast through me the way it would have otherwise. I skidded on the ice coating the street, but I managed to regain my balance and charge forward again.

But instead of heading toward the giants, I ran straight at the SUV. When I was in range, I leaped up onto the hood, then scrambled up onto the roof. Before the giants realized what I was doing, I raced forward and leaped off the vehicle's roof, pushing off hard and trying to get as high in the air as possible. Lucky for me, they'd parked close to the curb and the narrow sidewalk. A second later, my hands hit the top of the wall that fronted the mansion, and I dug my boots into the slick stones so that I could pull myself up onto the top of the wall. Fedora wasn't the only one who could do gymnastics.

I rolled off the top of the wall and dropped ten feet down to the other side. I paused a moment to palm one of the silverstone knives tucked up my sleeves, then darted forward across the lawn. The ice-crusted grass crunched like brittle bones under my boots.

The light spilling out from the office perfectly illuminated Fedora, who was fifty feet ahead of me and moving fast, her breath streaming out behind her in a trail of frosty vapor. She must have heard the disturbance out on the street because she picked up her pace, pulled a gun out of her trench coat, and shot through the lock on the patio doors with one smooth motion. A second later, she was inside the mansion.

"Hey!" a man's voice shouted from inside the office. "Who are you? What do you think you're doing?"

I didn't hear her reply, if there even was one.

Pfft! Pfft! Pfft!
Pfft! Pfft! Pfft!

More and more shots sounded behind me, but the giants weren't aiming at me anymore. Phillip must have gotten into the fight. He could take care of himself, so I focused all my energy on sprinting across the lawn, trying to get to the mansion, even though it was already too late.

Pfft! Pfft! Pfft!

Sure enough, gunfire flashed inside the office, as bright as the holiday lights had been earlier. Someone had just been shot.

A second later, Fedora stepped through the doors and out onto the stone patio. I squinted, but the office lights were behind her, and all I could really see in the darkness was the pale glitter of her eyes. She gave me a mocking salute with her gun before ducking back inside the mansion. Now that her mission was accomplished, no doubt she'd leave through one of the back doors and disappear into the woods. All without my even getting a look at her face.

I cursed. Even though I wanted to rush inside the mansion, I forced myself to slow down and approach the patio doors with caution, just in case she might be lying in wait to try to kill me too. I also grabbed hold of even more of my Stone power, hardening my skin as much as possible on the off chance that she decided to blast me with elemental magic *and* bullets. As a final touch, I reached out with my magic, listening to all the emotional vibrations that had sunk into the stone walls of the mansion.

Harsh, shocked mutters echoed back to me, from the shots the woman had just fired. Alongside that was a high, whiny chorus of worry, fear, and paranoia. But there were no sly whispers or dark murmurs of evil intent that would have signaled that she was hiding in the office, ready to put a bullet in my head the second I stepped inside. Whoever the woman was, she was long gone.

Still, I was careful as I eased my way into the office, my knife still in my hand, my other hand up and lightly glowing with Ice magic, ready to blast whoever might challenge me.

But only one person was in the office: the man I'd been watching.

Jonah McAllister, my old nemesis, lay sprawled across the floor.